I0608063

Operation Red X

Thomas Slatcoff

SLATCOFF AND **COMPANY** LLC

"I will stand with the *Muslims* should the
Political winds shift in an ugly direction."

The President of the United States of America

Description

A team of assassins conspired to destroy the succession to the Executive Office of the President of the United States of America, with the killing of all the Secretaries of the United States Presidential Cabinet. The conspiracy was carried out through a false flag operation that implicated the Republic of Poland as the perpetrator. Jan Sklodowski, Deputy Director, National Security Group, Poland National Police, was dispatched to the Embassy of the Republic of Poland, in Washington, D.C. From the Polish embassy, Jan and a team of hotshot investigators worked to counter the false flag operation.

About the Author

Thomas Slatcoff returned to private business after he served twenty-three years in federal law enforcement and retired as a Senior Criminal Investigator. He served The People of the United States of America from the Executive Branch -

U.S. Department of Justice
Drug Enforcement Administration - Diversion Control *and*
INTERPOL - U.S. National Central Bureau

U.S. Department of Agriculture
Office of Inspector General - Office of Investigations

U.S. Department of Homeland Security
Federal Law Enforcement Training Center - Counterterrorism Division

U.S. Department of Energy
Office of Special Operations *and*
Washington Regional Counterintelligence Office

As a Federal Law Enforcement Officer, Thomas was enriched through:

The diversity of assignments and tasks to execute and manage the day-to-day operations of crime-fighting. Focus areas included employee integrity, government program fraud, public safety, national security, continuity of government operations, and Protective Service Operations – the security, safety, and continuity for members of the Presidential Cabinet.

The diversity of co-workers, associates, and people from around the world who he had the good fortune to meet. Daily the personalities and cultures provided knowledge, experiences, and friendships to facilitate a global understanding of people and events.

Thomas used his diverse experiences, knowledge, and observations gained from private business, global government service, law enforcement, and life to create literary works to *Entertain, Inform, and Inspire*. For more about Thomas, please visit Slatcoff.com.

OPERATION RED X is a work of fiction.

The names, characters, and events in the book are the product of the author's imagination, or are used fictitiously and not intended as accurate representations of real incidents or people, living or dead.

Copyright © 2015 by **SLATCOFF AND COMPANY** LLC

All rights reserved.

In accordance with the U.S. Copyright Act of 1976, the scanning uploading, and electronic sharing of any part of this book without the permission of the publisher is unlawful piracy and theft of the author's intellectual property. If you would like to use material from the book, other than for review purposes, prior written permission must be obtained by contacting the publisher at Contact@Slatcoff.com.

Thank you for the support of the publisher's rights.

Published by:

SLATCOFF AND COMPANY LLC

Florida, USA

Contact@Slatcoff.com
www.Slatcoff.com

First Print Edition: January 2015
          Revised: June 2017-9-F1.2

ISBN-13-978-0-9971506-1-2

IN MEMORY

Mother,
Mary Elizabeth Sklodowski Slatcoff

And

Father,
Peter Slatcoff, Jr.

Angels then. Angels now.

Your example, continued patience, and unconditional love
built my foundation.

It supports me well. It is unshakable. It is timeless.

Thank you.

Love you.
See you when I get there.

Mary, Samantha, Lauren, Bethany

I am flattered by your belief I have something to offer others.

I am motivated by your support and enthusiasm for me.

I am inspired by your love for me.

Love you.

Thank you for your contributions to my literary journey.

Lauren Slatcoff

Your literary insight motivated me.
Your sharing inspired me.
I will forever cherish our coffeehouse conversations.

Julie Cook Slatcoff

You motivated me to pursue and finish this book.
You believed I had the ability.
You believed in me.

Wayne North

Our many years of friendship moved me to who I am today.
Our many conversations inspired me.
Your proofread of the manuscript was a huge help

All My English Teachers

Thank you for your patience and persistence.

I was born Muslim.
I support the Muslims.
I always have.
I always will.

The President of the United States of America

Fact News Center

29 September, Wednesday

USA, Washington, D.C.
Somewhere in underground tunnels

1530 Hours

"Abdul. Abdul," The faint voice said. "Are you there Abdul?"

"What are you doing here?" said a surprised Abdul. "And Bashir, you're here too. You two shouldn't be down here."

"Listen. I don't have a lot of time. Operation Red X will commence on October 1st. You'll be done by the end of October. Is that clear? This operation has to happen fast and furious."

The person talking in a faint voice turned to Bashir and continued, "Get it. Fast and furious. Just like the ATF gun-running operation you set up to get guns into the hands of my assassination team. Get it. Get it."

"Really. Come on."

"Okay," the faint voice continued. "I'll call Bashir with their schedules. Bashir will call you, so you'll know where to be and when. Do you have everything you need?"

"Yes," replied Abdul. "We have the last part of the deployment, the last van with supporters and equipment, coming from Michigan. It's on its way as we speak. They'll be here by Monday. I'll start Monday. You provide the names and schedule. My team will handle it from there. You don't worry about anything."

Abdul looked to Bashir. He briefly paused then continued.

"I'll take care of this as we planned in Kenya."

The faint voice said, "Your first attack will be on the 6ᵗʰ of October. I have the Secretary of Commerce going to Poland. Bashir will call you with the details."

"Very well. We'll be ready to go. Bashir is the cleanup team ready?"

"Yes, they're ready. You just worry about your part of the plan. I'll take care of my part. Okay."

"Well that guy you have in charge of the cleanup team, he doesn't seem capable. I'm just saying."

The faint voice interrupted.

"Okay. Okay. Will you two stop it? I don't need this. We must focus on the plan. We're one month away. Come on. In the name of Allah."

"For Allah," said Abdul.

Slowly, Bashir said, "For Allah."

"Let's go, Bashir, I have to get back."

1 October, Friday

Poland, Warsaw
Poland National Police
Warsaw District Office

"I'll meet you tonight at the Warsaw Café. Come alone. I know who you are. You don't need a description of me. Come alone Jan, or I won't come up to you," said the unknown caller.

Jan (pronounced Zun) had no idea with whom he had just arranged to meet at 2130 hours. Even more puzzling to Jan was how the unknown caller knew him. And 'come alone' was not how Jan wanted to meet someone unknown to him. The beeping of the analog, landline, desk telephone, the indication to cradle the phone handset, brought Jan out of his deep thought.

It was 1740 hours; the Warsaw District Office was empty. Jan was usually the one to stay late at the office. The fact of the matter, he was the only one to ever stay late.

Jan Sklodowski, a Senior Federal Agent, assigned to the Warsaw District Office of the Poland National Police, sat at his desk in a stark, cold, government office, in an aging building, near downtown Warsaw. Jan was employed by the Poland National Police for thirty-three years. He was the most senior agent and the oldest agent in the office. He was a decorated Federal law enforcement officer and proudly displayed his professional memorabilia in his office area. He received numerous awards, commendations, and countless accolades from Assistant Prosecutors with the Poland National Prosecutorial Office and foreign governments. Many of the investigations he conducted involved international aspects. Two notable awards were: The United States of America, Department of Justice presented him an award for his tireless efforts with the murder investigation of two U.S. citizens. They were murdered while on holiday in Krakow. On another occasion, the United States of America, Department of Agriculture, Office of Inspector General, Office of Investigation presented him with an award for his vital assistance with the apprehension of three Office of Inspector General felony fugitives wanted for conspiracy and false statements in a food adulteration scheme affecting the global food supply chain. Before the Poland National Police, Jan was a Police Officer with the Warsaw City Police Department.

In addition to Jan, the Warsaw District Office staff included a Supervisory Federal Agent, five other Federal Agents, and a Secretary.

Feliks Dubinski was the Supervisory Federal Agent for the Warsaw District Office and twenty years younger than Jan. Feliks was employed with the Poland National Police for seven years. His office was void of any professional memorabilia. He was not known to have received any recognition during his short law enforcement career. Jan remained puzzled as to how Feliks was promoted to a Supervisory Federal Agent so fast. When Jan checked with his counterparts at different district offices throughout Poland, he received the same comment, no comment. Jan's co-workers never answered the question and always immediately changed the subject. Jan theorized Feliks had issues with staff members and he was sent to the Warsaw District Office to be close to headquarters, under their watchful eye.

The five other Federal Agents, at various levels of their careers, were all younger than Mr. Dubinski, as he required his subordinates to address him. The work ethic of the younger agents was not to Jan's liking, and Jan was not motivated to get to know them or associate with them. The agents came to work, most often on time, and left at the 1630 clock strike ending their eight-hour tour of duty. Overtime was something the young agents rarely performed. At the end of their tour, Mr. Dubinski and his subordinates always ran off to happy hour at the local downtown Warsaw beer gardens. They packed together as though they did not know what to do if they were alone. This Jan knew, not because he went with them but from conversations with Olenka.

Olenka Wasniski, the Secretary for the Warsaw District Office, entered the workforce late in her life. The passing of her husband forced her to maintain employment outside the home. The need for money was the driving motivation. The survival benefits of the Poland Social Pension Plan were not enough to keep her at the standards to which she was accustomed. She also appreciated the professional socializing the employment provided. It was almost seven years since Olenka arrived at the District Office. She was hired by the previous Supervisory Federal Agent who a year later was promoted to a position at the Poland National Police Headquarters. Olenka missed his company and his office leadership. After Feliks had arrived, a rumor started that Olenka was only a housewife and did not qualify for the position of Secretary. She was only hired by the former Supervisory Federal Agent because of a romantic fling the two had which started before her husband's death. The office rumor grew to implicate the former Supervisory Federal Agent in the death of Olenka's deceased husband.

Olenka and Jan hit it off instantly upon Olenka's arrival. For one thing, Olenka and Jan were the same age. For another, they were both raised by parents that instilled within them a strong work ethic. Their bond was their upbringing. Their parents raised them with the motto, *Spare the rod. Spoil the child,* and it worked well. They respected people. They followed the rules and regulations. They gave an honest day's work. They committed themselves to the tasks given. Constant approval and praise were not needed. She too was not motivated to get to know the younger agents or associate with them. The way the young agents and the supervisor carried themselves and represented the Poland National Police was not to her liking either. Throughout her work days, Olenka constantly rolled her eyes in dismay at the comments and lack of a staunch work ethic displayed by the young agents.

As for the office rumors, Jan knew they were not true. He investigated the death of Olenka's husband and apprehended the vicious murderer who was found guilty and sentenced to life in prison, plus five years. Olenka was grateful for Jan's investigative tenacity. His investigation and the subsequent conviction of the murderer brought closure for Olenka. Olenka held a warm place in her heart for Jan.

It was now 1945 hours; Jan completed an electronic search of the past three years of intelligence reports. The search should have taken five minutes; however, Mr. Dubinski instituted a policy of always controlling the computer lock key to the Warsaw District Office intelligence computer. He controlled it by keeping it with him at all times. Jan had to go through the painstaking ritual of picking the computer lock to gain access when he needed intelligence information. This was just one of the policies established by Mr. Dubinski to reign control over the Federal Agents, to foster bureaucracy, and to hinder production.

Jan conducted a search of the Poland National Police Intelligence Report System, a country-wide system used by all the Poland National Police District Offices. Through a Mutual Use Agreement, the Poland National Police entered into with the International Criminal Police Organization (Interpol), Interpol provided a live feed to the Poland National Police Intelligence Report System. This arrangement provided an efficient and productive means to query intelligence information. Jan was prompted to conduct this search from a gut feeling, a strange feeling about the unknown caller. As a seasoned law enforcement officer, he learned from years of experience not to ignore his gut feelings. Gut feelings were an officer safety tactic, a tool for officer survival.

He entered a search for recent entries and recent inquiries for one year. In the space for Location, he marked World Wide. Because the system interfaced with Interpol, a window popped up for a password to allow the systems to talk to each other. Jan quickly entered the necessary password, and the system moved on. After a couple minutes, another window popped up to display the results, and it was blank.

Then the Poland National Police Intelligence System responded with the message NO MATCH FOUND. Nothing was found to take his gut feeling to the next level, a hunch.

It was now time for Jan to leave and conduct a pre-meet surveillance. Jan again contemplated going against officer safety protocol to meet the unknown caller alone.

Jan thought to himself, "What choice do I have? Should I call Mr. Dubinski and ask for assistance from other District Office Federal Agents? What good would that do, Mr. Dubinski's track record is to deny my requests."

As a Supervisory Federal Agent, Mr. Dubinski's primary management principle was – if we don't do anything, we can't do anything wrong, and we can't get into trouble. Utmost to Mr. Dubinski was staying out of trouble. He believed that was the key to his next promotion.

Jan also thought to himself, "What good would the assistance be. By now, the vodka has a hold on the Federal Agents. They are under the influence of Jan's beloved country's national drink – Polish Vodka."

To manage his officer safety, Jan did what he always did for the past seven years. He telephoned Olenka, briefed her on what he was going to do and then established a call-back time. If Olenka did not receive a phone call from Jan by the set time, Olenka called Jan. If Jan did not answer or if Olenka was not satisfied with Jan's answer, she phoned the Warsaw City Police Department and requested their assistance to check on Jan. For this meeting, the callback time was 2300 hours.

After he had made the telephone call to Olenka, Jan rose from his rickety, low back, metal, office chair and pushed it under his old metal desk. He surveyed the desk to ensure everything was in its place. The organization was one of his mother's golden rules. A habit his mother instilled in him since youth. He then checked himself. Once. Twice. Three times to make sure he had all his issued duty equipment. He walked through the hallway to the rear door of the building which led to the parking lot. He locked the office door behind him and double checked to make sure it was secured. He walked across the dimly lit parking lot to a government vehicle and used the ignition key to open the driver's door of the official vehicle, a dark blue colored BMW 530i sedan. He started the vehicle, selected drive, and operated the BMW to the main boulevard. He eased into traffic and was en route to the area of the Warsaw Café.

2145 Hours   Warsaw Café

Jan arrived at the Warsaw Café and immediately conducted a security sweep of the area. He looked carefully for anything that was out of the ordinary or unusual. He observed nothing and proceeded inside the café. The hostess greeted him and showed him to his table. Jan took the seat from which he watched the entire restaurant. Shortly, Jan sprang up from the table, and in a quick gait, walked to the restroom.

Instinctively, Jan went to the restroom to wash his hands before eating. As he washed his hands, a creepy man walked in and up to the sink right beside Jan.

Jan rolled his eyes and thought to himself, "Really. There are six other sinks in here, and this toad takes the one right next to me. Creepy! This is just creepy."

Jan did not give up any of his space and maintained his law enforcement pose.

The creepy man finished washing his hands and with a tactical shuffle step, moved away from the sink.

Jan, attentive of the tactical shuffle step, was suspicious now. He continued to watch the creepy man in the mirror hung cockeyed above the sink. Jan watched the creepy man as he slowly moved his right hand down to his right side. His left hand was raised in

28

an upright self-defense position. He slowly moved his suit jacket to the side.

Jan became concerned, and thoughts raced through his mind, "Is this the man I spoke to on the telephone? Is this a setup? Is someone trying to kill me because of one on my past investigations?"

Instinctively, Jan started to turn around and position himself for an offensive attack to jam the creepy man's assault. As he turned, he observed the creepy man pulled out a white, primly folded and ironed handkerchief. The creepy man shook it a few times to open it fully. He began to dry his hands. He looked directly into the eyes of Jan and said, "Damn restrooms, they never have paper towels. How do you wash your hands properly?" He walked away from Jan and exited the restroom.

Jan was stupefied. He stood there thinking, "I turned around to position myself to engage this man, possibly with lethal force and he pulled out a primly folded and ironed handkerchief to dry his hands."

Jan turned back to the sink to finish washing his hands. With the water still running, he cupped his hands to hold some. He raised his cupped hands to his face, and the water ran out of his hands before he rubbed the water onto his face to refresh himself. He took his wet hands and rubbed his face to make himself alert. He turned away from the sink to get a paper towel to dry his face and hands and to use as a barrier to turn off the water, so he did not re-contaminate his hands. He saw what the creepy man was talking about. There were no paper towels; the paper towel dispenser was empty. Jan turned back to the sink and raised his foot. Performing a balancing act, he turned the water off with his foot, so he did not have to touch the faucet handle with his washed hands. Jan vigorously shook and rubbed his hands together to dry them and used the corner of his suit jacket to open the restroom door. He returned to his table and continued to wait for the unknown caller as he sipped his bubble water.

At 2205 hours, still seated at the table eating his food, Jan was confronted by an individual who appeared to be of European descent. Jan moved swiftly to get up and out of his chair. He positioned himself to defend against any level of assault. He assessed the unknown man and immediately located his hands to determine if any weapons were displayed. His hands were empty. The unknown man stood approximately six feet two inches tall, weighed about two hundred pounds, muscular build, brown hair, brown eyes and clean shaven. He was dressed in a well-tailored suit, silk tie, and smartly shined, expensive looking, leather shoes. He sported well-manicured hands and hair. The creepy man from the restroom was nervous and constantly looked about.

The unknown man said, "I'm the caller."

"Hello, I'm Jan."

"I know who you are."

"What's your name?" asked Jan.

"That doesn't matter. What is important and worth a lot of money is the information I have."

"Okay."

"As I told you on the telephone, the United States government will be interested in the information. Very interested. I understand you can facilitate a meeting for me with the Inspector General for the U.S. Department of Agriculture."

"That's an unusual request. The Inspector General for the U.S. Department of Agriculture?"

"Are you not the hotshot Polish investigator that brought down an international cartel of food fraudsters? A conspiracy that involved a food adulteration scheme that affected the global food supply chain. Affected the global public safety."

"Well, I don't know if I would say it quite like that. That may be a bit overstated. How do you know about my involvement in that?"

"Do I have your attention now? I know. I just know," said the unknown man.

Jan replied, "Well, I may be able to help you. I'm going to need to know a lot more than I know now."

"I knew you were going to say that. I contacted you because I was told you were someone to trust to help me. The information put me in danger. When shared with you, you will be at risk too. Tonight, was just for us to meet. I wanted to be sure we were comfortable with each other."

The unknown man paused. He tried to hide his overt scan of the restaurant. Then he continued.

"I won't tell you anything else tonight. We won't talk tonight. I'm going back to my table now, and you should leave. I'll be back in touch."

The unknown man walked away.

At 2215 hours, as Jan drove home from the meet, he telephoned Olenka to tell her he was okay and that the meeting was over like he had done numerous times over the seven years Jan and Olenka worked together. Olenka asked no questions; she waited until the next morning when Jan was in the office to ask him how the meeting went. They always shared early morning conversation over coffee and paczkis.

USA, Washington, D.C.
1919 Connecticut Avenue NW
Washington Hilton

1000 Hours   Grand Ball Room

"Thank you, Mr. Secretary. Thank you for coming and speaking today at the North American Coal Council's Annual Meeting," said Tobey Zeglin Jr., the President of the NACC.

"You're welcome, Tobey. Thank you for the opportunity to speak," replied the Secretary of Energy.

"Mr. Secretary, you need to go. You have an eleven-fifteen meeting at your office," the Secretary's staffer said.

"Okay let's go," replied the Secretary

George broadcasted, "Hope from George."

Hope broadcasted, "Go George."

"We're moving."

"Copy."

Hope broadcasted, "Rich from Hope."

"Go, Hope."

"We're moving your way."

"10-4, all clear. We're at the drop point.

"Copy."

"Which way are we going?" asked the Secretary.

"This way Mr. Secretary," said Hope as she pointed to a side aisle that led to the rear of the banquet room and the doors the Secretary entered through earlier.

Retracing the route they followed into the grand ballroom, the Secretary's entourage continued down the hallway, down the escalator, and to the front door of the hotel.

Hope broadcasted, "Coming out."

"Copy. I have a visual. You're clear to come out," replied Rich.

The Secretary's entourage continued to move toward the Secretary's two-vehicle motorcade. Hope moved a little faster than the others and directly to the right rear passenger door of the Secretary's limo. She opened the door, and without delay, the Secretary continued to move and entered the limo. At the same time, Hope handed the door off to George. Hope then positioned herself three feet from the limo, faced the street, and looked for anything suspicious or out of the ordinary. The Secretary seated in the right rear seat, George closed the door. George opened the right front passenger door, entered, and took the right front position, then locked the limo's doors.

Hope moved to the follow vehicle as she continued to scan the area for threats. She opened the right front passenger door, entered, and took the right front position.

Hope broadcasted, "Move."

George broadcasted, "Make the notifications, arrival point Blue."

"10-4."

The Secretary of Energy's two-vehicle motorcade pulled away from the event site.

After a minute or two, Hope broadcasted, "Notifications made."

In the lead vehicle, the limo, was the Secretary of the U.S. Department of Energy, George, the Detail Leader and Dodge, the Limo Driver. Both the Detail Leader and the Limo Driver were Special Agents with the U.S. Department of Energy, Office of Special Operations. The second vehicle, the follow vehicle, had Rich, the Follow Vehicle Driver, and Hope, the Shift Leader. Both were also Special Agents with the U.S. Department of Energy, Office of Special Operations.

The U.S. Department of Energy (DOE), Office of Special Operations (OSO) housed the Executive Protection Program for the Secretary of Energy, the Security and Incident Investigative Unit, and the Information Systems Forensic Laboratory.

The function of the Executive Protection Program was to maintain and oversee the Executive Protection Detail and operations for the Secretary of Energy, senior Department of Energy officials, visiting dignitaries, and other select individuals, potential targets of a criminal or terrorist attack.

The function of the Security and Incident Investigative Unit was to oversee the conduct and disposition of investigations that involved personnel security, compromised or potentially compromised classified and unclassified sensitive information, alleged or suspected violation of the Atomic Energy Act, relevant federal laws, national security policy and Executive Orders or other security incidents of concern. Examples of investigations included: intentional infliction of threat of death or serious physical harm; penetration of classified automated information systems; threats of terrorism, sabotage or malevolent acts against DOE nuclear facilities; technical intercept of classified or unclassified sensitive information; lost, unaccounted for, theft or diversion of Special Nuclear Material, nuclear weapons and their components - tritium, plutonium or precious metals.

The function of the Information Systems Forensic Laboratory was to support the Security and Incident Investigative Unit with the ability to search and extract information from any technology or device pertinent to an investigation.

The OSO was created from the foresight of a Retired United States of America Air Force General who was then the Director of the Office of Security and Emergency Operations for the DOE. This was in December of 2000, ten months before September 11, 2001, and the terrorist attacks on the United States of America. However, in typical bureaucratic fashion, his idea to secure the department assets, both human and physical, was stymied from its conception. Stymied by co-workers who did not want him to succeed. Blocked by Federal civil servants' professional jealousy, ignorance to the evolving threats by the enemies of the United States of America, and flat out the lack of knowledge, skills, and abilities to start up a new component within the DOE.

Secretary of Energy Motorcade in transit

The two-vehicle motorcade moved through the heavy traffic in the District of Columbia. It was on its way to the DOE Headquarters Building, 1000 Independence Avenue Southeast, Washington, D.C. from the Secretary's 0900 hours event. The motorcade was stopped at the traffic light at Fourteenth Street and Independence Avenue, in a stacked formation, first the limo then the follow vehicle, both vehicles were in the left-hand turn lane.

George broadcasted, "Hope from George."

Hope broadcasted, "Go George."

"We're going through this intersection. Turn your emergency lights on."

"Are we permitted to do that? What's the emergency?"

In a stern voice, George broadcasted, "Turn on your emergency lights. We're going through."

With emergency lights engaged on both vehicles, the motorcade moved through the intersection and proceeded east on Independence Avenue.

George broadcasted, "Hope from George."

Hope broadcasted, "Go George."

"Get the vehicles washed and topped off with gas after we make the drop."

"10-4."

DOE Headquarters Building

When the Secretary of Energy's motorcade arrived at the arrival point, a DOE uniformed contract guard stepped into the roadway and stopped the northbound traffic with hand signals. The limo was pulled to the curb while the follow vehicle stopped on an angle to cover the Secretary's exit from the limo. The Detail Leader manually unlocked his door, emerged from the limo first, and closed his door. The Limo Driver locked all the limo doors electronically. George paused to scan the area for anything or anyone unusual. His eyes rapidly moved about the area, though the dark glasses shielded where and how long he scanned. He looked hard for threats, and when he believed it was safe, he tapped on the front passenger side door to signal the driver to release the locks. George opened and controlled the door for the Secretary to step out. The Secretary, with the Detail Leader in a right shoulder protective position, walked to and entered the DOE Headquarters.

George broadcasted, "Clear, we're in."

The motorcade moved off.

1600 Hours   OSO Security Room

George and Hope were in the OSO Security Room in the Secretary's Office Suite. This small room housed security camera monitors for camera coverage of the vast area of the Secretary's Office Suite. A point of continual observation for threats to the Secretary's security and safety. When the Secretary was in his suite, at least one of the five members of the Secretary's Protection Detail was in the room.

As usual, toward the end of the Secretary's work day, per the Secretary's Daily Schedule, George came to the room to wait for the Secretary's departure.

George said, "Hope, do you think the Secretary will leave on time today?"

"Probably, it's Friday. You know his wife likes him to be home early on Fridays," Hope replied.

"Why, what do they do on Fridays?"

"I think they always go to the same restaurant and his wife likes to be at the restaurant by six."

"What's the name of the restaurant they go to?"

"I don't know. That's a personal event, and we don't provide protection for personal events. We don't get information from his staff on his personal events."

"Yeah. That isn't right. Here comes the Secretary. We're moving."

Hope broadcasted, "We're moving."

Dodge, the Limo Driver, and Rich, the Follow Vehicle Driver replied with two clicks of their two-way radio mic.

Dodge and Rich were positioned in their respective motorcade vehicles since 1600 hours. The detail never knew the exact time the Secretary would leave for the day, though there was a time listed on the Secretary's Daily Schedule. This was the one time of the day the Secretary was not punctual per his schedule. He simply ended his day when he wanted to end it. To be prepared for his departure, everyone went to their assigned detail positions to wait for the Secretary. What the members of the Secretary's Protection Detail knew was the sooner the Secretary left for the day, and they got him to his residence, the sooner they ended their day and got to their residence.

The next announcement on the two-way radio was Hope.

"Coming out."

The entourage continued to move toward the motorcade in the underground garage.

At the motorcade, George opened and controlled the right rear door of the limo as the Secretary entered. George closed the door and entered the limo – the right front passenger seat, the Detail Leader's position in the motorcade. Hope was already in the follow vehicle – the right front passenger seat, the Shift Leader's Position in the motorcade.

Hope broadcasted, "Move."

Secretary of Energy Motorcade in transit

The Secretary's two-vehicle motorcade pulled away from the underground parking garage after a brief delay at the exit because of an upright barricade. The uniformed contract guard was checking a car into the garage and did not lower the barrier for a swift motorcade exit.

After a minute or two, Hope broadcasted, "Notifications made."

38

The Secretary's motorcade slowly moved through the heavy evening rush hour traffic in the District of Columbia, on its way to the Secretary's residence.

Finally, after the stop and go traffic caused by the rush hour traffic, the two-vehicle motorcade arrived at the Secretary's home in northwest Washington D.C.

George, the Detail Leader, emerged from the limo first. He closed his door and heard the electric door locks engaged at the Limo Driver's conditioned action. George scanned the area for anything or anyone unusual; he was looking hard for threats. When he believed it was clear, he tapped on the front passenger side door, and the Limo Driver released the electric locks. George opened and controlled the door, and the Secretary stepped out. The Secretary and the Detail Leader walked to the side entrance of the residence.

The Secretary said, "Thank you. Everyone have a good weekend. I'll see you all Monday morning."

The Secretary turned and entered his residence.

The Executive Protection Detail loaded back into the motorcade vehicles and drove off. They headed back to headquarters to return the government vehicles to the underground garage to end their shift and workweek.

While departing the Secretary's street, the Detail Leader telephoned the DOE Command Center and logged the Secretary at his residence for the evening and weekend. Then he took the detail out of service. The Secretary had no security on the weekends unless he attended an official event.

4 October, Monday

Poland, Warsaw
Middle-income residential neighborhood

0500 Hours

It was still dark outside. Jan turned the alarm off before it rang. Rarely did the alarm wake Jan up; his biological clock was extremely punctual. His usual routine had him up by 0500 hours to make coffee, shower, and dress. Jan's morning routine continued with him sipping his coffee and meditating. He enjoyed his black coffee flavored with a tablespoon of butter. This taste he acquired from his father. During this quiet meditation time, Jan prepared himself to enthusiastically charge the day.

This morning, as he did throughout Saturday and Sunday, Jan continued to reflect on meeting the unknown caller and the things the unknown caller said, both on the telephone and when they met in person. Jan was still at a loss as to what information the caller had and why the unknown caller called him to pass the information to the government of the United States of America. And give it to the U.S. Department of Agriculture (USDA), Inspector General (IG), was not what Jan expected. He pondered the connection to USDA.

It was 0630 hours, time for Jan to leave for the office. He checked himself for the third time to make sure he had, among other daily work necessities, his glasses, wallet, gun, ammo, handcuffs and Federal Agent credentials. As Jan did every time he left the apartment, he studied himself in the full-length mirror hanging on the wall next to the front door of his modest two bedrooms, two baths, apartment. He checked himself to ensure his clothing was neat and orderly. He double checked the grooming of his hair. The habits his mother instilled in him during his youth.

His mother, a wife of a coal miner and a homemaker, with only modest means, insisted her children dress in clean clothes pressed with sharp creases. This Jan's mother made certain from her painstaking Monday clothes washing days and Tuesday ironing days as a part of her well-organized household schedule. He smiled as he reminisced his happy childhood days in a small patch town in the Carpathian Mountains coal mining region of Poland.

Ready to charge the day, he headed out the door, locked it behind him and double checked that it was locked. He walked down the first-floor indoor hallway, of the two-story quad apartment building, in the middle-income, residential area of Warsaw. He exited the apartment building's front entrance and walked to the street where the official government vehicle was parked.

Since Jan was on government business, at a late hour and he did not pass the office returning from the meeting, Jan was permitted to take the government vehicle home. This policy was instituted by Mr. Dubinski when he became the Supervisory Federal Agent of the Warsaw District Office.

Jan waited for traffic to clear to enter the vehicle. He shook his head as he thought to himself, "Dubinski, what a toad. What a stupid bureaucratic vehicle policy that only serves to increase the level of bureaucracy and obstruct productivity."

On the drive to the office, Jan noticed a car was following him. Jan religiously varied his route to and from the office. This was a habit he developed early in his law enforcement career. He learned the value of personal security and environment awareness from his first partner at his first duty station when employed by the Warsaw City Police Department.

To be certain someone was following him, Jan quickly made a right-hand turn onto Fifth Avenue and increased his speed. The large black Mercedes-Benz followed and stayed with Jan.

Jan turned on his right turn signal but turned left onto Grand Boulevard. The black Mercedes-Benz started to turn right, then abruptly turned left onto Grand Boulevard and continued to follow Jan. The black Mercedes began to gain on Jan, and it began to flash its head lights. The front passenger stuck his arm out from the side window and motioned for Jan to pull over.

Though Jan made maneuvers to determine if someone was following him, he used a route that took him to the Warsaw City Police Headquarters on Grand Boulevard. He knew he could stop in front of the police headquarters building and at this time of the morning, many police officers would be coming and going for a change of shift. The mere fact of being in front of the Warsaw City Police Headquarters could be a deterrent to would-be assailants.

Also, Jan thought to himself, "If I have to stand and fight, this will be the best place to do it. Most of the Warsaw City Police Headquarters officers know me personally. Should an attack at any level occur they know me to be one of them."

As Jan approached the Warsaw City Police Headquarters, he started to slow the BMW. The large black Mercedes-Benz slowed in rhythm. He pulled to the curb and jammed the BMW into park. The BMW bounced front and back from the abrupt stop and not coming to a complete stop before jamming the transmission into park. In one smooth motion, he maneuvered the center consul, slid into the front passenger seat, and exited the vehicle on the passenger side.

The Mercedes-Benz came to a sudden stop in the roadway parallel to Jan's car.

As Jan took a position of cover behind the BMW front passenger tire and the engine block, he gripped his duty weapon and drew it from his right hip holster. He raised his duty weapon in the direction of the Mercedes-Benz, as the rear passenger side window went down, and a head appeared. It was the well-dressed, distinguished, unknown man from Friday night at the Warsaw Café.

The unidentified man waved at Jan to instruct Jan to come over to the Mercedes-Benz and get in.

Jan refused when he said, "I don't know who you are or what you're up to. If you want to talk, get out of the vehicle. We can go inside."

Jan now had his duty weapon at a low ready position alongside his right thigh. He continued to scan right and left for assailants. He was in a low crouched position, still behind the right front wheel and the engine block which provided the best cover in the event of an attack by the occupants of the black Mercedes-Benz S600 AMG. Racing through Jan's mind was the Mercedes-Benz could be a diversion and others may be in the area. Jan continued to assess the area to determine what was in the background and to the left and right of the Mercedes-Benz in the event he had to respond to gunfire.

Without warning, the right rear door of the black Mercedes-Benz opened and the unknown man from Friday night emerged. Instinctively, Jan, in one fluid motion, moved his duty weapon from behind his right thigh to a low ready position, transitioned from a one hand grip to a two-hand grip and eased the duty weapon close to his midsection. Simultaneously, Jan quickly located the unknown man's hands to determine if there was anything in them, particularly a gun. The unknown man's hands were empty. As he walked to the curb, again, Jan repositioned his duty weapon low and to the rear of his right thigh. He kept his gun out but concealed from view. All the while, Jan continued to scan the area, all 360 degrees, and the unknown man's hands. When he glanced to the rear, he noticed the familiar face of an approaching gentleman.

When the unknown man saw the same gentleman, the unknown man became visibly nervous. The unknown man looked deep into Jan's eyes and in a low tone exclaimed something that Jan did not understand. He pointed at the gentleman approaching and quickly returned to the waiting Mercedes-Benz. Before the door closed, the big, black, heavy, Mercedes-Benz sped away with disregard for the morning rush hour traffic. The abrupt departure caused some vehicles to brake hard and maneuver to avoid collision with it or other vehicles.

After Jan had greeted his colleague, who was oblivious to what Jan just negotiated, they made small talk to catch up.

Jan returned to the BMW at the end of the conversation and sat in the vehicle deep in thought about the early morning activities.

He said out loud, "Who is this unknown man?"

At 0755 hours, Jan wheeled the BMW into the Poland National Police office parking lot and parked near the light pole. He parked in a different location so not to set a routine. This was part of his officer safety vigilance.

Jan closed the door, pressed the lock function on the key fob, and walked toward the office building.

Today, he did not arrive at the office by 0700 hours as was his usual schedule. He did not have another cup of coffee nor paczkis with Olenka. He and Olenka did not share conversation.

USA, Maryland, Rockville
Interstate 270 Southbound

0500 Hours

Officer Martin broadcasted, "Unit 198 to dispatch."

Dispatch broadcasted, "Go Unit 198."

"Unit 198, 10-95 I-270 southbound Rockville Exit with a Mercedes-Benz Sprinter, extended, commercial, panel van, white

44

in color, no markings, occupied twice. Michigan Registration 1 5 7 Ocean Whiskey Lincoln. Out at 0605."

"10-4 Unit 198 0605 hours."

As Officer Larry Martin exited his cruiser, an unmarked green Chevrolet Camaro, the white Mercedes-Benz Sprinter van accelerated from the side of the road. With disregard for the heavy early morning rush hour traffic, the Sprinter van sped into the traffic and struck a vehicle in the right rear quarter panel. The impact caused that car to spin one hundred and eighty degrees, and it continued to roll backward. Two cars slammed on their brakes to avoid hitting the Sprinter van. Another skidded out of control from an attempt to avoid colliding with the vehicle rolling backward. The Sprinter van continued, accelerated its speed, and changed lanes with disregard to the other motorists. This erratic driving started a chain reaction accident scene. Vehicles, one after another, careened into the rear of the vehicles in front of them.

Officer Martin rushed back to his cruiser, entered, and picked up the two-way radio mic. He held the mic in his right hand as he took a deep breath. Office Martin, in disbelief, radioed dispatch and told them what was happening right before his eyes. He was momentarily awestruck. He took a second-deep breath. He hung up the radio mic and placed his left hand at the nine o'clock position on the black, leather-wrapped, steering wheel. He gripped the Camaro's floor mounted, leather-wrapped, gear selector with his right hand, squeezed the selector hard and slapped it into drive. His right hand quickly took the three o'clock position on the steering wheel and poised for defensive pursuit driving, he spun out in chase of the white Mercedes-Benz Sprinter van. As he maneuvered his cruiser through what now appeared to be a mile-long pileup, he observed the Sprinter van as it flipped into the air, landed on its roof, slid along the center concrete barrier, flipped over the median wall, and was struck by a northbound tractor-trailer rig. As the tractor-trailer rig braked hard to stop, it continued to push the Sprinter van down the roadway. When the vehicles stopped, the Sprinter van exploded into flames.

The quick-witted operator of the tractor-trailer jumped out when his rig came to rest before it exploded into flames. The impact and proximity to the exploding van caused the tractor-trailer rig to explode.

Officer Martin suppressed an adrenalin dump and radioed dispatch once more. This time he requested a fire truck and ambulance in the northbound lane approximately one mile from the I-270 Rockville interchange. When he arrived at the burning van, the heat and smoke were too intense for him to approach to render assistance. All he could do was watch as the van continued to burn and the occupants cried out.

The intensity of the fire became so great, the paint on Officer Martin's cruiser blistered. He abandoned his cruiser and backed away from the intense heat and toxic smoke.

The Rockville Station of the Montgomery Fire Department was slow to respond because of the volume of morning rush hour traffic. When they arrived, they too were held back from efforts to extinguish the raging fire and render aid to the unknown occupants. Following hours of containment, the emergency responders finally extinguished the flames after much effort. It was not until eight hours after the fiery collision that the Montgomery County Police Department Crime Scene Team technicians were able to approach the van, scour the carnage, and process the automobile accident scene.

Officer Martin's request for the crime scene investigation was from a hunch he had about the traffic stop. Though his Sergeant disagreed with him, the Sergeant reluctantly approved Officer Martin's request.

The crime scene technicians processed the van and discovered ten charred bodies, some fused together from the intense heat. The Montgomery County Coroner's Office personnel removed the charred bodies and transported them to the county morgue to conduct a thorough post-mortem examination. They hoped to identify the deceased individuals.

What the technicians found next was something Officer Martin never thought would result from his hunch. Ten handguns were found. They were holstered and fused one each to the bodies of the unknown deceased occupants. Also, the charred remains of ten military style shoulder weapons positioned in a gun rack installed to the inside of the van near the rear doors. At the scene, the makes, models, and calibers were not determined. The technicians took a series of evidentiary photographs, stripped the side arms from the deceased occupants and took the shoulder weapons from the gun rack. All the charred firearms were processed as evidence. Additional forensics at the crime laboratory was necessary to determine the makes, models, and serial numbers. There were charred remains of three computers, which were also processed as evidence. Lastly, there were the charred remains of five motorcycles for the crime laboratory to determine the makes, models, and vehicle identification numbers. That was the total inventory from the van. A van that was stopped by Officer Martin for an expired registration.

It was 2300 hours, and the crime scene technicians were still processing the scene. Three black Chevrolet Suburban vehicles, with tinted blacked out windows and blue law enforcement emergency lights flashing, arrived at the site of the carnage. The vehicles traveled at a high rate of speed and struggled to a stop. Alighting from the vehicles were twelve individuals clad in dark business suits, silk ties, and slicked back hair. Gold badges were on display hanging from their necks. One of the twelve people introduced all twelve as Special Agents from the Federal Bureau of Investigations (FBI) Headquarters, Washington D.C. Abruptly he asked, "Who's in charge?"

Officer Martin identified himself and stated, "I'm the officer in charge."

The Special Agent, in a condescending tone, without introductions, immediately instructed Officer Martin, "I am the Major Event Site Supervisory Special Agent. The FBI has declared this a Major Event Site in the interest of National Security. I will be taking over the investigation of this major event site."

The Major Event Site Supervisory Special Agent continued to instruct Officer Martin, "My team will secure all of the evidence from the site. My agents will complete the proper chain of custody forms for the crime scene technicians to transfer the evidence. We will take responsibility to clean up the site. You can release all the Montgomery County emergency personnel."

Office Martin stated, "Like hell, you will. The FBI has no authority or jurisdiction here. This is a motor vehicle accident site with fatalities resulting from the decedent's fleeing and eluding a traffic stop by the Montgomery County Police Department. I fail to see or understand how or why the FBI has the authority to take over the investigation of this event under the jurisdiction of the Montgomery County Police Department."

"This is a matter of National Security. I can only brief individuals with a clearance and need to know. You have neither. Office Martin, please call your Sergeant."

This was not the first time Officer Martin was embroiled in a turf war with federal law enforcement authorities for jurisdiction and control of a crime scene. What Officer Martin learned from his past experiences in these situations was to call his Sergeant.

Officer Martin stepped away from the unidentified Major Event Site Supervisory Special Agent, took out his cellphone, and called his Sergeant. It appeared to be an intense conversation from the nonverbal gestures.

Officer Martin returned to the scene as he holstered his cellular telephone. He announced to the Montgomery County Police crime scene team and all other Montgomery County emergency personnel, "We have been ordered to promptly turn over the crime scene, and all evidence gathered, to the FBI."

Officer Martin directed the team to clear the crime scene as quickly as possible and to cooperate with the crime scene transition to the FBI.

The unidentified Major Event Site Supervisory Special Agent thanked Officer Martin in a tone Officer Martin construed as condescending.

5 October, Tuesday

USA, Washington D.C.
DOE Headquarters Building

0600 Hours   Underground Garage

Four of the five Special Agents of the DOE's Secretary Protection Detail mustered in the DOE underground garage. Present from the five-person team was: George, the Detail Leader; Dodge, the Limo Driver; Rich, the Follow Vehicle Driver and Fred, the Advance Agent. Hope, the Shift Leader was late as usual.

With a concerned tone, George said, "Where's Hope? Does anyone know where Hope is? We have to get moving. We need to pick up the Secretary and be across town at the Rayburn Building for his nine o'clock meeting."

Dodge added, "Yeah if you're not ten minutes early, you're twenty minutes late. Where is she? We're going to have to leave without her. We can't wait. We can't wait any longer."

Fred moved off to the side and attempted to contact Hope on her government-issued, cellular telephone. There was no answer; it went directly to the voice mail and announced the caller to leave a message.

Fred hung up without leaving a message. With his smartphone still in hand, he moved back to the group and said, "You all go. I'll wait another fifteen minutes. If Hope shows up, I'll bring her to the Rayburn building when I go to complete my advance.

George replied, "Okay. Good. Thanks, Fred. We'll call you on the radio when we're five minutes out."

Scanning the rest of the detail, George said, "Let's go."

George and the other two team members, as they loaded themselves into the two-vehicle motorcade, were disgusted at Hope's tardiness. It seemed her lack of professionalism, and reoccurring tardiness was causing a morale issue. The Secretary of Energy Protection Detail collectively continued to express their concern about Hope to the Detail Leader. The sounding concern was that Hope represented a weakness to the detail and a risk to the Secretary's security and safety posture. George was beside himself with the issue and kept putting off taking any personnel action. It appeared to the other members of the Secretary's Protection Detail that George was an incompetent leader.

Shortly after the Secretary of Energy Protection Detail departed from the underground garage, Hope came riding down the escalator. She gyrated to the music she listened to through a full-size set of over the ear headphones and continued to rotate toward Fred. When she finally noticed him, she quickly stopped dancing and took the headphones off.

"Hope, where were you?" Fred asked as he rushed toward her. "The detail departed for the pickup at seven o'clock. The Secretary was scheduled on the hill for a nine o'clock meeting. You didn't answer my call to your government cellphone."

"We start at seven o'clock a.m. I don't turn my government phone on until seven a.m., "Hope replied. "Why didn't someone send the schedule to me? Why didn't George send it to me? If they wanted me here before 7 a.m., they should have called me, sent me a text. Somehow contacted me. It was not my fault."

"But you didn't have your phone on." Fred paused in frustration. "Okay. Okay. Come on, I'm to bring you with me to the hill when I go to complete the advance. We have to go now."

Hope replied, "Now! Right now? Can't I get a cup of coffee first?" And then in a frazzled manner, Hope ranted, "Let's go. Let's just go."

Fred and Hope climbed down into a government sedan. Careful not to twist their back the wrong way as they squeezed into the white, four-door, Chevrolet Caviler with government registration plates front and rear and flex-fuel markings on the rear molded bumper. To promote fuel efficiency, DOE retrofitted their government vehicles to run on natural gas. Though retrofitted to use natural gas as a fuel, the detail only used regular unleaded gasoline. Apparently, there were no natural gas refueling stations in the District of Columbia. One of the topics for the daily ridicule of the DOE's dysfunctional management style as perceived by the Special Agents of the Executive Protection Detail.

Fred in the driver's seat and Hope in the front passenger seat, Fred maneuvered the ominous government protection detail vehicle through the underground garage. They moved through the security checkpoint where the uniformed contract guard in the guard booth was awake. Through the open driver's door window, Fred greeted the uniformed contract guard with an enthusiastic hand wave. The contract guard nodded his head in reply as he pushed the necessary buttons to lower the security barrier to permit Fred and Hope to depart the DOE Headquarters garage en route to the Rayburn Building on Capitol Hill and their security advance.

USA, Washington, D.C. NW

0730 Hours   Secretary of Energy's Residence

The Secretary of Energy emerged from his house.

George greeted him, "Good morning, Mr. Secretary."

"Good morning George," replied the Secretary in an enthusiastic manner.

The Secretary entered the limo and in the same enthusiastic manner greeted Dodge.

"Good morning Mr. Secretary," replied Dodge.

After George closed the Secretary's door and was in the limo himself, he locked the limo doors and broadcasted, "Move."

Secretary of Energy Motorcade in transit

The Secretary's motorcade, two black vehicles, one a Cadillac Deville and the other a Chevrolet Suburban, both with dark tinted blacked out windows and nondescript District of Columbia registration plates. It moved down the narrow street lined with mature trees to merge onto the main city artery clogged with daily commuters. The Secretary's motorcade began a slow go to Capitol Hill.

George broadcasted, "George to Rich."

"Go George."

"Get us into this traffic."

Rich, with two clicks of the onboard, mobile, two-way radio microphone, acknowledged the command from the Detail Leader. He engaged the blue, law enforcement emergency lights affixed to the follow vehicle which halted traffic in the eastbound lanes at the intersection. Rich maneuvered the follow vehicle into a position that blocked the right-hand lane of the eastbound lanes and stopped the morning rush hour traffic. This allowed the limo to flow into the right-hand lane without stopping at the stop sign at the end of the street. Rich turned off the law enforcement emergency lights and stacked the follow vehicle directly behind the limo. The two-vehicle motorcade moved into the morning rush hour traffic, en route to the Rayburn building.

The Secretary sat in the right-hand rear seat and read the morning briefing papers. He was oblivious to the detail's daily duties.

Two miles from the Rayburn building, George broadcasted, "George to Fred."

There was no reply.

One and a half miles from the Rayburn building, George broadcasted, "George to Fred."

Again, there was no answer.

George whispered to Dodge, "Did you hear me?"

Dodge replied in a whisper, "Yes."

Rich broadcasted, "Rich to Fred."

"Go Rich."

"Did you copy George?"

"No."

"Call George."

"Okay. Clear. Fred to George"

"Fred, we're arriving. We're turning onto the horseshoe. What entrance are we using?"

Fred broadcasted, "I'm at the top of the horseshoe. Come all the way up to the doors. Stop on my mark. When you get out, follow me."

George replied with two clicks of his small, rectangular, molded, portable, hand-held, two-way radio microphone clipped to his left-hand French cuff.

Fred broadcasted, "Hope will show the drivers where to park and then meet us in front of the holding room."

Six clicks of the two-way radio mics sounded. Two each came from Dodge, Rich, and Hope.

Dodge continued his stoic poise and intense concentration on his task. Capitol Hill was always a challenge as the arrogant staffers rushed to work as if they were the only ones on the Hill. Dodge perceived an aura of elitism on the hill.

Washington D.C.
The United States of America Capitol Grounds
Rayburn House Office Building

The two-vehicle motorcade turned right onto the horseshoe driveway on the east side of the Rayburn House Office Building. The motorcade drivers gingerly navigated the narrow driveway to the bank of doors that handled the morning rush hour foot traffic of employees, guests, and tourists. The motorcade came to a stop at Fred's mark. George exited the limo and shut his door. There was a muffled sound of the electric locks engaged by Dodge. George acknowledged Fred's presence with a head nod as he scanned the area looking hard for threats. Then George tapped the passenger side door window. Again, there was a muffled sound of the electric locks unlocking the limo doors. George controlled the right rear passenger door for the Secretary to exit the vehicle.

When the Secretary saw Fred, he said, "Good morning Fred."

Fred replied, "Good morning Mr. Secretary, please follow me."

Fred turned and led the Secretary into the Rayburn building and to the hearing room where the Secretary was scheduled to testify before Congress. Such were some of the duties of an Advance Agent.

George closed the limo door and took the right shoulder protective position. George followed the Secretary who followed Fred who followed a uniformed police officer of the U.S. Capitol Police.

Once inside the Rayburn building, the uniformed U.S. Capitol Police Officer, with the wave of his hand, officiated the entourage's bypass of the security checkpoint. Once on the other side of the security checkpoint, the Secretary was joined and greeted by a member of his advance staff, one of his aides, and a DOE program specialist.

The uniformed U.S. Capitol Police Officer continued to flow through the lobby. He led the entourage to the bank of elevators which they rode to the fifth floor.

At the fifth floor, the entourage exited the elevator and proceeded to the Secretary's holding room adjacent to the hearing room. The Secretary and his entourage entered the holding room. Fred and George took positions outside the room by the door. The uniformed U.S. Capitol Police Officer went to tend to other business inside the hearing room.

George said, "Fred, why didn't you answer my radio call?"

"I didn't hear you," replied Fred. "You know the portable, hand-held, two-way radios are no good. They're a line of sight communication. We talk about that in our staff meetings all the time. The follow vehicle's onboard two-way radio has more power than the handheld radios."

"I know. I don't know what I'm going to do about our equipment. I keep telling management that we need better radios and other equipment. They don't authorize the purchase of new and better equipment. One of these days, we're going to have problems. It's going to be embarrassing. I just hope no one gets hurt."

George changed the subject.

"What time did Hope show up this morning?"

"Seven o'clock."

George noticed Hope walking down the hallway toward them. He motioned with his head in her direction, so Fred did not say anything else. George changed the subject.

"How long will we be here," George said to Fred.

"Per the Secretary's Schedule 11A. But the Secretary may stay for lunch in the Committee Chairmen's office. The Secretary's staff won't know until after the hearing. That's the best I could determine. You know the staff is always cagey with information and details about the Secretary's schedule."

"Okay," said George. "Now we wait. You didn't get us chairs Fred? Are we going to have to stand all this time? Geez."

As they continued to stand outside the holding room, Hope said, "How about that chain reaction, automobile accident on 270 yesterday? It looked bad. I saw some coverage of it on the local news last night."

Fred replied, "Yeah. I talked with my buddies at the Charlestown PD. They said it was bad. It tied up traffic and rerouted traffic all day, way into the evening hours. I took a different route home last night. When I came to work this morning, I saw the burn marks on the roadway. The one northbound lane was still closed. It looked like they were still processing or cleaning the scene this morning. It looked like a Federal agency was working the scene, which I thought was unusual."

"Yeah," said Hope. "I just talked to my friend who's with the Protection Detail for the Secretary of Commerce. He told me they didn't get the Secretary of Commerce to his White House meeting yesterday until one o'clock. He said the Secretary was mad."

"Where is the Secretary of Commerce residence?" asked George.

"I think it's in Rockville."

"Why was the Secretary of Commerce going to the White House? What kind of meeting did he have? Was it with the President?"

"I don't know."

Hope changed subjects.

"George, any progress with an intelligence unit in our detail? I know we talk about that from time to time."

"I know Hope. And I agree with you, we should have an intelligence unit. At least one person to handle that task on a full-time basis. I'm still working that issue. It's slow going with management. They fight me every step of the way and on everything I suggest. I get no respect from them. I have secret service training. I have experience from protecting the President of the United States. They think I don't know what I'm talking about when it comes to the security and safety of Secretary. It's frustrating for me."

The Secretary and his entourage, without notice, emerged from the holding room. Fred moved with ease to lead the entourage to the hearing room and then positioned himself at the rear doors outside the hearing room. A staff member guided the Secretary to his seat at the witness table. George followed the Secretary and positioned himself in the first row of seats, an aisle seat, directly behind the Secretary. Hope stayed outside with Fred because seating was limited.

Fred broadcasted, "Rich. Dodge. The Secretary is in the hearing room."

Dodge and Rich acknowledged Fred's broadcast with two clicks each. Dodge and Rich were posted in the vehicles to ensure no one sabotaged the motorcade and for the readiness to move the Secretary on demand, per the Secretary's Daily Schedule, an emergency or attack.

While inside the hearing room, the Secretary's advance person came up to George and said, "George, the Secretary will be going back to the DOE Headquarters. No lunch with the Committee Chairman. He also had a telephone call from the White House. He may be going to the White House for a one o'clock Cabinet meeting with the President."

"Thank you."

George stepped outside the hearing room and briefed Fred on what the Secretary's advance person just told him and then directed.

"Fred, you go back to the office and prep for an advance and arrival at the White House for the Secretary's one o'clock meeting with the President and other Cabinet members." He turned to Hope, "Assume the Advance Agent position for the balance of this movement."

George returned inside the hearing room and his front row, aisle seat behind the Secretary.

Fred left the fifth floor, returned to his ominous government Executive Protection Detail vehicle, the white, four-door, Chevrolet Cavalier, and returned to the DOE Headquarters. At the OSO office suite, Fred arranged for the change to the Secretary's Daily Schedule.

Outside the hearing room, Hope, in a three-way, cellular telephone conversation, briefed Dodge and Rich on the schedule change and possible move to the White House. Hope remained outside the hearing room. Hope was now tasked as the Shift Leader and Advance Agent due to staff limitations.

At 1230 hours, the doors to the hearing room opened. The Secretary's advance person led the entourage.

Hope rushed up to him and in a low tone asked, "What's going on?"

The Secretary's advance person informed Hope, "The Secretary has to go directly to the White House for the one o'clock Cabinet meeting."

Hope took the lead and proceeded to the elevator held by a uniformed U.S. Capitol Police Officer. The large entourage squeezed into the century-old elevator. The ride to the first floor was silent. When the elevator door opened on the first floor, everyone moved out.

In a hushed tone, Hope broadcasted, "Hope to Dodge."

"Go, Hope."

"We're coming out. Meet us at the drop point."

"What? You're on your way. We're still parked at the curb at the lower end of the horseshoe driveway. No heads up?"

Without any notice that the Secretary was coming out, Dodge and Rich scrambled and navigated the bustling foot and motor vehicle traffic in and about the horseshoe driveway to get to the drop point. As well trained and experienced law enforcement officers, both Dodge and Rich knew the Secretary should not wait outside for his limo. Anything less than a smooth flow of the Secretary into his limo created a security and safety risk to the Secretary as he was exposed.

Almost to the security checkpoint and the exit, the Secretary's cellular telephone rang. The entourage stopped along the wall, and the Secretary answered the phone. Hope and George took up positions on opposite sides of the Secretary and faced away from the Secretary. They looked for threats, maintained as much privacy for the Secretary as possible under the circumstances, and positioned themselves to keep the press or gawkers at bay.

After the brief telephone call, the Secretary looked to George. "I have to go directly to the White House as fast as possible."

"Yes, sir."

The entourage moved again. It passed the security checkpoint, exited through the automatic sliding glass doors, and moved to the waiting two-vehicle motorcade.

Hope opened the right, rear, limo door and then handed it off to George. George controlled the door, and the Secretary entered. As George positioned himself in the limo, Hope positioned herself in the right front seat of the follow vehicle and broadcasted, "Move."

The Secretary's two-vehicle motorcade crept through the narrow, congested horseshoe driveway and away from the Rayburn Office Building, for the United States House of Representatives.

George broadcasted, "We're moving directly to the White House. Hope, make the notifications."

Hope responded with two clicks. She telephoned DOE Headquarters and advised DOE Emergency Operations Center that the Secretary was en route to the White House for a meeting that was not on his Daily Schedule.

Secretary of Energy Motorcade in transit

As the Limo Driver led the Secretary's motorcade in a left-hand turn onto Independence Avenue, the Secretary, in a frantic voice and out of character, said, "George I need to be there now. Can you hurry this along?"

"Yes, sir."

The Secretary's motorcade passed First Street Southwest, and George broadcasted, "Engage emergency lights and expedite."

The Follow Driver, as conditioned, immediately checked his side mirror to determine if it was clear to set up an offset follow position. The offset follow was a protective position where the Follow Driver placed the center of the follow vehicle on the left or right rear corner of the limo. This protection driving tactic was used to clear lanes and make the motorcade more visible to the motoring public. A way to ask for more room to operate. The Limo Driver set the speed of and picked the lane for the motorcade. When a lane change was necessary, the Limo Driver used one flash of the limo's directional signals to request. The follow vehicle slid into the lane and held it open for the limo to use. After the limo had been repositioned, the follow vehicle re-established an offset protection posture.

With the lane clear and emergency lights operating on both the limo and the follow vehicle, the Secretary's motorcade expedited down Independence Avenue, en route to the White House. The motorcade still had to stop at all traffic control signals and posted stop signs if the intersection was not clear of traffic. Once the intersection was cleared, the motoring public gave the right of way to the motorcade, the motorcade proceeded without stopping.

While the Limo Driver, Follow Driver, and Shift Leader handled the logistics of expediting the Secretary to the White House, George telephoned Fred to obtain the plans for the Secretary's arrival at the West Wing.

From the caller ID feature on Fred's government issued cellphone, he answered the call with an enthusiastic, "Hello George."

Fred's game was on. He was rocking and rolling. The change in the Secretary's schedule represented a challenge to Fred. For Fred, that made his work days enjoyable.

George, with a slight panic in his voice, replied, "What's the plan?"

Fred calmly said, "I'm at the West Wing Parking lot. Come to the White House grounds and use the east entrance. The Secret Service Uniformed Division (UD) is expecting your arrival at that entry. UD will process the Secretary's motorcade through the White House grounds entry protocol."

George's narcissistic personality interrupted Fred, "Okay."

Fred continued, "Come straight back to the West Wing. When you turn up to the West Wing parking lot, look for me and stop on my mark. Parking is going to be tight. I think the entire Presidential Cabinet is here for the meeting."

George, still with a narcissistic tone, replied, "Okay. We are at the East Gate Security Checkpoint."

The telephone call was abruptly ended by George without notice to Fred.

The Secretary's motorcade flowed onto the White House grounds and was processed at the UD security checkpoint. When cleared, it continued the White House grounds to the area of the West Wing and stopped at Fred's mark. George exited the limo, shut his door, and opened and controlled the right rear door. The Secretary exited and continued to walk toward the West Wing entrance. George handed the door off to Fred and followed the Secretary into the West Wing.

The motorcade drivers eased away from the drop point and parked the vehicles with the assistance of Fred.

To pass the time waiting for the Secretary, Fred, Dodge, Rich, and Hope mustered outside the motorcade vehicles. Their conversation included many topics. All were on the lookout for celebrity, government employees. It was a comfortable fall day, sunny, blue sky, and a temperature everyone wished they had year-round.

At 1630 hours, George broadcasted, "He's out."

The protection team rushed to their respective positions in the motorcade, situated themselves, and eased the motorcade down the West Wing parking area to the Secretary. The Secretary and Detail Leader entered the limo, and the motorcade eased away.

Secretary of Energy Motorcade in transit

The Secretary quickly said, "George take me home."

"Yes, sir."

"To the house," George broadcasted, in a hushed tone into his left sleeve.

Hope sent two clicks of her mic to reply.

The Secretary of Energy's two-vehicle motorcade departed the White House grounds at the west entrance and proceeded through the District of Columbia rush hour traffic. As was typical, there was no conversation in the limo.

6 October, Wednesday

Poland Airspace
The United States of America Military Airplane

1300 Hours

The Military Flight Attendant said, "Mr. Secretary, may I take your coffee cup. We're on our descent to Warsaw. Please raise your tray table to the upright position."

"Yes, you may. Thank you," replied the Secretary of Commerce. "I'll prepare for landing."

"Thank you, sir."

The Secretary's Chief of Staff said, "Mr. Secretary, let me show you the revisions to your speech today. I have them here on my Blackberry."

"Already. Great. Let me look."

"Just hit the space key. The document will come up," said the Secretary's Chief of Staff as he handed his Blackberry to the Secretary.

"Okay. Press the key. There."

The Secretary pressed the space key, and at that instant, the United States of America military aircraft exploded into a fiery ball. The force of the explosion hurled pieces of the plane in multiple directions before the pieces plummeted to the ground.

USA, Washington, D.C. NW

0730 Hours   Secretary of Energy's Residence

The Secretary emerged from his house. George greeted him, "Good morning Mr. Secretary."

"Good morning George," replied the Secretary.

The Secretary entered the limo and greeted Dodge, "Good morning Dodge."

"Good morning Mr. Secretary," replied Dodge.

George closed the Secretary's door, entered the limo, locked the limo doors, and broadcasted, "Move."

Secretary of Energy Motorcade in transit

The Secretary's two-vehicle motorcade moved down the narrow street, lined with mature trees, to merge onto the main city artery and into the morning rush hour traffic, en route to the DOE Headquarters. The Secretary sat in the right rear seat and read the morning briefings.

George broadcasted, "George to Hope."

"Go George."

"Make the notifications, arrival point two."

After a brief lull, Hope broadcasted, "Notifications made."

The motorcade continued en route along the Potomac River. It slowly made its way to Independence Avenue. The two vehicles moved east on Independence Avenue when George noticed a large crowd gathered in front of the USDA building.

As the motorcade continued toward the DOE Headquarters Building, the crowd moved out into the roadway and blocked the motorcade. It came to an abrupt stop to avoid striking anyone. The follow vehicle struggled to come to a smooth stop and gently bumped the back of the limo. The sudden stop of the limo and the follow vehicle's bump to the limo caused the Secretary to slide forward into the back of the front seats and onto the floor. Occasionally, the Secretary did not affix his seatbelt as protection protocol required and as the Detail Leader briefed the Secretary when he first assumed his duties as Secretary. The crowd continued to occupy the roadway and started to surround the motorcade.

George in a panic said to Dodge, "Get us out of this. Get us out of this."

George engaged the electric locks which were already locked.

Dodge broadcasted, "Rich move back. Reverse out of this."

"I can't. The crowd surrounded the motorcade."

The crowd repetitively chanted, "Pass the farm bill. Raise the food stamp benefits."

Dodge continued to inch the limo along Independence Avenue. He was ever so cautious not to strike anyone, not even to touch anyone. The follow vehicle stayed tight to the rear bumper of the limo. It almost pushed the limo at times.

George broadcasted, "Stay on our bumper Rich. Don't let the crowd get between the two vehicles."

There was no response. Rich remained cool, calm, and collected: he knew what he needed to do. He brought protection detail experience from his training and work experience he used around the world when he was employed with the Dignitary Protection, with the U.S. Department of State.

George turned in his seat to look back at the Secretary. "Sir, are you alright?"

The Secretary rubbed his head. In a desperate tone, he replied, "Yes. What are we going to do?"

Dodge continued to inch the limo along Independence Avenue and was nearly to the second overhead arch of the Agriculture Building and the follow vehicle continued to stay tight to the rear bumper of the limo. Dodge took his right hand and placed it on the column gear shift selector. He moved the gear selector into neutral and gunned the engine causing it to roar. The roar of the limo's engine startled the crowd, and the group backed away from the limo. Dodge repeated the gunning of the engine. The people appeared to be confused and concerned and continued to move further away from the motorcade. This created an opening and Dodge dropped the gear selector into the low gear and accelerated through and away from the crowd. The follow vehicle was tight to the rear bumper of the limo. The motorcade cleared the crowd and expedited two more blocks to the DOE Headquarters Building.

DOE Headquarters Building

Dodge brought the limo to a smooth stop at arrival point two. George exited the vehicle and opened the Secretary's door.

George said, "Mr. Secretary, are you all right?"

The white-faced Secretary stepped out of the limo. He appeared to be shaken and concerned. He just looked at George.

George repeated, "Mr. Secretary, are you alright? Do you want to go to the Department nurse?"

A bit disgusted, the Secretary replied, "Yes. I'm okay. No, I don't want to go to the nurse's office."

The Secretary and George walked away from the limo. George led the Secretary into the building. This was not acceptable protection protocol, but given the staffing limitations, George had no other choice.

The Secretary, not far from the limo and with no warning, turned around and walked back toward the limo.

Dodge broadcasted, "He's coming toward the limo."

George turned and rushed to catch up to the Secretary.

The Secretary opened the right front passenger door of the limo, leaned in, and said, "Thank you, Dodge. Thank you. You did a good job getting us out of that. Thank you."

The Secretary did not wait for a response from Dodge. He closed the door, turned toward the building, and continued to walk to the entrance to the headquarters building.

Again, George stumbled about to get in step with the Secretary. This was not how George liked to perform his protection duties. The lack of smoothness frustrated George, a perfectionist.

1000 Hours   OSO Office Suite

George sat in his office. He was deep in thought about how the security detail reacted to the crowd this morning. He was not pleased. With respect for Chain of Command, he shouted to his Shift Leader, "Hope, can you come into my office."

Hope appeared in the doorway of George's memorabilia den and replied, "Yes."

Abruptly, George said, "Gather the guys. We need to have a meeting. I want to talk about this morning."

Hope replied, "What didn't you like?"

George, in an authoritative voice, said, "Gather the guys."

The members of the protection detail collected in a common area of the office suite of the OSO.

George emerged from his office. The smartly dressed, fashion conscious, Detail Leader professionally carried himself. He sported a short, well groom, slicked back, hairstyle combed straight back in a Mike Ditka style. His tie was reserved but added a splash of color to his professional ensemble. His usual white shirt, always starched and sharply pressed, was fitted with French cuffs which he accented with Office of the President cuff links he received while on the President's detail when employed by the United States Secret Service. Layered over his fashion statement was his duty gear. His issued duty weapon, a Glock Model 19 9-millimeter, rested on his right hip next to his belt clip, gold colored, law enforcement badge identifying him as a Federal law enforcement officer with DOE, OSO. His handcuffs were position on his left-hand side next to his two-way radio, two fifteen round capacity magazines and a collapsible baton. Draped neat and orderly over his chiseled bodybuilding physique, a cord led to his left ear and was connected to his custom molded earpiece. There was a concern on the face of George as he walked back and forth in front of the Special Agents of the protection detail. He looked up and looked at each person. He stopped at Dodge.

There, in front of Dodge, he just stared at him. This made Dodge uncomfortable; he became restless. Dodge's reaction to George's stare was out of character for the stoic Dodge.

George said, "I want to know why someone didn't call or radio the motorcade and tell me about the crowd on Independence Avenue by the Agriculture Building."

George paused a moment and then said, "Fred, where were you?"

70

"Easy George! I was right here in the office. I was the Advance Agent. I was not involved with the pickup."

Fred replied in a serious, authoritative tone. He showed signs of agitation which was out of character for him.

Fred, the oldest and most senior member of the protection detail, was the peacemaker for the team. When any member of the team became frustrated, Fred was there to calm the situation with the wisdom he possessed from his lengthy service to the United States of America. Fred first served his Federal government in the military, the Army. After ten years there, Fred came to the DOE where he served for twenty years. He served the DOE in various position throughout his twenty years. He dealt with the DOE's management shenanigans a lot longer than the younger members of the protection detail. Any of the other members. That included George, who in comparison to Fred was younger in age and with way fewer years of service with the DOE and the Federal government.

Fred tried to assist George. He provided suggestions on how to approach and present demands to DOE management. Fred really wanted George to be successful. Unfortunately, George did not listen to or follow Fred's advice.

George's only response to Fred, "I've worked for the Secret Service. I was on the Presidential Protection Detail. I was on the Secret Service Counter Assault Team. I was trained to manage an Executive Protection Detail."

So even Fred, the friendly, light-hearted Tennessean, was losing his patience with George. Fred did not tolerate someone who talked down to him or belittled him.

George continued, "Well, why didn't you know about the crowd forming on Independence Avenue?"

"Why would I? How would I?" said Fred still in an authoritative tone. "OSO has no intelligence. We aren't part of the intelligence community. We don't get the morning briefs to read. I keep telling you the detail needs a person in the DOE Emergency Operations Center (EOC), a place I'm familiar with from my various DOE assignments. I know the value of a person in the EOC. That person has access to the morning briefs and the daily intelligence traffic from the metro area, and national and international information. Also, it would behoove the detail to have someone at the Joint Terrorism Task Force, either in the District or in Baltimore. This would provide a real-time intelligence posture for the detail."

"We don't have the manpower for those positions," said George as he talked over Fred. "We only have the people in this room plus Rich who is on the floor, in the security room upstairs. That's five people. How can we put a body in those positions? What position do we give up?"

Still, with an authoritative tone, Fred said, "You have to ask for more bodies. We should have, at the minimum, two shifts of seven agents per shift. Plus, people for other positions like the DOE EOC, the Joint Terrorism Task Force, and Interpol. That's how. Those posts keep us in the loop with what's happening, with the intelligence around DC, and the places we go national and international."

"Okay, okay. We talked about this before Fred, "said George. "I'm not mad at you. I'm just frustrated. I can't get people here at the DOE to understand how a protection detail operates. The necessary equipment and staff."

George turned to Dodge and said, "You have any ideas? Maybe you could talk to the Secretary. He seems to be fond of you today."

Dodge just looked at George. There was a brief stare down before, in a sharp and snappy tone, Dodge said, "No, I don't have any ideas right now. I've been thinking. I want to research and gather some more information. Fred is correct, the detail needs more agents. But how are you going to hire Special Agents from the Federal law enforcement community when everyone knows we have no statutory authority. No one wants to take a job here. To come from other Federal law enforcement agencies with statutory authority, to one with no statutory authority. Then they have the embarrassment of the U.S. Marshal deputation. That's a huge problem for OSO. Not to mention the gun phobia here at DOE. And you're right George, management just doesn't get it."

"All right, we have to get ready for the next scheduled movement," George said.

George abruptly ended the meeting and walked away from the agents and back into his office. As the agents dispersed, Dodge motioned to Fred to follow him out of the office.

In the hallway, Dodge, in a low tone said, "Fred, let's move further down the hall. I need to talk to you."

They moved near the elevator bank.

Dodge said, "Fred, what's up with George? It's like he's blaming you and me for the shortcomings of OSO."

"I know," Fred replied in a discussed tone. "I don't know what to think. But I'll tell you this, he's not going to blame me for something I am unable to do because of the limited resources. Intelligence involves classified information with special rules and procedures. I don't think George understands he's at the DOE and not the Secret Service. The DOE does things their way. And why is he staring you down? What's going on between you two?"

Dodge shook his head.

"It was like he was jealous of me that the Secretary thanked me for getting the motorcade out of the crowd this morning."
Fred looked at his watch.

"Ten thirty-five. Dodge, I have to go. I have to complete the advance for the Secretary's luncheon this afternoon. It's his turn to host the Cabinet luncheon here at DOE. There'll be about eight or nine Secretaries here. I have to liaison with the advance agents from their details."

Dodge said, "Okay. I'll talk with you later. I better go push Rich. See you up there."

1045 Hours   Main Entrance

Fred was at the main entrance to the DOE Headquarters. He waited for the scheduled time to meet the advance agents from the details for the various Cabinet Secretaries who were attending the luncheon.

At 1030 a. m., Fred received a text from Hope.

"WE JUST RECEIVED WORD THAT THE SECRETARY'S LUNCHEON HAS BEEN CANCELLED. COME BACK TO THE OFFICE."

Fred replied.

"OKAY. ON MY WAY."

Back at the OSO suite, Fred said to Hope, "Do you know why the luncheon was canceled?"

"No," replied Hope. "You know the Secretary's staff never gives the protection detail any information or specifics. I don't bother to ask anymore."

Fred said, "I hear you."

1415 Hours   Main Entrance

"Fred to Hope."

"Go Fred."

"Hope, the Governor has arrived. We're moving your way. The Governor plus four. Copy."

"Copy. Governor plus four."

"We're in the elevator."

"Copy."

The elevator doors closed. With a chug and a clang, the elevator started to ascend. A bell sounded at every floor the elevator passed en route to the ninth floor in the express mode.

The elevator stopped at the Secretary's suite. The doors opened. Fred exited the elevator first, followed by the Governor and his staff. Fred led them down the hall to the Secretary's office.

Fred and the Governor's security officer moved to the side before the Governor, and his entourage entered the Secretary's foyer. As Fred and the Governor's security officer proceeded to the OSO security room, near the Secretary's suite, Fred heard the Secretary greet the Governor.

"Governor Schwartz, welcome to the Department of Energy. I'm glad you could come."

In a thick Austrian accent, Governor Schwartz replied, "Thank you Mr. Secretary. It's a pleasure to be here."

One and a half hours later, Governor Schwartz and his staff emerged from the Secretary's office. Fred and the Governor's security officer moved into place. Fred in the front to lead the group to the elevator. The Governor's security officer at the right shoulder of the Governor. When everyone was in the elevator, Fred pushed the button to close the doors. He used his key to express the elevator to the lobby. At the lobby, the elevator doors opened, and Fred emerged first, and the Governor and his staff followed.

Fred motioned to the DOE uniformed contract security guards at the security checkpoint. The security turnstiles were remotely activated to allow Fred, the Governor, and the Governor's staff to pass through unobstructed. Fred continued to lead them to the front glass sliding doors, through an open walkway, and to the Governor's waiting motorcade parked on the street.

Governor Schwartz, at the motorcade, turned to Fred, extended his hand, and the two shook hands. Governor Schwartz said, "Thank you, Fred. Thank you for your assistance."

The Governor and his staff entered the motorcade. The seven vehicles plus four District of Columbia uniformed, motorcycle officers moved.

Secretary's Suite

1600 Hours   OSO Security Room

"Hope to Rich."

"Go, Hope."

"We're moving your way."

"10-4, all clear."

Hope acknowledged Rich with two clicks to her mic.

The next broadcast on the two-way radios was Hope.

"Coming out."

The entourage continued to move toward the motorcade. George opened the right rear limo door, controlled it as the Secretary entered, and then closed it. George entered and sat in the right front passenger seat.

Hope, already in the follow vehicle right front passenger seat, broadcasted, "Move."

The Secretary of Energy Motorcade was in transit through Washington D.C. and arrived at his residence without incident.

Hope immediately exited the follow vehicle and positioned herself at the end of the driveway. She scanned the sidewalk and roadway for threats.

Without monotony, George emerged from the limo and closed his door. The Limo Driver electronically locked the doors. George scanned the area for anything or anyone unusual. He looked hard for threats. When he believed it was secure, he tapped on the window of the front passenger side door. The Limo Driver released the locks. George opened the door, and the Secretary stepped out. They walked to the side entrance of the residence.

The Secretary, as he never forgot to do, said, "Thank you. Everyone have a good evening. See you all in the morning."

The Secretary entered his residence.

The detail loaded back into the motorcade vehicles and drove off to return the government vehicles to the underground garage. They ended their shift for the day.

7 October, Thursday

USA, Washington, D.C. NW

0730 Hours   Secretary of Energy's Residence

The Secretary emerged from his house, and he and George greeted each other before he entered the limo. When the Secretary was seated, he and Dodge greeted each other.

After George closed the Secretary's door and was in the limo himself, the Limo Driver locked the doors electronically.

George broadcasted, "Move."

Secretary of Energy Motorcade in transit

At the Detail Leader's command, the motorcade moved down the narrow, mature tree lined street to merge onto the main city artery and into the morning rush hour traffic to the DOE Headquarters Building. The Secretary was in the right rear seat and read the morning briefings.

"George to Hope."

"Go George."

"Make notifications. Arrival point one."

After a brief lull, Hope broadcasted, "Notifications made arrival point one."

The Secretary's motorcade maneuvered through the District of Columbia morning rush hour traffic along the Rock Creek and Potomac Parkway, in the northwest area. The secure telephone in the rear of the Secretary's limo rang.

The Secretary picked up the handheld receiver and said, "Hello."

Through the rearview mirror, Dodge saw the Secretary listened attentively.

The Secretary spoke into the receiver, "Yes."

He continued to listen attentively now with concern in his eyes.

The Secretary replied, "Okay. Yes, I'll be there." He placed the secured telephone receiver back into the cradle. The click, when locked into position, echoed in the limo.

The limo glided past the Washington Monument as it approached the Agriculture buildings. Dodge continued to operate the limo with smooth ease and steered the limo into a right-hand turn to position it as far to the right-hand curb as possible in the busy morning rush hour traffic. Dodge positioned the limo for a flip to set the motorcade up for entry into the west entrance of the DOE underground garage. Dodge maneuvered the limo into position and began to enter the apron to the downhill descent into the garage and George engaged the emergency lights to notify DOE contract uniformed security guards to lower the barricades for an uninterrupted flow into the underground garage.

Once in the DOE underground parking, Dodge operated the limo to arrival point one. George unlocked the limo doors, opened his door, and stepped out. George closed his door and opened the right rear door and controlled it as the Secretary stepped out. When the Secretary cleared the door, George closed it and followed the Secretary through the security checkpoint. The Secretary was not required to submit to the departmental security protocol, and the entourage passed the security checkpoint unabated. With Hope in the lead, the entourage continued up the escalator to the lobby area.

They made their way through the lobby to the bank of elevators. Hope pushed the elevator call button, and they waited for the elevator doors to open. While they waited, DOE employees started to gather to wait for the elevator also. When the elevator doors opened, Hope entered first and controlled the elevator control panel. The Secretary entered the elevator with George directly behind him. DOE employees crowded into the elevator also. Hope pressed the ninth-floor button, and other floor buttons called out by the DOE employees.

After the slow ride up in the elevator, because it stopped at other floors requested by the DOE employees, the elevator arrived at the ninth floor. Hope exited the elevator first, followed by the Secretary, and then George. Hope led the entourage.

The Secretary looked back at George and said, "That was a scenic ride up today."

The Secretary proceeded down the hallway lined with the portraits of past DOE Secretaries and entered his office. George turned around and moved to the ninth-floor security room where Hope entered.

George said to Hope, "I'm going downstairs. I'll see you later."

"See you later."

1025 Hours   OSO Security Room

On the security camera monitors, Hope saw the Secretary coming out of his office with two other individuals. She jumped up and put on her jacket. She prepared to lock the security room door and follow the Secretary. She did not know where the Secretary was going. The Secretary's Daily Schedule showed him in his office.

Hope exited the room, closed and locked the door, as the Secretary and the two other unknown individuals passed the security room. She rushed to catch up.

The Secretary and the two unknown individuals passed the elevators and turned right at the first hallway. They continued to walk down the hall. Shortly, the Secretary and the two others walked into an office.

Hope entered the office and scanned the area, then stepped back into the hallway. Hope, at the door to the office and in the hallway, took up a position to secure the area and to wait for the Secretary to return.

At 1150 hours, the Secretary, by himself, emerged from the office. He retraced his route back to his office suite. As the Secretary walked by the security room, Hope paused and watched the Secretary proceed through his office foyer and into his office suite. Hope unlocked the door to the security room and entered. She took her post to continue her watch over the Secretary and the area from the security camera monitors.

At 1230 hours, Hope was pushed by Dodge. Dodge was now in the ninth-floor security room to relieve Hope so she could take a lunch break and have a change of tasks. This guarded against monotony and boredom which negated the vigilance that was critical to Executive Protection operations. Dodge continued the constant watch over the Secretary and the area of the Secretary's office suite.

It was 1445 hours. Dodge was still in the ninth-floor security room. He observed five individuals on the security camera monitors. They exited an elevator, walked pass the DOE contract uniformed security guard station, and down the hallway to the Secretary's suite. The people moved directly through the foyer of the Secretary's suite and into the Secretary's office. They did not stop at the reception desk.

Dodge reviewed the Secretary's Daily Schedule. No meetings were scheduled for this time; it reflected private time. Private time was a notation used by the Secretary's scheduling staff to show the Secretary was working on matters of his choosing, in his office, by himself.

Dodge thought to himself, "This is odd to have five individuals arrive at the Secretary's office during private time."

At 1600 hours, George arrived at the ninth-floor security room to push Dodge and to escort the Secretary to the motorcade for the end of the day departure.

George scanned the security cameras and observed the five individuals. They stood with the Secretary in the Secretary's outer office. It appeared they were just talking.

George said to Dodge, "What're those guys doing there? The schedule has the Secretary on private time."

"Yes. I don't know what this is about or who those guys are," replied Dodge.

"Hm."

"George, I'm going to the office to gather my stuff and move down to the limo to wait for the departure."

"Okay. I'll see you at the motorcade. You better hurry up; the Secretary is scheduled to leave in fifteen minutes."

"Yes. I'm hurrying."

At 1625, Hope arrived at the ninth-floor security room. She said to George, "Where is Dodge going? He sure is in a hurry."

"He's going to gather his stuff and then to the motorcade to wait for departure."

At 1800 hours, George said to Hope, "Here he comes."

George moved out of the security room and into the hallway. As the Secretary passed the security room, George fell in behind the Secretary's right shoulder and followed the Secretary.

Hope broadcasted, "We're moving your way."

Rich broadcasted, "10-4, all clear."

Dodge broadcasted, "10-4."

Hope acknowledged Rich and Dodge with two clicks of her mic.

In a rush, Hope locked the door to the security room and hustled down the hallway to join the Secretary and George at the elevator bank where they were waiting for an elevator. One of the six elevators arrived at the ninth floor, and the doors slowly opened. Hope scanned the interior of the elevator for any threats or anything out of the ordinary. She then entered and took a position by the elevator control panel. The Secretary came in next, followed by George. Hope pushed the Door Close button and the doors slowly closed. The elevator stopped at the lobby level, and the doors slowly opened. Hope exited the elevator first, then the Secretary, followed by George at the right shoulder protective position. Hope led the Secretary to a flight of stairs and directly to the caged motorcade parking area in the underground garage.

The entourage continued moving toward the motorcade. At the limo, George opened the right rear door and controlled it for the Secretary to enter. When the Secretary was seated, George closed the door, entered the limo, and sat in the right front passenger seat.

Hope, already in the follow vehicle right front passenger seat, broadcasted, "Move."

The Secretary's two-vehicle motorcade pulled away from the underground parking garage for a swift exit. At the preset speed, the doors of the limo automatically lock.

After a minute or two, Hope broadcasted, "Notifications made."

Secretary of Energy Motorcade in transit

The motorcade slowly moved through the heavy evening rush hour traffic in the District of Columbia on its way to the Secretary's residence.

When the motorcade arrived at the house, George followed standard Protection Operations protocol. He emerged from the limo first and performed the same ritual as his training conditioned him to do. He closed his door as he scanned the area for anything or anyone unusual. He looked hard for threats. When he believed it was safe, he tapped on the front passenger window, and the Limo Driver released the locks. George opened the rear door, and the Secretary stepped out. The Detail Leader escorted the Secretary to the side entrance of his residence. Greetings were exchanged, and the Secretary entered his residence.

The detail loaded back into the motorcade vehicles. They drove off to return the government vehicles to the underground garage to end their shift for the day.

8 October, Friday

Poland, Warsaw
Middle Income Residential Neighborhood

0500 Hours

It was still dark outside. As Jan always did, he turned off the alarm before it rang. His biological clock always had him up at 0500 hours.

Today was no different than any other day in Jan's lengthy law enforcement career. He made coffee, took a shower, and dressed.

Today as Jan sat at his kitchen table enjoying his black butter flavored coffee, his brain raced as he thought, "It has been a week since I talked to the unknown caller."

Jan was puzzled. He knew nothing about the unknown caller. He replayed in his mind what the unknown caller said.

"I have information that is valuable and worth a lot of money. The United States government will be very interested in the information. I need to talk with the IG for the USDA."

Jan was puzzled most by the expression on the unknown caller's face outside the Warsaw City Police Department on Monday last. Everything seemed to be okay until the anonymous caller saw Paweł Walinski, Chief of Intelligence, Warsaw City Police Department. The unknown caller's face went white. He mumbled something which Jan did not understand then fled the area.

Jan thought to himself, "The unknown caller left in haste. He tried to pull me over. He wanted me to leave with him?"

Trying to Jan, he had no leads to follow. None. He was at the mercy of the unknown caller to contact him in some way.

It was 0630 hours, time for Jan to leave for the office. He checked himself for the third time to make sure he had, among other things, his wallet, credentials, gun, ammo, handcuffs, and glasses.

He headed out the door for his routine 0700 hours arrival at the office. He was always in the office an hour before the others arrived. Today was Friday. On Fridays, Jan stopped at the best bakery in Warsaw, Munie's Bakery. Every Friday, Jan brought paczkis to the office for all his co-workers. Whatever Jan's opinion of the younger Federal Agents, he did what he knew was the right thing to do. As he was taught by his mother, he was always hospitable and respectful to people.

When Jan arrived at Munie's Bakery, he parked his personal vehicle in his usual spot, right in front of the fire hydrant. The spot was always open. He placed his blue law enforcement emergency light up on the dash and exited his personal vehicle.

As he walked toward the door to Munie's Bakery, he scanned the inside of the business through the large plate glass windows. It was a personal protection tactic made a habit from over 30 years of law enforcement work. He scanned the interior for anything unusual or out of the ordinary. His scan this morning disclosed an unknown man seated at Jan's usual table. He was talking to Munie, the owner of Munie's Bakery. This caused Jan to pause. He did not become rattled. As a seasoned law enforcement officer, Jan conditioned himself to respond to the unexpected.

Jan opened the door to Munie's Bakery and held it open for an enthusiastic elderly couple who were regular patrons at the bakery. Jan greeted them with a robust, "Good morning."

The couple in harmony replied with soft-spoken voices, "Good morning to you young man. Thank you." They giggled to each other as they continued out the door holding hands. Jan just smiled and entered the café.

Inside Munie's Bakery, Jan walked straight to the counter. Halfway there, a long-time smoker's voice shouted, "Jan. Good morning. The usual?"

Jan replied, "Yes Stanislawa, please."

At the counter, Jan was handed his order, a large cup of plain black, dark roasted, coffee and two paczkis on a dish with a fork. Stanislawa also gave him a brown paper bag with two dozen paczkis.

"Stanislawa, is this double bagged?"

Jan held up the brown paper bag of paczkis.

"Ah, damn it. No. Give me that back."

Jan handed the bag of paczkis back.

"Just go and sit down, I'll bring them to you in a minute."

"Thank you Stanislawa."

Munie and the unknown individual were still seated at the table talking. Jan watched their reflections in the large mirror positioned high on the wall behind the front counter.

Jan moved to his usual table and set his coffee and paczkis down. He bent over and greeted Munie with a big hug, a kiss on each of her chubby Polish cheeks, and a robust, "Good morning little sister."

Munie replied, "Good morning brother Jan. How are you?"

Jan, in an enthusiastic tone, said, "I'm doing just fine, just fine. I have your paczkis in hand. It can't get any better."

As Jan pulled out his chair to sit down, Munie said, "Let me introduce you to Josef Sklodowski, our uncle from Croatia."

Still standing, Jan exclaimed, "Our Uncle from Croatia! Hah. How are you? It's a pleasure to meet you."

Jan extended his hand and Uncle Josef rose from his seat and extended his hand. They greeted each other.

Uncle Josef said, "Please to meet you."

After a hardy handshake, they sat down at the table.

"I have to get back to the kitchen. I'll talk to you later," said Munie. She rose from her chair and pushed it under the table.

Both Jan and Uncle Josef quickly rose from their seats in respect to a lady leaving their presence.

Munie continued, as Jan and Josef remain standing, "Don't forget, you're eating Sunday dinner at my house, Uncle Josef. I'll call you with the time."

"Yes Munie," Uncle Josef replied. "Thank you again. I'm looking forward to Sunday and visiting with the family."

Munie turned to Jan, "And I'll see you on Sunday for dinner, too. Yes?"

"Are you making your *golabki*?"

"Yes. You know that's the regular Sunday meal with garlic mashed potatoes and green beans with diced ham."

Uncle Josef said, "Mm. Just like mother made. Your Grandmother made. That sounds so good. What can I bring?"

"Nothing. You just come for dinner and to catch up with family. It has been so long," replied Munie.

"I'll see you Sunday at church," said Jan. "Do you need a ride?"

"No. I'll walk. Such beautiful fall weather we're having here in Warsaw. I'll ride home with you, though."

"Okay. Good."

Munie walked away from the table, and the two gentlemen sat down.

As Josef was about to speak, Jan's cellphone rang. Jan looked at the display and said to Uncle Josef, "Excuse me, please. I have to take this call."

Jan rose from the table and walked outside to talk on the telephone. After the brief phone call, Jan returned.

Jan, in a calm, nonchalant manner, said, "Uncle Josef. I didn't know I had an Uncle Josef."

"No, you wouldn't know of me. I had left Warsaw before you were born. Things just got too complicated after the war. I had to go," replied Uncle Josef.

"What brings you back, Munie's *golabki*?"

"Well, that would be reason enough. Business brings me back."

"Business."

"Yes, business," replied Uncle Josef. "There's urgency to my business and to visit with Munie. I must apologize. I must excuse myself. I have a meeting at 1000 hours this morning. It's an important meeting about my business in Warsaw."

Uncle Josef stood to leave.

"I go now, I have a meeting. I'll see you at Munie's on Sunday, yes?"

Jan rose from his chair, in a show of respect for an elder leaving his presence.

"Yes. I'll see you Sunday. I look forward to visiting with you."

Uncle Josef pushed his chair under the table. He and Jan extend hands for a goodbye handshake. Uncle Josef turned and walked away from the table. He exited Munie's Bakery through the front door and walked to the curb where a black Mercedes-Benz met him in the roadway. It had all the show of a choreographed protection tactic. Uncle Josef entered the right rear passenger side of the black Mercedes-Benz S 600 AMG, and it sped off.

Jan sat at the table by himself. He raised his coffee cup to his lips, took a sip and immediately spat it back into the cup. It was cold. As he moved to get up to get a hot cup of coffee, he felt a gentle hand on his shoulder. It nudged him back down into his chair. The long-time smoker's voice, in a sexy tone, said, "I have a hot one here Jan. You don't have to get up. You see how I take care of you?"

"Yes. You always take care of me when I'm here. Thank you Stanislawa."

"And if you want, you can take care of me. You can take me to dinner and the movies tomorrow night to show your appreciation."

"Now Stanislawa, you know you're too young for me."

"That is what you keep saying. Here are your doubled bagged paczkis."

"Thank you, Stanislawa."

"Who was that gentleman you and Munie were talking with? I haven't seen him around here."

"Stanislawa, that was my Uncle Josef. I didn't even know I had an Uncle Josef."

"Uncle Josef! Oh no. I didn't recognize him."

"Do you know my Uncle Josef?"

"I don't want to talk about it. Your Uncle Josef, oh no. No."

In the hurried manner of a waitress, Stanislawa walked away from Jan shaking her head.

Jan finished his coffee and paczkis. He got up, pushed his chair under the table, and picked up the two dozen paczkis in the double brown bag. He rolled the bag tight as he walked out of Munie's Bakery to his personal vehicle. He entered his vehicle, took the blue light off the dash, and drove directly to his office.

Poland National Police
Warsaw District Office

Jan arrived at his office, and when he entered, he noticed everyone was in the secured conference room. He joined his co-workers.

Mr. Dubinski said, "Jan, glad you could join us. I hope it wasn't too much of an imposition to come into the office by 1000 hours. I'm surprised you took my telephone call earlier."

"Would anyone like paczkis?" replied Jan.

Jan unrolled the double brown bag and placed it in the middle of the conference table. The young agents jumped at the bag. They clamored to get a paczki, their usual response to Jan's weekly generosity.

Olenka sat off to the side. She laughed to herself as she observed Jan ignored his boss, as he usually did.

Mr. Dubinski said, "Okay. Okay. Focus here, guys. Focus. I called this meeting because I just received intelligence about a potential terrorist event. Our intelligence office has gathered limited information on a terrorist attack on a foreign government official. They analyzed this terrorist attack could happen here in Warsaw today, tomorrow or Sunday. Their information was sketchy, limited. This they picked up and examined from the signal monitoring."

He paused.

"This means we're *on-call* all weekend. I remind you since we're in an *on-call* status, we won't be able to consume any alcohol. You must answer your telephones, and there is no travel outside the Warsaw city limits without my authorization. Pack your jump bags tonight and keep them handy. I may call to detail you to assist other district offices. Remember, this is classified information."

Just then, the secure telephone rang. Mr. Dubinski raised his left hand and signaled for the group to stay. With his right hand, he answered the secure phone.

Into the phone, Mr. Dubinski said, "Yes sir."

Mr. Dubinski listened attentively and said nothing. After a short time on the secure phone, he hung it up.

He focused back to the group. In a startled tone, he said, "Okay that was my boss. The United States Embassy has confirmed a United States of America military airplane used by their Presidential Cabinet exploded in the air over Gdansk on Wednesday. Apparently, the military plane was descending for its landing in Warsaw. The U.S. Presidential Cabinet Secretary of Commerce and his staff members were on the aircraft. There appeared to be no survivors. The United States, Department of Justice, Federal Bureau of Investigation, sent personnel to investigate."

As the information was relayed to the group, the group took on a more serious demeanor and listened attentively to the information their boss conveyed. When their boss said no survivors, the group became somber knowing lives were lost, most likely due to terrorism.

"We're still on alert. There is no change to my previous order. Any updates I will pass on to you. I don't expect any updates until Monday. That's all for today. Jan, could I see you for a minute. Everyone else can go."

Typical of law enforcement officers, humor was used to deflect the harsh reality of life they experienced daily. As a defensive mechanism to the volume of mayhem they witnessed in comparison to the civilian population, they defaulted to jocularity to ease and manage the stress. So, when they got up to leave, and their boss told Jan to stay behind, they all jeered Jan and called him the pet.

After the room had cleared, Mr. Dubinski looked intently at Jan and said, "Close the door, please."

Jan rose out of his chair and closed the door. He continued to stand.

Mr. Dubinski, in his usual condescending tone, said, "Jan sit down."

Jan replied, "I'm okay. I'll stand."

Jan was uneasy. He may be reprimanded again for his tardiness to the office this morning. Reprimanded by a micromanaging Supervisory Federal Agent.

Mr. Dubinski said, "Jan, my boss told me you were selected by our organization to aid the U.S. Department of Justice with this terrorist event."

Mr. Dubinski paused in expectation of a comment from Jan. Jan said nothing and Mr. Dubinski continued.

"You'll be the one to assist them and command any team. I'm sure we'll provide assistance, probably with a ten-person team."

Surprised, Jan replied, "Thank you for the heads up. Please tell your boss I appreciate the confidence he has in me to select me to lead the assistance, alone or with a team."

"I will," Mr. Dubinski said. "If I need you over the weekend, I'll call you. That's all."

Jan turned and left the conference room. He went directly to his office, sat down in his rickety metal office chair, rested his hands on his desk, and stared off as he contemplated what Mr. Dubinski just told him. Jan knew selected for such an assignment was a good thing for his career.

USA, Washington D.C.
50 Massachusetts Avenue NE
Union Station

0800 Hours

Fred stood post outside Union Station. He observed the area for anything out of the ordinary or suspicious in anticipation of the Secretary's curbside arrival and subsequent departure from Union Station. He just finished his advance work for the Secretary's train ride to New York City. The Secretary and his wife were going to New York City to visit their daughter over the weekend. The Secretary had official government business on Monday. Fred's attentiveness to detail was interrupted by a radio broadcast.

"George to Fred."

"Go George."

"Five out."

"10-4. All clear for arrival. Stop on my mark. One greeter."

"10-4."

"Making the last turn, do you have a visual?"

"10-4. All clear for arrival. Stop on my mark. One greeter."

The Secretary's limo was brought to a smooth stop on Fred's mark on Massachusetts Avenue outside Union Station. The Secretary and his wife were transported from their residence.

When the Secretary's limo stopped, Fred moved around the rear of the limo to control the left rear door and to synchronize breaking the limo seal, the opening of the limo doors. This per protection protocol when the Secretary's wife accompanied the Secretary in the limo.

When Fred saw George open the Secretary's door, he opened the left rear door. The Secretary's wife stepped out. She said, "Good morning Fred."

Fred replied, "Good morning."

Fred followed the Secretary's wife around the back of the limo and into Union Station, positioned at her right shoulder. Likewise, George was positioned at the Secretary's right shoulder. The entourage followed the Secretary's staffer who led them to the gate to board the train.

For security purposes, Fred arranged early boarding for the Secretary and his wife and for them to bypass the security checkpoint by using the VIP entrance to the boarding gates and tracks. This expedited their move through Union Station.

The Secretary and his wife boarded the train car and settled in for their ride to New York City. George also boarded the train and settled in for his security responsibilities. Fred remained outside to stand post until the all aboard call.

"Fred to Dodge."

"Go Fred."

"The packages are in, waiting for departure."

"10-4 standing by until departure."

"10-4."

At 0830 hours, the Conductor exclaimed, "All aboard!"

Notice of departure was also given over the stations' public-address system.

Fred boarded the train and settled in for his security duties. The squeal from steel wheels rolling on steel rails sounded as the train started to chug away from Union Station.

When the train cleared the depot, Fred broadcasted, "Fred to Dodge."

"Go Fred."

"Cowcatcher up."

"Cute Fred. Cute. 10-4"

With the Secretary under way, Dodge drove off from Union Station en route to DOE Headquarters to park the government vehicle in the underground garage.

When Dodge arrived at the entrance to the DOE underground garage, he was waved through the security checkpoint and drove down the ramp. The limo tires squealed on the concrete floor as he negotiated through the maze of concrete support columns and positioned the limo to back it into the secured cage area, next to the follow vehicle which was not used today due to staffing limitations. Hope and Rich were in New York City to conduct the advance. They left for New York City last night after their shift. Such a tight and demanding schedule was not to the liking of any of the Special Agents assigned to the detail. The tight and demanding schedule was due to the small number of staff members and was an officer safety issue discussed by the Special Agents in many meetings and casual conversations with George.

Dodge parked the limo and secured the cage area. He proceeded through the drab off light green painted concrete hallways of DOE Headquarters on his way to the elevator and to the fifth-floor OSO office suite.

When Dodge entered the fifth-floor office suite, he noticed Barb, the Administrative Assistant, and Brad, the Acting Director for OSO, watching the television used by the detail to keep current with the latest news and events, worldwide. Open source intelligence was the predominant means by which the detail to gather intelligence.

Brad noticed Dodge entered the office suite and shouted, "Come here. Get over here and look at this."

Dodge joined Barb and Brad in front of the television. They were watching a Fact News Center report.

The news broadcaster said, "A United States of America military airplane crashed near the coastal city of Gdansk, Poland. The Fact News Center has limited information. This breaking news just came into the Fact News Center, Washington Bureau from our London Bureau. London reported the U.S. Military aircraft may have been transporting the Secretary of Commerce."

Fact News Center went back to the regularly scheduled programming.

Brad looked at Dodge and in an excited tone said, "What are you going to do about this?"

Dodge calmly replied, "What do you want me to do Brad?"

Still excited, Brad said, "Shouldn't you check this out?"

Dodge replied, "For what? Why? How? We have no agents assigned to any of the intelligence agencies. We have no one assigned to the DOE EOC, DOE Intelligence or Counter-Intelligence offices nor the Joint Terrorism Task Forces or Interpol. We're not on the distribution list for any of the DOE intelligence components, and we have to beg to get an intelligence briefing before we go on travel, both domestic and international."

Dodge paused. He thought, "I should stop and walk away."

Dodge continued.

"Remember Brad, no one at the DOE wanted Special Agents at OSO. Even DOE OIG tried to have our series changed. They said we didn't conduct criminal investigations. OSO was limited to the news media, open source information on the Internet, and other open source resources. And the statutory authority issue. You said DOE's statutory authority only applied to the contract uniformed guards. For the love of God, contracted employees. Employed by a private contract company. How about the U.S. Marshal Service special deputy authorization? What is the status on that? Brad, you said foul play caused the alleged downing of the U.S. aircraft in Poland?"

"Fact News Center reported that the Secretary of Commerce may have been on the plane."

"That's right Brad; Fact News Center said the Secretary of Commerce may have been on the plane."

There was a pause. Brad said nothing more and walked away from Dodge.

Dodge looked at Barb in bewilderment. Barb just shrugged her shoulders, and they both went to their respective offices.

As Dodge made his way to his office cubicle, his government cellphone rang and announced the caller as George. Dodge pressed the answer button.

"Dodge this is George."

"Yes."

Excited, George said, "Did you see the news? Did you see a military plane is down? A military plane with the Secretary of Commerce on board."

"Yes," replied Dodge. "I saw the report on Fact News Center. I didn't see any pictures. They didn't show any pictures."

"Did you tell Brad?"

"I watched the news report with Brad."

"What did Brad say?"

"He wanted me to check it out."

"How are you going to check it out? We're not the Secret Service."

"I told him I can't check it out. Well, I didn't tell him like that. But I told him."

"Okay. Keep watching the news outlets. We may have to come back from New York before Tuesday morning. We may have to come back Sunday morning. You may have to pick us up at the train station Sunday afternoon. Stay by your phone."

"I won't be available Sunday."

"What do you mean you won't be available Sunday?

"You know I have no car on Sundays. My wife takes it to work. She works a 12 to 14-hour shift on Sundays. You know that. Do you want me to take the limo home for the weekend in case I have to pick you all up at the train station on Sunday?"

"No. I can't authorize that. You know how DOE is on their vehicle take-home policy, with us using government vehicles. You won't be able to do that."

"We talked about this time coming. OSO ill-prepared to handle an emergency of any nature or level. The equipment OSO needed -- guns, cars, radios, ballistic vests -- nothing!"

"Yeah, I know."

"If you come back Sunday, you'll have to take a cab I suppose."

"Can't you get your wife to call in sick? Can you take her to work and have the car?"

"No, I can't. And you forget I have my son to watch too."

There was silence on the telephones.

Finally, George said, "Okay Dodge. I have to go."

"Talk to you later," replied Dodge.

1700 Hours   Commute home

Dodge's shift ended, and he departed the DOE underground garage in his personal vehicle for his commute home. He wound his way out of the District of Columbia to the Baltimore –

Washington Parkway, to the Washington D.C. beltway and then onto Interstate 95 North.

As Dodge was accustomed to doing during his commutes, he listened to satellite radio. The volume was high. The music was loud. He slow crawled through the bumper to bumper commuter traffic on Interstate 95 northbound, a major commuter artery in the Washington D.C. area. It was Friday, and every Friday the rush hour traffic was heavy and slow. The federal government's plan to reduce rush hour traffic by offering a compressed work schedule of four ten-hour days, which provided federal employees Mondays or Fridays off, did little to ease the commuter's woes. It was worse when there was an accident or construction on any of the major commuter arteries in the metro area. Inclement weather snarled traffic as many of the commuters could not drive in adverse weather conditions, rain or snow.

While he sang along to the satellite radio, Dodge felt his government cellphone vibrate against his side. He retrieved the phone and looked at it as he drove. The display identified George as the caller. He answered.

"George this better be good. I'm in traffic, on a Friday, and I'm listening to my music. What's up?"

"Did you see the news? The latest news on the crash."

"No, I'm on my way home."

"That military plane that went down in Poland, the Secretary of Commerce was on it. The Fact News Center reported that the U.S. Ambassador to Poland confirmed the Secretary of Commerce was on the plane and there were no survivors. None."

"Oh, my."

"And the Secretary was concerned. I've never seen him like this before. I thought he was going to ask to come back today."

"What do you think he's going to do?"

"I don't know. I really don't know. His wife isn't here right now. She's out shopping with their daughter. Fred is with them."

"Okay. Keep me informed."

"Okay."

Washington D. C. Suburbs

Dodge arrived at his residence after a one hour and fifty-minute commute. He got out of his vehicle and went into his house and immediately turned on the television. Dodge expected all the news outlets to be reporting on the military plane crash. He flipped through all the news channels his expanded cable plan had but found no news outlet reporting on the alleged downed military aircraft. He found this unusual and flipped through the channels again. Nothing.

His distant stare was interrupted by his wife. "Honey, where are we going for dinner tonight?"

Warsaw City Limits

Jan spent the rest of his Friday work day in his office. He did not even take a lunch break. Since his meeting with his boss this morning, all Jan thought about was assisting in the terrorism investigation. From his past experiences, he knew the intensity of such an investigation, especially since it involved the United States of America. His work experiences with law enforcement officers from that country were mixed. Some were so congenial to work with. Others were on the edge of a diplomatic incident.

Jan arrived home at 1730 hours. Throughout the evening, his mind continued to race. It raced with how to help the U.S. law enforcement officials. He knew he had to help them. His second line supervisor was just waiting for the request which had to come through the proper diplomatic channels. His mind raced with conspiracy theories. It even raced with a conspiracy theory that involved his Uncle Josef.

Jan thought to himself.

"Could it be that Uncle Josef participated in this event? Until today, Uncle Josef was unknown to me. According to Uncle Josef, he left Warsaw after World War II. Why? Munie knew him, but Munie never mentioned him to me. Why? Stanislawa seemed to know of him. Though she seemed disturbed he was back in Warsaw. What was that all about? If involved, he wouldn't get any special treatment. Relative or not. That was it. I have to stop thinking about this for tonight."

9 October, Saturday

USA, Maryland, Germantown
Residence of the Secretary of Education

1200 Hours

The Secretary of Education and his wife left their Washington D.C. suburban townhouse in Germantown, Maryland. They went out the front door, and the Secretary locked it behind them. They proceeded down the short sidewalk to their assigned street parking to enter their white Chevrolet Suburban for the short two-mile drive to the Seneca Valley High School football stadium. Today, their son's football game was at home and kickoff was 1300 hours.

The Secretary opened the right front passenger door and assisted his wife into the Suburban. Seated, he closed her door and walked around the rear of the Suburban as he looked up to the bright blue sky. His expressions showed enjoyment for the perfect fall day. As he opened the driver's door, he dropped his keys. He bent down and picked them up and continued to enter the driver's seat and closed the door. He started the Suburban, fastened his seat belt around him, gently placed the column-mounted gear selector in reverse and eased out of his assigned parking space. He paused briefly to allow two motorcycles with passengers to pass by first.

While he waited for the motorcycles to pass, the seat belt chime sounded. He looked at his wife and said, "Honey, fasten your seat belt. I don't want anything to happen to you. You know most accidents happen within two miles of a person's home."

The Secretary's wife fastened her seat belt while she gave her husband a seductive smile for his loving concern.

The Secretary backed out of the parking space, gently placed the gear selector in drive, and drove two blocks to the heavily traveled four-lane cross street, Wisteria Drive. He stopped the

104

Suburban, turned on his left turn signal, and checked traffic. When traffic cleared, he made a left turn onto Wisteria Drive, stayed in the left-hand lane, and accelerated to the posted speed.

The Secretary traveled east on Wisteria Drive. When he crossed the bridge, two motorcycles with passengers approached from the rear at a high rate of speed. The occupants of the motorcycles were dressed in black military-style clothing and light blue colored helmets with a dark tinted, full face shield. As the motorcycles reached the Secretary's Suburban, one motorcycle drove on the edge of the road and maintained a position on the left-hand side. The other took a position on the right-hand side of the Suburban and stayed on the roadway. Briefly, both motorcycles maintained the speed of the Suburban. They held their positions at the front doors of the Suburban, then fell in behind the Secretary's Suburban.

The Secretary and his wife looked at each other and shook their heads. The Secretary said, "Those motorcycle drivers can be aggressive at times. I'm going the speed limit. They're lucky my protection detail isn't here."

The Secretary slowed the Suburban for a stop in the left-hand turn lane of the intersection of Wisteria Drive and Crystal Rock Drive. He waited for traffic to clear to turn onto Crystal Rock Drive en route to the Seneca Valley High School parking lots. Traffic cleared and the Secretary started to turn when one of the two motorcycles pulled in front of him and blocked his path. The Secretary braked hard to avoid hitting the motorcycle. His wife was thrown forward, and her seat belt restrained her.

At the same time, the other motorcycle pulled up to the driver's door window. The passenger raised a military style long rifle and began to fire in a fully automatic sequence. The rounds instantly shattered the driver's door window. Many of rounds hit the Secretary and caused him to twitch in his seat. The impact of the multiple rounds threw him in the direction of his wife. His seat belt kept him in the driver's seat. Blood spattered throughout the interior of the Suburban and onto the Secretary's wife. The

Secretary was bleeding profusely from his upper torso, mouth, and head from multiple gunshot wounds. He slumped over with his head turned toward his wife. His lifeless, wide open eyes stared at her.

The Secretary's wife screamed hysterically as the motorcycle drove off. She was in shock from witnessing the violent assassination of her husband. She remained motionless as she screamed. Her eyes locked onto her murdered husband's lifeless eyes.

The motorcycle that blocked the roadway appeared in the driver's side window. The passenger threw an object into the Suburban, and the motorcycle sped off.

Momentarily, the Suburban violently exploded. The explosion raised the Suburban off the road. As it landed, burning debris flew into the air then landed on the roadway. The Suburban became engulfed in flames.

The two motorcycles continued to roar off in the westbound lanes of Wisteria Drive. A short distance away, the motorcycles stopped, and all four riders looked back at the carnage they caused. They appeared to look carefully as if to determine if anyone survived the attack. The motorcycles roared off from their victory without resistance.

The nearby motorists and pedestrians were fear struck. The few motorists and pedestrians who had a presence of mind to render aid were kept at bay by the intensity of the fireball Suburban. It continued to burn and spew an excessive black smoke. The area filled with a noxious odor of burning petroleum products and flesh. The good Samaritans were unable to do anything except watch from a distance. A few of the horrified spectators were on their cellular telephones. They tried to call 911 and were unable to connect.

After approximately ten minutes, the Montgomery County Police Department arrived at the scene and set up traffic control. Within another ten minutes, a Montgomery Emergency Services fire truck and ambulance reached the scene. All the emergency services were kept at bay by the intense heat and spewing toxic smoke of the fully engulfed vehicle. The firefighters applied a fire-retardant foam to snuff out the fire and bring the scene under control.

Once the site was brought under control, the first officer to arrive, the investigating officer, Officer Larry Martin barked out orders. He ordered officers to set up a perimeter. Larry ordered other officers to direct traffic away from the intersection. Other officers, he ordered to distant intersections to route traffic away to reduce the traffic jam that ensued.

After the aggressive work of the Montgomery County Fire Department firefighters, the fire-retardant foam cooled the vehicle enough for Officer Martin to approach and review the scene close up. What he observed stopped him in his tracks. No training or years of experience prepared a law enforcement officer for such a scene. He saw the remains of two human bodies charred and dismembered beyond recognition in the remains of a bombed, burnt out, melted automobile. He turned around and walked away. He waved back other approaching officers. As he was careful with his approach, he was careful with his departure. He did not want to disturb the debris, which included body parts. He knew he was to declare the scene a crime scene, which included all the wreckage.

A short distance away from the burnt-out vehicle, Officer Martin radioed dispatch.

"Unit 198 to dispatch."

"Go Unit 198."

"Unit 198 request the coroner's office to transport two."

"10-4 Unit 198. Stand by."

Officer Martin stood by and moved around the crime scene to look at the rear of the vehicle. He hoped to get a registration number for the vehicle from a rear license plate. The front license plate was not there. He suspected it melted from the intense heat of the inferno caused by the apparent explosion.

Though the burn markings toward the rear of the vehicle were not as intense as in the front, there was no rear license plate either. What Officer Martin found painted on the back of the Suburban was a large red X with the number 16 painted next to it. This was unusual to Officer Martin.

"Dispatch to Unit 198."

"Unit 198 go dispatch."

"Unit 198 coroner's office en route."

"10-4. Now requesting Crime Scene Team."

"10-4. Stand by."

While Officer Martin waited for dispatch to confirm the Montgomery County Police Department Crime Scene Team was on its way, he gathered the officers and informed them, "This is a crime scene."

He directed the officers to set up a perimeter to maintain the integrity of the crime scene per the department's regulations and directives. The officers swiftly moved into action. They took up positions a distance away from and around the bombed, burnt out, vehicle.

"Dispatch to Unit 198."

"Unit 198 go dispatch."

"Unit 198 crime scene team en route. Time 1243 hours."

"10-4."

While Office Martin waited for the crime scene technicians and personnel from the coroner's office, he observed two black Chevrolet Suburban SUVs, with blacked out windows and blue law enforcement emergency lights flashing. The vehicles eased through the crime scene perimeter and made their way to the site of the carnage.

Officer Martin thought to himself, "Now what's this?"

He walked up to the parked emergency vehicles and abruptly stopped. He said to himself, "This can't be happening."

Walking toward him were the same Federal Agents led by the same Major Event Site Supervisory Special Agent from the FBI that took control of his crime scene on Monday.

The Major Event Site Supervisory Special Agent said, "Officer Martin. We meet again. The FBI declares this as a National Security Major Event Site. I'm taking over the investigation of this major event site. Do you want to call your Sergeant?"

Officer Martin replied, "Well, of course, I have to call per our policy. I think we both know what he'll say. How do you guys get here so fast?"

The Major Event Site Supervisory Special Agent ignored Officer Martin's question. He sarcastically said, "Please make the call so I can get to work."

Officer Martin stepped away, took out his cellular telephone and dialed his Sergeant. The phone call was short.

Officer Martins returned to the Major Event Site Supervisory Special Agent and said, "The crime scene is yours. I'll dismiss all Montgomery County Police and Emergency services that are present."

"Thank you, again," replied the Major Event Site Supervisory Special Agent.

10 October, Sunday

Poland, Warsaw
Warsaw City Limits

In downtown Warsaw, at the ornate, large wooden Byzantine Catholic Church, with three gleaming gold-covered onion domes, each supporting a gold three bar cross, parishioners filed out of the front doors of the church at the end of the 1030-hour liturgy. Father Thomas was outside to greet the parishioners as they left.

"Good morning Father Thomas," said Munie. "It was a beautiful liturgy today, as always. I really enjoyed your homily. You enjoy your week."

Father Thomas replied, "Thank you Munie. You have a good week too."

"By the way, when are you, the Deacon and the nuns coming over to the café for breakfast? You haven't been there for some time."

"No, we haven't. Look at me." He gently patted his plump belly. "I'm trying to watch what I eat. The doctor has me on medications, and I may have diabetes. I have to lay off the baked goods."

Munie shook her head. "Well, you come by anyway. Have coffee with us and visit."

"Okay. I'll come by this week."

"Good morning Father Thomas," Jan said.

"Good morning, Jan. Good to see you. What do you know about the U.S. plane going down? I know. I know. You can't say anything."

Both Father Thomas and Jan laughed as Father patted Jan on the back.

Jan followed Munie to the parking lot and opened the front passenger door for her. Munie got into his car, and Jan closed the door and walked around the back. He greeted fellow parishioners as he made his way to the driver's door. He opened the door, got in, and drove off from the church parking lot to Munie's house.

About a block away from Munie's house, Jan observed a large black car parked in front of the house. As he approached, he saw it was a black Mercedes-Benz S, the same vehicle used by Uncle Josef.

Jan parked his car in the driveway. Simultaneously, he and Munie got out and close their doors. They saw Uncle Josef seated on the front porch and they called out.

"Good morning, Uncle Josef."

Uncle Josef replied, "A good morning it is."

Munie and Jan climbed the front porch steps. On the porch, Munie greeted Uncle Josef with a big hug and a kiss on each of his cheeks. Uncle Josef returned the cheek-kissing. In turn, Jan and Uncle Josef greeted each other with a big hug and cheek-kisses. The three entered Munie's house.

Inside the house, Jan said to Josef, "Are the other two guys going to stay in the car all afternoon?"

Josef replied, "Yes. They're okay. They'll leave soon and come back when I call them."

"Make yourselves at home. Let me change out of my church clothes. I'll be right down," Munie said.

Munie climbed the squeaky, ornate, oak, staircase to the second floor.

Jan and Uncle Josef went into the living room off the large foyer and took seats opposite each other.

Jan said, "You seem distant Uncle Josef. Is something troubling you?"

Uncle Josef replied, "Yes Jan. I'm deeply troubled and bothered by the information I have. The fact of the matter is an event Wednesday afternoon corroborates the information."

To be funny, Jan said, "Is it the downing of the U.S. military plane near Gdansk on Wednesday?"

Uncle Josef replied, "Yes Jan, it has a lot to do with that event. That event and a marking at that event corroborate information I have."

Jan was shocked. He was just trying to be funny. With concern and excitement, Jan said, "You were at the wreckage site on Friday? You accessed the site? How? You accessed the site?"

Calmly, Uncle Josef replied, "Jan, I have to start at the beginning. I'm sure the last week has been puzzling to you."

Uncle Josef was interrupted by Munie. "Should I get the wine? This is going to take some time."

Munie continued to descend the oak staircase, walked across the large foyer, and into the living room.

Jan looked to Munie. He looked to Uncle Josef. He looked back to Munie and exclaimed, "What! What's going on here? Am I the only person in the dark?"

Uncle Josef looked at Munie as she looked at him. They broke into loud laughter.

Starting to control her laughter, Munie said, "Well if anyone is in the dark that would-be Uncle Josef."

Munie and Uncle Josef continued to laugh in a low tone. With their laughter under control, Munie said, "Let me tell him, Uncle Josef. Let me tell him."

Uncle Josef said, "Oh. Okay."

"Jan, we're laughing because you say you're in the dark. Well, your Uncle Josef is the one in the dark, so to speak," said Munie. "He works black operations for Poland's Federal government, for the Poland Federal Police. Since the early 1950s. Jan, your Uncle Josef works for the same law enforcement organization you do."

Uncle Josef presented his law enforcement credentials to Jan.

"Yes, Jan. I work for the Poland National Police. I work in the National Security Group, a component of the Poland National Police. To know about me and the investigations my component handles, you must be cleared for the highest level of security Poland has. I cleared you for that level."

Uncle Josef paused.

"I trust Dubinski told you this was going to happen."

Jan still held Uncle Josef's law enforcement credentials as he slid back into his chair. He was flabbergasted. He tried to speak, but he couldn't. He looked to Munie. He looked to Uncle Josef. He looked at Uncle Josef's credentials. He looked carefully at the picture. He read out loud, "Director National Security Group." He exhaled deeply. He tried to speak. Nothing sounded. He looked at Uncle Josef again. It was the same person whose picture was on the credential. Jan mumbled, "Director."

Jan thought to himself, "Throughout my law enforcement service, I heard stories of this component, but I never met anyone from it. I never dealt with it. I never saw them in action. And I worked with a lot of law enforcement agencies throughout the European law enforcement community and the world. This component actually existed."

Munie moved over and stood by Jan. With her hand on his shoulder, she said, "Jan, you should be proud of yourself. I am. Your Uncle Josef is. Mom and dad would be so proud. I'm sure they look down from heaven and are proud of you. This is a great honor for you."

Jan, somewhat composed and still holding and looking at Uncle Josef's law enforcement credentials, replied, "I don't know what to say. Thank you, Uncle Josef. Thank you."

Uncle Josef reached his hand out to Jan. They shook hands. They each rose at the same time, embraced each other, and patted each other on their backs. They cheek-kissed.

Uncle Josef said, "Congratulation Jan."

Jan turned to Munie and hugged and cheek-kissed her.

Munie also said, "Congratulations."

As Jan turned to Uncle Josef and handed him his law enforcement credentials, Munie said, "Okay. Okay. Enough of this hugging and kissing, there are *golabki* to eat. Come and sit. Uncle Josef, please pour the wine. This will be the only celebrations of your accomplishment Jan. Let's enjoy."

Munie walked back and forth from the kitchen to the dining room. She positioned all the food on the large, oak, dining room table. She joined Jan and Uncle Josef who were already seated. She reached out, the three held hands as Uncle Josef said grace.

As they started to pass the serving plates and bowls between them, Jan sat back in his chair and said, "Wait a minute. Hold on. If I need the highest level of security clearance to work with

115

you, Uncle Josef; if I need the highest level of security clearance to know about the Poland National Police National Security Operations, how does Munie know? Why do you talk so freely in front of her? What's going on here?"

The room became silent. No one said anything. The clanging of the plates and utensils stopped. Munie rested her hands on the edge of the table near her plate, her fork in her right hand and her knife in her left. Uncle Josef looked up from his plate overflowing with *golabki*, garlic mashed potatoes, and green beans with ham. He raised his left hand with his knife in it, finished chewing, and swallowed. With his knife pointed at Jan, he said, "She's our boss. Your sister is the Secretary-General of the Poland National Police, National Security Group. And she is a damn good Secretary General. Has been for some time. That café is just a cover."

Jan's jaw dropped. His mouth opened. He found himself speechless again. Twice within an hour. He looked at his sister then to his Uncle Josef.

Then, in what seemed to be a gene of the Polish people, Munie and Uncle Josef roared with laughter. Uncle Josef laughed so hard he slammed his hand on the dining room table and made the blue and white Sunday dishware bounce on the oak table. Munie covered her mouth, doing her best to maintain her femininity as she continued what can only be described as the Polish roar of laughter.

Finally, Uncle Josef and Munie gained composure. Uncle Josef said, "Just kidding with you Jan. We're just joking. Munie does have a clearance. She has an authorization that allows her to know what I do. Not the details, just where I work and an understanding of what I do. She's my lifeline. When I need to come out of the dark for a breather, you know to get away from work, Munie is my cover story. Should something happen to me while working, she provides a means for me to come out and heal. In the case of my demise, while serving Poland, she's in charge of my funeral. She'll be your cover too."

"That's enough for now," said Uncle Josef. "Let's eat and enjoy. This will be your last day of leisure for some time Jan. You'll hit the ground running tomorrow morning at 0700 hours. I'll pick you up at your house in the morning. The pieces of information I have are coming together. I have a lot to tell you tomorrow."

Uncle Josef put down his fork and reached for his wine glass. He looked to Munie and then to Jan. He raised the glass of wine and said, "*Hospodi Pomilui Nas*, Poland and the United States of America."

The three touched glasses and took a drink to solidify Josef's toast to an old Slavonic salutation. God Bless us, Poland and the United States of America.

Before they set their wine glasses back on the dining room table, Munie raised her wine glass and said, "*Sto Lat!*"

The three again touched wine glasses and repeated "*Sto Lat!*"

They took a drink of the wine to solidify Munie's toast. A salutation used in Poland to wish someone one hundred years.

They set their wine glasses down on the dining room table and continued to eat and socialize.

USA, Maryland, Ocean City

Back from 1030 morning service at the First Presbyterian Church, Mrs. Parker changed her twin daughters and herself into their Sunday casual fall fashion beachwear. Mrs. Parker descended the broad staircase in her two-story, grand, colonial, beachfront home and made her way to the grandiose center kitchen. She greeted the house staff.

"Good morning everyone."

The staff replied in unison and with Hispanic accents.

"Good morning Mrs. Parker."

The house staff was busy with the duties of the day. It was Sunday. Mrs. Parker insisted on a large family meal at noon with only her husband and her twin daughters, no house staff, no guests. After the three-person staff prepared the meal and staged it for serving, they were relieved of their duties. The staff was given liberty to enjoy their Sunday anyway they wished to enjoy it. The only stipulation, they had to leave the house and grounds. The staff did not have to resume their duties until 0700 Monday morning. At that time, they had to be back at the house to prepare for the return trip to Washington D.C.

This was the routine for the Secretary of Defense, his wife, his twin daughters, and the house staff since the Secretary took the oath of office during the swearing-in ceremony and reception at the White House Rose Garden three years ago. Mrs. Parker demanded this from her husband to manage the stress of his position, for her, their children, and her husband, and to maintain a level of normalcy to their life.

Since this routine did not involve government business, the Secretary's protection detail was not responsible for the Secretary. The detail did not contact the Secretary and his family until 0700 hours Monday morning. At that time, the Detail Leader telephoned the Secretary's Chief of Staff to determine the Secretary's arrival time back in Washington D.C. Based on the time, they prepared to transport the Secretary from his Washington D.C. residence to the Pentagon. If the Secretary needed the detail, he had the telephone number to contact the Duty Agent.

The Secretary always acquiesced to the wishes of his wife. Growing up in a politically active home, Mrs. Parker was aware of the demands that surrounded such positions and how the requirements of the position extended to the entire family, even the children. Luckily, her twin daughters were too young to be deeply involved in the daily demands and rigors of the political position, except for the continual photo opportunities. Though the political advisors called them photo opportunities, they were all staged and choreographed. This Mrs. Parker liked; she had control.

After Mrs. Parker greeted the house staff and ensured all was progressing for the noon meal, she moved into the den. Her husband did not go to church with her and the twins. Though he was raised Catholic, he had not attended church since he took a world religion course during his freshman year in college. Except for Christmas. He considered himself a non-practicing Catholic. This disturbed Mrs. Parker. She persisted in encouraging him to attend church services on a regular basis.

Instead, the Secretary spent his Sunday morning in his den until the family meal at noon. So, she knew she would find her husband there. She hoped he was relaxing watching the pregame analysis shows for the Sunday football games.

When Mrs. Parker entered the den, that was not how she found her husband. She found him watching the Sunday morning political shows and on the telephone. She cleared her throat.

The Secretary noticed his wife and said into the telephone, "I must go. My sweetheart is here. Thanks for calling, and I'll see you Tuesday. I look forward to working with you and your staff on the funding requirements for the Department, Senator."

The Secretary hung up the telephone and said, "Good morning honey. Did you enjoy the service this morning? How was Reverend Marsh?"

Mrs. Parker straightened the pillows on the chairs.

"Yes, I did. Reverend Marsh asked me to say hello and to bring you to service next Sunday."

Her tone changed to sarcastic.

"How is your morning going? Are you working? It's almost time for the Sunday meal with your favorites."

She ended her sarcastic tone.

"I'm going to take the girls down to the beach before the meal. I'll see you in about an hour. The house staff is leaving now."

"Okay. See you in a little bit."

The Secretary began to flip between the numerous Sunday morning political programs. One of the shows caught his attention, and he stopped on that channel. He quickly became irritated at the show's host and guest who talked about the Department of Defense bloated budget. The show's guest was the head of a not for profit government watchdog organization. He insisted the Department of Defense was filled with waste, fraud, and abuse which caused the department's bloated budget.

Disgusted, the Secretary threw a pillow at the television and said out loud.

"You don't know what the hell you are talking about."

He got up, walked over to the television, and picked up the pillow. He returned to his favorite over-stuffed chair.

As he sat back down in his chair, in his peripheral vision, he noticed a black-clad figure coming into the den rushing toward him. The black-clad figure had a military compact rifle in the high ready position and trained on the Secretary. The Secretary was startled and froze in his favorite overstuffed chair. He immediately started to plead with the lone intruder.

"Please don't hurt me. Please don't hurt me. What do you want? Do you want money? I have money in the safe. I'll get it for you."

The Secretary started to rise out of his chair. The lone, black-clad ski-masked intruder, who was now in arms reach to the Secretary, dropped his weapon from his hands and it hung from his body on a sling. The lone intruder reached out and pushed the Secretary back into his chair. He said nothing though his mouth was exposed through an opening in the black ski mask.

Again, the Secretary pleaded with the lone intruder. He trembled and there was a tone of panic in his voice.

"Please don't hurt me. Please don't hurt me. What do you want? What can I do so you don't hurt me?"

His voice turned to a tone of pity.

"Please. Please. I'm the Secretary of Defense for the United States of America. God help me!"

Through the eye openings in the black ski mask, the intruder and the Secretary locked eyes. The Secretary heard muffled gunfire. It was the muffled sound of a fully automatic rifle fired by the intruder. It caused his body to twitch in the chair. The Secretary instantly felt an intense pain in his abdomen. His hands clutched the arms of his chair from excruciating pain. He looked down and saw he was bleeding profusely; the result of the proximity of the fully automatic weapon and the numerous rounds the intruder fired. He went into shock.

A second time, without warning, the lone intruder fired his fully automatic weapon into the Secretary's body until the gun's slide locked back signaling an empty magazine. The Secretary's lifeless, bullet-riddled, body rested in his favorite overstuffed chair. Fibers from the chair's stuffing lofted in the air. His hands still clutched the arms. There was a distance look on the Secretary's face. His blood spewed from his lifeless body and flowed down the chair and onto the hardwood floor.

Instantly, the lone intruder, with the precision of a well-trained soldier, smoothly and effortlessly, disengaged the empty magazine from his weapon. It fell to the floor. With his left hand, he removed a fully loaded magazine from a pouch on his black ballistic vest. He reloaded his weapon with the loaded magazine. There was the sound of metal on metal when he slammed the slide forward to charge the weapon. He scanned the area. He scanned the area again. A loud voice at his eleven o'clock took his attention away from the Secretary. He rotated and simultaneously aligned the weapons sights and trained the compact, military weapon in the direction of the voice. He looked down the sights. The voice came from the television. It was an advertisement that illegally increased the volume for an attention grabber. He quickly returned his focus back to the Secretary. His weapon moved with his eyes.

With the Secretary still lifeless, the lone intruder, with his left hand, pulled out a rag from his left rear pocket. He stooped down by the pool of blood and soaked the cloth in the Secretary's blood. All the while, the lone, masked, intruder retained his right hand on the trigger of his military weapon now positioned in the low ready. With the dripping, blood-soaked, rag, the masked intruder drew a large red X on the bloodstained hardwood floor between the feet of the lifeless Secretary of Defense. Also with the blood-soaked rag, next to the large red X, he wrote the number 6.

Slowly and cautiously, the lone masked intruder rose to an upright position, and the blood-soaked rag dropped out of his hand to the floor. He scanned the area once, twice, always moving his compact, military, weapon in the direction that his eyes looked, the weapon now back into a high ready position. The lone intruder, with an abundance of caution, retreated away from the lifeless Secretary of Defense and out of the den.

To retraced his entrance through the Secretary's house, the intruder cautiously moved out of the den to the oversized hallway. He signaled over a portable, two-way radio for his sentry at the front door to fall back for extraction. The two intruders moved cautiously through the oversized hallway and through the grandiose center kitchen. They paused at the archway to the mudroom. In a Middle Eastern accent, the first intruder broadcasted on his portable, two-way radio, "Two coming out."

In a Middle Eastern accent, a return broadcast declared, "Clear."

The two black-clad ski-masked intruders move through the mudroom and out the rear door held open for them by a sentry, a third intruder.

The three black-clad, ski-masked intruders moved through the manicured backyard and were joined by two other black-clad ski-masked individuals at the pathway to the beach. In military style formation, the five-person team moved down the beach path, past the lifeless bodies of the Secretary of Defense's wife and twin daughters and across the course light brown color sandy beach. They met up with a sixth black-clad ski-masked individual who was positioning a military style, motorized, black rubber raft into the ocean. The five intruders jumped onto the black rubber raft as it began to motor out to sea. They fled from the assassination undetected.

Maryland Suburbs

"Come on. That was no penalty. Get some glasses," said Dodge as he fidgeted in his lounge chair in the basement of his townhouse. He was watching the Baltimore Ravens and Pittsburgh Steelers football game. It was just him and his one-year-old son. His wife was at work.

The Ravens were about to receive the kickoff from the Steelers as the Steelers just scored. The Steeler touchdown and the subsequent extra point made the score 14 to 13 for the Steelers.

Dodge's government cellphone rang and vibrated and move about the coffee table. Dodge looked at the screen. George was identified as the caller.

123

Dodge answered, "Hello, George. Are you watching the Ravens?"

"No. I'm standing outside a restaurant in Manhattan. Who's winning?"

"The Steelers. They just scored. It's 14 to 13. The Steelers are winning. What's up?"

"It looks like the Secretary will be back on Tuesday. I have a chance to call now and update you."

"Okay. Are you coming back in the morning or the afternoon? Do you have a time and train number yet?"

"I don't have the specifics yet. When I do, I'll call you."

"Okay. Just a reminder, I won't be able to meet you all on the tracks. You know it's only me here. The rest of the team is with you. I'll try to get the Secretary's staff to come to Union Station and meet you all at the tracks and lead you out to the limo. Also, Fred will have to use the metro or a cab. I won't be able to stage the follow vehicle for him. Do you have anything else?"

"Did you see anything else on the downing of the U.S. Military Aircraft with the Secretary of Commerce?"

"No, I didn't. When I arrived at the house on Friday evening, I flipped through the news channels. I didn't see anything about a downed U.S. military aircraft."

"Yeah. I've watched too. I haven't seen anything either. The unusual thing was the Secretary hasn't said anything about it since Friday afternoon after he had a telephone call with the White House."

"That's unusual. Do you have anything else?"

"No. What's your hurry?"

"George, the game is on."

"Okay, I'll talk to you later."

Dodge looked at the television and said out loud.

"Come on ref that was holding. The Steeler was holding. Throw the flag. Throw the flag. Come on."

Dodge threw his government cellular telephone onto the coffee table.

11 October, Monday

Poland, Warsaw
Warsaw City Limits

0500 Hours

It was still dark outside. Jan turned the alarm clock off before it rang. His biological clock always had him up at 0500 hours.

Today was different than any other day in Jan's lengthy law enforcement career. There was so much excitement in the air for Jan. Today he started to work at the National Security Group for the Poland National Police. He did not believe the good fortune that came his way.

The excitement did not alter Jan's routine. Like every work day, Jan made coffee, took a shower, and dressed. He then sat at the kitchen table and sipped his buttered flavored coffee. The excitement hit him again, and he thought to himself.

"Today I'm waiting for Uncle Josef to pick me up and take me to work at the National Security Group."

It was 0700 hours. There was a knock at the door. Jan went to the door and looked through the one-way security peephole. He saw it was Uncle Josef and opened the door,

"Good morning Uncle Josef. How are you?"

"Good morning Jan. I'm well. The first thing I must tell you today, don't call me Uncle Josef. From today forward, just call me Josef. No matter where we are. No matter what we're doing, just call me Josef. Okay."

"Yes. Just Josef. Josef, would you like a cup of coffee?"

"No thank you Jan. We have to go. We have a lot to do today."

Jan checked himself for the third time to make sure he had his wallet, credentials, gun, ammo, handcuffs, and glasses. He took a quick look at himself in the long mirror hanging on the wall by the door and picked a small piece of lint off the front of his suit jacket. He walked out the door, closed it, and locked it behind him. He checked the door to make sure it was secure.

They left through the front door to the apartment building, and Jan followed Josef to the black Mercedes-Benz S 600 AMG at the curb. Josef entered the rear right door. Jan walked around the back of the Mercedes and entered the left rear door. The Mercedes drove off.

Poland National Police
National Security Group
Clandestine Office somewhere in Warsaw

They arrived at an industrial building. The driver pressed a button on the review mirror, and a large, steel, overhead, garage door opened. The driver pulled in and pressed the button again. Jan heard the steel door clatter as it lowered behind them. When it finally closed, the driver pressed another button on the review mirror. A second large, steel, overhead, garage door opened in front of them. The driver pulled through and pressed the button again and the garage door lower behind them. When it stopped, Josef got out. Using that as his signal, Jan got out and followed Josef.

They walked to the first man door. Josef placed his right hand on a screen next to the man door. The electronic lock disengaged. Josef looked to Jan and said, "The door is controlled by a biometric electronic security lock." Josef opened the door and walked in with Jan in tow.

The door automatically closed behind them, and Jan heard a magnet attached to metal. The distinct sound of an electronic door lock engaged.

Jan looked up and was in awe. There were television screens on every inch of the walls. There was an enormous, thick, oak, conference table in the middle and plush, high back, black, leather, chairs. At the perimeter of the room was a series of continuous workstations, also with plush, high back, black, leather, chairs. Each workstation was equipped with a thirty-inch computer screen.

Josef said to Jan, "Pretty impressive. Yes."

"Yes, Josef, impressive."

Josef, in a loud, mild manner, voice, announced to the dozen workers, "Let me have your attention people. Please gather at the conference table."

All the workers stopped what they were doing at their individual workstations along the walls. They got up and moved in unison to the oak conference table. They all took a seat and waited for Josef.

Jan thought to himself, "Unbelievable. Unbelievable. These people are organized, obedient and appear to be motivated to work. Now, this is refreshing."

Josef pointed to an open chair and motioned Jan to take it. Jan navigated the room.

Josef sat in a chair at the table and addressed the group.

"The newbie is Jan Sklodowski. He'll be working with us now. As you have a chance, please introduce yourself to him. Yes, I believe in nepotism, and that is the introduction of and for the new person."

Josef continued.

"Now for the business at hand. Zeke, bring up the pictures from the downed U.S. military plane."

There was a brief pause as they looked at the carnage.

"The plane was exploded by a missile. Do we know what type?"

A voice from the table sounded out, "No sir. Not yet."

"Keep working on that please."

The next series of pictures showed there were no significant pieces left of the plane.

"Have we determined the location from which the terrorist fired the missile?"

A different voice from the table sounded out, "Yes sir. They were off Highway 5 on the west side of Gdansk. They moved off Highway 5 at kilometer marker 35.4. They went north for 2.5 kilometers. They stopped in a heavily treed area. Analysis of that crime scene disclosed six different people were there. They used two different vehicles. One a light-duty pickup truck and the other a larger heavy-duty transport vehicle. Specific makes and models were not determined. They left no debris behind. Nothing. Tire prints and footprints only. That was all sir."

Josef continued, "Thank you. This third series of pictures was concerning and telling. After the crime scene team had analyzed the wreckage at the crime scene, Wednesday, they were able to piece some of the smaller pieces of the airplane debris back together. They could do this because, during their crime scene analysis, small pieces of the plane had red colored markings. What they pieced together was what you see in this last picture. It appeared to be a red X with the number 10 written beside it. Now, this was concerning because?"

A third voice came from the table. "Information from three proven reliable informants, all independent of each other, disclosed a terrorist operation to assassinate all of the members of the United States of America Presidential Cabinet. The informants were very clear about this. They all were specific the plot was a false flag operation designed to kill all the members of the U.S. President's Cabinet and point to Poland as the perpetrator of the operation. That was all sir."

Yet a fourth voice chimed. "Point of reference: By the codified laws of the United States of America, there are eighteen positions in succession to the President of the United States. Fifteen of these posts are from the U.S. President's Cabinet. In order of succession, the numbers and Presidential Cabinet titles are

4. Secretary of State
5. Secretary of Treasury
6. Secretary of Defense
7. Attorney General
8. Secretary of Interior
9. Secretary of Agriculture
10. Secretary of Commerce
11. Secretary of Labor
12. Secretary of Health and Human Services
13. Secretary of Housing and Urban Development
14. Secretary of Transportation
15. Secretary of Energy
16. Secretary of Education
17. Secretary of Veterans Affairs
18. Secretary of Homeland Security

The first three, in order of succession to the Presidency, their titles and numbers are

1. Vice President of the United States.
2. Speaker of the House of Representatives.
3. President Pro Tempore of the Senate.

Again, the large red X seemed to represent the Executive Protection operation protocol of moving the protectee off the X, the spot of an attack. The number 10 seems to signify the Secretary of Commerce who is tenth in the line of succession to the Presidency. It appeared the attackers taunted and visibly gloated their success to their foe, the United States of America. That was all sir."

Josef said, "It was confirmed by the United States of America, Ambassador to Poland, the Secretary of Commerce was on the down U.S. military airplane. He was en route to what the Ambassador termed a 'U.S. Classified Diplomatic Mission.' The Ambassador gave no other information about the mission. None of this information was released to the public by the U.S. government. The U.S. government was determining how to release the information. What they wanted to say. No statement was made to the public. They wanted to make notification to the family of the late Secretary and the relatives of the deceased U.S. government staff also on board the airplane. That's all for now. Thank you."

The workers dispersed from the oak conference table and went back to their workstations around the walls. Josef motioned for Jan to follow him.

Josef and Jan went to Josef's office. Josef shut the door behind them and spoke.

"We have a morning briefing every day. Some days, we have an afternoon briefing too. The individuals whose workstations are along the walls are analysts, all with a different responsibility. People contribute when they have something to contribute. They're intelligent and proficient. The rest of the group you have already met."

Jan looked puzzled. "I've met the rest?"

Josef said, "Yes. The rest of the group members are the two gentlemen in the car and me."

Surprised, Jan replied, "Oh. That's all."

Josef continued.

"Our job is to resolve matters that impact the national security of Poland and her people. By design, our charter keeps us small. The staff keeps us efficient and effective. Our authorization comes from the Foreign Intelligence and Surveillance Act of 1949. We search out and find perpetrators for other agencies to swoop in and apprehend. Sometimes those agencies are from other governments from around the world. One way to look at our mission: we work to take out of society, by incarceration or other means, all individuals, foreign or domestic, that want to do harm to Poland as a country, Poland's government officials or citizens of Poland. This may seem like a broad spectrum, but again, we search out and find perpetrators of acts that fit into the charter's three categories. Other agencies within Poland's government and other foreign governments from around the world take the individuals out of society. Our mission, for the most part, is non-transparent. We don't want any attention. Therefore, everyone in the group must pass a rigid security screening and sign a Non-Disclosure Agreement. The Non-Disclosure Agreement carries the penalty of immediate incarceration if there is a perception an individual violates the agreement. The incarceration is for life if it is proven the person violates the Non-disclosure Agreement. Proceedings for these violations are handled by Poland's Confidential Court with no appeal rights. Sometimes domestic and foreign media outlets refer to it as the 'secret court.'

Josef paused for a short moment.

"The drafters of the law were cautious not to refer to the court as secret anything. The framers of the legislation lived through World War II and remembered from firsthand knowledge how powerful, and out of control, a *secret police* organization can get. They referred to the German Stasi, the German State Security Service. The drafters of the legislation used the term *confidential court.*"

Josef briefly paused again.

132

"And that is precisely what we must maintain, a confidential posture, so we can carry out our critical mission. Here's a Non-disclosure Agreement for you to read and sign for your final step for processing in."

Jan took the document and said, "I don't have to read it."

He turned the pages of the Non-Disclosure Agreement until he came to the signature page. He signed the document by his name and handed it back to Josef.

"Here, it's signed. Let's get to work."

Josef took the document from Jan.

"Thank you. Indeed, let's get to work. Your first task is to determine your best confidential source from the United States government to contact to learn what their government knows about the terrorist plot to kill every member of their Presidential Cabinet. I know I don't have to remind you, but I will feel better by saying, be ginger with the United States. You know how sensitive they are when their shortcomings are pointed out to them. They get so indignant because they think they are the superpower of the world and no one will ever attack them, no one will ever harm them. Even post September 11, many U.S. government officials still believe that."

"Yes, I know what you mean. I'm going to get started."

"Oh. One last thing, your office is next to mine."

"It is. I thought I had a workspace along the wall?"

"Oh no. The Deputy Director's office is next door. Go settle in."

Jan left Josef's office and went into his. It was massive in comparison to his office at the Poland Federal Police, Warsaw District Office. It was plush with a large, oak, desk; a black, high back, leather chair and current computer equipment on a separate side desk. There was also an oak bookcase and an oak credenza. And everything matched. There was a small round conference table with high back, leather chairs and a small lounge area furnished with leather couches and chairs and end tables with lamps. Jan was overwhelmed as he sank into the leather couch to take in his surroundings and absorb his first day. His first day as Deputy Director of the Poland National Police, National Security Group.

"Hey. What are you doing? Are you sleeping on the first day of the job?" asked Josef.

Jan jumped to his feet.

"No. I was just taking it all in."

"I'm just joking with you. But, come with me. One of the analysts has information we must see now."

Josef and Jan walk over to the large, oak, conference table where the rest of the group was already assembled.

Josef said, "Go."

A voice from the large conference table said, "I went back out to the satellite feeds we have. I wanted to look at the crash site again. I wanted to zoom in on the area to make sure we didn't miss anything. When I typed the coordinates in, I saw this."

The voice paused to allow the group to study the image that was up on the large screen.

The voice continued, "The entire crash site, crime scene, was cleaned. There were no signs of the airplane debris or the tracks we saw yesterday. Nothing was there. It was if someone cleaned up the site so no one would know it happened. That was all sir."

Another voice chimed in, "Please watch what the U.S. Ambassador to Poland is saying today about the crash. He's

134

walking himself back from yesterday's comments. Today he's saying it was a U.S. unmanned drone that self-destructed. That is all sir."

Josef said, "Okay. This isn't the first time for this during one of our investigations. Thanks for the update. Let's keep moving forward. Remember, we're involved because we have credible information the assassination of members of the U.S. Presidential Cabinet is being carried out as a false flag operation implicating Poland as the perpetrator. We must gather facts to disprove Poland is doing this. Let's keep moving forward."

USA, Washington D.C.
950 Pennsylvania Avenue NW
U.S. Department of Justice

Main Justice
Attorney General's Office

The Attorney General, his Chief of Staff and his Detail Leader, left the Attorney General's office suite and walked through the Main Justice building to the courtyard.

As they walked, the Chief of Staff said, "At your request, the news conference is in the courtyard. You're right; it's a beautiful fall October day. This should make for some great photos of you for the media to use. I will record this and provide a copy of the recording to the select news media outlets."

"Thank you. The President called me. He told me to move the press conference outside to the courtyard. It was his idea to record it and provide copies to a small group of press people he handpicked. I was told he paid good money to control the press."

"Yes. I know the President does and he uses tax payer's dollars. I can't believe he can get away with that. Okay, for today, there'll be about twenty minutes for you to speak. I'll give you the signal when it's time for you to stop and leave. There'll be no questions, there's no audience. The courtyard serves only as a backdrop. The President's idea is brilliant. I don't know why I didn't think of this. We have a backdrop, but we don't have to answer any questions. I just say it's time to go and you don't have time for questions and answers. This is brilliant."

"Good," said the Attorney General. "You know the press can be brutal. Brutal I tell you. The President is such a knucklehead the press comes down hard on me. Some of the things he says he wants to do are just simply asinine, not to mention they violate the Constitution. I tell him, and I tell him. He just doesn't listen to me. Hell, he doesn't listen to any of his Cabinet members. You saw how he cussed out the Secretary of Defense last week over his four-day workweek schedule. Two days later, he's telling the Secretary of Defense he can continue his four-day workweek schedule. Sometimes I think the President is working for our enemies."

The Detail Leader followed the Attorney General from the rear right shoulder protective position. The group made their way through the building to the exit for the courtyard. There, the Detail Leader broadcasted, "Coming out."

Main Justice Courtyard

His broadcast was acknowledged with two clicks from the mic of the Advance Agent who conducted a security sweep of the Main Justice Building courtyard before the choreographed news conference. The Advance Agent remained posted in the courtyard area to maintain the integrity of the location and the arrival of the Attorney General. Though there were no Federal employees at the building because it was a Federal Holiday, Columbus Day, the detail still covered the Attorney General since he was performing official government duties. Today, it was just a two-person team.

The small group was met by the Advance Agent who gave a warning.

"Mr. Attorney General, please watch your step onto the platform. The steps are a little steep and narrow."

"Thank you."

The Attorney General used a quick gait to scale the stairs. He planned to speak about the successes the Department of Justice had combating terrorism worldwide. He proceeded directly to the podium and looked out to an empty courtyard.

"Good afternoon everyone. Thank you for coming out today on such a beautiful fall day. Today, I want to highlight the great success the Department of Justice is having combating terrorism worldwide."

At that moment and without warning, a giant cloud of smoke started to roll into the courtyard from the direction of its main entrance controlled by U.S. Department of Justice Police. Out of the cloud of smoke appeared five individuals all clad in black, military-style, garb and a light blue colored helmet with a dark-tinted, full face, shield. The individuals had a military, fully automatic, long rifles in the high ready position. They began to fire automatic volleys.

The Attorney General was shocked. His mouth was open, and it appeared he tried to say something, but nothing came out.

Two of the five attackers broke formation and quickly advanced toward the platform. They moved with tactical balance which positioned them to avoid a crossfire situation.

In the sudden mayhem, the Attorney General's two protection detail Special Agents were stunned to realize the Main Justice building security was breached. The two Agents attempted to counter the attack. The Advance Agent took a concealed position to the left of the stairs but was not able to return fire before gunned down by an advancing attacker.

The Detail Leader, his Glock Model 19 9-millimeter, semi-automatic pistol in hand, fired suppressive rounds in the direction of the attackers. He moved up the stairs and across the platform to cover and evacuate the Attorney General off the X. He reached the Attorney General in time to catch him as he started to fall. The Detail Leader was unable to maintain a grip on the Attorney General who slipped through the Detail Leaders hands due to the coating of blood from the profuse bleeding of his multiple gunshot wounds. He hit the platform floor with a loud thud, and his lifeless body did not move. His eyes stared up at the Detail Leader. Immediately, blood pooled around his motionless body.

The Detail Leader, without hesitation and his 9-millimeter, semi-automatic pistol still in hand, grabbed the Attorney General under his shoulders and dragged him toward the stairs of the platform, an effort to recover the Attorney General into the building. When the Detail Leader got to the top of the stairs, he stood face to face with one of the attackers. The attacker was in an offensive attack posture; his military rifle at the high ready position. Their eyes locked through the dark tinted, full face, shield of the light blue motorcycle helmet. The Detail Leader dropped the Attorney General to counter the attacker. The attacker fired first with an automatic volley of rounds that hit the Detail Leader. The force of the multiple rounds instantly knocked him back. Incapacitated from the multiple gunshot wounds, he was unable to control his backward stumble, and he fell to the platform floor. His lifeless body did not move.

The attacker turned his focus to the Attorney General and fired an automatic volley of rounds into his dead body. The attacker tactically walked around the dead Attorney General, scanned the platform area for any signs of life and threats to him. Then he repositioned his military weapon to a low ready position and retained his right hand on the gun. With his left hand, the attacker took a rag from his left rear pocket. He stooped down by the Attorney General and soaked the rag in the Attorney General's pool of blood. The attacker, with the rag saturated with the blood of the Attorney General, drew a large red X on the platform floor by the Attorney General's lifeless body. Also with the blood-soaked rag, next to the large red X, he wrote the number 7. All the while, the other four attackers continued surveillance of the courtyard and looked for counter threats.

When finished, the attacker quickly stood up and rapidly moved off the platform. The formation of five attackers regrouped and tactically moved to the front entrance of the courtyard. There, they mounted the waiting motorcycle as passengers. In a roar, the five motorcycles drove out the gate and onto Pennsylvania Avenue into the congested city traffic.

Washington D. C.
711 4th Street NW
Jerrard F. Young District of Columbia Lodge #1
Fraternal Order of Police

Sarge was at the lodge for about two hours now. His usual retirement routine was to have a leisurely lunch and then a few drinks. It never failed, his fellow co-workers, some retired some not, were usually at the lodge too. They all enjoyed each other's company. Today the crowd at the lodge was light due to the Federal holiday.

It was 1545 hours and over the television came a news flash:

"We interrupt your regularly scheduled programming to bring you a special announcement."

The big, red, word *ALERT* streamed across the bottom of the picture.

The news alert grabbed Sarge's attention, and he watched the television behind the bar.

Fact News Center continued to report a news alert:

"I am Kate McGuire for Fact News Center. We just received shocking news. This was awful," said Kate McGuire, the female reporter of Now What's Happening in Government.

She advised this News Alert may be too graphic for some viewers and listeners.

"We just received information the Attorney General of the United States of America was assassinated. It appeared there has been a terrorist attack at the Main Justice Building in Washington, D.C. I can't believe this; the Attorney General was killed. His lifeless body was still on the platform from which he gave a news conference on the great success with combating terrorism worldwide.

I was told we were to cut to live footage placed on InstaTube by an unknown source. Wait. Wait. No, I have now been told the InstaTube live footage was a hoax, Fact News Center will not air it.

So that's what we have right now. The Attorney General may have been assassinated.

Wait. Wait. We're going live to the scene.

Hale! Hale! Can you hear me, Hale?"

"Yes. Yes, Kate, I can hear you. Can you hear me?"

"Yes, I can hear you, Hale. What's the scene like?"

"Kate, I'm over at the old post office building. That's as close as I can get to Main Justice. A large area is cordoned off around Main Justice. It looks to continue over to the FBI Headquarters Building. From here, it appears emergency personnel is flooding the scene. The blare of emergency sirens seems to come from across the District, but all I see are emergency vehicles coming from the underground garage at the FBI Headquarters. Those emergency vehicles are moving to the scene. This is odd. Wait a

140

minute Kate, I have to let this big blue and white tractor-trailer rig pass by before I can talk more."

"Hale. Hale. Did Hale drop off? We'll keep trying to contact Hale. Until then, again I say..."

"What? Why was she cut off like that?" said Sarge.

Sarge was confounded. He stared straight ahead at the television which no longer had a picture, just a black screen. Shaggy, the bartender, took the remote control and changed the station to other channels. Nothing, all the channels were the same, a black screen was all that displayed.

Sarge said to Shaggy, "You can quit trying. There won't be any broadcasts now for a day or two. During events like this, Homeland Security shuts down communications. No one will be able to transmit or receive any signals. A defensive mechanism they use to protect the President and permit emergency services to move about without concern of the attackers tracking them. Only law enforcement, fire departments, and medical emergency teams will have communications now, on secure channels the public cannot access."

"Oh, really!" replied Shaggy.

Shaggy slid his cellular telephone from his left rear pants pocket, checked his service, and found his screen was black. He was surprised he had no service.

"You doubted me? I told you. The Homeland Security blacked out communications."

"I believed you. That was just a human nature reflex to check. Can I get you another Sarge?"

"Yes, please. I won't be going anywhere soon. The district is going to come to a standstill. No one will get in. No one will get out. All the employees, private and government, will shelter in

141

place. It could last a couple of days. There'll be an enforced curfew. Unless you have a life-threatening reason for being out and about on the streets, law enforcement will order you off the streets. Give me another indeed."

"I won't be able to go home? I won't be able to call my family? Come on Sarge, the Federal government wouldn't do all that?"

"Oh yes and no one will know. You are in what I call the EZ, the elite zone. It's an area where high-ranking federal government officials create an oasis of pleasure for themselves. They let the press call it *inside the beltway*. Every time they read or hear it described like that in the news, they laugh their asses off. The District of Columbia is a playground for the élite. The rest of the country, the rest of the world, is where they house their peasants."

"Talking like that Sarge, maybe you had enough? Maybe I should shut you off?"

Both Shaggy and Sarge laughed. Then Sarge abruptly stopped and glared at Shaggy.

Shaggy continued to laugh alone until he noticed Sarge's glare, then he slowly stopped laughing.

Sarge continued to sip his drink.

12 October, Tuesday

Poland, Warsaw
Poland National Police
National Security Group
Clandestine Office somewhere in Warsaw

Jan was still taken aback by his new assignment with the Poland National Police, National Security Group. It was his second day, and he was again driven to the office from his residence. He was a little stunned from the fuss.

When Jan arrived at the office, he rushed directly to his office. He had to call a friend formally employed at the Interpol-United States National Central Bureau, Washington D.C., J. T. "Sarge" Yonkers.

Jan met Sarge when Jan worked a high-profile murder investigation that involved six victims who were citizens of the United States of America. The murders were related to an international child slave trade controlled by the Russian mafia. The two worked together on the investigation of the crime for over two years and became good friends. They even vacationed together in the south of France when Sarge and his friend, the IG for USDA, were on a side trip to visit Interpol Headquarters in Lyon, France.

Sarge was employed by the FBI. Though Sarge retired a few years ago, Jan and Sarge stayed in touch and maintained a personal friendship. Jan knew Sarge was still well connected to the Federal law enforcement community. He was aware that Sarge could help him with an introduction to a Federal law enforcement officer to assist in the investigation of what appeared to be a well-organized, false flag, operation to kill all the members of the United States of America Presidential Cabinet and blame the Republic of Poland as the perpetrator.

Jan thought to himself, "Maybe Sarge would come aboard and work for the government of Poland to help investigate this case."

For the balance of the morning, Jan prepared for his telephone call to Sarge. He reviewed all the information in the National Security Group case file.

USA, Maryland, Germantown
Residence of the Secretary of Education

It was 0630 hours. The Secretary of Education's protection detail arrived at the Secretary's house to pick him up for his commute to the Department of Education, Maryland Avenue, Southwest, Washington D.C. The two-vehicle motorcade stopped to let the Detail Leader out. He positioned himself to receive the Secretary when he came out of the house. The motorcade moved off to turn around and re-position for a swift departure once the Secretary was in the limo.

The motorcade sat for ten minutes after repositioned.

The Limo Driver broadcasted, "Where is he? We have to go to stay on schedule."

"I don't know. It's not like him to be late. I'm going to knock on the door," replied the Detail Leader.

The Detail Leader walked up the walkway to the front door and stepped onto a small porch area of the Secretary's townhouse residence. He used a reserved knock. There was no answer. He knocked a second time, again a reserved knock. No answer.

The Detail Leader talked into his left sleeve. "I can't believe this."

The Detail Leader knocked a third time, this time louder. He heard footsteps coming toward the door. The door opened slowly, and the Secretary's son said.

"Can I help you?"

144

The Secretary's son recognized it was his father's Detail Leader and continued.

"Oh. Good morning. My Father isn't here."

"What? Your Father isn't here. Where is he?"

"I don't know. I hadn't seen my father or mother since Saturday morning when I left for my football game."

"Did they go away for the weekend again? When did he leave? How did he leave?"

"Dude, when I came home about an hour ago, no one was here. I assumed my mother went to work and you all picked up my father. Maybe he drove my mother to work and then went to work himself. The Suburban was gone."

The Secretary's son started to close the door.

"Wait a minute. When was the last time you saw them?"

"Before I went to my football game on Saturday I told you."

"Did you see them Saturday night when you came home?"

"I came home an hour ago. I spent the weekend with friends. I didn't get any calls from them. I didn't need to call them."

The Secretary's son changed his tone to condescending.

"Look, I have to go. I have to get ready for school. My father's protection detail loses him."

The Secretary's son shook his head left to right.

"Do you even have his telephone number? Do you want me to get it for you?"

"I have his telephone number, thanks."

The Detail Leader turned and walked back down the steps and walkway to the waiting two-vehicle motorcade. He got into the limo.

"He's not here."

The Detail Leader cocked his head toward the Limo Driver.

"The Secretary isn't at home for our pickup. I can't believe this. This is the first time this has happened to me. Let me call his cell phone."

The Detail Leader dialed the Secretary's cellular telephone number. The cellphone rang one time and went to the automated answering system. The Detail Leader listened through the automated announcements, and when prompted he left a message.

"Mr. Secretary this is your Protection Detail Leader, please call me or have one of your staff members call me, please."

The Detail Leader hung up and looked over to the Limo Driver.

"I don't know what else to do. Do you have any ideas?"

"No, I don't. The Secretary's not here?

The Detail Leader broadcasted, "Let's move."

The two-vehicle motorcade moved away from the Secretary's residence toward Wisteria Drive.

"Where're we going?" asked the Limo Driver.

"Back to the building unless I get a call on our way. This is unbelievable."

The Secretary of Education's two-vehicle motorcade motored through the roads of Germantown to Interstate 270 south and continued back to the Department building in Washington D.C.

When they arrived at the building, the Detail Leader immediately went to the Secretary's office suite in search of the Secretary's Chief of Staff. He met the Chief of Staff coming out of the Secretary's private office.

The Chief of Staff said, "The Secretary won't be coming in today. He'll be on a special National Security assignment for the White House. Until he returns, the protection detail isn't needed."

The Detail Leader replied, "You're just telling me now."

"I was just notified. It was classified, and I had to take the call from the White House on a secure telephone. I was coming out of the Secretary's private office, and I was just coming to tell you. The FBI picked him up Saturday afternoon and transported him to a secure location."

"Okay. Thanks. Please let us know as soon as possible when we will resume our duties."

"I certainly will. When I know, I'll let you know. And there won't be any daily schedules to pick up until the Secretary returns."

"Thank you."

Poland National Police
National Security Group
Clandestine Office somewhere in Warsaw

It was 1500 hours Warsaw time, which was nine o'clock in Washington D.C., a six-hour time difference. Jan picked up the telephone and first dialed one, the country code for the United States of America. Then the three-digit area code. Then the seven-digit number for Sarge's personal cellular telephone.

The cellphone rang once, twice and a voice answered in a protective tone.

"Hello."

Through a speakerphone, Jan said, "Is this Sarge?"

Cautiously, Sarge replied, "Yes. Who's this?"

"Sarge this is Jan from Poland."

"Jan, how are you? I haven't heard from you for a while. How are you?"

"I'm doing fine. How are you?"

"Very well, thank you. Where are you calling from? My caller ID did not display the telephone number I have on my contact list for you."

"Sarge, I have a lot to tell you. But first, I need you to call me back. I don't want to say anything over an unsecured line. Do you have a piece of paper to write a number down?"

"Yes. I'm ready."

"011 48 551 8999 1468."

Sarge repeated, "011 48 551 8999 1468."

"Yes, that's it. We hang up. Then you call me. Oh, give the operator the code 011911."

The call was disconnected.

Sarge mashed the CALL END button on his cellphone a couple of times to ensure the call ended. He waited two minutes and dialed the phone number Jan gave him. There was a moment of silence. Then the telephone rang once and immediately answered.

"For Polish press one, for English press two, for French press three, for Spanish press four, for Arabic press five."

Sarge pressed two for English. Immediately an English-speaking voice said, "Type the code now."

Sarge pushed the keypad numbers corresponding to 011911.

An English-speaking voice said, "What is the first name of the party with whom you wish to speak?"

"Jan."

There was silence for a couple of minutes. Then a voice said, "Hello."

"Jan."

"Yes, Sarge?"

"What's going on?"

"A lot is going on Sarge. Sorry for the confusion. I have a new job with the National Security Group within the Poland Federal Police. There's a need for the utmost security. That's why you had to call me back. We're now talking over a secure telephone system which can't be tapped by even the NSA of your country."

"Oh. Are you sure?"

Sarge and Jan started to laugh.

"Well, that's what my country tells me," replied Jan.

Jan continued.

"Sarge, I was brought into the National Security Group on Monday. On my first day, they briefed me on false flag operation to assassinate all the members of the United States of America Presidential Cabinet. Yes, you heard me correctly, all the members of the United States of America Presidential Cabinet."

Sarge interrupted Jan. "What? No way. All the members of the President's Cabinet have a protection detail. That is impossible. If an attempt is made, the detail will move their guy off the X. No one can get to our Secretaries, our Presidential Cabinet."

"Sarge, you know I have a lot of respect for you. For your law enforcement abilities. However, this plot to assassinate all the members of the United States of America Presidential Cabinet is real. It's in the attack phase. I have the evidence, the facts, to prove this to you and any officials you tell me to share the information. That's precisely the reason for my outreach to you. I need your help again. I know you're retired. I need your help. Will you help me, please?"

"Yes, of course, I'll help you. Your assertion is a surprise. Do you know what this means to the National Security of the United States of America?"

"I think I do. The important question to ask is, who in the Federal Law Enforcement community is going to understand what this means to the National Security of the United States of America? So that's my first request Sarge, to whom are you going to refer me? Keep in mind, this must be a trusted individual. You see Sarge, we have information, credible and reliable information. Our informants say the perpetrators of this operation are carrying it out in such a way as to make it look like the Republic of Poland is doing it. That Poland is assassinating the members of the U.S. Presidential Cabinet."

Sarge expanded breath and said, "Oh my God. I can't, I can't believe this is happening. Poland is a longtime ally of the United States. This is diabolic."

"Yes, Sarge, I know this sounds unbelievable. Again, I have the evidence to prove not only is there a terrorist attack by someone, a group or a state, we now believe it's in the attack phase. The terrorist operation is being carried out now, on U.S. soil and foreign soil. The evidence discloses a well-trained and well-financed operation."

"Jan can you give me the highlights starting from the beginning."

"In July of this year, our first informant, a reliable informant, came forward and provided preliminary information about a possible operation to assassinate the United States of America Presidential Cabinet. Informant number one lived and worked in Great Britain. Through his contacts, he dealt with members of terrorist organizations. He gleaned details of the false flag operation. Candidly, what caught our attention and why we continued to follow and investigate this matter with all our resources was the mention of a false flag operation in which Poland was going to be blamed for the terrorist activity. This had the potential to be extremely disruptive and damaging to Poland. Not only with the United States of America but many other countries as well. This had the potential to affect our national security and to change our relationship with the United States of America and other allies too.

We continued our investigation by cultivating informant number two who was tasked to develop specific information. That task first corroborated a false flag terrorist operation rapidly approached the attack phase. That was the beginning of September. In late September, from the monitoring of various communications, we gathered positive information the false flag terrorist operation was going to be carried out and soon. We did not develop a specific or approximate time.

So, here we are, it's October, and we believe we have an investigation of the first attack of the false flag terrorist operation to kill all members of the United States of America Presidential Cabinet."

Jan briefly paused then continued.

"The first attack was on Polish soil. Perhaps you heard about the downed U.S. military plane over Poland, near Gdansk?"

"No. I haven't seen any coverage of such an event from the media here."

"Well, that does not surprise me. We believe your government, the close inner circle of advisors to your President, are still trying to figure out how to spin the facts to make your President look good and not damage his Presidency. Although they may be notifying next of kin before they make a press release.

Unusual was what the U.S. Ambassador to Poland told my country's government yesterday. Your government wanted to notify next of kin before they made a press release. But today, the U.S. Ambassador walked back everything he said yesterday. Today he said a military drone went down. That it was a drone that exploded and not a military plane. The U.S. media outlets and foreign media outlets were not covering the story. Have you heard of any other events in the U.S. germane to this investigation?"

"No. Is there anything else I need to know right now?"

"No. You have the highlights. Will you help me?"

"Yes. Of course, I'll help you. Tell me what you want me to do. You are familiar enough with our law enforcement community and its levels from working through Interpol. I need a little time to digest the information to provide any suggestions. As ideas come to me, I'll tell them to you so we can discuss them and you can decide how you want to proceed. Wait. I'm retired now.

Okay. I'm going to have to work around that. What do you want me to do?"

"First, I need to know what your government knows about the false flag terrorist operation. Second, I need to know if there are events in the U.S. related to this false flag terrorist plot. Please don't take it the wrong way, Sarge. Well, we know each other well enough I can be candid with you. I wonder if your government is covering up events, so the world does not see the United States of America as vulnerable. Susceptible to the point an enemy state would see an opportunity to attack the United States of America on your own soil. You and I both know the killing of members of a Presidential Cabinet of any country is embarrassing and disruptive. The citizens of the country could quickly lose confidence in the ability of their government to govern and protect them from threats both foreign and domestic. Do you think you can get any information to help me? Help Poland?"

"I must try. I must help you. Let me digest the information. I'll get back to you as soon as I have something to report. Should I contact you the same way I did for our conversation today?"

"Yes. That'll provide us the quickest and most secure way of communicating. Sarge, thank you. Your assistance is invaluable to me, the government of Poland, and the Polish people. Thank you."

"Not a problem. Glad to help. You are my friend Jan, you know I'll help you any way I can. My reply time is going to be a little bit slower since I'm retired. I'll call you as soon as I know something. Let me get to work."

The two gentlemen ended the call.

Sarge fell back into his favorite lounge chair and stared off. He pondered all Jan told him. He thought to himself, "I can't imagine the catastrophic impact such an attack would have on the United States of America."

Sarge thought about what he did not share with Jan.

"If the terrorists were successful in carrying out the operation and assassinated even a few of the fifteen Secretaries in the Presidential Cabinet, it was possible there would be no individuals to be Secretaries in the President's Cabinet out of fear of assassination. The Secretaries and the Deputy Secretaries scared into a mass resignation. The departments and agencies left leaderless. The United States of America without a Presidential Cabinet and without a succession to the Presidency. Something the United States of America never experienced during its existence."

It was now 1130 hours. Sarge stood by the kitchen sink. He finished his coffee as he stared out the kitchen window, still stunned by the implications of the information Jan had just told him. Sarge placed his coffee cup in the sink, collected his glasses, cell phone, retirement watch, retired credentials from the FBI and his Glock 9-millimeter. Post 911, the Law Enforcement Officers' Safety Act permitted retired law enforcement officer at all levels to continue to carry a firearm based on their issued retired credentials. He double checked himself, so he had everything and walked toward the door. It was a sunny, warm fall, day in the northern Virginia suburbs. Sarge was on his way to the Fraternal Order of Police Lodge in Washington D.C. for lunch and to think how to help Jan.

USA, Washington D.C.
Fraternal Order of Police Lodge #1

Sarge finally arrived at the Fraternal Order of Police (FOP) Lodge #1 after a grueling drive of fifteen miles which took one hour and forty minutes. He got caught in a Presidential movement. It appeared the entire city was shut down for the Presidential motorcade. While stopped in traffic, Sarge turned on the radio and learned the President was at the Department of Interior.

154

Sarge parked his car on the street, got out and put money in the parking meter. As he walked to the entrance of the lodge, he snickered to himself and rolled a memory.

"When I was on active duty with the FBI, I just placed the law enforcement placard on the dash with a blue light. I didn't pay for parking. Now retired, I had to diligently pay for parking or risk a parking ticket. Sometimes my retired credentials provided professional courtesy from the Parking Enforcement Officers. Sometimes it did not."

Just then, booming down the street was Lizzy, a District of Columbia Parking Enforcement Officer.

Sarge said, "Hi Lizzy. How are you? You look radiant today."

In a high-pitched voice, zaftig Lizzy, with her long jet-black hair bouncing with her walk, replied, "You better ease back Sarge. You keep talking like that, and you, and I are going to have to dance. You know what I mean Sarge? All these years we know each other. I think you're all talk."

Sarge laughed as did Lizzy as she reached out, grabbed Sarge, and pulled him into her for a long embrace and a cheek kiss. They greeted each other in this jovial manner for years.

Lizzy, in a stern voice, said, "Sarge, did you put money in your meter? Those retired credentials don't mean anything to me. You know that, right?"

"Come on Lizzy, cut me a break. Sometimes I think I'm going to have to take you to a dinner and a movie, so you don't ticket my car."

"Now you know, I could construe that to be a bribe. Sarge, are you trying to bribe a government official?"

"Oh no. Oh no. I wouldn't do that for fear you would lock me up?"

"I'm going to lock you up all right. And then I'm going to restrain you. Mm. Hm. I'm going to lock you up all right. Get out of here. I have work to do. It's lunchtime. All the freeloading Congressmen are coming off the hill to have lunch. Well, have lobbyists buy them lunch. They think they can just park anywhere and not pay because they have congressional plates. Well, honey, I don't mind educating them. Oh. No. I don't mind at all."

Lizzy beat her hand with her ticket book.

"Good to see you, Lizzy. You have a good day."

Lizzy stood and watched as Sarge walked away.

"You too Sarge. Mm. Hm. You look fine. Mm."

13 October, Wednesday

USA, Virginia, McLean

It was 0530 hours in the Washington D.C. suburb of McLean, Virginia. A warm fall morning. Slightly humid. Sixty-three degrees.

Every day, rain or no rain, hot or cold, humid or mild, the Secretary of Agriculture went out for her daily morning run. She went for her morning run every day at the same time, 0500 hours, and took the same route. Her usual route took her fifteen miles in total. It wound through residential and business areas throughout McLean.

This was against the professional advice she received from her Executive Protection Detail during her security briefing after being appointed to and assuming the duties of Secretary of Agriculture. Her protection detail advised her to buy some type of aerobic machine for her house and stop running outside, alone, in the morning, at the same time each day and the same route every day. The protection detail further suggested if she continued to run outside, to change and vary her routine and schedule as a security practice.

The Secretary of Agriculture dismissed the advice of her protection detail. She instructed them, "This is what I've done all my life and no job, private or public, is going to change my routine and desire to run outdoors."

She quickly signed a memorandum. It stated she understood the advice from the Executive Protection Detail and released the detail of any responsibility for her security and safety when she ran outside without her protection detail.

The detail even offered to have a Special Agent on her right shoulder as she ran. The balance of the detail to follow in vehicles. The Secretary's reply to the suggestion was short and blunt, "You have my signed memo."

The Secretary was on her return, and she approached a high-volume intersection in the business area of McLean when she heard motorcycles approaching. She slowed to a jog in place at the intersection. The pedestrian control sign displayed the Do Not Walk figure. As she jogged in place, she checked her time and heart rate. She became oblivious to the sound of the motorcycles as they got closer. The intersection cleared, she resumed her run and crossed against the light as she did every day.

As the Secretary's stride carried her through the intersection, five motorcycles appeared and each had two riders, all dressed in black, military, fatigues, with a light blue helmet with a dark-tinted full-face shield. The Secretary's heart began to race. She increased her speed. As she did, one of the motorcycles fell in behind the other four and positioned itself in the intersection the Secretary just ran through. Another motorcycle sped to the end of the block and took a position at that intersection. The other three paced the Secretary down the block while they drove in the left-hand lane.

The Secretary was now running as fast as she could. Her heart pounded in her chest from the exertion of running and the stress created from anticipating the unknown actions of the light blue-helmeted motorcycle occupants.

One of the motorcycles broke formation. It pulled up alongside the Secretary. The Secretary, from a quick look over her shoulder, saw the passenger fidgeting with something. Then without warning, the light blue-helmeted passenger on the motorcycle raised a military, shoulder, weapon and fired an automatic volley at the Secretary. The Secretary jerked from the rounds entering her body. The force of the multiple shots pushed her forward. The blue-helmeted motorcycle passenger fired a second automatic volley. Again, the shots hit the Secretary, and the force from the bullets knocked her to the sidewalk. She began to moan in agony as she tried to get up but fell back down.

The motorcycle pulled up alongside her. The light blue-helmeted passenger dismounted and tactically advanced on the Secretary. The passenger's shoulder weapon was in the low ready position. The passenger fired point blank at the Secretary until the magazine went dry. The Secretary's body jerked from the force of the rounds. Her body became lifeless as blood flowed from it, onto the street, and toward the gutter. The red blood was in distinct contrast with the white tinted concrete sidewalk.

The light blue-helmeted passenger tactically changed magazines. He pulled the empty magazine out, reversing it, and forcefully rammed a loaded magazine into the receiving slot. The two magazines were taped together making the reloading fast and efficient. The attacker slammed the slide forward to charge the firearm. All the while, the attacker scanned the street for any threats or countermeasures.

With no countermeasures observed, the light blue-helmeted passenger, with his left hand, took a white rag from his left rear pocket. He stooped down by the pool of blood formed by the bullet-riddled, lifeless, Secretary and soaked the rag in the Secretary's blood. With the blood-soaked rag, the passenger drew a large red X on the concrete sidewalk between the feet of the Secretary of Agriculture. Next, to the large red X, the passenger wrote the number 9. The passenger stood and dropped the bloody rag.

All the while, the passenger retained control of the military style shoulder weapon with his right hand, in a low ready position and his finger on the trigger.

The passenger shuffle stepped back to the motorcycle, continued to watch for any signs of a counter assault and mounted the motorcycle. It motored off and joined the other motorcycles. The passenger on the lead motorcycle motioned signals to the other motorcycle operators, and all the motorcycles roared off into the rising sun and the dawn of the day.

USA, Virginia, Arlington

0600 hours. Sarge was up early this morning after a sleepless night. He continued to ponder the information Jan shared with him yesterday and the brief news report of the assassination of the Attorney General of the United States of America on Monday. Sarge was eager to turn on the television to see what the news outlets were reporting on these events.

Sarge was puzzled. He thought he would have a brutal night on Monday, finding it difficult to navigate the District of Columbia and surrounding suburbs after the assassination of the Attorney General. He was wrong. His travel home was not delayed or interrupted. There was no police activity out of the ordinary. To his surprise, it appeared the Attorney General was not assassinated. There were no signs of the city on lockdown due to such an event.

Sarge was a little troubled that he did not mention to Jan the brief news coverage of the assassination of the Attorney General on Monday. Sarge thought to himself, "I was just so surprised with everything I was being told."

Sarge, without making his coffee first, turned on the television and broadcasts were running. He turned immediately to Fact News Center for coverage of the assassination. He listened and watched for twenty minutes. Nothing. No report on the killing. He flipped to the Central News Network and watched again for about twenty minutes. Nothing. No story of the killing. Even the headline band on the bottom of the screen for the two most popular cable news outlets was void of any reference to the assassination of the Attorney General. He flipped through a couple of local channels. It was all the same, no news coverage of the killing.

Now Sarge was befuddled. How something so newsworthy was not reported was beyond him. He wondered, "Why no coverage of the assassination?"

He sat back in his favorite lounge chair. He talked out loud to himself.

"I don't understand this. The news outlets reported on lesser matters. The sting operation for food stamp trafficking that involved two Democrat Senators and a former Democrat mayor of Washington D.C. They were indicted. That was covered. There was a lot of coverage of the former Secretary of Agriculture charged with accepting bribes from a major chicken processing company. Those stories were covered by the news outlets. But the assassination of the Attorney General was not covered."

Sarge paused briefly and then continued silent thoughts.

"Okay, first things first. Who am I going to call to help me help Jan?" Sarge had a Eureka! Moment. "I'll call Slatski. Thomas Slatski. Jan may even know Tommy from his handling of the FBI cases at the INTERPOL Washington Central Bureau. This may work out well."

Still puzzled by the lack of news coverage on the assassination, Sarge picked up his cellular telephone and reached out to his associates at FBI Headquarters.

After he had called his associates at the FBI, Sarge was bewildered. He discovered no one at the FBI was talking about the assassination of the Attorney General. No one confirmed or denied it happened. No one confirmed or denied the FBI was investigating, as all his contacts phrased it, an alleged assassination of the Attorney General. Sarge pressed them as hard as he could, given their relationships and his status as a retired FBI Supervisory Special Agent.

Sarge's vast experiences did not diminish during the few years of retirement. He knew if the agents talked about the assassination they risk criminal prosecution or worse, in-house reprisal. He was sure an investigation of the assassination of the Attorney General required the investigating agents at all levels to sign a

Non-Disclosure Agreement. Perhaps that was the resistance he met.

Sarge said to himself, "Now how do I find Slatski? Let me see if this old number in my telephone contacts still works."

Sarge dialed the number. It rang once and immediately went to an automated answering system.

"Hello. Thank you for calling. I hope I'm out fishing. Please leave your name and number; I'll call you back. Enjoy the day!"

Sarge left a message.

"Really. Come on. I'm trying to reach Thomas Slatski. If this is his number, please call Sarge. You have my number under missed calls. Thanks."

Sarge hung up and eased back into his lounge chair deep in thought.

USA, Florida
Somewhere between Deland and Palatka

Northbound on the Amtrak 98 Silver Meteor, somewhere between Deland and Palatka, Thomas "Tommy" Slatski noticed he missed a telephone call. He did not recognize the number. He attempted to check his voice mail. But there was no cellular service. He placed his cellphone back on his seat back tray and continued to write.

USA, Washington D.C.
The White House

2030 Hours   Oval Office

"Sir, with all due respect, you have to address this issue." Said Romahn "Joey" Enumahn, Chief of Staff. "The longer you let it go, the worse you are going to look. Please think about the party. There are some very close races this November. The Democratic Party must win seventy percent of the elections to regain control in the Senate and take control in the House. If this gets out, it will most certainly impact the elections. It could be ruinous to you and the Party. Imagine the ramifications to the Presidential race."

"Well Joey, thank you for telling me what I already know," said the President of the United States of America. "If we go public with this, it's going to appear I can't secure the citizens of the United States of America. In all probability, I won't be able to get anyone to come forward and apply to or accept Cabinet positions. If I have Cabinet members start to resign, the global governments are going to take that as a sign of weakness. Some of those global governments may consider attacking the United States of America. No, I won't go public now. I need to buy time to handle this. Furthermore, how many Cabinet members have been assassinated so far? What is the FBI doing?"

Joey replied, "Five. Sir. Five of your Cabinet members have been assassinated."

"And what is the FBI doing about it?" asked the President.

"They are investigating is all the Director of the FBI will tell me. He doesn't provide any details, even when I press him for more information. He says he's briefing you directly. He doesn't like me. He never did."

"Quit your whining and complaining. You sound like a Republican. You're not thinking about quitting on me? You owe me. You owe me a lot for all I've done for you back in Chicago. Besides, you don't want to end up like Blago, do you?" said the President.

"I'm not complaining," replied Joey. "I won't quit on you. It's just difficult keeping all your lies straight. I'll see you tomorrow."

In a teasing tone, the President said, "All my lies. Get out of here. Good night, Joey."

14 October, Thursday

USA, Pennsylvania, Pittsburgh
530 William Penn Place
William Penn Hotel

0630 Hours

"Good morning Mr. Secretary. This is your protection detail with your six thirty wake-up call. Will you have breakfast in your room or at the restaurant?" asked the Detail Leader.

The Secretary replied, "Thank you. I'd like to have breakfast in the restaurant today. My wife will be joining me."

"Very well sir. I'll make the arrangements."

"Thank you. I'll see you in about forty-five minutes."

"Yes, sir."

The Detail Leader, in his hotel room, turned to the members of the Secretary of Veterans Affairs Executive Protection Detail.

"Okay. The Secretary is going to be moving in forty-five minutes. He's going to have breakfast in the hotel restaurant with his wife. Then we'll follow the Secretary's Daily Schedule. You have your assignments. Let's go."

The five-person protection detail moved out. The Limo Driver and Follow Vehicle Driver proceeded to their vehicle, both parked in front of the hotel. They both waited in the motorcade vehicles for the Secretary to emerge from the hotel. The Advance Agent went directly to the hotel restaurant to sweep the area for any possible threats. He remained there to maintain the security integrity of the site, to greet the Secretary and his wife and to show them to their table. The Detail Leader and the Assistant Detail Leader stayed on the floor. They waited for the Secretary and his wife to emerge from their hotel room.

At 0730 hours, the Secretary and his wife appeared. The Assistant Detail Leader led the group to the elevator, and the Detail Leader followed the group. At the elevator, the Assistant Detail Leader pressed the elevator button to summon the elevator. There was no conversation. The Secretary's wife did not function in the morning without first having two cups of coffee.

The elevator chimed as it passed each floor on its way up to the twenty-third floor. When it arrived, the Assistant Detail Leader assumed a defensive posture between the elevator doors and the Secretary. The Detail Leader assumed a defensive posture on the right shoulder of the Secretary. The defensive shield was engaged effortlessly, and the Secretary and his wife did not know it was happening.

The elevator doors parted to open. The Assistant Detail Leader scanned the elevator for anything out of the ordinary, and when he assessed the elevator safe, he led the group in and positioned himself by the control panel. When the group was all in, he pushed the close button while the Detail Leader placed himself in front of the doors. The Assistant Detail Leader then pushed the lobby button. The elevator descended, and the chimes sounded as the elevator passed each floor on its descent to the first floor. The elevator stopped at the seventeenth floor, the doors parted to open, and four young adults waited to get on the elevator.

The Detail Leader announced, "This elevator is being used for official government business, please take the next one. Thank you."

The elevator doors closed in perfect rhythm as the Detail Leader finished. The Assistant Detail Leader had pressed the close door button as soon as the doors opened completely. The elevator continued to descend, and the chimes continued to sound as it passed each floor.

166

The elevator came to a stop on the first floor. The doors opened, and the Detail Leader scanned the area for threats as he moved out of the elevator. The Secretary and his wife followed. The Assistant Detail Leader followed after all three.

The Advance Agent quickly met the group and said, "Good morning Mr. Secretary and Mrs. Block. Please follow me."

The Advance Agent led the entourage through the lobby of the William Penn Hotel to the Terrace Room dining on the first floor. As they got close to the Terrace Room doors, the hostess came out, greeted the entourage, and escorted them to their table.

USA, Washington D.C.
935 Pennsylvania Avenue NW
U.S. Department of Justice
Federal Bureau of Investigations

Headquarters
Director's Conference Room

"Okay. One more item before we end our Case Status Meeting. Susan, did everyone sign a Non-Disclosure Agreement about the next matter for discussion?" said Bashir Bashshar al Bazir, Director, Federal Bureau of Investigations.

"Yes, sir," Susan replied. "I have signed Non-Disclosure Agreements from everyone, sir."

"Good. Now we can talk freely about this matter, and we don't have to ask anyone to leave the room. Thank you all for your cooperation with the signing of the Non-Disclosure Agreements. Walter, what's the status of the investigations of the assassinated Presidential Cabinet members?"

"Sir, there was no change. When we last talked, the update was to get the surveillance camera footage from the cameras in and around the crime scenes. When the tech team went out to gather the footage from the various government entities that control the surveillance cameras, everyone was cooperative and signed the Non-Disclosure Agreements. However, the tech team's review of the footage at the times of the assassinations disclosed no images. It appeared the cameras stopped working before, during and shortly after the assassinations."

Director al Bazir said, "What? That can't be. Did you go out and double check the tech teams work?"

"Yes, I did sir. My personal review disclosed the same. It appeared the surveillance cameras stopped working before, during and after the assassinations. It was the same for all the locations that had security camera coverage. The custodians of the surveillance cameras were baffled by, what they called, a malfunction."

"Walter, you don't believe it was a malfunction, do you?"

"No, I didn't. I felt the cameras were compromised. It appeared to me the cameras were turned off for the duration of the assassination and then turned back on. That was my observation from my visit and request to review the records from all the government entities in which the assassinations occurred. One other thing, the Secret Service visited all the government entities before our tech team. When I pressed the custodians of the surveillance cameras for the details of the Secret Service's visit, all the individuals immediately said they couldn't talk because they signed a Secret Service Non-Disclosure Agreement."

"What's the Secret Service doing? They don't have jurisdiction in this matter."

"No, they don't. But each Presidential Cabinet member whose department or agency has an Office of Inspector General has jurisdiction. The Inspectors General have full statutory law enforcement authority post-September 11. This may complicate the investigation."

"Well, Walter, it's your job to keep it simple. I believe you can do that. One last note. The President is asking about this. That's all for today everyone. Thank you all for coming."

The Director of the FBI stood and exited the conference room with his two assistants and the Deputy Director and his personal assistant who followed behind. The balance of the senior management team began to leave.

William Penn Hotel Lobby

The Secretary of Veterans Affairs and his wife finished their breakfast. They left the Terrace Room and proceeded to the bank of elevators. The security detailed followed. The Secretary kissed his wife goodbye and said, "I'll see you later. Do you still want to dine on Mount Washington tonight?"

Mrs. Block replied, "Yes, honey. That would be delightful. Everyone says it is a spectacular view of the city. Yes, I would like to do that. How about you?"

"That'll be fine. I'll have staff make a reservation."

"Good."

"Are you still going to the museum today? What's the name again?"

"The Andy Warhol Museum. Would you like me to wait for you and we could go together later in the afternoon?"

"No. You go and enjoy yourself. Take your time and enjoy."

The elevator chimed, and the doors opened. Over the right shoulder of Mrs. Block, the Assistant Detail Leader scanned the elevator for threats as Mrs. Block entered. The Assistant Detail Leader followed and positioned himself by the control panel and operated the controls. Mrs. Block stood in the middle of the elevator for the ride up to the twenty-third floor to return to her room and freshen up before heading off to the museum.

The elevator arrived at the twenty-third floor uninterrupted. The Assistant Detail Leader positioned himself in front of the doors. When the doors opened, the Assistant Detail Leader scanned the area for threats. He cautiously moved out of the elevator and continued to scan for threats. Mrs. Block followed, and as she continued to walk down the hallway, the Assistant Detail Leader repositioned himself at her right shoulder. He continued to be on the alert for threats.

At Mrs. Block's room, the Assistant Detail Leader moved in front of her. He used the electronic key card and opened the door for her.

Mrs. Block entered, turned to the Assistant Detail Leader and said, "I have a few telephone calls to make, I'll be about an hour."

"Okay. I'll be in the hallway here when you're ready to go."

Mrs. Block closed the door.

The Assistant Detail Leader was sleepy. He stayed up and watched the entire Monday Night Football Game rerun of the Steelers versus the Cowboys. He decided to go to his room to rest. He knew a half hour power nap would take the sleepy edge off. As he was about to lay down, he heard faint screams from a woman in distress. He jumped up from the bed and ran out of his room. As he moved up the hallway toward Mrs. Block's room, he observed individuals coming out of her room. They carried a large black bag.

The Assistant Detail Leader shouted "You. You in the light blue helmet and black fatigues. Stop. Stop."

At that moment, the Assistant Detail Leader was cut down by a blaze of automatic gunfire. The sound muffled by a silencer affixed to the military weapon.

The Assistant Detail Leader worked alone. He had no partner or a team of agents to counter the assault. He did not have a chance to defeat his assailants. From the expression on his face, he was not surprised he was ambushed on the twenty-third floor of the William Penn Hotel.

His assailant was joined by another assailant. The two assailants placed the deceased Special Agent in a large black bag. The assailants carried the bag down the hallway and join up with two other individuals dressed in black military fatigues and light blue colored helmets with a dark tinted full-face shield. They briefly mustered at the doorway to the stairs as they position two large black bags for carrying. The four individuals moved into the stairwell, and the heavy metal fire door closed behind them, with the echo of a loud thud.

Secretary of Veterans Affairs Motorcade in transit

The Detail Leader broadcasted, "Fifteen out."

He turned to the rear seat of the limo.

"Mr. Secretary, as we anticipated, there's a huge crowd at the site. Your protection team will be close to you during this stop."

"Okay. Thanks for the heads up. By the way, what is a Gooskis?"

The Secretary's aide said, "Gooskis is a local bar in the Polish Hill District of Pittsburgh. It is frequented by many Polish veterans from many of the wars. It is a high-visibility venue for your speech and an excellent backdrop for a photo opportunity. The other option was the Immaculate Heart of Mary Roman Catholic Church given the ties to the community. But, with this administration's contempt for Christians, that site was not considered."

"Good choice to stay away from the Catholic Church. The President told his Cabinet members not to use Christian religion backdrops or Christian references in our speaking engagements. You kept me out of the President's crosshairs. Will lunch be served?"

"Yes." The Secretary's aide said. "You'll be having a sit-down lunch with the owner of Gooskis, the head priest of the Immaculate Heart of Mary, the Pittsburgh City Councilwomen for District 7 and the President of the VFW Post 6675 which is in the Southside area of Pittsburgh. All will be questioning you about the President's agenda for the veterans. They want more resources to address the mental health of veterans from all wars."

"Okay. What are we having for lunch?"

"Sir, you'll be having Pierogi."

"Pierogi! What are Pierogi?"

"It is likened to an Italian ravioli. A variety of fillings is used. It could be cheese mashed potatoes, prunes, dry cottage cheese or fried cabbage and onions. They are first boiled and then cooked in a lot of butter. And usually, they are served with caramelized onions."

"Prunes. I don't want any prunes. You make sure I don't get any prunes. Prunes."

"Yes, sir."

The Detail Leader broadcasted, "Twenty-Eighth Street Bridge for Brereton."

Clicks of the two-way radio mics came across the radio earpieces to acknowledge the location.

As the Secretary of Veterans Affairs two-vehicle motorcade passed over the Twenty-Eighth Street Bridge, the roar of motorcycles attracted the attention of the Limo Driver. He scanned his mirrors to determine from what direction the sound came. In the rearview mirror, he observed the follow vehicle had remained at the beginning of the bridge. With his scan, he saw it explode into a ball of fire. Out of the smoke from the explosion, he observed five motorcycles closed the distance to the limo. The Limo Driver stomped on the accelerator to the rented Suburban. After a lag, the suburban gradually picked up speed as it continued to cross the bridge.

The Detail Leader nudged the Limo Driver and whispered, "Slow down, we have plenty of time."

The Limo Driver motioned for the Detail Leader to check the mirrors.

The Detail Leader immediately checked his mirror and observed five motorcycles had surrounded the limo. The Detail Leader focused back to the roadway in front of him. He saw the road was blocked by a large light blue and white tractor-trailer. It was stopped and blocked all lanes of travel. The Limo Driver started to slow the limo anticipating the need to perform a J-turn to escape the attack.

Two of the motorcycles paced the limo. The passengers reached out and placed an object on the limo at four different locations.

The Limo Driver and the Detail Leader said nothing. They knew what was placed on the vehicle and they had no defensive maneuver or tactic to defend against four explosive devices magnetically attached to the limo. The limo, a Hertz rental car, was not armored. It was not re-enforcement. It had no ballistic windows. There was no one to call. There was no police escort. There was no counter-assault team to save the day.

When away from the Washington D.C. metropolitan area, the Presidential Cabinet motorcade moved from point to point through traffic using daily rental vehicles. They were not equipped with emergency equipment or protective armor. Local or state police staffing dictated if a police escort was provided. Today, no police escort was provided.

The limo was still moving toward the light blue and white tractor-trailer rig as the rear door to the attached trailer automatically raised. When the overhead trailer door was fully opened, it exposed a horrifying scene. Inside the trailer was the lifeless body of the Secretary's wife. As the Secretary turned his attention to the front of the limo, he saw his dead wife hung from the ceiling of the trailer. He screamed at the horrific scene and went into shock staring at his wife. The limo exploded at that moment.

The force of the explosion raised the limo off the roadway. It came to rest on the bridge in a ball of fire. The heat so intense, the sheet metal melted into a different shape. The force of the explosion and the limo hitting the roadway shattered the glass from the windows. The glassless windows provided a plethora of oxygen that fueled a fireball that engulfed the limo. The glassless windows acted as fully open dampers, and the air created a furnace effect on the interior of the vehicle and intensified the inferno.

The motorcycles stopped at the midpoint of the bridge. Four of the motorcycles turned to view the carnage, one faced away on the lookout for a counter-assault. Another motorcycle raced back to the burning motorcade. The passenger dismounted, moved cautiously to get as close as possible to the exploded limo. With a can of spray paint, the attacker painted a large red X and the number 17 on the roadway. Then, the attacker ran over to the tractor-trailer, jumped up into the trailer, took down the Secretary's wife, and threw her into the fully engulfed limo. The attacker went deeper into the trailer and returned with a large black back. He struggled a bit due to the weight but managed to throw the bag into the fully engulfed limo. The attacker jumped down from the trailer and ran back to the waiting motorcycle. He remounted, and it was driven back to join the others.

The formation of five motorcycles, with two occupants each, all clad in black military fatigues and light blue colored helmets with dark tinted full-face shields, preceded toward the carnage, back across the Twenty-Eighth Street Bridge in the direction of the tractor-trailer rig. In single file formation, they passed the raging inferno, once a Suburban. The motorcycles roared up an automatic ramp deployed from the rear of the blue and white tractor-trailer. As it chugged away from the carnage, the ramp was automatically retracted and the overhead door automatically closed.

USA, Pennsylvania, Philadelphia
Thirtieth Street Train Station

The Amtrak 98 Silver Meteor pulled into the Thirtieth Street Train Station and jerked to a stop. The conductor announced the train station stop and disembarking instructions.

Thomas "Tommy" Slatski, groggy from a restless night of trying to sleep in a coach seat, excused himself to get by the obnoxious female passenger who occupied the aisle seat next to him.

Tommy had an uncomfortable, sleepless night and a long train ride. The obnoxious female passenger, who got on the train in Savannah, Georgia, immediately took over. After she had stowed her luggage, she extended her seat in the fully reclined position, took her shoes off, and braced her feet against the seat back in front of her. She quickly fell asleep and started to snore. Not loud but soft and annoying snore which continued throughout the entire night. She tossed and turned. Her legs slipped off the seat back and came to rest touching Tommy which Tommy thought was done intentionally.

With his luggage in hand, Tommy disembarked the Amtrak 98 Silver Meteor, negotiated the track walkway to the escalator,

175

which took him to the main lobby at street level. Tommy waited for his connecting train to take him to his destination, his hometown to visit family.

While he waited, Tommy did the touristy thing. He took random pictures of the train station with his cellular telephone camera. Then he realized he just risked confiscation of his cellphone by the Philadelphia Police Department in the name of Homeland Security. Overtaken with the architecture, age, and sheer beauty of the grand old building, he thought nothing of taking pictures. With no one running toward him, he settled in to wait for the departure of the Amtrak Pennsylvanian.

A big smile came to Tommy's face. He remembered he packed sandwiches. As he ate his cheese sandwich, he reminisced about the road trips he took with his father and mother, Diane, his then future sister-in-law and Annie, his brother's then future mother-in-law. The trips were during football season to watch the Generals of Washington and Lee University in Lexington, Virginia and to various cities throughout the south, home to their opponents. Sometimes his mother packed sandwiches to eat along the way to save time from stopping. He chuckled to himself and caught himself before he laughed out loud. He chuckled remembering his father's famous line, *"Pour me a nip."* Meaning he wanted a cup of coffee from his Stanley thermos that had a heavily used patina the result of his father's use, day after day, year after year, as a Teamster card carrying Truck Driver.

Tommy remembered he received a telephone call yesterday in Florida. He retrieved his cellphone and scrolled to the phone number that was unknown to him. Tommy decided to call it. He pushed the send button. It started to ring. One ring. Two rings. Three rings.

A voice answered, "Hello."

Tommy said, "Hello."

The voice replied, "Hello, is there anyone there?"

Tommy said, "Yes. Hello. Hello. To whom am I speaking?"

The voice replied, "I don't know, you called me. To whom am I speaking?"

"I called this number because I missed your call yesterday. I don't know who you are. My name is Thomas Slatski. Are you trying to get a hold of me?"

"Tommy. This is Sarge. Sarge, from Interpol. How are you? Yes, I called you. I have to talk to you. It's very, very important."

"Okay. I have time now. How about you?"

"No not over these telephones. Can you get to a secure phone?"

"Sarge I'm retired from federal service. About four years now. I don't have access nor a clearance. What could you possibly want from me? What could I do for you?"

"Okay, that's enough. I'll figure out how to get you to a secure line. I'll call you back."

"If it helps, I'll be in Maryland in a few days. Do you want to meet someplace? Are you still in the Washington area?"

"I'm still in Northern Virginia. We may do that if I can't get you to a secure phone. Where are you at now?"

"Tomorrow, I'll be about 80 miles east of Pittsburgh, PA."

"Do you think you can get to Pittsburgh if I can get you into the FBI field office there?"

"Yes. I can do that."

Okay. Let me call you back. Tommy, this is important. I really need your help."

"Sarge, anything I can do for you, I will. You should know that from our days at Interpol. I'm just surprised since I'm retired from federal service. Call me back."

"Thanks, Tommy. I'll call you back. Thanks."

Tommy hung up. He rested his hand, still holding his cellphone, on his leg. Deep in thought about his phone call with Sarge, he was brought back to reality when he faintly heard an announcement in the background.

"Amtrak 43 the Pennsylvanian to Pittsburgh and stops in between. Now boarding on track seven."

Tommy gathered his luggage and walked off to find a Red Cap to expedite his boarding to business class.

Pittsburgh
Twenty-Eighth Street Bridge

Detective Slatski broadcasted, "10-3 Stop transmitting. 10-80 Explosion Twenty-Eighth Street Bridge

Pittsburgh Bureau of Police Dispatch broadcasted, "10-4 Okay. All units 10-23 standby. All units 10-23 standby. Break. Dispatch to the last unit, identify and repeat."

"Unit 54 10-80 Twenty-Eighth Street Bridge. A lot of smoke coming from the Twenty-Eighth Street Bridge. En route from 2600 block of Liberty Avenue to investigate."

"10-4 Unit 54 go to channel 9."

"10-4 channel 9."

"Unit 54 to dispatch."

"Go Unit 54."

Detective Slatski broadcasted, "One vehicle fully engulfed at the west end of the Twenty-Eighth Street Bridge. Obstructed roadway. Request assistance, fire department, emergency medical. A second vehicle fully engulfed on the east end of the Twenty-Eighth Street Bridge. Request assistance. Fire department. Emergency medical. Emergency personnel approach required from respective ends of the bridge. The bridge blocked on each end. Repeat, engulfed vehicles, bridge blocked on each end."

Dispatch broadcasted, "10-4. Standby Unit 54."

Precinct Shift Sergeant broadcasted, "Unit 54 from Shift Sergeant."

"Go for Unit 54."

"Unit 54 set up a crime scene perimeter. Hold prospective witnesses. Repeat. Set up crime scene perimeter. Hold potential witness."

"10-4."

"ETA 15 minutes."

"10-4."

Poland, Warsaw
Poland National Police
National Security Group

1950 Hours

Jan shut down his computer as he readied to leave work for the day. Ever since his promotion to the National Security Group, Jan worked twelve-hour days. As Jan reached for the light switch, Josef appeared behind him.

"Jan, not so quick. I need about a half hour with you. I need to show you something."

"Sure Josef. Here or your office?"

"Here will be okay. Look at this."

Josef handed Jan a nondescript white piece of paper. Jan looked it over and studied it for a minute or two then looked to Josef.

"Okay. I give up. It's a list of dates and cities. What should this mean to me?"

"This is a list of dates and location of assassinated Presidential Cabinet members of the United States of America."

"How did you get the list? Is this list credible? With respect sir, are you sure?"

"Jan, I'm sure. The National Security Group collaborates with the FBI of the United States of America. We jointly monitor data from a satellite. It cross-references with the U.S. and Poland local law enforcement communications. It's a program the two governments have been using since 11 September terrorist attacks in the U.S. Apparently, the FBI has information that some of the local law enforcement agencies in the U.S. have information about the assassinations. Some of those local departments didn't share that information with the FBI."

"What do we get for our assistance? Do you suspect our local law enforcement agencies are doing the same? Not sharing vital intelligence?"

"What do we get out of it? Intelligence. Do I think our local law enforcement agencies withhold information to the National Security Group? Yes, I do. Poland collaborates on this effort, so the U.S. has deniability."

"What do you mean deniability?"

"If the U.S. citizens, or worse, the U.S. local law enforcement community ever find out their Federal government monitors their own people and state, county and local law enforcement agencies, it would be embarrassing to the U.S. government. The U.S. government can blame it on Poland and say they didn't know the Poland government monitors U.S. citizens and state, county and local law enforcement."

"Why agree to that? We risk embarrassment and the loss of credibility in the European Union. Around the world, if this is ever disclosed."

The Great Country of Poland will figure out how to handle that if it's ever disclosed. It's something Poland has to do to keep her edge. It's the real world, the global community, Jan."

Jan said, "Okay. The list has six alleged assassinations.

6 October	Gdansk, Poland
	Secretary of Commerce
9 October	Germantown, Maryland
	Secretary of Education
10 October	Ocean City, Maryland
	Secretary of Defense
11 October	Washington, D.C.
	Attorney General
13 October	McLean, Virginia
	Secretary of Agriculture
14 October	Pittsburgh, Pennsylvania
	Secretary of Veterans Affairs"

Josef said, "Within a few days, we'll have imagery of the event scenes to examine."

"Obviously I don't know the full capabilities of the National Security Group, so I'm going to ask, do we have access to the street surveillance cameras in the U.S.?"

"Not here in Poland. Our co-workers in the U.S. do."

"I'll check on that."

"Good. Now go home already."

"Good night. See you in the morning," replied Jan as he turned the lights out, closed his door, and left the private office.

15 October, Friday

USA, Washington D.C.

Secretary of Interior Motorcade in transit

2030 Hours

"Move."

The two-vehicle motorcade for the Secretary of Interior departed 1849 C Street NW under the command of the Detail Leader. The Secretary's motorcade moved slowly as it navigated the District of Columbia morning rush hour traffic to Route 66. From there, it continued to the Theodore Roosevelt Memorial Bridge, to the George Washington Memorial Parkway, to the 495 Capital Beltway, to the 270 spur, to 270 Dwight D. Eisenhower Memorial Highway, and then to route 15 north, the Catoctin Mountain Highway to business Route 15, Taneytown Road. The motorcade was en route to Gettysburg, Pennsylvania. The Secretary was scheduled for a luncheon at the Gettysburg National Military Park and then a speech.

It was a bright, sunny, fall morning in the Washington D.C. metropolitan area. The same was expected in Gettysburg. The Secretary snuggled into his seat in the right rear of the limo, directly behind the Detail Leader. He planned to read his morning briefs and to review his speech while en route. This, of course, between catching a nap, which the Secretary enjoyed when on a long-distance drive.

To transport the Secretary by motorcade for long distances was not the preferred method for the protection detail. The logistics of such a security transport were daunting. Of grave concern was the number of hospitals and safe havens to move the Secretary to in the event of a medical emergency or attack. All along the route, facilities had to be identified and located. Contact had to be made to establish a point of contact. A security analysis had to be conducted.

A Protection Plan was written by a two-person advance team following protection protocols. It placed one of the Advance Agents at the event site, and the other Advance Agent in the motorcade follow vehicle. In the case of a medical emergency or an attack, the Advance Agent directed the Limo Driver to the nearest hospital or safe haven, at any point along the route. Creature comforts, based on the Secretary's preferences, were also located and noted in the Protection Plan. A simple plan based on the available resources, both human and physical, the Secretary of Interior's Executive Protection Detail had to use.

The limited resources of the Secretary's protection detail were consistent with, and a constant complaint of all the Presidential Cabinet members' protection details. Contrary to Hollywood drama, Presidential Cabinet members had no access to a fleet of helicopters or jets like the President. Such thoughts were perpetrated by Hollywood fiction.

This was going to be a long ride and a long day.

The motorcade progressed at a nice pace. Five miles from the outskirts of Frederick, Maryland and on route 15 north the Secretary said, "I need some coffee. I checked Google. The nearest Dunkin Donuts is about seven miles from here. Does anyone know where that is?"

The Detail Leader replied, "I'll check Mr. Secretary."

"I can Google it again and get directions for you to follow as I read them out loud."

"That won't be necessary. We'll handle it."

"Okay. Just trying to help."

The Detail Leader, into his left sleeve, broadcasted, "Detail Leader to Advance."

"Go."

"Where is the nearest Dunkin Donut shop from our current location?"

"About five miles. It's an on/off deviation. A total of six miles off route. We have to get off at the West Patrick Street exit and go west."

"10-4. Direct the Limo Driver. We'll be taking this deviation. The Secretary wants coffee."

"10-4. Break. Advance Agent to Limo Driver."

The Limo Driver responded with two clicks of his two-way radio mic.

"In two miles, exit onto the West Patrick Street exit, Route 144 west. It will take you to a stop light with a merge lane for westbound traffic to keep moving."

The Limo Driver responded with two clicks of his mic.

"This is the exit."

The motorcade flowed around the exit ramp to the westbound traffic lane. The follow vehicle engaged emergency lights and held traffic for the limo to flow into the right-hand westbound lane without slowing or waiting. The follow vehicle, emergency lights still operating, continued to hold traffic.

The Shift Leader broadcasted, "One left."

The Limo Driver maneuvered the limo into the middle lane of a three-lane roadway.

Again, the Shift Leader broadcasted, "One left."

Again, the Limo Driver without hesitation or looking steered the limo into the left-hand lane and the motorcade continued westbound.

The Advance Agent broadcasted, "At the fourth red light, make a U-turn. Go back a half of block to the Dunkin Donuts. Traffic will be heavy there. The Dunkin Donut parking lot is small. Expect congestion."

The Limo Driver responded with two clicks of his mic.

The Shift Leader broadcasted, "One left."

The Limo Driver glided into the left-hand turn lane at the traffic signal without looking. The Limo Driver just followed the directions, the continued assistance, given by the Shift Leader or Advance Agent.

When the green left turn arrow displayed, the motorcade moved with a U-turn and then turned right, into the parking lot. The Limo Driver stopped the limo as close to the main entrance that traffic congestion permitted. The follow vehicle stopped immediately behind the limo, offset to protect the Secretary and Detail Leader when they got out of the limo.

The Shift Leader, from the right front seat of the follow vehicle, was first out of the motorcade. He scanned the area looking for any signs of threats. He completed his hard scan from behind blacked out sunglasses.

The Shift Leader broadcasted, "Clear."

With that broadcast, the Detail Leader, from the right front seat of the limo, emerged and closed his door. The Limo Driver electronically locked all the doors. From behind blacked out sunglasses, the Detail Leader scanned the area for threats. When the Detail Leader felt confident there were no threats, the Detail Leader tapped on the front right passenger door window and the Limo Driver to unlock the doors. The Detail Leader opened the right rear door and controlled it until the Secretary got out. As the Secretary got out, the Shift Leader positioned himself to take the door from the Detail Leader. The Detail Leader moved with the Secretary. The Shift Leader closed the door and remained at the door to control it when the Secretary returned or in the event of an attack.

While he moved to the entrance to the donut shop, the Detail Leader broadcasted, "Position the motorcade for departure."

Clicks of the two-way radio microphones sounded in response to the Detail Leader's orders.

The Advance Agent left the rear seat of the follow vehicle and moved directly to the entrance door. He scanned the interior of the Dunkin Donuts and signaled to the security team all was clear. He controlled the entrance door for the Secretary and Detail Leader to enter without delay. From this post, the Advance Agent was prepared to control the door in preparation for the Secretary's exit and to be on the lookout for threats or anything unusual.

As the motorcade was repositioned for departure, the Shift Leader took a position at the corner of the building. From this post, the Shift Leader was on the lookout for threats and anything unusual. When the motorcade returned, the Shift Leader positioned himself by the right rear door of the limo in preparation to control the door as the Secretary entered the limo.

A happy clerk sounded, "Can I help you, sir?"

The Secretary meandered toward the counter while he studied the menu, then replied, "Yes. I'll have an extra-large coffee with extra cream and sugar. I also would like two apple fritters and two Boston cream filled donuts."

The happy clerk, as she worked the register, said, "Yes sir. That'll be $8.76."

"Oh. I'm an AARP member. Here's my card. I believe I get a free donut."

"Thank you. Yes, you do. One of your donuts will be free. Let me take that off. Now that'll be $7.53."

"Here you go. Keep the change."

"Thank you, sir."

Another not so pleasant clerk handed the Secretary his extra-large coffee followed by his donuts in a bag.

"Thank you all."

The Secretary walked away from the counter toward the exit doors.

The Advance Agent opened the door in preparation for the Secretary and Detail Leader to exit. The Secretary walked through the door and continued toward the limo. The Detail Leader followed the Secretary at the right shoulder protective position. As the Detail Leader passed the Advance Agent, he faked a punch at him. The Advance Agent did not fall for the jocularity known to come from the Detail Leader, a typical part of law enforcement work. The Advance Agent followed behind and moved to the left rear door to enter the follow vehicle.

As the Secretary walked toward the limo, the Shift Leader opened the right rear door and controlled it while the Secretary entered. He handed it off to the Detail Leader and moved near the front passenger door of the follow vehicle to stand watch. After the Detail Leader entered the limo and closed his door, the Shift Leader, now seated in the follow vehicle, broadcasted, "Move."

The motorcade drifted to the end of the parking lot to merge onto West Patrick Street to retrace its route back to Route 15 north. At the exit, the follow vehicle positioned itself along the left-hand side of the limo. With emergency lights engaged, the follow vehicle crept into traffic. The traffic yielded the right of way to the emergency vehicle. The follow vehicle held traffic as the Limo Driver steered the limo to the right onto West Patrick Street. The follow vehicle fell in behind the limo with emergency lights still flashing. It was positioned in an offset escort until the motorcade was northbound on Route 15.

On route 15 north and in the left-hand lane, the motorcade sped by the first exit for Thurmont, Maryland, as five motorcycles came up the on-ramp. The motorcycles entered the highway and maintain the posted speed. This kept the motorcycles one-half mile to the rear of the motorcade. The Follow Vehicle Driver monitored the motorcycles as he watched any other traffic in the event he had to interrupt the flow of traffic to maintain the integrity of the motorcade. The motorcade stayed the course and continued northbound on Route 15.

As the motorcade approached Emmetsburg, Maryland, the Secretary said, "I need to use a restroom. That coffee went right through me."

"Detail Leader to Advance Agent."

"Go Detail Leader."

"Restroom."

"Government facilities next exit. The National Fire Academy. Four miles total deviation."

"10-4. Direct the Limo Driver please."

The Advance Agent was about to broadcast to the Limo Driver, but he was interrupted by the roar of approaching motorcycles. In the right-hand lane, the five motorcycles raced by the motorcade at a high rate of speed. Their approach was so fast, the Follow Driver could not take any defensive maneuvers without the risk of collision. The motorcycles sped by the motorcade as it slowed to exit the highway to follow a deviated route for a restroom stop.

At the end of the exit ramp, the limo merged into the left-hand turn lane. The follow vehicle, with emergency lights engaged, drifted to the right-hand side of the limo and continued to roll into the travel lanes of the rural road that led to the National Fire Academy. This allowed the limo to continue to move onto the rural road. The follow vehicle pulled back into formation behind the limo, and the two-vehicle motorcade resumed a stacked formation.

After a short distance, the motorcade turned right off the rural road and through an unchecked, unsecured entrance. The road zigged by a helicopter landing pad, mature trees, and early nineteenth century buildings that were once used as a seminary and monastery. On the broadcasted directions of the Advance Agent, the limo stopped. As the follow vehicle came to a stop, the Advance Agent exited the vehicle and rushed to the lead position to lead the Secretary to the restroom facilities at the main administration building of the National Emergency Training Center. He knew his way from the advance work he completed.

When the limo stopped, the Detail Leader exited the limo and went through the same ritual he did every time the Secretary exited the limo. He manually unlocked his door only. He exited the limo and closed his door. The Limo Driver electronically locked all the doors. He scanned the area from behind his dark tinted glasses for any potential threats. On the Detail Leader's command, a tap on the front right door window, the Limo Driver electronically unlocked all the doors to the limo. The Detail Leader opened the right rear door to allow the Secretary to exit the vehicle. Once the Secretary started to walk off, the Detail Leader handed the limo door off to the Shift Leader who controlled the door. If attacked, until the Secretary was halfway to the entrance, he would go back to the limo for evacuation. At or past the midpoint, the Secretary would continue to the building and a predetermined safe room.

The Advance Agent led the Secretary and Detail Leader into the building and directly to the men's restroom. The Advance Agent moved ahead and entered to perform a security sweep. It was empty. If there were individuals present, the Advance Agent would quickly control them and direct them to leave when finished. Until cleared, the Secretary would be held outside by the Detail Leader.

With the security sweep completed, the Advance Agent rushed to control the restroom door for the entry of the Secretary and Detail Leader. The Advance Agent posted himself outside, in front of the door, while the Secretary was inside. After a security sweep, the Detail Leader posted himself outside the restroom with the Advance Agent.

When the Secretary was finished, the Detail Leader broadcasted, "Coming out."

As they emerged, the Advance Agent controlled the door, then swiftly moved by the Detail Leader and the Secretary, once again to take the lead position to lead them out of the building and back to the limo.

As the Secretary exited the building, the Shift Leader moved to the rear right door of the limo. When the Secretary reached the halfway point, the Shift Leader opened the limo door for the Secretary's reentry into the limo. As the Secretary entered the limo, the Shift Leader handed the door off to the Detail Leader. The Shift Leader posted himself three feet away from the limo and faced away, and through dark tinted glasses, scanned the area for potential threats. The sound of the limo door closed by the Detail Leader did not break his concentration. He waited for the broadcast from the Detail Leader.

"Secured."

When the Shift Leader heard the command, he entered the front right seat of the follow vehicle. Once seated and the door closed, the Shift Leader responded, "Secured."

The Detail Leader waited for the response of the Shift Leader. The response that signaled the entire motorcade was ready to move. It was the command from the Detail Leader on which the Limo Driver proceeded.

"Move."

The motorcade retraced its route back to Route 15 north to continue onto Gettysburg and the Secretary's event. Once on Route 15, the motorcade glided into the left-hand lane, quickly accelerated to seventy miles per hour and maintained that speed and lane position.

The motorcade traveled approximately ten miles when the Advance Agent broadcasted, "In two miles, exit right."

Clicks of the two-way radio mics acknowledged the Advance Agent's directions.

Running at seventy miles per hour, in one mile, the follow vehicle was positioned in a right-hand offset to allow the limo to glide into the right-hand lane for the right-hand exit.

As the limo moved into the right-hand lane, the follow vehicle repositioned in a left-hand offset to block any vehicles from approaching and/or overtaking the limo.

Though the motorcade was slowing, it did not stop at the end of the exit ramp. The motorcade kept moving making it more difficult for any would-be attacks. Mainly a sniper attack. As the motorcade came closer to the end of the exit ramp, the follow vehicle eased passed the limo on the right-hand side and with emergency lights engaged, positioned itself to block traffic. This defensive maneuver allowed the limo to negotiate the left-hand turn without stopping. Once the limo made the left turn, the follow vehicle fell in behind it. The two-vehicle motorcade continued in a stacked formation.

Calmly, the Shift Leader broadcasted, "Obstruction right. Obstruction right."

This was a command to the Limo Driver to safely move left to create distance between an obstacle, a potential threat to the limo. Parked on the right-hand side of the roadway was a long tractor-trailer rig. A light blue tractor attached to a long white trailer blocked the right-hand lane.

Instinctively and without effort, the Limo Driver eased the limo to the left and traveled down the middle of the roadway. The follow vehicle was in a right offset position with its emergency lights flashing. When the motorcade passed the long tractor-trailer rig, the limo eased back into the right-hand lane. The follow vehicle fell in behind. The motorcade disengaged their emergency lights.

The motorcade continued Taneytown Road and negotiated a rise in the roadway from a bridge. As it started down the other side, the Limo Driver saw roadblock spikes stretched across both travel lanes. In a calm composed manner, the Limo Driver whispered to the Detail Leader, "Do you see that? I can't avoid it. I'm going to hit and run. I'm going to push through to the safe haven at the event site."

The Detail Leader replied, "Yes. Keep moving. Don't slow down."

The Limo Driver, unable to take evasive action, sped up. The position of the roadblock spikes and the narrow rural roadway provided no space for a defensive maneuver. There was a slight jar to the limo when it ran over the spikes. The limo was equipped with run-flat tires which allowed the Limo Driver to continue to drive north on Taneytown Road toward Gettysburg. He accelerated the speed. The motorcade was under attack.

The Detail Leader, in a calm whisper, broadcasted, "Attack. Attack."

The Shift Leader broadcast, "We hit it. We're hit!"

The Limo Driver and Detail Leader looked back through the mirrors and saw the follow vehicle get smaller. It did not keep up with the limo. It did not have run flat tires because of budgetary constraints imposed by the continuing resolution. Congress did not pass a budget.

Then came the roar of four motorcycles. They surrounded the limo. Each occupied twice by individuals dressed in black military fatigues and light blue colored helmets with dark tinted full-face shields. The passengers were armed with long military weapons.

The Limo Driver continued to accelerate the limo. It labored. The run flat tires were unable to handle the high speed. Though designed to keep the limo rolling, they were not designed to sustain high-speed evasive driving.

The Secretary woke up from his nap. He said, "What're the motorcycles doing? What's going on here?"

At the same time, all four motorcycles swerved toward the limo and paced the speed of the limo. When in arms reach, all four of the passengers reached out and place small rectangular blocks on the limo. They veered away from the limo and quickly reduced their speed. With the limo at a high rate of speed, this quickly created distance between the limo and the motorcycles.

Through the rearview mirror, the Limo Driver saw a fifth motorcycle joined the other four. They sat on the side of the road in what appeared to be a formation.

The Detail Leader shouted to the Limo Driver, "What're you going to do? Do something. Do something."

The Limo Driver replied, "What do you want me to do?" There was a brief pause. "Brace yourself. I'm going to stop the vehicle. We all need to jump out."

The Limo Driver jammed on the breaks. A loud noise came from the anti-lock brake system, and the limo slowed.

In a frantic voice, the Limo Driver shouted, "Okay. Jump! Jump!"

The Secretary shouted with panic, "I can't jump. The car is still moving."

The Detail Leader disengaged his seatbelt and jumped into the rear seat. The Detail Leader said, "I got you Mr. Secretary. I got you. I'm going to open the door. We're going to jump together."

The Limo Driver shouted again, "Jump. Jump."

The Detail Leader clutched to the Secretary, reached for the door handle and opened the right rear door. As the Detail Leader positioned to jump out of the limo with the Secretary, the right rear door closed.

The Detail Leader repositioned himself with the Secretary. He opened the door again. The limo moved slower. There was an explosion, and the force propelled the Detail Leader and the Secretary out the open door. The two bounced along the side of the roadway and continued to roll into the grassy area adjacent to the edge of the road.

When they stopped, the Secretary did not move. The Detail Leader was conscious, but disoriented from the explosion and bouncing and rolling along the ground. The Detail Leader looked up to see the limo come to rest in a grassy field a few hundred yards away. It then exploded again and was now fully engulfed in flames.

As the Detail Leader tried to get up, he fell to the ground. It was as if he had no legs. With apprehension, he looked down. His legs were there, though he was unable to stand. He tried again and fell again. He started to fade in and out of consciousness. In desperation, he looked for the Secretary. With blurred vision, he saw the Secretary about thirty yards away. He started a belly crawl toward the Secretary.

As the Detail Leader belly crawled, he heard the roar of motorcycles as they progressed closer. With instinct, he reached to draw his issued duty sidearm. He panicked. His sidearm was not in the holster. He slowly continued to regain his composer. He continued to crawl on his belly toward the Secretary. The roar of the motorcycles turned to an idle. He looked toward the Secretary and saw two of the motorcycle riders stood over the Secretary and pointed their military-style long weapons at the Secretary. The Detail Leader saw the recoil of the guns, but he heard no sounds. A second time, he saw the recoil of the military weapons indicative of multiple rounds of fully automatic weapons. Still, he heard no sounds. Both times, he saw the Secretary's body twitch from the rounds that entered his body. Then without warning, the Detail Leader felt the burning sensation of multiple bullet wounds. His belly crawl stopped. He tried to turn around, but he expired.

The attackers regroup at the motorcycles. They all remounted the motorcycles except one. That attacker, without concern, walked to the side of the roadway. On Taneytown Road, the attacker spray painted a large red X and the number 8 beside it. The attacker stood, surveyed the carnage and returned to his motorcycle. The formation of five motorcycles roared away east on Taneytown Road.

USA, Northern Virginia

1045 Hours

Sarge was seated in his favorite lounge chair. He drank his morning coffee and watched Fact News Center. He had a telephone call to the FBI Headquarters and waited for a return call to see if he could get a secure phone at the Pittsburgh Field Office so he and Tommy could talk freely about Jan's request for assistance.
Sarge's cellular telephone rang.

He mumbled to himself, "I hope this is the FBI so I can talk to Tommy already."

He looked at the display which read NUMBER NOT AVAILABLE.

Sarge mumbled, "What. Who could this be? I better answer it."

"Hello."

"Hello. Who's this?"

"Who are you looking for?"

"Sarge! Sarge is that you?

"Yes. Is this Jan?"

"Yes. How are you today?"

"Good. How are you?"

"I'm good. I'm calling to see if you have any information for me."

"No, not yet. I thought you were the call I was waiting for to help me get to a secure telephone so I can talk to a friend about this."

"Do you need a secure phone?"

"Yes."

"Would you mind going to the Embassy of Poland? I don't know how far that may be from you. If you wish to go there, I can get you to a secure line. Then you can call any telephone number, landline or cellular, anywhere in the world and it will be safe. Will that help?"

"Yes. That would help a lot. Can you do that?"

"Yes. Let me go. I'll call the embassy. I'll call you back."

"Thank you."

Sarge and Jan ended their call.

Sarge placed his cellular telephone on the coffee table. He rose from his lounge chair, walked to the kitchen and topped off his coffee. Sarge returned to his chair, fell back into it and continued to watch Fact News Center. He picked up the remote control and scrolled through the news channels. Sarge desperately looked for some open source reporting on, if nothing else, the alleged assassination of the Attorney General. At the FOP lodge, though brief, he and Shaggy saw and listened to a news report on the alleged assassination of the Attorney General. There was no mistaking that for him. He stopped at Central News Network and continued to watch the news.

Sarge's cellphone rang, and the vibration mode made it dance on the coffee table.

Sarge quickly picked up the cellphone and again viewed NUMBER NOT AVAILABLE on the screen. He answered it anyway. He thought, "It may be Jan. Though how Jan could have organized the assistance of the embassy so quickly."

"Hello."

"Hello, again Sarge. Jan is here. Okay. All is arranged. When you go to the embassy, tell the guard you are there to see Bertha.

You'll have to wait in the reception area for Bertha. When she greets you in the reception area, she'll ask to see your retired FBI credentials. When she asks the password say pierogi."

"That was quick. Okay, I'll ask for Bertha. The password is pierogi."

"Yes. You got it. I've organized everything for you. Bertha will take you to a secure telephone, and you can make your call."

"Good. Oh, Jan, are we on a secure line?

"Yes."

"There is nothing on open sources about an alleged assassination operation or the murder of any of the Presidential Cabinet members. The only thing I saw was a four-minute report on Fact News Center about the assassination of the Attorney General. With all the information you gave me on Tuesday, I forgot to tell you. On Monday, 11 October, when I was at the FOP lodge, there was a short emergency newscast about the assassination of the Attorney General. The FOP bartender, Shaggy, also saw the news broadcast. At this point, I have to call that an alleged assassination. I found no information to corroborate the assassination of the Attorney General. My sources in the government came up dry. No one said anything. Though my hunch, they knew something."

Jan replied, "My count of assassinated Presidential Cabinet members is at six. I have a list of six.

6 October	Gdansk, Poland
	Secretary of Commerce
9 October	Germantown, Maryland
	Secretary of Education
10 October	Ocean City, Maryland
	Secretary of Defense
11 October	Washington, D.C.
	Attorney General

13 October	McLean, Virginia
	Secretary of Agriculture
14 October	Pittsburgh, Pennsylvania
	Secretary of Veterans Affairs"

There was silence on the telephone.

Finally, Jan said, "Sarge. Are you there Sarge?"

With a shaky voice, Sarge replied, "Yes. I'm here. I can't believe what you say. You say that information is credible?"

"Yes, very reliable."

"I don't know what to say. You say six assassinations. I saw no open source information on them. I'm stunned. What is the date of the Attorney General's assassination?"

"11 October."

"That's the day I was at the FOP lodge. Shaggy and I heard the short news report of the assassination of the Attorney General."

"Okay, I'll note that in the file."

Jan continued, "We're dealing with something big here Sarge. At times, I have a hard time putting my arms around this. And when I think I understand it, something else happens. It slips away from me. You can see why I need your help."

"Yes, I can," said Sarge. "Again, I pledge my assistance to you. You know I'll help you in any way I can."

"Thank you, Sarge. Thank you. Go see Bertha now so we can continue."

"I will. I'm going as soon as we hang up. Goodbye, for now, Jan."

"Good-bye, Sarge."

Sarge ended the call and placed his phone in his pants pocket. He turned the television off with the remote control and threw it onto the lounge chair. He picked up his coffee cup, an Interpol mug, and walked to the kitchen. He rinsed it out and placed it in the dishwasher. He turned the coffee pot off, grabbed his coat and put it on as he went out the back door to the garage for his car. He was off to the Embassy of Poland to meet Bertha.

On his slow drive to 2640 16th Street NW, Washington D.C. he telephoned Tommy.

"Hello."

"Tommy, I'm on my way to the Embassy of Poland. It has access to a secure telephone to call you. Our conversation will be secured then.

"That's good."

"There'll be no need for you to go to an FBI office."

"Good. Though you know, I would have if necessary."

"I know. Will I be able to call you in about an hour or hour and a half?"

"Yes. I'll be waiting for your call."

"Great. Thanks, Tommy. Talk to you soon."

"Yes, sir."

Sarge slowly made his way across the Fourteenth Street Bridge. He continued Fourteenth Street, crossed over Independence Avenue and passed the U.S. Department of Agriculture buildings on his right and left. Sarge continued up Fourteenth Street to K Street and turned left onto K Street. From K Street, he turned right onto Sixteenth Street and scanned the street numbers. He saw he was two blocks away from the Embassy of the Republic of Poland. He looked for street parking and noticed a car pulled away from the curb. He signaled to take the spot. After parallel parked in the 2500 block, he got out, locked his car and put the proper coins in the meter and laughed to himself remembering his friend Lizzy, the Parking Enforcement Officer. He crossed the street and walked the final block to the Embassy of Poland.

USA, Washington D.C.
2640 16ᵗʰ Street NW
Embassy of the Republic of Poland

Sarge was greeted by a security checkpoint at the Embassy of Poland. He emptied his pockets and passed through a full body x-ray scanner by holding his hands above his head. On the security guards cue, he exited the machine and was given the okay to proceed to the reception area. Sarge gathered his belongings and reorganized himself on his way.

At the reception area, he was greeted by the receptionist.

"How may I help you?"

"I'm here to see Bertha."

"Please have a seat over there."

The receptionist pointed to an area with plush furniture, two televisions, and about a dozen people.

"Thank you."

Sarge walked to the reception area to wait for Bertha.

No sooner Sarge sat down in one of the large plush chairs a female voice sounded.

"Sarge?"

Sarge sprang back up and looked over the plush chair. He saw the towering, blue-eyed, vivacious, blond hair, Polish lady booming his way.

"Yes, I'm Sarge. Are you Bertha?"

"Yes, I am. Jan told me you would be right over and here you are. May I see your credentials, please?"

"Yes."

Sarge presented his retired FBI credentials to Bertha.

Bertha gave them a good review to include a look at the picture and a look at Sarge to make a thorough comparison.

"And the password?"

"Pierogi."

"What is it?"

Sarge a little nervous, but with confidence, replied again, "Pierogi."

"Yes, pierogi. Did you ever eat any?

"No, I haven't. I didn't know it was food."

"Well, we're going to have to fix that."

Bertha handed Sarge his credentials.

"I see you are retired."

"Yes, I am."

"Good for you. Follow me. Oh, I almost forgot, here are your Poland government credentials. They give you access to the embassy so you can bypass the security checkpoint. There's also a key card for your office."

"Bertha slow down a little. I'm only here to use a secure telephone."

Bertha interrupted Sarge with disregard for his comment.

"Please display your Poland Embassy credentials. The embassy security has a zero-tolerance policy. Anyone who isn't presenting credentials is placed in handcuffs, willing or not, and then given the opportunity to produce their credentials. You don't want to go through that on your first day or any day."

Sarge clipped the Poland Embassy credential on his coat.

"Bertha, I appreciate all your assistance. All I want to do is make one telephone call."

"Yes, I know. But you will have to make two. Your first call will be to your U.S. counterpart. Your second call will be to Jan. He requests you to telephone him after you finish your first call."

"Oh."

"I'll give you the tour tomorrow. Today, make your calls from your office and call me when you're done. I'll escort you out."

Surprised, Sarge stuttered, "Oh. Okay."

Bertha led Sarge to an elevator which took them to the sixth floor. They disembarked the elevator, turned right and went halfway down the hallway.

"Here we are. This is your office. Let's see if your key card works. Please use it to open the door."

Sarge became overwhelmed with the progression of this afternoon. He fumbled for the key and the use of it.

He thought, "I so want to tell Bertha you know I'm retired."

On the third try, the key card opened the lock and Bertha pushed the door open and entered the office. As she held the door open for Sarge, she said, "Here it is. If there's anything you need, you call me. Okay."

"Yes. Thank you."

"To dial out, press nine then one and the 10-digit number for U.S. telephones, landline or cellular."

"Thank you."

Bertha left the room. She closed the door behind her.

Sarge, taken aback by everything, fell into the plush, high back, desk chair behind the large, oak, desk. His mind wondered.

"What's going on here? Did Bertha get Jan's message crossed? Call Jan after I call my counterpart? This is your office? I am holding Poland government credentials? Embassy credentials? Okay. Okay. I must call Tommy."

Sarge picked up the telephone and dialed as Bertha instructed. The phone rang.

Tommy answered, "Hello."

"Hello, Tommy? Sarge here. We can now talk freely. We're on a secure line. I'm calling you because I need help with something that is unfolding as big. I mean huge. I know you conducted executive protection for members of the Presidential Cabinet."

"Yes. I was assigned to Executive Protection Detail with the Agriculture's Inspector General and when I was with the Office of Special Operations with the Department of Energy."

"Good. But now you are retired?"

"Yes, I'm retired from the federal law enforcement."

"Okay. Do you know anyone who's working on a protection detail for any member of the Presidential Cabinet?"

"Let me think now."

"While you think let me bring you up to date. Right now, I'm sitting in the Embassy of Poland in Washington. I'm talking to you on a secure telephone from a sixth-floor office. I have a friend, his name is Jan, who's now with the Poland National Police, their National Security Group. It's kind of like our CIA. We know each other from my Interpol days. Jan contacted me and asked if I could assist him with an investigation. I explained to him I was retired from the FBI, but I would help him. He wanted me to reach out to some of my counterparts. Someone who had information on, you ready, on an operation, to assassinate all the members of the President's Cabinet. I made some telephone calls to my associates at the FBI. I received no information. My hunch, they knew something, but they were not telling me anything. Then I remembered you work Executive Protection for the Cabinet members, so I reached out to you for help."

"Okay."

Sarge continued, "Oh. Oh. This was interesting. Two things. I watched open sources, mainly news outlets, for any information related to an assassination attempt of the President's Cabinet members. The only thing I saw and heard was when I was at the FOP lodge one afternoon. The 11th of October to be precise. The bartender and I were watching Fact News Center. The regularly scheduled programming was interrupted for a special report on an alleged assassination of the Attorney General. There was a four-minute report before the Secret Service shut down the airwaves and the television went blank. Then today, Jan shared a list of six Presidential Cabinet members who have been assassinated to date. His list included the Attorney General on 11 October. So, I'm convinced something big happened."

"Wow. Let me absorb this for a couple of minutes. A couple people quickly come to mind. Can I think on this overnight and call you in the morning?"

"Yes. I think that would be a good way to proceed. Thanks, Tommy."

"You're welcome, Sarge. On what number should I call you?"

"Ah. I don't know. Can I just call you again? I'm sorry. I don't know what number I'm calling from. Did it come up on your screen?"

"No number came up. When you called, it showed NO NUMBER AVAILABLE."

"Can I call you around eleven o'clock tomorrow? No. Let's make that Monday morning. Is Monday morning okay for you?"

"Yes. I'll be expecting your call Monday morning. I'll figure out who we can call."

"Good. Thank you. I'll talk to you Monday."

"Talk to you Monday."

They both hung up.

Tommy slouched back in the wooden glider on the front porch of his brother's house. He continued to rock back and forth mulling over in his mind everything Sarge just told him. Tommy thought to himself, "Could there be some type of international conspiracy to assassinate the members of the Presidential Cabinet of the United States of America? Could it be one of the terrorist groups identified by the U.S. Department of State? Maybe it is a country hostile to the United States of America? But no press coverage? That is concerning. Very concerning. Could the current administration be so diabolical as to keep this from the citizens of the United States of America? Is it possible for the Federal government to instruct the press not to report this and have them follow the order?"

Tommy was brought back to reality by his brother Jeff.

"Tommy. Hey, Tommy."

"Yes."

"Come on, let's go to Rizzo's for dinner. Is that okay with you?"

"Oh yes. I can always eat at Rizzo's. You know, of all the places I have eaten Italian food, Rizzo's is the best. Let's go."

They walked to the car, opened the doors, got in, and buckled up.

Tommy said, "Hey, is Diane coming with us."

A voice came from the back seat.

"Yes, I'm going."

Tommy quickly turned around. Diane was already in the car.

"Oh good. You must be hungry. How long have you been sitting in the car?"

"Since I got home from work." Laughing, Diane continued, "No. I'm just kidding. It's clear Jeff, you can back out."

Jeff said, "You seemed to be deep in thought after the telephone call. Who was it?"

"A gentleman I worked with when I was assigned to Interpol in Washington. Sarge. He's also retired. Apparently, a friend of his from Poland asked for his help on a matter I'm not at liberty to talk about right now. Sarge wanted me to assist his friend."

"La-di-da. That sounds important," said Diane.

"I don't know, Diane. A little strange to me. I haven't worked with the government for five years now. Haven't talked with Sarge for, well longer than that. And then, out of the blue, he called. Strange."

Jeff circled the block for a third time looking for a parking space. Finally, someone pulled away from the curb.

With sarcastic humor, Tommy said, "Boy, I thought we were out touring the town like our younger days. You kept going around and around."

Jeff and Diane laughed as they got out of the car and waited for traffic to clear to cross the road.

"Maybe you still work for the government," said Diane. "Maybe you are a spy now. The whole retirement thing is just a cover."

"Maybe. Maybe Diane."

"You government guys."

The three of them laughed as they walked into Rizzo's and approached the hostess.

"I'm hungry," said Tommy. "They better have a lot of gnocchi or as they call them here, cavetelli."

Embassy of the Republic of Poland

Sarge held down the button in the handset cradle to disconnect the telephone call. He then clicked the button up and down a few times to make sure the last call was disconnected. He dialed Jan's number. The number rang. It rang again. Then again.

Sarge mumbled under his breath, "Where are you Jan? You tell me to call. Then you're not there."

The number was still ringing.

With no answer to a dozen rings, Sarge hung the receiver up. He got up from the desk chair, looked around to make sure he did not forget anything and started to walk out of the room. As he did, the telephone rang.

Sarge glared at the phone. He thought, "Is that Jan? Should I answer it? This is too much already."

Sarge walked back to the desk and picked up the telephone. He answered reluctantly.

"Hello."

A chipper voice was on the other end.

"Hello, Sarge. This is Jan."

"Hello, Jan. How are you?"

"I'm doing fine. How are you?"

"As well as a confused person can be."

Jan laughed.

"How do you like your office?"

"My office? Why do you and Bertha keep saying that?"

Jan continued to laugh.

"Well, Sarge, the Poland National Police want to contract your services. We want you to work with us to help us solve what may, what could be, the biggest conspiracy law enforcement will ever know."

"What are you talking about? Work with you? With the Poland Federal Police."

"Yes. Why not? I can speak for your abilities. I know what you can do. And you will report to me and only me. What do you say? Yes, I hope."

"I don't know what to say. This is suddenly. You people move fast."

"Yes, we do. I know you can keep up with us. That's why I want you to work with us. What do you say? Oh, you can bring two other people with you. Do you have anyone in mind?"

"Jan, slow down. I haven't said yes yet."

"Sarge think about it over the weekend. Monday, come back to the embassy. Come back to your office. Call me and let me know. How's that?"

"Okay. That'll work."

"Very well. Do you have a couple of people who can help you?"

"I think I do. I think I might. I'll call you late in the morning or early in the afternoon my time on Monday."

"Great. You have a good weekend."

"Yes. Thank you and you the same."

They hung up from each other. Sarge stood in the office. A lot was going through his mind now. His thoughts were interrupted by a knock at the door.

"Yes, hello. Come in."

Bertha entered the room.

"Were you able to make your telephone calls?"

"Yes. Thank you for your help Bertha."

"You're welcome. Are you going to help us?"

"What? What do you mean?"

"You talked with Jan, yes."

"Yes."

"Well, are you going to help us? Sarge, I too work for the Poland National Police, the National Security Group. Jan and I are working this case together. Come on, you have to help us."

Oh. I told Jan I would give him an answer on Monday."

"Very well. If you are finished, I'll walk you out."

"I'm ready to go."

Sarge, a gentleman, held the office door open and motioned with his arm extended for Bertha to exit first.

Sarge exited and closed the door behind them.

Bertha turned and said, "Make sure it's locked, please."

Sarge tried the closed door, and it was secured.

Sarge followed Bertha down the hallway to the elevator. They entered the waiting elevator, and Bertha waved her identification card in front of the reader. She pressed the button to close the doors and then the lobby button. The doors quickly closed and the elevator descended smoothly. When it stopped, Bertha pushed a well-worn button, and the lobby area appeared on a screen. She studied the image and then pressed the button to open the doors. The doors opened, she exited the elevator and Sarge followed.

She turned to Sarge and said, "Thank you for coming over today. I look forward to working with you. The exit is straight ahead. Keep your Poland Embassy identification card; you'll need it on Monday."

"Thank you for everything. I'll see you Monday morning. Enjoy your weekend," replied Sarge.

Bertha turned and walked away.

Sarge walked straight ahead and exited the Poland Embassy. He walked to his car parked on Fuller Street Northwest. When near the driver's door, Sarge leaned up against the car, expelled a deep breath and remained there as he thought about the events of his day. He then entered and drove squaring the block back to Sixteenth Street Northwest. He turned right for his cross-town jaunt to the FOP Lodge.

18 October, Monday

USA, Washington, D.C.
Federal Bureau of Investigations
Headquarters

0830 Hours   Director's Office

"Good morning Bashir," said Walter. "How was your weekend."

"Relaxing, Walter. Just stayed around the house doing nothing," replied Bashir.

"Bashir, you said if anything, anything at all came up about the assassinated Secretaries to the Presidential Cabinet, you wanted to know immediately. That's why I stopped by."

"What do you have Walter."

"Sir, it has been reported to me the Inspector General from the Department of Agriculture was inquiring into the assassination of the Secretary of Agriculture. His inquiry was based on a Congressional request."

"That's not good. Not good at all. The President is not going to like this," replied Bashir "Do you know the name of the Congressman?"

"No," said Walter. "I know nothing more. As you know, this is a sensitive issue. I'm discrete with my inquiries. I won't be the one who lets this information to the public."

"How do you plan to follow up on this?"

"I plan to continue to monitor the matter. As you know, the FBI has its network of informants who have infiltrated the Inspector General community. They provide a daily brief of all activities at the Inspectors General offices."

"Those damn Inspectors General. Carter really tied our hands with that move. Then Bush just had to give them all full law enforcement authority after September 11. Keep me informed."

"Yes, sir."

0920 Hours

The three-person Executive Protection Detail, for the Secretary of Housing and Urban Development, was in place. The Advance Agents were now the Limo Driver and Follow Vehicle Driver. The Limo Driver was in the Secretary's vehicle and positioned on the street in front of the main entrance to the Westin Book Cadillac Detroit. The Follow Vehicle Driver was also in position. He was in the follow vehicle parked behind the Secretary's limo. They waited for the Secretary and the Detail Leader to emerge for transit to the Masonic Temple, approximately one mile away.

The Limo Driver was in mental practice. He visualized the route just as he had rehearsed it the multiple times he drove it during his advance work. Right onto Cass Avenue. Left onto Ledyard Street, pass the rear of the temple. Right onto Second Avenue and right onto Temple Avenue for a right-hand drop.

As the Secretary and the Detail Leader emerged from the lobby of the Westin, the Detail Leader broadcasted, "Change of plans. The Secretary is walking. I repeat we're walking."

The Limo Driver looked into his rearview mirror. He saw the Follow Driver shaking his head. Based on their advance work, this was the last thing the two drivers wanted to happen. In the security briefing to the Detail Leader last night, both drivers were emphatic the Secretary should not walk. They explained to the Detail Leader Cass Avenue was a surface street known for crime. They both emphasized their Detroit Police Department contact advised against even driving down Cass Avenue because vehicles stopped at traffic lights were approached by prostitutes and beggars. The beggars were known to be persistent and at times blocked traffic or were hostile and hit, kicked and spat on vehicles that did not give them money.

The Secretary met his Chief of Staff who was standing outside the Westin talking on his cellphone. The Secretary interrupted the phone conversation.

"Hey, I'm going to walk. Such a beautiful fall morning. You don't mind?"

"No, sir," replied the Chief of Staff. "It's quite a beautiful morning for a walk."

The Chief of Staff lowered his telephone to his side.

"It'll give us a chance to discuss your morning meeting with the Detroit business leaders and your afternoon event."

The Chief of Staff returned his attention to his telephone.

"He's here. I'll call you back."

The Chief of Staff pressed the end button on the screen of his smartphone and holstered it. He walked with the Secretary.

The two of them walked south on Michigan Avenue. The Detail Leader followed behind the Secretary in the right shoulder protective position. The two-vehicle motorcade, staffed with one security agent per vehicle, slowly trailed the group along the street curb.

The Secretary, his Chief of Staff, and the Detail Leader turned right onto Cass Avenue.

The Follow Vehicle Driver broadcasted, "Be alert people. Local support report street traffic on Cass includes prostitutes, beggars and street drug dealers. The area of Cass Avenue under Interstate 75 is a known area for strong-armed robberies."

The Detail Leader responded with two clicks of his mic.

The group stopped at a red traffic light at the intersection of Cass Avenue and West Adams Avenue. The pedestrian Do Not Walk indicator light was displayed. The two-vehicle motorcade came to a stop with four cars in front of them.

The Detail Leader, in a nervous tone, broadcasted, "I need help up here. Now."

The Follow Vehicle Driver replied, "10-4 on my way."

The Follow Vehicle Driver mashed the accelerator. All four wheels chirped as he forced the commercially rented Chevrolet Tahoe SUV to jump the curb. Parked on the sidewalk, he instinctively reached for the emergency light switches. There were no emergency lights in the rented vehicle used during movements away from Washington D.C. In a hurry, he exited the vehicle and ran to join the Detail Leader. He arrived at the group and apparently, his mere presence dispersed street people who appeared to be approaching the Secretary and the Chief of Staff. He remained until the traffic light changed and the Secretary, Chief of Staff and Detail Leader walked across the intersection.

The Follow Vehicle Driver turned and started to run to return to his vehicle, the Detail Leader broadcasted, "No. No. Stay with us. I need your help here. We'll get the vehicle later."

The Follow Vehicle Driver reversed himself and ran to catch up with the group which was now halfway into the intersection. He had to negotiate pedestrians. He excused himself to them as he bumped into some and knocked over others as he made his way to the group.

With the focus on assisting the Detail Leader, no one in the three-person security team noticed nor heard the roar of five motorcycles, each with two riders abreast. The occupants were outfitted in black military-style uniforms and light blue colored helmets with a dark tinted full-face shield. Riding in a formation, the motorcycles were half a block to the rear of the two-vehicle motorcade. The roar of the motorcycles intensified as they broke formation and maneuvered through the vehicle traffic to close the distance to the Secretary's limo. As the motorcycles passed the secretary's limo, the last one stopped at the left rear bumper and held that position. The other four continued toward the Secretary.

The four motorcycles neared the Secretary and his group, and two circled the group. First, the motorcycles were close while circling them. Gradually, the two motorcycles increased the distance. Their driving and the continued roar of their engines disoriented the pedestrians and caused them to move away.

Instinctively, the Detail Leader took control of the Secretary. He physical grabbed his belt in the middle of his back with his right hand. With his left hand, a hand full of the suit at the Secretary's left shoulder. This gave the Detail Leader total control to move the Secretary in the direction necessary to escape the attack.

The Detail Leader, now fused to the Secretary from the protection technique, turned the Secretary and started to move the Secretary toward the Follow Driver in anticipation of an emergency exit route instinctively created by the Follow Driver. Instead, the Detail Leader saw the Follow Driver disoriented and stunned from the noise of the motorcycles and what was assuredly an uncontrolled adrenaline dump. The Detail Leader shouted to the Follow Driver to pull him out of the hypnotic state caused by the roar of the motorcycle' engines, the engine fumes, and an adrenalin dump within his core. The shouts from the Detail Leader did not bring the Follow Driver back to reality; back to a state of function. The roar of the motorcycle engines, the fumes, the commotion, and an adrenaline dump, rendered the Follow Driver useless to his protection responsibilities.

Still fused to the Secretary, the Detail Leader shouted again to the Follow Driver to bring him out of the hypnotic state. The Detail Leader saw the Follow Driver thrust backward from a volley of automatic gunfire hitting its mark, the center of the Follow Driver's torso. There was no time to look up to survey the cause of the Follow Driver falling to the ground and bleeding profusely from his chest.

At the same time, the Detail Leader felt the Secretary getting heavier which undoubtedly was caused by the Secretary witnessing the gruesome murder of the Follow Driver. The Detail Leader shouted to the Secretary, "Stay with me. Stay with me. Everything is going to be alright. I'll get you out of this." The psychological protection tactic worked, the Secretary became lighter to allow them to move more freely as one.

The Detail Leader still fused to the Secretary, moved as one. He started to turn and to run away from the last known direction of gunfire. As he did, the Secretary became weighty again. This time caused when the Secretary witnessed the gruesome murder of his Chief of Staff.

Again, the Detail Leader shouted to the Secretary, "Stay with me. Stay with me. Everything is going to be alright. I'll get you out of this."

This time, the psychological assurance did not make the Secretary lighter. The Secretary continued to get heavier and heavier. The Detail Leader did not have to survey the scene to know what happened. The attackers, for a third time, hit their mark. The steady stream of automatic gunfire murdered the Secretary of Housing and Urban Development.

The dead weight of the Secretary pulled the fused Detail Leader to the ground. As the Detail Leader fell, he crawled to position himself on top of the Secretary. He performed one last protection

219

tactic. He made one last stance to protect the Secretary from harm. His heroic actions moved to slow motion. There was a warmth over his back. He did his best with what resources he was given and permitted to use. He knew what happened to him. The automatic gunfire hit its mark a fourth time.

The Detail Leader will not go home tonight to his loving wife and her warm, enthusiastic greeting. His two daughters will no longer have two outstretched arms to jump into and hold them. He will not be there for Stormy, the Great Dane family protector to crouch with her chest touching the floor, her back arched, her buttocks high and her happy tail wagging out of control positioning herself to lunge and hug him.

His family will no longer receive his timely presence. His spouse will only receive the flag draped over his coffin, condolences from those who knew him and those who pretended to know him, and a death benefit payment for a Law Enforcement Officer Killed in the Line of Duty. His last honor, when the law enforcement community etches his name on the wall of the National Law Enforcement Officers Memorial.

A silence came over the area. The automatic gunfire stopped. The roar of the motorcycle engines brought to an idle. One of the attackers commanded by motion to another attacker to come over to him. When together he said, "Go and make sure it was done."

"Yes, sir."

The willing accomplice, with his military long rifle in the mid-ready position, tactically moved to the Follow Driver and delivered two gunshots to his head. He moved to the Chief of Staff and twice shot him in the head. He stood over the Detail Leader and fired two more rounds. Without hesitation, he twice shot the Secretary. He walked back to the motorcycle operator who gave him the command. They simultaneously nodded to each other in an affirmation that the task was completed.

The motorcycle operator said, "And the Limo Driver?"

"Taken care of the same," replied the willing accomplice.

The seated motorcycle operator said, "Go mark it for the FBI."

The willing accomplice returned to the bloody bodies. He knelt on one knee by the Secretary. With his left hand, he retrieved a white rag from his left rear pocket. He sponged up the Secretary's blood and scrolled a large red X near the Secretary's bullet-ridden, lifeless body and wrote the number 13 near the large red X. The blood-soaked rag left on the ground, the attacker sprang up from the task and quickly returned to the motorcycle. Again, in affirmation, the driver and the accomplice nodded to each other. The accomplice mounted the motorcycle, and in a formation, the five motorcycles drove away from the attack.

Many of the bystanders were in shock from the horror they just witnessed. They just stood and stared at the murdered bodies. Immediately, a flurry of police activity descended on the scene of the massacre. The criminal street element fled. They knew when the police arrived they would be abused. They would be detained. Taken to the local district police station and questioned. Held for a day or two. They wanted no part of that.

Some of the bystanders tried to operate their cellular telephones to call for help. The phones were inoperable. They repeatedly tried with no results. They were unable to swiftly report the carnage to the police and wondered to themselves how the police responded so quickly.

USA, Washington D.C. NW
Embassy of the Republic of Poland

"Good morning Sarge," greeted the uniformed guard standing outside the door to the Embassy of Poland.

"Good morning."

"If you wish, you can go directly to elevator number six. The attendant will take you directly to your floor. Enjoy your day."

"Thank you."

Sarge walked through the door held open by the uniformed guard. With some hesitation that he would be stopped by one of the uniformed guards at the security checkpoint, he cautiously walked in the direction of elevator number six and stopped short of entering. Unsure he should, he waited for the attendant to acknowledge him.

The chipper elevator attendant said, "Good morning, Sarge. Come in. Let's get up to your office, there's work to be done today."

Sarge entered the elevator, and the doors quickly closed behind him. The attendant pushed a button. The elevator ascended and chimed as it passed floors. It stopped at six. The doors opened, and Sarge moved out.

The chipper elevator attendant said, "Have a good day sir."

"You too," replied Sarge.

Sarge turned right and went halfway down the hallway to his office. Using his Poland Embassy credentials, he opened the door and entered. He hung his suit coat up and sat down in the desk chair. The telephone rang as he gathered his thoughts.

Instinctively, Sarge picked up the receiver and said, "Hello.

"Well hello to you Sarge. Good morning. How are you today?"

"I'm fine, thank you. How are you?"

"Very well. Sarge this is Jan."

Sarge thought to himself, "How did he know I was in the office?"

"It's Monday morning. I'm calling to see if you will help us. I need to know now. I really need your help."

"Yes, I will, Jan."

"Great. Thank you, Sarge. How about your team? Do you have anyone in mind?"

"Yes, I do."

"Who is it?"

"A gentleman I worked with at the Interpol – Washington National Central Bureau. He worked protection operations for members of the Presidential Cabinet. He will know the ins and outs of security operations for the Presidential Cabinet."

"Great! When can you all start?"

"I can start now. Today. I'll have to check with Tommy."

"Okay. Give Tommy's full name to Bertha so she can get him Republic of Poland government credentials. This is fantastic. Let me know as soon as you can if Tommy is on board with us. I want to have a secure conference call with the four of us, to bring everyone up to date on this matter and to establish a path forward. We need to hurry this along."

"I will."

"Sarge, are you curious about your compensation for your help?"

"I briefly thought about that."

"You'll receive four thousand US dollars per day plus expenses. You'll have an Embassy car to use with an Embassy credit card for gas. You'll have an on-site Embassy suite until we finish. Tommy will have the same. Is that fair?"

"I think that's fair."

"Good. That's that. You have the authority to make that offer to Tommy. Oh. If you two use the airlines for any travel, you go first class. A little different than those civil service days."

"Yes."

"And the embassy staff will take care of everything for you. If Bertha doesn't anticipate what you need, just ask her. She'll handle everything with the embassy staff. I must go now, call me as soon as you know if Tommy is a part of the team. Leave a message, please. I'll be in meetings the rest of the day."

"Okay."

"And again, thank you for helping us, Sarge."

"You're welcome."

Sarge ended the telephone call. He leaned back in his high back, plush, leather chair to ponder the conversation. He picked up the phone receiver and dialed Tommy's number.

It rang once. Twice. Three times before it was answered.

"Hello," said Tommy.

"Good morning Tommy. This is Sarge."

"Hey. Good morning Sarge. How are you?"

"I'm doing well. Thank you. And you?"

"I'm doing well also."

"Tommy, are you willing to help me? Us? Them? Will you assist the Poland government?"

"Yes, Sarge. I'll help you help the Poland government."

"Good. Poland will pay you four thousand US dollars per day, plus expenses. You'll be housed in the embassy quarters on-site here until we're finished. You'll be given an Embassy car to use with an Embassy credit card for gas. Fair?"

"Yes, that's fair."

"Okay. I need to call Jan back and tell him you're on board with us. He wants to have a secure conference call with us tomorrow. Will that work for you?"

"Yes. I'll be available anytime. Just call."

"Very well. Thank you, Tommy. We'll talk tomorrow."

Sarge hung up. The telephone immediately rang. He answered, "Hello."

"Hello, Sarge. This is Bertha. How are you today?"

"I'm well. Thank you. How are you?"

"I'm well too. I'm calling because it's lunchtime. Would you like to join me?"

"I have to call Jan and leave a message. Yes, I'd like to join you for lunch."

"Make your call. I'll be by your office to get you. We'll eat here at the embassy dining room. Is that okay?"

"Oh yes."

"Good. See you in a few minutes."

Sarge held the receiver button down to disconnect the call. He dialed Jan's number to leave a message about Tommy's willingness to help.

"Jan, Tommy said he will help. I presented the offer. He too was pleased. He'll be available when we make the conference call tomorrow. Talk to you tomorrow."

Sarge hung up the telephone receiver as a knock came from the door.

"Yes. Come in."

The door opened. It was Bertha. "Are you ready?"

"Yes, and I'm hungry."

"Good. This will be authentic Polish cooking. You'll get your pierogis."

Sarge moved from behind his desk, gathered his suit coat and threw it over his shoulder. He shut the lights off, closed the door and double checked to ensure it was locked. He joined Bertha in the hallway. They walked off.

USA, Washington D.C.
200 Independence Avenue SW
U.S. Department of Health and Human Services

Secretary's Suite

"Mr. Secretary, it's time to make that call," said the Chief of Staff.

"Yes. Thank you," replied the Secretary.

"I'll wait in the outer office."

"Okay."

The Chief of Staff rose from his chair. He looked to the Secretary and said, "Mr. Secretary, are you alright? Are you feeling okay today?"

"Yes," replied the Secretary. "I'll come and get you when I finish the telephone call."

The Chief of Staff walked out of the Secretary's private office to the outer office to wait.

Shortly, the Secretary appeared in his outer office. He walked over and sat down across from his Chief of Staff.

"Why do you think the President is sending me to London to represent the United States of America at a conference on the latest outbreak of mad cow disease in the United Kingdom? You would think he would send the Secretary of Agriculture."

"Did you mention that to him?"

"Yes. The President said, 'I want you to go.' To which, well, what could I say," said the Secretary. "I mean there is a nexus to the department, but Agriculture has always taken the lead on this matter. And how do you say no to the President of the United States of America."

"When do you have to go?"

"Wednesday. I leave Wednesday. The meeting is Thursday morning. He said if I wanted to stay through the weekend and take my family, this might be a good time to do that."

"Well, what are you going to do?"

"I'm going to go. I'm not taking the family. Just me. I want to return right after the meeting. You set all that up."

"Yes, sir. Should I request military flights or use commercial flights?"

"You have to use military flights. The President was adamant about that."

"Adamant? A year ago, we couldn't use the military planes per his orders."

"Yes. I know."

"Mr. Secretary, are you alright? You seem distant."

"I'm all right. I don't know about the President, though."

"What do you mean?"

"He has changed a lot over these last three years of his second term in office. I said that in your confidence."

"Yes, sir. On a confidential basis always. Since friends in the old neighborhood. Yes, sir, you have my trust. Let me go and make the travel arrangements. Oh. Do you want any members of your protection detail to go with us? You know how much of a burden they are."

"Yes, protection is a burden. And you see nothing in return for the cost. I don't know. Let's take two. And don't let Security convince you more is needed. Two protection agents, that's all."

"Yes, sir. I'll get right on this. Should you call the Secretary of Agriculture just to touch base? Get a feel for what she thinks of this, of you going and not her?"

"I was thinking the same thing. I'm going to call the Secretary right now. Sit back down."

The Secretary pushed the speaker button on the telephone and then the speed dial button for the Secretary of Agriculture. The phone rang once and was answered.

"Hello. This is the Office of the Secretary of Agriculture. How may I help you?"

"This is the Secretary of Health and Human Services calling for the Secretary of Agriculture."

"The Secretary is not in today. May I have her return your call?"

"When will she be in?"

"The Secretary is not in today. May I have her return your call?"

"Is she due back in the office today?"

"May I have her return your call?"

"No, I'll call later."

The Secretary hung up the telephone and shook his head.

"You got to be kidding me. I'm the Secretary of Health and Human Services. I'm put off by, well, I don't know who. I can't get in touch with the Secretary of Agriculture? Really."

"Okay. I'm off to make the travel arrangements."

"Okay. Thank you."

19 October, Tuesday

USA, Washington D.C. NW
Embassy of the Republic of Poland

0830 Hours

Tuesday morning in Washington D.C. Fall. The fresh morning air will break into a mild, blue sky, sunny day. The smell of fall was in the air. The leaves started to change colors. Washington took on a whole different look.

Tommy made his way through the morning rush hour and arrived outside of the Embassy of the Republic of Poland. He reminisced, "I forgot the fun the commute to the city provided. The people were still interesting and provided a distraction for the metro ride. Never a dull moment when you observed humans. Each ethnic group had their own idiosyncrasies. Interesting."

Standing outside of the Embassy of the Republic of Poland, it suddenly dawned on Tommy; he was not given the time to arrive or how to contact Sarge. He stood on Sixteenth Street paused for a decision. Then he saw Sarge.

"Sarge. Good morning."

"Tommy. How are you?"

Their hands extended as they walked up to each other. The outstretched hands clasped together like the linkage of two railroad cars attaching. The joy of seeing each other after many years pulled them into an embrace. There on Sixteenth Street, in front of the Embassy of the Republic of Poland, two lawmen reunited. They rekindled *the blue bond*. Lawmen that stood on the thin blue line drawn between right and wrong, between good and evil.

Talking over each other, they both paid each other the same compliment.

"You're looking well."

And simultaneously, they said "Yes. I'm doing well. Thank you."

Their excitement was quickly interrupted with a raspy voice.

"Okay. Okay. Break it up. I'll have none of this in front of my embassy."

Both Tommy and Sarge turned to look in the direction of the voice.

Sarge said, "Bertha, good morning. Let me introduce you to Tommy. Tommy, this is Bertha. Bertha, Tommy. Tommy will be helping us."

Bertha said, "Hello. It's my pleasure to meet you. Welcome. Thank you for your willingness to help the government of Poland, the people of Poland."

"It's a pleasure meeting you. Thank you for the opportunity to help," replied Tommy.

Bertha continued, "Let's go inside. Time is of the essence here. Let's go inside where we can talk freely. Tommy, we have to brief you into this matter."

Bertha led the way, and the three walked into the Embassy of Poland. They passed the security checkpoint. Sarge fumbled for his credentials.

The security guard said, "Sir, that's okay. I know who you are. Please continue through."

Bertha looked in the direction of the security guard.

The security guard said, "Yes, Bertha. He's with you too?" The security guard motions toward Tommy.

"Yes, he is."

"Good morning everyone and welcome to Poland."

The threesome passed the security checkpoint to the bank of elevators. Bertha led them into the elevator car. When all three were in, she waved her credential in the direction of the control panel and the elevator doors closed, engaged, and the elevator ascended to the sixth floor.

When the elevator doors opened, Bertha said, "Please follow me. We need to use a highly secured room for the briefing."

Sensitive Compartmented Information Facility (SCIF)

Bertha led them down the hallway and stopped at a nondescript door. She waved her credentials and the door automatically opened. She entered. Sarge and Tommy followed her into a small room. Bertha reached and closed the door behind them. She then waved her credentials by a pad near a second door. The door opened automatically. The three of them entered a large windowless room. The room was furnished with a big, round, black, wooden, conference table with overstuffed, high back, ergonomic, black leathered, chairs. Each position was fitted with a personal handheld tablet computer.

Tommy said, "Bertha, should I leave my cell phone outside?"

"No Tommy that won't be necessary. Your device won't work in this room. There's no need to leave them outside. Thank you for asking."

"Oh." Tommy looked to Sarge. "Have we been away that long?"

The three laughed in unison only to be interrupted by a voice.

"What's all the laughing about? Do you think you should be more serious about this?"

With surprise, Sarge and Tommy looked toward the voice coming from the direction of the door. Jan walked into the room.

Sarge said, "Jan you're here. I didn't."

Jan talked over Sarge.

"Yes, I'm here. I wanted to meet Tommy. And it appeared this case will require my efforts here in the United States. We have a lot of work here in the United States."

Sarge introduced Tommy.

"Jan, this is Tommy. Tommy, Jan."

Simultaneously, Jan and Tommy said to each other, "Hello. Pleased to meet you."

Jan continued, "Welcome to Poland. Thank you for your willingness to help Poland."

Tommy replied, "You're welcome. Thank you for your confidence in me that I will be able to help you. Help Poland."

Jan looked in the direction of Bertha. "Good morning Bertha. How are you today?"

"Good morning, Jan. I'm fine. Thank you. I trust your travel was uneventful."

"Yes. Thank you for all your assistance for my late-night arrival. Okay. Let's start. Please. Everyone sit. This is the team. The four of us.

Jan continued.

"Here's where we are. Poland is being targeted. We don't know by whom or why. Poland is being implicated, in a false flag operation, as the country that is assassinating members, the Secretaries, of the United States of America, Presidential Cabinet. We know as of last night the total murders are eight. Eight members of the United States of America, Presidential Cabinet. They are:

6 October Secretary of Commerce, Official Business, Military Aircraft, in flight over Poland

9 October Secretary of Education, Personal Business, Personal Vehicle, Germantown, Maryland

10 October Secretary of Defense, Personal Business, Personal Residence, Ocean City, Maryland

11 October Attorney General, Official Business, Courtyard, Main Justice, Washington D.C.

13 October Secretary of Agriculture, Personal Business, Route of morning run, McLean, Virginia

14 October Secretary of Veterans Affairs, Official Business, Motorcade, Pittsburgh, Pennsylvania

15 October Secretary of Interior, Official Business, Motorcade, Gettysburg, Pennsylvania

8 October Secretary of Housing and Urban Development, Official Business, Walking to event, Detroit, Michigan

Jan spoke from memory, no notes or aids. He maintained eye contact with the other three. He noticed Sarge and Tommy kept glancing at each other.

"Comments?"

Sarge replied, "Jan, eight members of the Presidential Cabinet assassinated and nothing, nothing in the news. There wasn't one network, not one cable news channel that carried this story. If…"

Jan interrupted Sarge.

"Not if. This has happened. These Secretaries have been killed. Assassinated on the streets of America and on foreign soil. And, yes, no news coverage."

Sarge replied, "The Poland government should take this information to the U.S. authorities. The Secret Service? Maybe the FBI? Perhaps your Ambassador here should have a meeting with the U.S. government. I don't know. This sounds far-fetched. Jan, you have my trust and confidence. I'm … I don't know what I am. Tommy."

"I don't know either," replied Tommy. "Eight Secretaries? How about the protection detail members? Were there casualties there?"

"Tommy our sources said there were. Members of the Secretaries protection details were also killed," Jan said. "And in some cases, family members of the Secretaries. It appeared whoever was with the Secretary at the time was also murdered. They didn't leave witnesses behind."

Sarge said, "How? How is something this big covered up? A cover-up of this size; there's no comparison. I'm aware of nothing this large, a conspiracy this big. And no news media coverage? Come on."

Jan said, "You two may not know, but I know for a fact that your government, the government of the United States of America pays the open source news media outlets to present or not to present information to the public. Your government pays off the media not to report certain information to the citizens of the

United States. You may find that hard to believe with your constitution and the first amendment. But it's so."

Tommy replied, "Okay. Let's not churn up all this drama. Let's start with the basics, prove or disprove. We have to prove or disprove it is happening."

"How?" asked Sarge. "Where do we start?"

"We'll go to their residences and see if they're home. Alive. A basic approach," replied Tommy.

Jan said, "Good idea. Well done. Do you want to see the videotapes? We discretely did that. We, the government of Poland, with a U.S. company owned and operated by U.S. citizens of Polish descent, Polish heritage. The company diligently worked to locate these people to get pictures of them. We thought this may be a radical Muslin terrorist group who was just saying they assassinated the Secretaries in a false flag operation to blackmail the government of Poland. Photographs of the Secretaries alive would negate any extortion attempts. All efforts were negative. We placed that information in the Prove Column."

Tommy replied, "Oh. Okay."

"Has the government of Poland been contacted by anyone?" asked Sarge.

"No," replied Jan. "The long and the short of it is, Confidential National Security Sources (CNSS), with a history of being reliable, provide information to the government of Poland on this matter. The CNSS, daily, sometimes on the hour, provide information. What's today, Tuesday, something is to happen on Wednesday, tomorrow. Another Secretary is to be assassinated. Which one of the seven remaining Presidential Cabinet members? We, our CNSS, don't know. Poland can't afford this to happen. So, I'm asking us to think. Think of a resolve. What can we do to pronounce Poland is not involved?"

Tommy said, "I'm not comfortable to sit back and do nothing when we know another, other Secretaries, law enforcement officers, and U.S. citizens are targets for assassination."

Sarge raised his hand and counted on his fingers. He said, "Okay, we have to establish a prioritized list to follow. I suggest we continue to prove or disprove. We need evidence to prove or disprove; one, the false flag theory, two, the assassinations, three, the cover-up. If we can do that, we can package the evidence and take it to someone who'll listen to us."

"Good," replied Jan. "We focus on three points. I have the right people. Fresh eyes. Tommy, what do you think?"

"I like it. This is good. Damn Sarge, you still have it."

"Bertha, your thoughts?" Jan asked.

"Yes. That lays the case out. Fresh eyes, you are right again Jan."

Jan said, "What's that Bertha. Speak up, please. Did you say I'm right?"

Both Bertha and Jan smiled at each other and briefly stared into each other's eyes.

Sarge chimed back in, "Me too. I'm not comfortable with the possibility or the fact that another or more or all the other Secretaries could be assassinated. Now I'm just going to say this, just put this on the table. What if we kidnap the remaining Secretaries to take them out of harm's way? Obviously, we have a huge, huge, cover up. So, the U.S. Government will have to continue to keep, what will be missing Secretaries, out of the news. The people committing the assassinations will be taken by surprise which may cause them to do something stupid which may provide evidence for us. That's the plan. That's the easy part of the plan. Putting it into operation will be the challenge."

Bertha replied, "How would we penetrate the Secretaries' security?"

"There's not a whole lot of Secretary security to penetrate," said Tommy. "The assassination of the Secretaries is easy for me to believe. They're soft targets, very soft targets. The cover-up. A massive cover-up. That's what I have a hard time putting my head around. No Bertha, we could penetrate the secretaries' security."

"I think that might work," said Jan. "We may be able to pull this off. What do you think, Tommy? Kidnap the secretaries to protect them?"

Deep in thought, Tommy replied, "Hmmm. Maybe. Just maybe. This may just work. But there'll be a lot of planning to do. A lot."

Sarge said, "Hold that thought. For the evidence. It would seem the quickest way to gather evidence would be to interview the CNSS. We could correlate all the facts they provide."

In unison, Jan and Bertha blurted out, "Hold on. Hold on."

Jan continued, "That'll never happen. The interviewing and parading of the CNSS to the world. No. That's not going to happen. Please appreciate the precarious position the government of Poland has with this matter. We're not going to give up our CNSS to the world. No. Never."

Sarge replied, "Jan, Bertha, it was just an idea. I didn't mean any disrespect."

Jan said, "Please, Sarge. Bertha and I just get a little excited. It's the love for our country that shows through here. Please, we want ideas. All is well?"

Sarge looked to Bertha then back to Jan. "Yes, all is well. And that idea won't work."

There was light laughter in the room.

Sarge continued, "Back to the protective kidnap plan. What Secretary is a target for Wednesday, tomorrow?"

Jan replied, "We have no details. Who, what, where, why or how. Nothing more at this time."

Tommy asked, "Okay. Once we have the Secretaries, where are we going to keep them? How are we going to feed them? What'll we tell them? There's a lot to plan here in a short time."

Bertha replied, "Jan, how about that place? You know, that place."

"Bertha they have the highest clearance, equal to you and me. We can speak freely. Do you mean our Continuity of Operations facilities?"

"Well. Yes. The COOP facilities."

"That could work. That could work," said Jan. "Our Continuity of Operations facilities. The government of Poland built a Continuity of Operations facilities here in Washington D.C. Post September 11 brought changes in the U.S. and the government of Poland built a facility in the event Washington D.C. was attacked by traditional or nontraditional warfare or by biological, chemical or nuclear bombs. We wanted a facility to shelter in place. This embassy built a five-story facility under the embassy. This five-story facility was added to the sub-basement right here with three different points of entry/exit. This could be the place to house them. I want to think on that for a little bit. Great idea Bertha."

Tommy and Sarge, in unison exclaim, "Really! Five stories underground! Here in Washington D.C. It was just built?"

239

"Yes," said Jan. "From what I was told, many of the embassies along embassy row here in Washington did the same thing. This was at the encouragement of your government. It was a part of the U.S. Embassies Protection Plan. In fact, your government, through the Department of State, funded part of the efforts."

Tommy and Sarge, again in unison, exclaimed, "Really!"

Sarge said, "That's something. When we were still working, there were no such provisions for civil servants. You have the food, facilities, water, everything to sustain them?"

Jan replied, "Yes we do."

Sarge said, "For how long?"

Bertha replied, "For as long as we need if there are no other events that require activating our COOP plan. Absent such events, we can continue to move provisions into the facility. Though I don't see that being necessary; it is set with a two-year supply."

Sarge said, "For how many people? How many people will it sustain for two years?"

Bertha replied, "One hundred and sixty people. The entire staff of the Poland Embassy and their families."

Tommy said, "Good because we're going to have to take the Secretary, the staff with them and the entire Secretary's protection detail. So that brings us to, what do we do with the vehicles? There'll be two vehicles per Secretary. Maybe, a third."

Bertha replied, "We have to store them at a different location. There is no space for more vehicles here at the facility. We can store the cars at the security company's office in Georgetown."

Sarge said, "Another quick thought, for planning purposes, where are we going to get the human and physical resources to carry out the protective kidnappings? This might not be such a good plan."

"That's easy, we can use the security company staff," replied Jan. "They'll have the necessary equipment to conduct the protective kidnappings."

"What?" said Sarge. "You're going to use a private contract security company to execute this plan? Do they have the necessary training? The skills? Can we trust them to something like this?"

Jan replied, "Oh yes Sarge. The security company is a cover. The staff is trained in Poland. They receive continued training from Poland military staff. Some of the training is done here in the U.S. Most of it is conducted in Poland. They have the necessary training, skills, and equipment. The Embassy of Poland doesn't rely on the U.S. government to protect us. We let your Secretary of State think he's protecting us, but we don't trust him. We don't trust this current President. Sorry. I'm not trying to be insulting. Poland takes its responsibility seriously to protect its citizens, in our country and abroad. Your President is not concerned with your citizens. Remember Benghazi? Your Secretary of State said it was caused by a YouTube video. But if I recall correctly, she told her daughter something else. Really! Trust me, I have a team that can handle this task."

Sarge said, "Okay. We have the facility. We have the resources. Now, all we need is a plan."

Jan replied, "Yes. We'll leave it to the security company. I'll give them the task. They'll handle it. They'll tell us when they have a Secretary in the facility. We won't trouble ourselves with that matter. After all, that's a protection issue. I'm only doing it because you and Tommy are worried about not sharing intelligence information with your beloved country. I understand that. I respect that. Remember, we have a lot of investigative work to do. We need to stay focused on that."

Jan continued.

"We need to gather evidence to prove Poland isn't responsible for the deaths of the members of the U.S. Presidential Cabinet. We, Poland, may not hold the current U.S. administration in the highest regards, but unlike your current President, our leadership will not behave like an immature, inexperienced leader. The President of Poland has this matter at his highest priority. I'll also share this, Poland has indisputable proof the U.S. government waged a propaganda blitz on the Israeli government to discredit them on the world stage during the Iran nuclear proliferation treaty talks. Poland will not idly stand by and let the United States of America or any other state or ruling party wage a negative propaganda blitz on Poland. Ally or no ally.

Okay. It is 1130 hours. I think that brings us to lunchtime. Shall we all go to the embassy dining room?"

Everyone agreed and prepared to leave the SCIF.

Jan said, "You go ahead. I'm going to call the security company and get things started with them. I'll catch up. I want to call them from the secure telephone in here."

Bertha, Sarge, and Tommy left the SCIF for the embassy dining room.

USA, Washington D.C. SW
U.S. Department of Health and Human Services

1145 Hours   Secretary's Suite Conference Room

"Good morning everyone," said the Secretary of Health and Human Services. "I'm sorry I didn't catch you all earlier. Today's luncheon briefings are canceled. I have to clear my

242

schedule. Please accept my apology. I hope this isn't too much of an inconvenience to you. Just one item to note, I'll be traveling to Great Britain tomorrow for a two-day trip. We don't meet on Fridays. I'll see you all on Monday. Thank you."

The Secretary exited the conference room ahead of the staff. He was followed by his Chief of Staff.

At his office, the Secretary opened the door. He held the door open, turned to his Chief of Staff and said, "Come on in, please."

The Chief of Staff entered. The Secretary closed the door behind them. The Secretary motioned to a grouping of plush, leather-covered, chairs with a large round glass top coffee table in the center. He said to the Chief of Staff, "Please, sit down. I need to talk to you."

"Yes, sir." The Chief of Staff sat down. "What is it Mr. Secretary?"

"I have a meeting with my personal attorney. I don't know how long the meeting will last. I'm going to see him myself. I'm not taking you or any of the protection team. I have a hunch about something that's big. It's huge if my hunch is correct. I don't want to involve anyone else in this matter. My wife doesn't even know. I'm telling you in case something happens to me. I want you to make sure my attorney gets the information to the right people. He may need help with the bureaucracy. I don't even know who the right person or people would be or who could be trusted if my hunch is correct. I will be telling my attorney to use you to help him get the information to the right government people. Will you do that for me?"

"Sure Mr. Secretary. You know I will. But you are starting to scare me. What's this all about?"

"I won't tell you any more than I have. You only need to know my personal attorney may reach out to you to help him. At that time, my lawyer will tell you everything. That's all you need to know for now so you can maintain your integrity. Please don't ask me anything else."

"Okay. As you wish Mr. Secretary."

"Thank you. I'm beaten down from this administration's fight against the Affordable Care Act. The President doesn't listen to me or follow any of my advice. He listens to the brats on the hill. Those lily whites who know nothing about how the American people live day-to-day. They don't know anything about what the America people really need when it comes to their health care. They simply do what they have to do to get votes, so they don't lose their positions and all the money that goes with that position. Half of that massive law is tax increases. Okay, sorry for the rant. I need to go to my meeting. I'll talk to you later today."

"Yes, sir. I'll talk to you later." The Chief of Staff rose from the chair and walked out of the Secretary's office.

USA, Washington, D.C.
Eye Street NW

1400 Hours

The Chief of Staff for the Secretary of Health and Human Services answered his government-issued cellular telephone.

"Hello, Mr. Secretary. How are you? How did your meeting go?"

The Secretary said, "My meeting went well."

The call abruptly ended.

The Chief of Staff looked at his phone. The oversized screen on his smartphone displayed CALL ENDED in big white letters with a red background. He hurried to redial the Secretary's cellular number. It rang once and then nothing. He redialed the Secretary's number. Again, it rang once and then nothing. A third time, he redialed the Secretary's number. It rang once. Nothing.

The Chief of Staff thought to himself, "Now what?" He became nervous. "Could something have happened to the Secretary? Kidnapped. Shot. With what he said to me this morning, I don't know what to think."

He became upset to the point he had to sit down. Just then, his phone rang. In his nervous state, he fumbled to swipe the screen to answer the call. The phone rang a second time. Finally, he swiped the screen correctly and said, "Hello, Mr. Secretary."

The Secretary replied, "I don't know what happened there. Anyway, I'm finished here and on my way back to the office. I'll see you when I get back."

"Okay, Mr. Secretary."

They both hung up. The Chief of Staff fell back into his desk chair and remained deep in thought.

Embassy of the Republic of Poland

1430 Hours   SCIF

The four-member team, after dining on authentic Polish cuisine, returned to the SCIF to continue their conversation to counter the false flag operation. To investigate the assassination of the United States of America Presidential Cabinet members.

Jan said, "Did everyone have enough to eat? This dining room here, the food is just like in the home country. What do you think, Sarge?"

"It's good, but that one restaurant you took me to in Warsaw is better."

"Munie's."

"Yes. Munie's Bakery. Oh, that place has delicious food."

"Yes, it does."

Jan continued.

"To keep everyone in the loop, I wanted to report on my telephone call before lunch to the security company. I tasked them with the protective kidnapping as we discussed. They said they would handle it. They also stated that they'll continue to monitor the activities of the Presidential Cabinet members in case I ask for further assistance. The company has learned that the Secretary of Health and Human Services leaves tomorrow for Great Britain. They said they planned a protective kidnapping for tomorrow, somewhere along the Secretary's route from his residence to Andrews Air Force Base. I asked that they report their progress as events develop."

Bertha injects, "Hell. The Secretaries are better protected now than ever. They have the Poland Security Company providing protection."

Jan laughed. Tommy and Sarge looked at each other with a puzzled look.

Jan said, "I think we all had enough for today. I just wanted to come back to the SCIF and update you all on my telephone call to the company. I wanted you to know that Poland will do what we can to protect the remaining members of the Presidential Cabinet."

"Sarge and Tommy, Bertha will show you to your embassy suites that you'll use for the duration of your assistance to Poland. We'll meet at 0700 hours tomorrow morning at the embassy dining room for breakfast. Are there any other questions or comments?" asked Jan.

No one had any questions or comments. It was apparent that they all were fading for the day. They welcomed the break. Everyone left the SCIF. Tommy and Sarge followed Bertha so she could show them to their suites. Jan was off to his embassy suite as well. His travel from Poland to the U.S. started to wear on him. He looked forward to a few hours of relaxation; a relaxing workout at the embassy gym and a good night sleep.

20 October, Wednesday

USA, Washington, D.C. NW
Embassy of the Republic of Poland

SCIF

After breakfast in the embassy dining room, Jan, Bertha, Sarge, and Tommy made their way to the SCIF to continue their investigative strategy session.

They settled into the SCIF, and the secure telephone rang.

Bertha answered, "Hello. Yes. Yes. Hold please."

Bertha pushed the hold button. She looked to Jan and said, "You have to take this."

"Who is it?"

"You have to take this. I think we need to leave while you talk."

"Who is it? Bertha, we're all on the same team here. Who is it?"

"It's the Security Company."

"Already. The Company has to report already?"

"Yes."

"Put it on speaker."

"Are you sure?"

Sarge interrupted, "Jan if you want us to leave, we can. It's no big deal if you have to take this call in private."

"No. Bertha put it on speaker."

"As you wish."

Bertha pushed the hold button, then the speaker button.

"This is Jan. Good morning."

A voice replied, "This is the Security Company. Can we talk freely?"

"Yes. There are four of us here. All are cleared. Go ahead."

"We have one. Repeat. We have one."

"What? Already? Everything secure?"

"One of the attackers. We had to decide this morning, kidnap the Secretary for his protection or subdue one of the attackers. We made the decision to subdue the attacker. We believed the attacker a greater value to the investigation. There was the potential to gain much intelligence from the attacker."

"Thank you. I'll be down momentarily."

The call was ended. There was dead silence in the SCIF. No one said anything until Jan broke the silence.

"Well. That was quick. And it was a bit of a surprise too. This could be a huge development for the investigation."

Sarge and Tommy sat there. They didn't know what was going on. They didn't know what to say.

Tommy broke his silence.

"Good. But the Company let the Secretary go on? They didn't get the Secretary knowing he's in danger?"

"Tommy, remember they were out there," responded Sarge. "They were the ones who engaged the operation. Like Jan said, this could be huge."

Tommy stared off in the direction of Sarge. His eyes displayed deep thought. He was settling in himself what may very well be the loss of more U.S. citizens at the hands of a rogue state or state-sponsored terrorism. His interbeing meditated to understand and justify the reality. His law enforcement wisdom prevailed.

"You're right," said Tommy. "Now we decide, are we going to talk to him? Do we think he has useful information for us? He must know about the fate of the other Secretaries. How could he not?"

Sarge said, "I think we should talk to him."

Bertha said, "Yes talk to him. It could only help us. This could be a big break for us, in that it has come so quickly in our investigation. This could move this investigation right along."

Jan said, "I too think we should talk to him. We all agree on that. Now, what's our approach? May I suggest, let one of the security company people talk to him first. We can watch and listen to the interrogation from here. One of us can always play good cop later."

Jan reached out and pressed a button. A wall opened and exposed a large television screen. He asked, "Everyone agree?"

Everyone nodded in agreement.

"Okay. I'll call down and tell the Company to talk to the attacker."

Shortly, a buzzer sounded in the SCIF.

Jan said, "They are going to start to interrogate the attacker. Let's watch."

The team repositioned their chairs for a better view of the television screen. The four of them were affixed to the screen. They listened to every word and paid close attention to the attacker's nonverbal communication. It was the nonverbal communication that most interested the four. This gave them information for additional avenues of interrogation.

The attacker was visibly nervous and was not convinced no harm would come to him. He was scared. He said nothing of value. The Company ended the interrogation of the attacker.

As the group repositioned their chairs back to the large round wooden conference table, Bertha said, "Did I hear him correctly. Did he allude to the assassination of members of the Presidential Cabinet? Did I hear him say that more than once?"

Tommy replied, "That's what I heard."

Sarge added, "Yes. And his nonverbal signs were indicative of fear, being scared. Other nonverbal signs showed an openness, a willingness to talk."

Jan added, "Almost to the level of relief. Like he finally could talk about the assassinations. I think that was a relief for him."

Bertha said, "Now we wait for the results of the checks in numerous databases worldwide. We have a photograph, DNA and his fingerprints to run. Let's see if we can identify this man. What leverage can we gain for the next round of interrogation?"

"Let's get back to our strategy session," said Jan.

The telephone in the SCIF rang.

"Again," said Jan somewhat discussed. "Are we going to be able to continue today?"

251

Jan pressed the speaker button and said, "Hello. This is Jan."

A voice announced, "Jan, this is Josef. How are you? How's it going over there?"

Jan's tone changed to excitement. "Josef. Good to hear from you. All is well. Everything is moving along just fine. You're on an open speaker."

"Oh. Okay."

"Joseph, I would like to introduce you to Sarge and Tommy. Sarge and Tommy this is Josef Sklodowski, Director, National Security Group, Poland National Police. He's my boss."

Together, Sarge and Tommy said, "Hello Josef. Pleased to meet you."

Josef replied, "Nice to meet you both. Welcome to Poland and thank you for your willingness to assist the government of Poland with a matter sensitive to our national security. Thank you."

"Josef, how can I help you?" asked Jan.

"I wanted to personally relay information to you. It was confirmed by our intelligence that a U.S. military aircraft exploded off the coast of Scotland on its descent into the Glasgow International Airport for a refueling stop. The plane transported the U.S. Secretary of Health and Human Services. There were no survivors. We dispatched a staff member from Glasgow who reported back there were no signs of this event. Let me repeat. There were no signs of this event. That's all the information we have right now."

"Okay. Thank you."

"If you need anything from me, call. We'll talk later."

"Okay. Thank you."

Jan pushed the speaker button to end the call. The room went quiet. Everyone thought about the information they just heard and the events of this morning. For Tommy and Sarge, the stark reality of the vast terrorist operation to assassinate the members of the United States of America Presidential Cabinet became clear and apparent and real.

Jan broke the silence and said, "People we must maintain our focus. We must continue without emotions. We have a job to do. The security company made the decision this morning that they did. We won't second-guess them. We won't second-guess ourselves. We will prevail. We will bring to justice all those responsible for this slaughter. This senseless, despicable crime. We can only do that if we set our emotions aside to conduct the investigation."

The group became attentive. Jan continued to lead the group in discussions to establish a sound investigative strategy.

"Tommy and Sarge, this is mainly for you two. Do we have anyone in the U.S. government to reach out to for assistance, for information about the Secretaries? Can you give that some thought for tomorrow, please? This would be most helpful. This is what we have to this point.

1. A list of Secretaries who have been assassinated.
2. A videotape of the Secretaries' residences that show their absence. They are not coming or going from their residences. Where are they?
3. One of the attackers in our custody. What does he know? What will he tell us?

We don't have too much."

Sarge blurted out, "Let's leak this to the press. What if we call a journalist and provide them the information that these Secretaries

253

aren't here. They aren't around their departments or residences. Only that they are not around."

Bertha said, "Yes. We could use the press to dig up information. That may work. That may generate more people to come forward."

Tommy replied, "What if the press doesn't write an article. Suppose they wait for a lot more information. The information we are looking for? Suppose they choose not to act. Jan says the current administration pays some news agencies to control what they broadcast and what they don't broadcast."

Bertha said, "That could happen, but that would not stymie the investigation any more than not contacting them. This contact will have to be given the status of a Confidential National Security Source. The press will have to fact check the information."

Sarge said, "We're talking about a 'deep throat' type informant to the media? Like the guy from the 1970s with Watergate?"

Bertha replied, "That may just work. Will the journalist want a face to face meeting or could we do this through social media? A Twitter account or a Facebook account? This might just work. Technology could maintain the anonymity we need in the short term."

Jan said, "Okay. Now we're getting somewhere. Put that on the list. But make sure the account is not traceable. Everyone okay with that?"

With an affirmative head nod, everyone motioned their agreement.

"Good. Bertha you'll coordinate this with our cyber specialist to set up an account that can't be traced. Please remind cyber of the NSA shenanigans so they can counter them."

Bertha replied, "Yes I will focus on both points Jan. NSA. Come on."

"We still need more information. We need someone who's suspicious that something is going on. Someone who's credible and reliable. How do we find someone like that?" asked Jan.

Sarge replied, "I'm going over to the FOP lodge tonight. Let me ask around. Let me see what I can find out."

"Good. Hopefully, you'll turn something up."

Jan continued, "I think we had a productive day. We accomplished a lot. Let's stop here for the day. Tomorrow morning first thing, we'll review our investigative strategy and update our list."

Everyone tidied up the workspace. The team rose from the chairs and pushed them under the table and left the SCIF for the day.

21 October, Thursday

USA, New York, New York City
Manhattan

Fact News Center

"We interrupt our regular programming for developing news. The Washington Era reports a plot to assassinate the Secretaries of the Presidential Cabinet. This is shocking. Please excuse my emotions. I just cannot believe that the superpower of the world, the United States of America, is under attack, yet again," said Bryan Hallmark, Co-host and News Reporter, Now What's Happening in Government, Fact News Center.

"Bryan. It's okay, "consoled Mary Kraft, Co-host and News Reporter, Now What's Happening in Government, Fact News Center.

Mary then directed her attention to the red light and the worldwide audience. She looked into the camera and said, "Breaking news just into the news center. The Washington Era reports a plot to assassinate high-level U.S. government officials. That's all we know right now. That's all we have. When we get more information, we will interrupt the Concert in the Street and report it to you. Now back to Hall and Oats, our featured artist for our fall Concert in the Street series."

In New York City, on the news set of Now What's Happening in Government, Fact News Center, in a startled tone, Mary said, "Bryan, are you okay? You look very nervous and shaken. What's the matter with you? It's just the news. It's just a story. This is what we do. We report the news. We tell the world what's going on in the world. On my god!"

Bryan replied, "Mary, you don't understand."

In an annoyed tone, Mary said, "What do you mean I don't understand? What's there to understand? I will tell you what you need to understand, our ratings. Falling apart on the set is not going to move our ratings up. That's what I understand, Bryan."

Bryan replied, "Mary. You don't know do you?"

Still excited, Mary said, "Know what? Know that our ratings may fall because of your emotions. Come on. Man up already."

Bryan replied, "You really don't know. I hope you don't know. That will excuse your insensitivity toward my feelings. My display of emotions."

Starting to lose her patience, Mary said, "What are you talking about?"

Bryan, now sniffling a little, replied, "My mother is the Secretary of Agriculture. I haven't seen her nor spoke to her since the 11 of October. We never go more than four or five days without at least talking on the telephone. Usually, we have dinner together every two to three days. She either flies up to New York City, or I take the train to Washington D.C. I don't know what's going on with her. This is very out of character for her. Mary, my mother and I are close. Very close. It's like she fell off the face of the earth."

Bryan was interrupted by a faint, extremely excited voice that said, "Stop! Stop!" The voice got closer and continued to say, "Stop! Stop" It now caught the attention of Mary also. Simultaneously, Bryan and Mary turned their heads in the direction of the voice. They saw one of the producers frantically running toward them. He continued to exclaim, "Stop! Stop!" His hand motioned a cutting gesture to his neck. Both Mary and Bryan froze. They knew what was happening.

The producer was directly in front of them now. He continued to motion a frantic cutting gesture to his neck. It was more intense and rapid now. He said nothing. He immediately reached for Bryan's microphone and ripped it off his body. He fumbled with it momentarily and finally managed to turn the microphone off.

The frazzled producer looked up at Bryan and exclaimed, "Really! Really! An open mic? An open microphone. That was such a rookie mistake. Everything you said was broadcasted to the world. The world! The whole wide world!"

Bryan again became emotional. He started to shake. Tears welled in his eyes. He began to sway back and forth. Then he fell to the floor like a rock. There was a big thud when his limp body hit the concrete newsroom floor. He did not move.

The producer exclaimed, "Great! Just great! Someone call the nurse."

Mary froze in place. She said nothing. There was a blank, distant, stare on her face. Her mouth was open in ah. She tried to talk, but there was no sound.

The producer looked at Mary and said, "What? What did you say? What did you say?"

There were no words from Mary. She remained frozen in place. When she tried to talk again, her words were faint.

She said, "My ratings."

The producer moved closer to Mary to hear what she was saying. He immediately jumped back from her.

"Come on," the producer said. "Not you too. Someone call maintenance to clean this mess up."

The event was too much for Mary. The stress of her ratings falling because of Bryan's open microphone was too much for her to handle. Her continual self-imposed self-demands to keep her ratings high, to be the number one news anchor in New York City, was just too much. What she thought was determination, hard work, dedication, and ambition crumbled her. It served only to build a tsunami of stress that hit her hard. Very hard. Though she was left standing, she was standing in her own urine. It was the pressure of the tsunami of stress that left Mary in a state of urinary incontinence right there on the set of Now What's Happening in Government, Fact News Center.

"Hey. Where're you going? Don't you have a show to produce here today?" said Wayne Norchenski as the producer hysterically passed him.

The producer, in a threatening tone, said, "What? What did you say? Who are you and what are you doing on my set?"

Mr. Norchenski said, "Well let me introduce myself. Again. We met yesterday at lunch. I'm Wayne Norchenski. I work with Fact News Center as a News Analyst. Today I'm here to be a guest on Bryan's show and discuss the latest government waste, fraud, and abuse. You know, government mismanagement."

"What? Who?" the producer said. He continued in a disturbed disgusted tone, "You know, I don't have time for this. There'll be no more show today for Bryan or Mary. Very well may be no more show for Bryan and Mary ever. Anywhere. They surely don't need a guest today."

"Well, now that's not what I wanted to hear. I traveled all the way from Seattle to be a guest on the show. That's not good. Is there anyone else who could do the show?"

"Look over there. I have one host of the show flat on his back. The nurse is checking him out. The other host of the show is standing, still standing in her own urine. No there's no one else. The whole world has heard my co-host breakdown on live television. Really!" said the producer as he shook his head in an obvious sign that he was fed up with everything.

In a mocking tone, Mr. Norchenski said, "I see that. I don't know why that would cause you to be rude. You're still standing, on a dry floor. Here, take my bottle of water. It's half full. You have a beautiful day."

USA, Washington D.C. NW
Embassy of the Republic of Poland

0730 Hours   SCIF

The team settled into the SCIF to convene their investigative efforts from where they left off yesterday. Jan noticed Sarge fidgeting with his neck. Jan was amused and continued to watch Sarge fidget. Bertha noticed Jan watching Sarge and started to watch too. Bertha nudged Tommy. Now all three watched Sarge fidgeting with his neck. After a minute or two, Jan, Bertha, and Tommy roared with laughter.

The laughter startled Sarge. He quickly looked up and around the room. He saw the other three were looking at him. He said, "What? What are you all looking at? I cut my neck shaving."

"Cut your neck shaving," Jan replied. "That's really bleeding. Do you have to go to the nurse's office little boy?"

The roar of laughter returned to the room as Sarge talked over it.

"Funny. Real funny. I think I can manage. I expect a little more compassion from this group."

Tommy said, "Yeah. Right. That was compassion."

Sarge replied, "Are right. Are right. Let's get started."

Jan said, "Okay. Continuing from yesterday."

Jan was quickly interrupted by Sarge.

"Excuse me Jan. Before we start, I just want to say how impressed I am with Bertha's efforts."

Bertha jerked her head up from some papers in front of her on the conference table. She trained her eyes on Sarge. Her eyes and face expressed puzzlement, confusion. Tommy was also focused on Sarge in anticipation of what Sarge was about to say.

Sarge continued, "Yes. She was given the task to create a shadow Facebook or social media account. We wanted to reach out to the press to see if a news story generated information for us. Well, she got it done literally overnight."

Bertha interrupted Sarge. "What are you talking about? I haven't completed that task yet. I spoke to the cyber people last night after we left here. I'm waiting for their telephone call today. Yes, they're working on it. It's not in play yet."

"Hmmm. What?" Sarge mumbled. "Am I the only one that watched the news this morning?"

At the same time, Jan, Bertha and Tommy said, "I watched the morning news."

"Maybe it was not the same channel. Maybe all the news outlets didn't pick the story up," said Sarge. "The channel I watched reported a breaking story about the assassination of the Secretaries of the Presidential Cabinet. I just wanted to applaud Bertha's quick and decisive action with one prong of our investigative strategy."

Looking in the direction of Bertha, Sarge continued, "Good job Bertha."

Bertha replied, "Sarge, that investigative tactic isn't in play yet. I know it's not in play yet. Are you sure you heard the news correctly?"

With a touch of sarcasm, Sarge said, "Yes, Bertha. I'm not that old. I know what I heard. Do you all want to watch it?"

In a surprised tone, Jan said, "Watch it? Watch what? How?"

261

Sarge got up from his chair. He walked to the technology cabinet, retrieved a thumb drive from his right front pants pocket, raised the thumb drive in the air, and waved it around. He said to the team, "So you think I'm crazy. You think I'm old. I'll show you."

With a smirk on his face, Sarge opened the technology cabinet doors. He turned the power on, which automatically opened the wall and exposed the big screen television. He plugged the thumb drive in and with the remote control turned the device on.

Sarge said, "Watch."

The team positioned their chairs to watch the big screen television and this is what they heard.

"We interrupt our regular programming for developing news. The Washington Era reports a plot to assassinate the Secretaries of the Presidential Cabinet. This is shocking. Please excuse my emotions. I just cannot believe that the superpower of the world, the United States of America, is under attack, yet again."

"Breaking news just into the news center. The Washington Era reports a plot to assassinate high-level U.S. government officials. That's all we know right now. That's all we have. When we get more information, we will interrupt the Concert in the Street and report it to you. Now back to Hall and Oats, our featured artist for our fall Concert in the Street series."

The picture turned to the Hall and Oats.

"Bryan, are you okay? You look very nervous and shaken. What's the matter with you? It's just the news. It's just a story. This is what we do. We report the news. We tell the world what's going on in the world. On my god!"

"Mary, you don't understand."

"What do you mean I don't understand? What's there to understand? I will tell you what you need to understand, our ratings. Falling apart on the set is not going to move our ratings up. That's what I understand, Bryan."

"Mary. You don't know do you?"

"Know what? Know that our ratings may fall because of your emotions. Come on. Man up already."

"You really don't know. I hope you don't know. That will excuse your insensitivity toward my feelings. My display of emotions."

"What are you talking about?"

With the remote control, Sarge paused the video. He looked at each team member as he said, "Now listen to this. Listen to this. You're not going to believe this. Listen."

Sarge resumed the video.

"My mother is the Secretary of Agriculture. I haven't seen her nor talked to her since the 11 of October. We never go more than four or five days without at least talking on the telephone. Usually, we have dinner together every two to three days. She either flies up to New York City, or I take the train to Washington D.C. I don't know what's going on with her. This is very out of character for her. Mary, my mother and I are close. Very close. It's like she fell off the face of the earth."

"Stop! Stop! Stop! Stop"!

The video ended. The picture on the big screen television went black. There was complete silence in the room. No one said anything.

The silence was finally broken by Sarge. "Bertha. That wasn't the result of your efforts?"

Bertha shook her head and indicated no as she said, "No. That wasn't me."

Tommy quickly chimed in, "If it wasn't you, then who? Who was it?"

Jan looked to Bertha and said, "Did cyber do something without you knowing about it?"

"That wasn't cyber. I was explicit with cyber not to do anything until I cleared it," replied Bertha. "They know how sensitive this investigation is to the government of Poland."

Jan leaned back in his chair, gave a big sigh and said, "Wow."

After a pause, he continued, "Sarge what possessed you to record it? How were you able to get it all recorded like that?"

"I made a mistake last night when I set my recorder to record the sitcoms I like to watch. I thought if I got a chance I'd watch the recordings. I set the correct time, but I hit AM, not PM. So, this was recorded."

The room went silent again. The team knew what a break this was for the investigation. The hotshot investigative team also knew, from over a hundred and forty years of combined investigative experience among them, it was a type of event that broke an investigation wide open. It was just dumb luck.

Happenstance. Unexplainable. It did not matter. Investigators ran with this kind of information. They used it to parlay additional information and leads. In this case, to prove to the world that the government of Poland did not assassinate the members of the United States of America Presidential Cabinet.

Snapping back at it, Jan said, "Who wants to go to New York? We have an interview to do. What a break. What a break!"

Sarge motioned to Tommy and replied, "We'll go. We'll take care of it."

"Good. Thank you," said Jan.

Jan paused in thought. Then said, "Sarge, how did you make out at the FOP lodge last night?"

"I was so excited about the news broadcast, I forgot about last night. It was interesting. Nothing substantial. Nothing direct. But there was a lot of discussion about something going on in the city at the Federal government level. Many of the Federal agents at the FOP were talking. Well, they were speculating about a massive conspiracy, a massive cover-up of something. A few of the Secret Service agents believed it reached into the White House. As they put it, 'reached the highest levels in the White House.' They didn't come out and say it, but they insinuated the President and Vice President were involved in whatever was happening."

Jan acknowledged, "Interesting. Do you think you'll be able to gather any pointed information? Any direct information?"

"It'll take some time. Probably longer than we have. I spend a lot of time there, I'll continue those efforts."

"Please," said Jan. "Let's see where we are before lunch. Then you guys can leave for New York. Bertha will get with Intel and call you to let you know where the news reporter is so you can talk with him."

Jan stood from his chair, walked over to the whiteboard and said, "This is what we have.

1. Video footage from the Secretary's' respective departments and residences showing the lack of their presence.
2. An attacker who knows something.

3. Two people, Sarge and Shaggy, who saw and heard a news broadcast that reported the assassination of the Attorney General.
4. The U.S. Federal Agents eluding to a massive cover-up or conspiracy that may involve the President and Vice President.
5. The video, with audio, of the Secretary of Agriculture's son who admitted his mother was not available to him, which can be corroborated with video footage from number one.

Pulling another whiteboard close to the one he just wrote on, Jan continued, "Here's the list of the nine Secretaries whom we believe have been assassinated. We're getting someplace. We still have a long way to go. We're getting someplace, though."

The team mustered about the room to leave for lunch. Tommy and Sarge knew they were not coming back to the room. They pushed their chairs under the table and positioned everything about their table space to present a well-organized and maintained workspace. The team left the SCIF.

Jan and Bertha headed in the direction of the embassy dining room.

Tommy and Sarge walked to the embassy garage to retrieve their vehicle. They left for New York to interview the son of the Secretary of Agriculture. They planned to take Pennsylvania Avenue to the Baltimore-Washington Parkway, 295, then onto Interstate 95 north. Since they passed by Mangialardo and Sons, they decided to get sub sandwiches for lunch and keep driving.

As Sarge navigated the embassy vehicle out of the embassy garage and onto Sixteenth Street NW, he declared, "Tommy, I'm getting the *G-Man* sub on a hard roll. Mm. I can't wait. What are you getting?"

"The same Sarge. No meat, just cheese and the vegetables."

In a surprised tone, Sarge said, "No meat? Why?"

"I don't eat meat anymore."

"Why not?" asked Sarge.

"For my health," replied Tommy. I'm hoping the small things I do will add up to big savings health-wise."

"Okay. I'll try not to make fun of you for that," said Sarge.

The United States Department of Justice
Federal Bureau of Investigations
Headquarters

1145 Hours   Directors Conference Room

"Okay. As is becoming typical, we have one more item before we end our Case Status Meeting. As a reminder, you all signed Non-Disclosure Agreements," said the Director of the FBI.

"Walter, what's the status of the investigation of the assassinated Presidential Cabinet members?"

"Sir, the investigation just got complicated. We have a videotape of the son of the Secretary of Agriculture announcing to the world, on an open microphone he didn't know was on, that he has not talked with his mother since the 11th of October. He further announced this was very much out of character for his mother in that they talked with each other every two to three days."

The Director adjusted himself in his over-stuffed, high back, black leather upholstered conference table chair. "Walter, I asked you to ensure this did not get complicated. How did this happen? What has gone on here?"

"Sir, her son is a mess. He calls the Department of Agriculture every day. He pleads with them to tell him where his mother is,

267

to give her a message to call him. They continue to tell him she's on a National Security trip and they can't tell him the details because he doesn't have a clearance. They then say they'll pass his message to her. That's what our source in the Inspector General office is telling me."

"Should we take him off the street? Should we have him committed to a mental hospital for his continued harassment of Federal government employees? What about the other Department's IG, are they kicking up their heels yet? That damn Patriot Act. Congress just had to give them all statutory authority."

"Not that I'm aware. I'm in daily contact with them."

"It appears they all have bought the story I told you to tell. The Secretaries are sequestered by the President at an unknown location to work on a National Security matter. I said that would make a good cover story. You can hide anything under the label of National Security and the mythical clearance levels. What a joke."

"Yes, Mr. al Bazir. It appears your cover story is working well. You are right. It's a good cover story."

"What is the update on the Secret Service involvement is this? They don't have jurisdiction in this matter. Are they still looking into this?"

"Sir, I don't know. I have no means, nor sources to talk with, from that organization. I have no update on the surveillance footage."

"Okay."

"I still believe the cameras were compromised. It appeared to me the cameras were turned off for the duration of the assassinations and then turned back on. That was my observation from visiting and requesting to review the recordings from all of the entities who had the possibility of recording the assassinations."

"Walter, forget the surveillance camera footage. You checked for it. It wasn't there. It won't be a problem for us."

"Yes, sir."

"It seems your biggest challenge is keeping this matter from getting complicated," said al Bazir. "Last point, the President is involved in this case. Every time I see him, he asks me about it. Golf last Saturday. Right on the course. What will I tell him about the Secretary of Agriculture's son?"

Walter quickly replied, "I plan to go to New York today, right after this meeting. I want to meet with the son and assure him all is well with his mother. I also want to assess his mental state. He could be a threat to the President. In which case, I'd have to refer that issue to the Secret Service for them to have the son undergo a physiological evaluation for a Mental Health Commitment Order. If the mental health evaluation discloses he's a threat to the President, the Secret Service can deal with that matter. That gets it out of our hands."

"I like that," said Mr. al Bazir. "That's good. Excellent Walter. I have the right man on this matter. Let me know tomorrow how your meeting with the son goes. That's it for today, everyone. Thank you all."

Mr. al Bazir got up from his chair and exited the conference room. His two assistants, the Deputy Director and his personal assistant following behind. The balance of the senior management team left the room as well. Walter remained behind, still seated, deep in thought.

Walter Noarc came from a long line of government servants. Following that proud family tradition was not what he wanted to do. He aspired to be a professional baseball player. That was not to be. He was unable to stand up to the family pressure. The

269

constant pressure was overwhelming. He finally acquiesced to the family pressure with a compromise. The compromise was a promise to himself that he also made known to his family and to which they agreed. He told his family he would not be a member of anyone's Cabinet. He would not be a Secretary of any department. When his father announced at the Thanksgiving Day family gathering in Ocean City Maryland that the President gave the family one Secretary position, he reminded his father of the promise, of the condition he set for himself to follow the proud family tradition of government service. His father tried to change his mind. Walter stayed his ground on his decision. So, his father gave the Secretary of Defense position to Walter's brother-in-law, Jeremy Parker. That was three years ago. Walter's sister was not happy with her father when he gave the Secretary position to her husband or with her husband when he accepted it. To the family, she said nothing openly. To her husband in private, she vehemently voiced her thoughts. Those conversations led to a compromise of her own with her husband.

Walter enjoyed a strong sibling bond and relationship with his sister. A bond and relationship that lasted over the years in part to what they jokingly referred to as their 'pinky swear.' That was their promise to each other that they would talk to each other on Tuesday nights and Saturday mornings every week no matter where they were, no matter what they were doing. This was done as a ritual. It was their way to stay close to each other and ground themselves to ward off the pressures of a wealthy politically connected family. His loving sister was vocal in her support of his stance on how far he would go in government service. In support of his sister, he too vocally disagreed when their father gave the Secretary of Defense position to her husband. He was not heard by the egos and narcissistic personalities of the other family members.

Interstate 95 Northbound

Sarge's cellular telephone rang when they were about ten miles outside of New York City. Sarge quickly answered.

"Hello. This is Sarge. Yes. Yes. Okay. Thank you, Bertha."

Sarge ended the telephone call, looked at Tommy and said, "Amazing. This is amazing. Bertha's Intel people trace this guy down through his cellphone. She's texting me the address. It's in Manhattan."

"Where he's at right now?"

"Yes. Amazing. Simply amazing."

"Really, where he's at right now? That is amazing. You have to ask yourself, how are there fugitives, people with outstanding warrants, still out there? You just have to wonder."

New York City, 5ᵗʰ Avenue, Manhattan

1830 Hours

"This should be the text," said Sarge as he reached for the vibrating cellphone. He swiped the screen and revealed the text. "Yes, this is the address."

He studied it.

"Let's go. I know where this is."

He navigated the embassy vehicle into the slow Manhattan rush hour traffic. They inched along with the never-ending New York City traffic.

"Here we are. Now to find parking. Can I be that lucky? Can I get that one? Okay. You can't beat that. Three doors down."

Sarge clicked on his right turn signal and stopped to let a parked car merge into the traffic. As the parked car eased out of the parking spot, Sarge eased the big black Mercedes-Benz up to position it to park parallel in the street parking space.

With the vehicle parked, Sarge said to Tommy, "Come on. I'm hungry after that long drive."

Sarge and Tommy got out of the embassy car. They walked up to the restaurant and were about to enter when Sarge said, "There he is. There's the son of the Secretary of Agriculture sitting in the patio area, in the company of another gentleman. I wonder who that is. We need to get a table outside to watch this for a little bit before we approach him."

Just then, the gentleman seated with the son of the Secretary of Agriculture quickly stood and briskly walked in the direction of Sarge and Tommy. He looked hard in their direction. He waved his hand and called out, "Tommy. Tommy. How are you?"

Surprised, Sarge looked at Tommy and said, "You know that guy?"

Tommy gave him a hard look.

"Yes, I do. That's Wayne. Wayne Norchenski. He and I worked together at Agriculture."

"Get him to take us to the table, so we can all sit together."

"I'll try."

As they got closer, their hands extended. When they meet, their outstretched hands clasped with the energy and joy of seeing each other after many years. As athletes, they pulled themselves together for an embrace. Two lawmen reunited. They rekindled *the blue bond*. Lawmen that stood on the blue line that was drawn between right and wrong. Between good and evil.

Simultaneously, they announced to each other, "You're looking well. Yes. I'm doing well. Thank you."

The excitement was quickly interrupted when Tommy looked toward Sarge. "Sarge, this is Wayne. Wayne this is Sarge. Wayne and I worked together at Agriculture."

Sarge quickly extended his hand for a firm business style greeting. "Nice to meet you, Wayne. You're the Coast Guard guy from Seattle. I sent Tommy out to Seattle to do an Interpol Outreach presentation to that IG organization you were involved with."

In a firm, but friendly tone, Wayne said, "Yes you did. It's my pleasure to meet you, Sarge. Tommy spoke well of you."

Sarge looked back and forth from Wayne to Tommy.

"He better or I'll kick his ass."

Wayne laughed at Tommy and said, "Please come over and join me. Join us at the table."

"No. It looks like your friend doesn't want any other company," said Tommy. "Is he all right?"

"He'll be okay. Do you remember who that is?"

"He looks familiar. I can't place him, though."

"He's the son of the current Secretary of Agriculture. You should remember him from our days at Agriculture. When we were there together, he went on some of the trips with the Secretary. His mother was then the Under Secretary for Food Safety. We always thought he had a weird relationship with his mother. Do you remember how they acted together? Some of the strange things they did. You always said they were sleeping together."

"That's Bryan. What's his last name? Bryan. Bryan."

"Yes. Bryan Hallmark."

"Do you think he remembers me?"

"He remembers you. He pointed you out to me when you were walking up the street."

"Is that so? Hm. After all those years. You never told him I thought they, he and his mother, were lovers, did you?"

"No. I don't think I did."

Sarge laughed. "What went on over at Agriculture?"

"Come on. Join us," said Wayne.

Tommy looked to Sarge and asked, "Sarge, is that okay with you?"

Sarge replied, "Yes. Sure. I just want to eat already. I hope I don't let it slip that you think he and his mother are lovers."

Wayne laughed and said, "Good. Come on over."

The three of them walked to the table where Bryan was still seated.

At the table, Tommy quickly extended his hand to greet Bryan.

"Bryan. Hello. Nice to see you."

Bryan stood, shook Tommy's hand and replied, "Good to see you. How are you? It's been awhile."

"I'm fine. Thank you. It sure has been awhile."

Tommy looked to Sarge. "This is Sarge. Sarge, Bryan."

Sarge and Bryan shook hands and exchanged greetings while Tommy said, "Bryan, you don't mind that we join you and Wayne?"

"No, I don't mind. Don't be funny," replied Bryan.

"Thank you."

"I saw you walking up the sidewalk and pointed you out to Wayne. I told Wayne to invite you to sit with us. I remembered how close you and Wayne were when you two worked together at Agriculture. We always had so much fun on those Department trips. You and Wayne never judged my mother or me. You two were always so pleasant and fun to be around. And when you two needed to be, you both were serious about your jobs. These two were real professionals Sarge. Real professionals. You may not know, but you two were well-liked at Agriculture. Well-liked by many, many people, at all levels. My mother included. She always had kind words for you two with the IG."

And then Bryan broke down and started to cry.

Tommy looked at Wayne. Wayne looked at Tommy. Tommy looked at Sarge who fought to hold back from laughing. Tommy kicked Sarge's foot under the table to signal to him not to laugh.

Wayne finally broke the silence, "Bryan, maybe we should go. I'll take you home."

In a soft feminine sounding voice, Bryan replied, "I'm sorry Wayne." He looked up from the table toward Tommy. Then Sarge. He continued, "Guys, I'm so sorry. An emotional event upset me today. I'm just not myself. I'm out of the loft, spending some time with Wayne to clear my mind. It's not helping. I just can't help myself. I'm just beside myself thinking about it all the time. I think I should go."

As Bryan got up from the table, Wayne said, "Bryan, I'll take you home. I'll get us a cab."

Tommy said, "No. We can give you a ride. We're at the curb. We can take you home."

Wayne replied, "No you don't have to interrupt your evening for us."

Bryan echoed the same as Wayne.

"No," said Tommy. "We're taking you home Bryan. That's that. Let's go."

Sarge turned to retrace his path from the patio to the front door to the car. Wayne helped Bryan as they started to walk. Bryan followed Sarge. Wayne followed Bryan. Tommy followed them all.

They made their way to the car where Wayne helped Bryan into the rear seat. He closed the door, looked at Tommy and said, "Sorry about all this."

They were then interrupted by a man dressed in a finely tailored suit, silk tie, slicked back hair and sharply shined leather shoes.

The man said, "Excuse me. I need to talk to that man."

Tommy and Wayne looked at each other. They looked back at the unknown man. A total stranger who just came up to them on a New York City street and announced he had to talk with Bryan. Simultaneously, they shook their heads. They continued to look at the man.

Wayne said, "Oh yeah. You do. Who are you?"

Wayne and Tommy both slid into a defensive posture.

"Oh. I'm Walter. I'm with the Federal Bureau of Investigation." said the man.

"Oh. Really," said Wayne in a sarcastic, bothered tone. "Last name? Perhaps some identification. I'm thinking a photo ID and a badge. Maybe."

The man was startled. It appeared he was never talked to in that manner before. There was smugness on his face. A nonverbal to say, how you dare question me. I'm an FBI Special Agent.

Through the rearview mirror, Sarge observed the finely dressed man. Sarge emerged from the vehicle and walked around the front of the car to make his way to the stranger.

Sarge announced, "What's going on here? Who's this guy?"

"We got it, Sarge. We got it. Let's just all get in the car and go," said Tommy.

The man fumbled to retrieve something from the inside breast pock of his suit jacket. He said, "Go. You can't go. I need to talk to Bryan. This is important."

The man continued to fumble under his suit coat. As conditioned, Wayne and Tommy shuffle stepped and positioned themselves at opposite forty-five-degree angles to the man. A defensive posture they mastered from their days as Defensive Tactics Instructors and undercover roles, working the street combating food stamp trafficking up and down the eastern seaboard. On the streets of Pennsylvania – Philadelphia, Harrisburg, York. Maryland – Baltimore, Oxon Hill, Forest Heights, Suitland. Washington D.C. The bowels of drug infested, poverty-ridden triangle in Virginia - Newport News, Hampton, Norfolk.

Finally, the man retrieved the item he fumbled with and presented his government credentials to Wayne.

"There. There are my credentials." In a meek authoritative voice, he continued, "I'm here to talk to Bryan. This is a matter of vital national security."

Sarge, now standing behind Tommy in a stacked defensive tactics position, said, "National security. Just what is the national security matter?"

"I'm not at liberty to discuss this issue with you. You know I can only talk with people with the proper clearance level and need to know. You don't have either. I'm here to take Bryan."

Tommy exclaimed, "Take Bryan! Take Bryan where? You just said you wanted to talk to Bryan. Do you want to talk with Bryan or do you want to take him?"

The man became nervous. His hands started to shake. He fumbled taking back his credentials from Wayne and stowing them in the inside breast coat pocket. In an anxious demeanor, the man said, "Let's not make a scene here. All I want is Bryan. You give me Bryan. I leave. You all can leave. We go our own ways." His voice changed to a meek authoritative voice as he continued, "I'm Walter Noarc, a Federal Agent with the FBI. I demand you turn Bryan over to me. Now!"

Laughing, Wayne said, "Really. That sounds like a line from a movie. You're starting to annoy me."

"Well Mr. Noarc," said Sarge. "Tommy and I are employed by the Republic of Poland. We are here on official business for the Republic of Poland. Wayne and Bryan are assisting us. Therefore, they are agents of the Republic of Poland. This vehicle is the property of the Republic of Poland. All of us, it, and its contents enjoy diplomatic immunity. As a retired Federal Agent from the FBI, I know you know that means you have no jurisdiction over us, the vehicle or the contents of the vehicle. Bryan is the contents. We're leaving in our diplomatic vehicle, with its diplomatic contents, as the treaty between the Republic of Poland and the United States of America grants us respectively. Right?"

There was an uncomfortable silence. The meek manner Federal Agent started to tremble. His actions were indicative of someone who never worked a day on the streets in the real world. He did not present himself as a seasoned law enforcement officer. Rather, he appeared to be a career, administrative, bureaucrat. Someone who sat at a desk and second-guessed, after weeks of studying an event, the actions of law enforcement officers who in milliseconds processed the event and acted.

Sarge, in a gesture of pity, broke the silence.

"In the spirit of cooperation between countries, what I can do is, I'll bring this matter to the attention of Poland's Ambassador to the United States of America. I'll explain to the Ambassador the events leading up to tonight and tonight's meeting with you. I'll ask the Ambassador. No. I'll encourage the Ambassador to contact the Director of the FBI and request a meeting to discuss this matter between the two of them. How's that?"

Walter became even more nervous. He tried to speak but only stuttered. The situation had him frazzled. He thought to himself, "This situation is out of control. This whole operation is out of control."

Flashing through his mind was all the deceit and deception at the highest levels of government. Weighing heavily on his conscience was the loss of life, the loss of innocent citizens of the United States of America.

He finally conceded in a calm composed tone, "Yes. You're correct sir. You all do enjoy diplomatic immunity. I can't stop you from leaving and taking Bryan with you."

He reached into his right outside suit coat pocket and retrieved his business card. He extended his trembling hand with his card.

"Please take my card. My cellular telephone number is on it. Should the Republic of Poland wish to cooperate with the government of the United States of America, please contact me.

But only me. Please don't talk to anyone else in the FBI about our meeting tonight. Talk to only me. I ask for your professional courtesy. Obviously, I have before me three intelligent, astute fellow brothers in law enforcement. An unusual situation brings us together here tonight. Again, if you wish to assist the United States of America, please call me. But only me. Thank you."

Sarge took the business card from Walter. Walter slowly shuffle stepped away. Then turned and continued to walk down the street. His gait started to slow. He stopped and looked back. His facial expression was one of deep concern. He lowered his head, turned back, and continued to walk away.

Hustling around the front of the Mercedes, Sarge commanded, "Get in. Get in the car. We need to get out of here. Let's go now."

Wayne looked at Tommy and said, "What the hell is going on? What is happening? What are you involved in now?"

Though Wayne's tone was of concern, he displayed a smirk crafted from the excitement of what just happened. Reminiscent of when Tommy and Wayne worked together on the streets of the real world. For that instant, for that night, on the streets of Manhattan, the Tommy and Wayne Show presented once again.

Wayne said nothing else. He hustled around the rear of the Mercedes, opened the left rear passenger door and entered. Tommy followed as the front passenger. With the sound of the last door closed, Sarge accelerated away from the curb and into the traffic. He received a reception of sounding horns from other drivers who expressed their displeasure with being cut off. Sarge paid no mind to the traffic. He was focused on getting back to Washington. Back to the embassy and the safety it offered to all four of them.

Sarge, in a controlled rush, wheeled the embassy vehicle through the Manhattan traffic. Even at the late hour of the night, traffic was heavy.

Oblivious to the heavy traffic, his precision driving skills wheeled the Mercedes through the streets of Manhattan with persistence to make his way to Interstate 95. As he drove, no one said anything. All the occupants were in complete silence. All were thinking their own thoughts about the evening's events. Surely, one thought consistent with them all was – why did the FBI want to take Bryan?

Coming up on the ramp to Interstate 95 South, Sarge broke the silence.

"Tommy, do you think we should take 95 or stay on the surface roads? The surface roads will be slower, but if the bureau is looking for us, they will probably be looking on the interstates."

"Go 95. We need to get back as fast as we can. Besides, there won't be any bureau agents out tonight. If anything, they'll send out a message for the locals to pick us up. You know how the bureau works. They get other agencies to do their job and then take the credit. But the locals can't touch us either. We have diplomatic immunity. I doubt they send out a notice. I don't think we'll have any problems tonight. We need to get back to the embassy with Bryan. 95. Take 95."

"Okay. Here we go."

Sarge wheeled the embassy vehicle onto the southbound ramp to Interstate 95. At the merge lane, he accelerated the vehicle to the speed of the traffic and effortlessly flowed into the traffic. Sarge signaled and moved over three lanes to the furthest left-hand lane. He accelerated the vehicle to eighty-five miles per hour and set the cruise control. This the dominant travel position for law enforcement officers to push the traffic out of their way. He adjusted the electric seat for a comfortable position for the late-night drive to the nation's capital. The big, black, Mercedes-Benz floated southbound toward Poland.

Tommy turned in his seat to see Wayne and said, "How're you doing back there Wayne?" He looked to Bryan and said, "Bryan, are you okay?"

Wayne replied, "Fine. Thanks for asking. I don't suppose there's any chance of turning around and taking me to my hotel so I can get my toothbrush?"

A roar of laughter ensued from them all. It was a deep gut laugh and roared on for about two minutes. Then as quickly as it started, it ended. It was silent for about thirty seconds. Then the roar of the deep gut laughter returned.

Finally, Tommy composed himself enough to say, "No. No, Wayne, that's not going to happen tonight. We'll retrieve your things and have them delivered to the embassy."

Taking a moment to gain his breath from the laughter, Tommy continued, "Wayne, we've known each other a long time. I ask for your patience with me. When we get to Philly, we'll find a place to eat. I'll tell you the details there. Bryan, you too. Bryan, you know how Wayne and I work. I ask for your cooperation too. Please."

"I stayed in the car back there because you and Wayne were handling that guy," said Bryan. "For right now, I'll do what I'm told."

"Thank you, Bryan. I appreciate that. Thank you," said Tommy. "Let's relax until we get to Philly."

As they continued southbound on Interstate 95, the cabin of the heavy Mercedes afforded a quiet chamber. It was periodically interrupted from Bryan's shallow snoring. When Wayne had enough of the snoring, he nudged Bryan and Bryan repositioned himself, so the snoring stopped.

Tommy looked over to Sarge and observed Sarge's bored, glazed over eyes. Sarge was fidgeting at this point, an attempt to relieve his boredom. The early start to the day, the late hour of the day, the fact that he had done all the driving today, and of course he was hungry. He had not eaten since lunch. That was some ten hours ago now.

"Are you hungry?" Tommy asked Sarge.

Sarge jerked his head to look at Tommy. "I'm beyond hungry."

"We ate lunch, I don't know how you could be hungry. You even had the *G-Man*. How could you be hungry?"

"Oh. I'm hungry. I'm starving."

There was a groggy moan from the rear seat.

"You had a *G-Man*. A *G-Man*. The sub? From that sub shop, a few blocks from the Capitol? On Pennsylvania Avenue?" said Wayne.

"Yes. Do you remember how good those subs are?" Replied Tommy.

"I certainly do. You guys had those without me! Ah. Man! *G-Man* subs. I could go for one of those. Maybe two."

And then a soft moan chimed into the conversation. "Are we going to eat tonight?" said Bryan.

Tommy said, "Okay people. Oh, my. Let me see what I can find on the internet. We're about twenty-five miles from Philly."

Tommy retrieved his smartphone from its holster. He said out loud, "Philly Steak Sandwiches, Philadelphia PA."

From the back seat, Wayne talked over Tommy, "Okay. Geno's or Pat's?"

Tommy replied, "What?"

"Geno's or Pat's. I have them up. These are the first two listed. When I click on the sites, I recognize the pictures as being the ones I would go to with the King of Prussia office. Geno's or Pat's?"

"Oh. I see. I suggest Geno's. That's the one with the long lines on the food shows. If there are long lines, the food must be good. Those persnickety Philadelphians. Those people from the east side of PA aren't going to stand in line for bad food."

Sarge said to Tommy, "What're you going to eat there?"

"I don't know," replied Tommy. "I'll find something."

Wayne said, "What do mean? He's going to have a Philly Steak sandwich with everything on it. What else. He'll probably have two if I remember correctly."

Snickering, Sarge said, "Tommy here's a vegetarian, Wayne. Did you know that?"

Wayne said "A vegetarian. A tree hugging vegetarian. Let me guess, you believe in global warming. Are you on Al Gore's email newsletter list too?"

Sarge laughed so hard he jerked the steering wheel which caused the big black Mercedes-Benz to swerve back and forth. He twice had to correct the vehicle back onto the roadway from the berm. Wayne too was into an uncontrollable roar of laughter.

"Okay. Okay," said Tommy. "Everyone had their fun at my expense. That's okay. Ah, Sarge, you just missed our exit."

Silence came over the vehicle. Sarge under his breath sounded some profanities ending with, "I don't know how much longer I can wait. I'm so hungry."

Tommy said, "Yeah. See, you missed the exit because you laughed at me. Now, take the next exit coming up. Please."

The cellphone navigation sounded its reset.

"Turn here," said Tommy. "It's three blocks up."

It was 0130 hours. Sarge brought the embassy vehicle to a stop at the underground garage door to the Embassy of Poland. He engaged the automatic down feature for all four windows and turned on the interior lighting to assist the security guard.

The security guard alighted from the guard hut and walked over to the driver's window. She shined her flashlight as she studied the occupant's faces. In a polite, but an authoritative tone and a thick Polish accent, she said, "Good evening Sarge. What do we have here?"

Sarge presented his and Tommy's embassy identifications and replied, "The Republic of Poland will have two guests tonight. Code 50."

The Security Guard said, "Code 50. Very well. I'll notify the Guest Quarters Supervisor. Please sign them in. Guest Quarters will give them a temporary identification badge until tomorrow morning. In the morning, you'll have to take them and finish their processing. Remember they can't be unescorted until they are processed in."

Sarge replied, "Yes. Okay."

The security guard took back the paperwork and walked back to the guard hut. The heavy steel garage door slowly opened to the right. When completely opened, Sarge crept the Mercedes-Benz into the garage. The heavy steel door started to close behind them.

Sarge navigated through the underground garage to find a parking space near the elevator. He steered the Mercedes-Benz into a parking stall, turned the car off and announced, "And that was a long day. Let's get in and process Wayne and Bryan with Guest Quarters."

USA, Washington D.C. NW
Embassy of the Republic of Poland

0630 Hours   Dining Room

"Good morning, Sarge," Bertha said.

"Good morning, Bertha," replied Sarge as he struggled to get the greeting out.

"You look tired. What did you do last night?" Bertha asked.

Sarge raised a beautiful Polish Boleslawiec stoneware coffee cup to his lips. He gently blew over the hot, black, steamy, coffee then took a gentle sip. His face curled up from the intense heat of the coffee. He set the coffee cup down on the saucer, looked over his glasses and said, "Bertha, I had a wild day yesterday. A wild day. I can't go into the details here. We'll have a lively and interesting conversation this morning in the room."

"Okay. Jan and I had a long, but interesting afternoon yesterday too, "Bertha replied. "It's going to be quite a morning in the room. Who's with Tommy?"

Sarge turned in his leather upholstered, dining room chair. Sarge turned back to Bertha and nonchalantly said, "Oh, that's Wayne. Wayne Norchenski. He and Tommy know each other from Agriculture. That's all part of the busy day yesterday. More about that in the room."

"Who's that with them?" asked Bertha.

Sarge slowly turned, turned back to Bertha and again nonchalantly replied, "Oh, him. That's Bryan Hallmark, Co-host of the Now What's Happening in Government for Fact News Center. The guy from New York. Son of the Secretary of Agriculture."

With a bewildered look on her face, Bertha fumbled her speech.

"I know. I recognize him from watching his morning show. He's now on Poland's soil. You know what, we need to go. We need to get into the room. Obviously, there's a lot to do today. He's here? You know he's the son of the Secretary of Agriculture."

"Well, yes," replied Sarge with a tired moan. "That's why we went to New York City yesterday."

United States Department of Justice
Federal Bureau of Investigations

0700 Hours   Headquarters

There were no windows, no natural light. The overhead, often flickering fluorescent lights were off. The small desk lamp with the illegal tungsten energy inefficient bulb brought from home set the ambiance for the stark government office of Walter Noarc, Chief Compliance Officer, Office of Integrity and Compliance. Walter's job evolved from a U.S. Department of Justice, Office of Inspector General Report that disclosed FBI personnel were noncompliant with laws and policies that governed the use of National Security Letter authority. The Office of Integrity and Compliance was given the mission to develop, implement and oversee a program to ensure there were processes and procedures in place to facilitate FBI compliance with both the letter and spirit of all applicable laws, regulations, and policies.

Walter set down the large three-ring binder, lifted himself up and adjusted himself in his flimsy government executive chair, leaned back in it, and rubbed his hands together. He started to play with his wedding ring as he stared at his FBI insignia ring. He stopped fidgeting with his hands and focused on the FBI ring. Over and over he read the words inscribed in the FBI symbol -

Fidelity, Bravery, Integrity. As he continued to concentrate on the phrase, it became apparent what he must do.

Walter picked up the telephone and pushed the speed dial button for his sister's phone number. It rang once and immediately went to a voice answering prompt. He listened and then spoke into the phone.

"Liz. Walter. Hey. Pick up. I need to talk with you. I sure hope you're not mad at me. Anyway, I must do something, and I want to tell you first. You always support me. I hope you'll continue to support me when you find out what I must do. I know this is going to be devastating to you and the family. Dad will probably disown me, but Liz, I must do this. I'm finding it harder and harder to live with myself. Knowing what I know. I just can't do it anymore. Liz, I love you. I'll call you later. Take care of yourself."

Full of emotion and fighting to hold back tears, he ended the call and hung up the receiver.

Walter leaned back in his flimsy office chair. He closed his eyes and took a deep breath and exhaled. He took another deep breath and exhaled.

"What am I doing?" Walter said to himself. "She's dead."

Walter got up from his chair, looked around his stark government office and the framed mementos. He reached over and turned the desk lamp off, and the room went dark. Walter had no problem navigating the lightless room to the door, after years in the office. He opened the door and left his FBI office for what he knew was the last time. The door closed behind him. Today, he did not bother to lock it. He slowly walked down the hallway of an aging, decaying federal building that housed the premier law enforcement agency recognized around the world. He headed for the nearest exit. He knew what he had to do. He was aware that, for the love of God and country, he had to do it.

Embassy of the Republic of Poland

0730 Hours   SCIF

"Let's get started. Good morning everyone," Jan said.

Bertha, Sarge, and Tommy replied in unison and in a joking manner.

"Good morning, Jan."

Jan smirked at the team's humor and said, "First, yesterday afternoon, Bertha and I, interrogated the assassin that was captured the other day.

The assassin admitted he was a member of an assassination team that was hired to kill all the Secretaries of the U.S. Presidential Cabinet. The team started out with twenty-five members. It lost ten members in an automobile accident in Montgomery County on 4 October, and with the one down below, the assassination team was down to fourteen people. The assassin said for every Secretary they assassinated, they were paid one billion US dollars."

Jan paused.

"They take their orders from, are you ready for this. Sarge, it pains me to report this, but they take their orders from the Director of the Federal Bureau of Investigation."

Sarge was visibly moved by this information. He adjusted himself to the edge of his chair and sounded.

"No. No way. I want to talk to this guy. That just can't be. That law enforcement agency is steep in honor. In integrity. I don't believe that."

Sarge fidgeted in his chair.

Jan replied, "Sarge I didn't believe him either. Trust me, we asked the assassin that question three times, three different ways. We were convinced he told us the truth.

He believed the operation to assassinate all the Sectaries reached the White House. He said the President of the United States of America knew about these attacks and may have ordered the attacks. He gave us no specifics on the President's involvement, but he believed the President was involved from the conversation his team leader had with the Director of the FBI. The assassin overheard the conversation one night, when, in a restless sleep, he laid awake in his bedroll. No one knew he overheard the conversation. If someone knew, he would be dead now."

"If I may inject here, Jan," Bertha said.

"Yes. Please."

"This assassin became credible to us when he said that. He also said, with much emotion in his words, *I'm a dead man. I don't know what you will do with me, but I'm a dead man.* He explained his name was already placed on the list of people to assassinate simply because he was captured. He explained it was for that reason, the van full of assassins fled the traffic stop on 270 in Rockville on 4 October. They knew they only had one option. That option was to get away to stay alive. He also said *Talking to us will be the last thing he does on earth. So now, he was going to do what he wanted to do.*"

Jan continued, "The assassin explained that the team leader got a telephone call from the FBI Director and the Director told the team leader when and which Presidential Cabinet member, which Secretary to kill. He was also told where the Secretary would be. The team took this information and planned the assassination of the Secretary. For a year, the assassins planned the false flag operation. All along October was the target month to complete all the assassinations. Initially, the assassination team thought this to be a challenging assignment. As they started

291

to do their intelligence gathering and reconnaissance, the job unfolded to be simple. They found the Secretaries were soft targets. Very soft targets. Their protection was insufficient and ineffective due to three reasons: the details were not adequately staffed to perform the security task, they were not properly equipped, and they were not properly trained. They found Presidential Cabinet protection was a joke. He explained how a member of one of the details kept referring to protection as *a matter of what was perceived. Security was a matter of perception. What people thought was done.* The assassin laughed when he told us that. It was the big joke among the members of the assassination team. They kept mocking that Special Agent."

"Let's see what we have now. What does our evidence look like now?"

He pulled up the list and displayed it on the large television screen. He continued.

1. Video recording of the Secretaries residences and departments showing their absence. They are not coming or going from their homes or offices.

2. Sound recording of Bryan Hallmark's admission on his television program that his mother, the Secretary of Agriculture, is missing.

3. Testimony from one of the assassins who stated:
    a. There is an assassination team.
    b. It started with twenty-five people. It now has fourteen people.
    c. Its mission is to assassinate all the members of the Presidential Cabinet.
    d. The assassination team takes its direction from the Director of the FBI.
    e. The assassination operation may reach into the White House with the President being a part of the operation.

292

      f.   For each assassination, the team is paid one billion
            U.S. dollars.

Sarge said, "Let's continue with what Tommy and I learned
yesterday.

4.   Testimony of Bryan Hallmark
      a.   Bryan Hallmark is the son of the Secretary of
           Agriculture
      b.   Bryan has not talked with his mother for eleven
           days.
      c.   It is out of the ordinary for Bryan and his mother not
           to talk at least every five days or meet for dinner at
           least once a week.
      d.   When Bryan calls the Department of Agriculture,
           he's told his mother is away handling a National
           Security task, and she can't call him.
      e.   That has never happened during the previous three
           years his mother has been Secretary of Agriculture.

5.   FBI involvement via Walter Noarc
      a.   The FBI has information about the assassination
           operation.
      b.   The FBI showed up to take Bryan Hallmark the
           same time we came to talk to Bryan Hallmark, after
           Bryan's admission on his television show.
      c.   The FBI agent was very nervous during our
           encounter on the street in New York.
      d.   The FBI agent did not want Poland's Ambassador to
           the United States to contact the FBI Director.
      e.   The FBI agent wants us to call only him to talk
           about this matter.
      f.   The FBI agent is dispatched from Washington D.C.
           and not the New York Field Office.

That is all."

Immediately, Sarge fell back into the high back, black, leather
chair. He started to shake his head and mumbled, "I can't believe
this. I can't believe this. This can't be happening."

Tommy said, "Sarge, what's the matter?"

"It's confirmed, the FBI is involved in the conspiracy."

"What do you mean? How is it confirmed to you?"

"The FBI is running this case out of their headquarters. They're running this case out of the Hoover building right here in Washington D.C."

"How does that confirm it for you?"

"It was a long-standing policy not to run case investigations out of the Hoover building. J. Edgar himself established that policy many years ago. Hoover instituted that policy to keep himself clean. He was always in the position to blame the management and subordinates of the field offices when something went wrong. In that fashion, he stayed in the good graces of the Congress, which he had to do to build his kingdom. Each and every director since Hoover saw the value in that policy and enforced that policy."

"So that was why Noarc was in New York last night?"

"Yes. That's what I think. That's what I believe."

"We're getting someplace," replied Jan. "The evidence is starting to build. Next steps, should we contact Noarc? Should we get the Ambassador to communicate with the Director of the FBI? What should we or can we release to the press? We haven't given them anything yet."

"Did the captured assassin say anything about a false flag operation, a Poland false flag operation?" asked Tommy.

"No," replied Bertha. "That was not a question we asked. We stopped for the day to absorb the information we were given. We knew we were going to regroup today. We decided to correlate all the information to formulate a second interrogation session."

"Thoughts on how we proceed?" Jan asked.

"We need to interrogate the captured assassin again," Bertha replied. "We need a list of questions to make certain we cover everything."

"Wait a minute, let's get this on the board as we go," said Jan.

23 October TO DO

1. Interrogate the captured assassin.
2. Compile a list of questions for the interrogation.
3. Determine the value of Bryan Hallmark to the investigation.
4. Determine what to release to the press.
5. Contact Noarc, ask for his cooperation or tell him the Embassy of Poland is going to the Director of the FBI.

The telephone rang, and Bertha immediately answered it.

"Yes. Yes. Okay. Yes. I'll be up directly."

Bertha slowly placed the telephone handset back in the cradle. She still had her hand on the cradled handset as she shook her head back and forth. Bertha looked at the team members.

"Oh. You aren't going to believe this. You guys aren't going to believe this. Guess who's upstairs in the reception area? You're not going to believe this."

In unison, the team said, "Who? Who?"

"Walter. Walter Noarc. Can you believe that?"

Jan, Sarge, and Tommy fell back into their chairs. A silence came over the SCIF. Jan finally broke the silence.

"No, I can't believe that. What're we going to do?"

Tommy immediately responded. "Interrogate him. Interrogate him is what we're going to do. That guy is so weak he'll tell us everything he knows."

"We're not ready to interrogate him," said Jan.

"Hold him in the embassy. Just hold him here until we're ready to interrogate him. Just like the assassin," said Sarge.

Jan replied, "Slow down Sarge. Slow down. Noarc is a U.S. government employee. There's a bit of a difference between the two."

Belgium, Brussels
Regentlaan 27 Boulevard du Regent
Embassy of the United States of America

1630 Hours

The Secretary of State and his Chief of Staff entered the large black armored Chevrolet Suburban SUV with blacked out windows. With a local police escort of four motorcycle uniformed patrol officers, all with light blue colored helmets with a dark tinted full-face shield, the three-vehicle motorcade moved away from the Embassy of the United States of America en route to the hotel.

Secretary of State Motorcade in transit

The silence in the armored vehicle was broken when the Chief of Staff said, "Mr. Secretary, your protection detail advised against your bicycle ride tonight around Brussels Park."

The Secretary of State replied, "Yes, I know."

"So, what're you going to do tonight? There's the Museum of Instruments if you would like to take in some culture. There's the Loft if you would like to relax away from the hotel with a drink. The Boston Café would be another option for dinner and a drink. A little home away from home perhaps."

"I'm going for a bike ride. I think you should go too."

"Sir, with respect, you should not go for the bicycle ride if the protection detail says not to go. They know the security posture of the area, given the high-level nuclear disarmament meetings you're having. Your Detail Leader is quite adamant that you don't go on a bicycle ride. Come on. Let me find a nice bar for you to go and relax before tomorrow's meetings."

"No. I want to go on the bike ride. That's what will relax me for the meetings. Set it up," replied the Secretary. "Besides, I don't believe there are people out there who want to harm the United States. This administration is doing a lot to set in motion a foundation for a Global government to benefit the less fortunate people of the world. This President is remarkable."

"Okay. But I don't think you should do this," said the Chief of Staff.

"And you're going with me."

"What? Come on. I have material to review for tomorrow's meeting. Remember, I'm the one who provides you all the information at the negotiating table. Don't you think I should cram tonight for the meetings tomorrow? Come on. You know as well as I, these meetings wouldn't be going as well as they are if not for me."

"No." The Secretary reached up over the front seat and tapped the Detail Leader on his left shoulder. "In fact, let's see how good my protection team is. I want to go in one hour. I'm going to change into my bike riding clothes as soon as we get back to the hotel."

The motorcade arrived at the hotel. As completed so many times before, the protection detail members flowed into what a bystander could only call, a team that choreographed their movements to utter perfection. The security team glided through their routine to get the Secretary out of the armored vehicle, into the hotel and up to his room. It was so routine it was effortless.

Arriving at the Secretary's room, the Secretary and his Chief of Staff entered. The door closed behind them, and a local uniformed Brussels police officer stood post at the Secretary's door. The protection team moved directly to the adjoining security room, soon to be joined by the balance of the protection team members once they parked the motorcade vehicles. They waited for contact from the Secretary's Chief of Staff to finalize the Secretary's activities for the balance of the day. All along, the Detail Leader hoped the Chief of Staff talked the Secretary out of a bike ride.

The Chief of Staff was unable to talk the Secretary out of the bike ride, and he thought to himself, "Oh. Here we go again." He picked up his cellular telephone and called the Detail Leader.

The Detail Leader said, "Hello."

The Chief of Staff replied, "Hello. The Secretary wants to go on a bicycle ride, in Brussels Park, in one hour."

"Again, I advise you and the Secretary not to go on the bike ride. Intelligence indicates that Brussels has a large number of demonstrators in town for the meetings. The local police believe they are looking for the attendees to the meetings. When they spot them, they're going to call a flash mob. It is unknown what these flash mobs will do to demonstrate the meetings."

"I know that. You know that. The Secretary knows that. We are not going to convince him not to go. So, we'll see you in front of his room in one hour. Thank you."

"Okay. How many people are going?"

"Just the Secretary and myself."

The Detail Leader knew the Chief of Staff was not a physically active person and detested physical exercise. But he never told the Secretary no. The Detail Leader worked hard to hold back his laughter and only said, "See you all in one hour."

The Detail Leader hung up from the call and turned to the room full of special agents. He closed his eyes, took a deep breath, opened them and announced, "The Secretary is going on a bicycle ride."

All the special agents started to moan and complain. Given the intelligence information provided, they all knew he should not go on the bike ride.

One of the special agents expressed, "Is this guy nuts?"

The Detail Leader immediately replied, "Enough. I don't want any more of this. We have a job to do. We're going to do it. We're going to do it to the best of our ability, with the equipment we have and with the number of agents in this room."

The room went quiet. So, quiet, you could hear a mouse fart. The silence was broken by the same voice that caused the silence.

"DL, I apologize to you and the team. I'm ready to go. My head is straight."

The Detail Leader said, "Thank you. Thank all of you for your commitment. Now here is what we need to do. There are six of us. I want to cover the Secretary this way: The Assistant Detail Leader and I will be on the Secretary's right shoulder at all times. We'll each take half the park and switch each other out when we come to each other. That'll give us a rest. As you all know, the Secretary goes for about a fifty-mile ride. That's a lot of circling of the park. Likewise, the rest of you will team up in two. That gives us two more teams of two. The teams of two will lead us. Each team will take half the park, switching each other out as we circle the park. This will give you all a rest. We'll take our local uniformed motorcycle police officers and position them an equal distance apart in the middle of the four sides of the park. We will post the medical emergency crew in the middle of the park. We need to put two of the motorcade vehicles in the park. Position them, one on each end. Place the keys on the left front tires. Are there any questions?"

The room was silent.

The Detail Leader continued, "Let's go and suit up. See you all in the lobby when I come down with the Secretary. We'll all ride together to the park and split off there to take up our positions."

The Detail Leader looked to the Assistant Detail Leader.

"Please brief the local police on this movement."

"Yes, sir."

The special agents filed out of the security room. They went back to their hotel rooms and changed their clothing for the bicycle ride.

About forty minutes later, the security team started to assemble in the lobby. The Assistant Detail Leader surveyed the area. Everyone from the security team was there except the Detail Leader.

The Assistant Detail Leader broadcasted, "Detail Leader from Assistant Detail Leader."

"Go."

"All set."

"10-4. Moving your way."

"10-4."

The Assistant Detail Leader made eye contact with every detail member to acknowledge they all received the two-way radio traffic. The detail members filed outside and mounted their bicycles. They set up the formation and waited for the Secretary. All other resources were staged in the park as directed.

Shortly the lobby elevator doors opened. The Secretary emerged, and the Detail Leader followed him at the right shoulder protective position. The Chief of Staff followed to the left of the Secretary. The Assistant Detail Leader led the group through the hotel lobby to the bicycles outside. They all mounted the bikes and pedaled away from the hotel to Brussels Park. At the park, the protection team followed their established plan.

As the other security detail members moved to their positions, they noted the local uniformed motorcycle patrol officers were posted as requested. They wore their light blue helmets with a dark tinted full-face shield and standard uniforms. They straddled their police motorcycles and scanned the area for potential threats.

Two-way radio chatter during the bicycle ride was non-existent until the twenty-third lap. One of the special agents announced, "Number twenty-three. Lap twenty-three."

Multiple clicks came from two-way radio mics to acknowledge the broadcast.

On the twenty-third lap, as the Secretary passed one of the local uniformed motorcycle police officers, the officer started his motorcycle with a long and loud revving of the engine. This startled the Secretary to a point he almost lost control of his bicycle. This appeared to be a signal to the other three motorcycles to start their engines too. The motorcycles were driven to the rear of the ambulance, and the rear doors opened. Four individuals dressed in black, military style, uniforms, and

301

light blue colored helmets with dark tinted full face shields emerged from the ambulance. They held their automatic military weapons in a low ready position. They mounted the motorcycles as passengers, and in a formation, the motorcycles moved to the motorcade vehicles. At each motorcade vehicle, a motorcycle passenger retrieved the car keys from atop the front tire.

The Detail Leader, with panic in his voice, broadcasted, "What's going on? What's happening?"

After a pause, the Assistant Detail Leader broadcasted, "Form up. Form up. To the motorcade vehicles. Attack. Attack."

All the members of the protection detail pedaled toward the Secretary. As they got close, doing their best to control their adrenaline dump, they heard the roar of motorcycle engines gaining on them and the Secretary.

As the motorcycles advanced on the entourage, there came the sound of faint pops, the automatic weapon fire from the riders on the motorcycles. Two of the special agents dropped from their bicycles. Their bodies went lifeless from numerous bullet wounds.

The motorcycles continued to gain on the Secretary, the other four members of the Secretary's protection detail and the Chief of Staff. The Secretary looked to the Detail Leader and showed a horrified gaze in his eyes. The Detail Leader pedaled faster to get closer to the Secretary to comfort the Secretary. The Detail Leader knew there was little to do at this point. The Secretary of State's protection detail had too few resources, both human and physical.

Two of the four remaining Special Agents started to fade from the group. The Detail Leader glanced back and saw the two Special Agents dismount from their bicycles. They took cover behind huge oak trees and took one last stance to stop the attack. Their 9-millimeter Glock Model 19s with a total of sixteen rounds, fifteen rounds in the magazine and one in the chamber, were no match for the military style fully automatic long guns. The motorcycles swiftly surrounded the two Special Agents and cut them down with a volley of automatic gunfire. Their lifeless bodies, riddled with bullets, fell to the ground as the volley of suppressed automatic fire faintly echoed through the park.

The motorcycles regrouped and roared off and in an instant, caught up to the balance of the entourage. Over the roar of the engines, came more of the suppressed popping sound of automatic gunfire. The entire group, to include the Secretary, took rounds. First one Special Agent fell to the ground and remained lifeless. Then the Chief of Staff fell into the path of the other Special Agent. They both fell to the ground. Neither got up. They were dead. The Secretary and the Detail Leader continued to pedal in an attempt to outrun the bullets. Outrun the motorized bicycles. Finally, the Detail Leader and the Secretary of State fell to the ground. The Detail Leader, riddled with bullets, bled profusely and struggled to crawl to the Secretary. With one last attempt, the Detail Leader covered the Secretary's body with his own. The Detail Leader tried to draw his weapon. He had no strength left. His bullet wounds drained his body of its life-sustaining fluid. The Detail Leader expired with his hand on the grip of his holstered duty weapon. His body laid across the Secretary.

The four motorcycles came to a stop by the lifeless Detail Leader and the Secretary, in a semi-formation and idled. One of the passengers dismounted and brought his military long gun to a high ready position and looked down over the weapon. With a shuffle step, the assassin tactically moved toward the lifeless bodies. He crouched down on one knee and pulled the dead Detail Leader off the Secretary. The assassin shimmied closer to the Secretary to check for signs of life. There were none. The assassin slowly reached around with his left hand, pulled a white rag from his left rear pocket and soaked the white rag in the pool of blood from the Secretary's lifeless body. With the blood-soaked white rag, he drew a large red X on the concrete sidewalk next to the deceased Secretary. By the large red X, he wrote the number 4.

The assassin stood erect and gazed at the scene as the bloody, white rag fell to the ground. It was as if the assassin admired the results of the attack. The assassin moved swiftly and remounted the motorcycle which roared away from the Brussels Park in a formation. They passed emergency vehicles rushing to the scene of the assassination.

Embassy of the Republic of Poland

1015 Hours   SCIF

"Bertha will go and bring Mr. Noarc down to the SCIF. We'll ask him the nature of his visit and listen to his response. Listen to what he says. Are we in agreement?" Jan asked.

In unison, Bertha, Sarge and Tommy replied, "Yes."

Bertha eased her high back conference style chair away for the large conference table. She slowly rose from the chair, stepped behind it, and slid it under the conference table. She paused, took a deep breath and walked briskly to the door of the SCIF. She quickly tapped the keypad positioned on the wall. The sound of the electronic lock disengaging echoed through the SCIF as did the noise of the door closing behind Bertha.

The other team members started to shuffle through papers laid out in front of them. They also scoured their computer tablets that rested on the conference table. This was all in preparation for Walter Noarc's unannounced, unscheduled visit.

They heard the keypad after what seemed an eternity. Then, with a thud, the electronic lock disengaged. The SCIF door opened, and they heard Bertha say, "After you, Mr. Noarc."

Mr. Noarc replied, "Thank you." He entered the SCIF and Bertha followed.

Once in the SCIF, Bertha closed the heavy metal door. There was a loud sound as the latch mechanism was engaged and magnets secured the door.

Jan immediately looked up from the conference table. When he saw Mr. Noarc, he slid back into his leather chair and stared at him. Jan was spooked by who he saw. This was Mr. Noarc. He worked for the U.S. Department of Justice, Federal Bureau of Investigations.

Jan saw Mr. Noarc was uncertain where to sit and said, "Here, sir. Please sit here. May I get you a bottle of water?"

"Thank you," replied Mr. Noarc as he pulled on the high back, black, leather, conference table chair. He sat and said, "Yes, I'll have a bottle of water. Thank you, sir."

Mr. Noarc sat in the chair, grabbed the edge of the conference table and pulled himself closer. He fidgeted in the chair to make himself comfortable.

Jan, with the bottle of water, walked back to Mr. Noarc and placed the bottle on a coaster in front of Mr. Noarc, along with a short style glass.

Mr. Noarc looked up and saw it was Jan. He slowly said, "Thank you, sir. How are you?"

"You're welcome. Fine, thank you," Jan replied. "I thought you were going to get in touch with me?"

Jan suppressed his excitement of meeting the unknown caller from the Warsaw Café again. He extended his hand for a professional greeting. The two shook hands.

Jan continued, "You've already met Bertha. I understand you met Sarge and Tommy in New York the other night."

Sarge, Tommy, and Bertha looked to each other. They looked to Mr. Noarc and then looked to Jan. There was a puzzled look on their faces. They were unable to follow the conversation Jan was having with Mr. Noarc.

Mr. Noarc replied, "Yes. I do know everyone in the room. Meeting you here Jan is quite a surprise."

In a surprised tone, Jan said, "You're surprised. I'm surprised. What were you doing in Warsaw? You wanted to talk to me over there? You needed me to pass information to the Inspector General of the Department of Agriculture? When you worked for the FBI?"

"What's going on here?" asked Sarge. "Mr. Noarc in Warsaw? When?"

Jan said, "Sarge, Tommy, Bertha. The short version. Mr. Noarc reached out to me in Warsaw. He called me at my Warsaw District Office. We met at the Warsaw Café. And we met on the street in front of the Warsaw City Police Department. He wanted my help to pass information to the Inspector General of the Department of Agriculture."

Mr. Noarc kept his head lowered.

"I guess we'll all find out together what information he wants the United States government to know. Right, Mr. Noarc?"

Noarc raised his head some, but he did not make eye contact with anyone.

"Thank you for taking the time to receive me this morning without an appointment."

He looked about the room. He made eye contact with Jan first, then Bertha. When he got to Sarge and Tommy, he said, "Good morning, Sarge. Tommy."

Sarge sarcastically replied, "Good morning."

Tommy warmly replied, "Good morning. Good to see you again."

Jan took a cue from Tommy. With the desire to gain Mr. Noarc's trust and confidence, Jan changed his tempo and flow to professionalism and said.

"Mr. Noarc, welcome to Poland. What brings you to our great country this morning? How can Poland help you?"

Mr. Noarc took the bottle of water, opened it and poured some into the short glass. He filled the glass half full. He turned the lid back onto the bottle and repositioned it on the coaster. He picked up the glass and took a drink and returned it to the coaster. He cleared his throat and spoke.

"This is tough for me. I've been under a lot of pressure and stress since February. There is no one I could trust to help me. I don't know what my family or friends will think of me. I must end this now. I believe Poland, you people, are the ones to help me stop this. Stop this now."

Mr. Noarc became nervous, and his hands shook. As he reached for the short glass of water, his trembling hands knocked it over.

Tommy said, "Let me wipe the water up for you."

Tommy quickly moved around the conference table with napkins in hand. When Tommy got to Mr. Noarc, he pulled out the chair from the conference table and dabbed up the water. Tommy pulled the chair into him and sat down beside Mr. Noarc.

Tommy placed his hand on Mr. Noarc's shoulder and said, "Relax. Take a deep breath. We're here to help you. Take your time and tell us what you've come to tell us. Your thoughts must weigh heavily on you as your nervousness is showing us."

Mr. Noarc turned his head toward Tommy and looked deep into his eyes.

"Thank you, Tommy. Thank you."

Mr. Noarc took a deep breath and continued.

"I appreciate your patience with me and your willingness to help me with the predicament in which I find myself."

He looked away from Tommy. Again, he hung his head low and looked down at the conference table in front of him. He spoke but did not look at anyone.

"I'm the Chief Compliance Officer, Office of Integrity and Compliance, Federal Bureau of Investigations. I make certain all employees of the FBI abide by the Constitution of the United States of America and all laws, rules, regulations and internal FBI policy."

He paused for a moment.

"In February, during the regular FBI Director case status meeting, I was asked to sign a Non-Disclosure Agreement before the Director of the FBI briefed us on a false flag operation. The goal of the false flag operation was to make it look like Poland assassinated all of the members of the United States of America Presidential Cabinet."

Sarge rose from his chair in a show of indignation. He stood and leaned over the conference table. He pointed his right index finger at Mr. Noarc.

"No way. I'm retired from the FBI. There's too much honor in the agents for something like that from that federal law enforcement organization. Why are you here? Are you trying to get to get to Hallmark's son like in New York City? Someone in which we have an interest. And today you're here. You expect us to believe this cock-and-bull story. Come on."

Jan interrupted. "Sarge! Sarge. Relax. Come on. Relax. Sit down. Let him speak."

Sarge replied, "Sit down. His story is insulting. It's insulting."

Mr. Noarc, in a soft-spoken controlled voice, said, "Insulting. Not true. You, a retired FBI agent, who was stationed at FBI headquarters for many years. You investigated such events when you were in Chicago. You and the guy who went to Agriculture to be the Inspector General. You had a reputation at FBI headquarters."

Sarge replied, "You know what. You just go on. Just go on."

Sarge sat back down and leaned back in his chair. He crossed his arms over his chest and cocked his head a little to the right.

Mr. Noarc continued.

"Sarge, I'm sorry this disturbs you. May you get a feel for how heavy this weighs on me?"

Mr. Noarc paused. He took a deep breath and continued.

"I signed the Non-Disclosure Agreement thinking it was just some operation typically handled by the FBI. A necessary formality. Oh, no. The Director laid this bombshell on his staff after everyone signed them. You know how it was Sarge. You were in those meetings. You signed those agreements. At that level, that many years invested, no one was going to give up their retirement. I wasn't. It became too much for me, so I came here. I contemplated what my family was going to think. My wife. My children. And Sarge that was why you left FBI headquarters and spent many years at Interpol, the Washington National Central Bureau. You grew weary of what headquarters was doing."

Sarge replied, "Your father will take care of you. Who are you trying to kid? You could leave the FBI tomorrow. Your family wealth would provide for you. Hell, you're probably drawing from a family trust right now."

"My father. What do you know about my father? He won't take care of me. When he learns what I'm doing, he won't take care of me. He'll only take care of himself," Mr. Noarc said. "So, if you don't believe me Sarge, to whom do I go?"

Mr. Noarc faced Tommy.

"It was because of him that I came here. When we were in New York City, I sensed I could trust him. That's why I came here today."

Again, Tommy placed his hand on Mr. Noarc's shoulder and said, "Relax. Take a deep breath. We're here to help you. Take your time and tell us what you need to say. This is good for you."

Jan interrupted, "Okay. Let's take a break. Let's just listen to what Mr. Noarc has to say to us. Mr. Noarc, please continue, tell us facts to back up your admissions. Facts to prove the United States of America is in the midst of a false flag operation to implicate Poland as the country that is assassinating the members of U.S. Presidential Cabinet."

"Okay. I'll continue. One fact is the absence of many of the cabinet members. Which ones do you see on the news this month of October? Either for activities in the United States or international.

Fact two: I believe you were in New York City to pick up Bryan Hallmark because of the open microphone incident. You probably thought he had valuable information to provide regarding his mother, the Secretary of Agriculture. I was dispatched to New York to pick him up so no one else, you or anyone else, talked to him. The FBI was assessing whether they

310

needed to apply for a mentally unstable commitment order to put Hallmark away, so he didn't talk to anyone. Discredit him of course, in the interest of National Security. You know how that worked Sarge, right?"

Sarge said nothing in reply. His nonverbal signs displayed smugness. He briefly glared at Mr. Noarc then cocked his head back to the right.

Fact three: "You need to talk to Officer Larry Martin with the Montgomery County Police Department. See what he has to say about the FBI taking over incidents the Montgomery County should be investigating. See what he says. With those events, the FBI imposes a gag order so no one can talk about them. Again, in the interest of National Security. The FBI has a team that shows up at the assassination sites and cleans the sites. They take everything from the assassination sites and burn it. See what Officer Martin says about the traffic accident on I-270 near Rockville and an incident in Germantown.

Fact four: You already know about the United States military plane going down in Poland. Did that make the news? No, it didn't.

Fact five: I was in Warsaw to lead the cleanup team to clean that site. I volunteered to go to Poland with the cleanup team. I planned while I was in Poland to get help in a foreign country to get this off my chest. I fumbled that attempt. I didn't coordinate it well. While I tried to right this wrong in Poland, with you Jan, at the Warsaw Café on Friday and in front of the Warsaw City Police Department on Monday, I threw myself off schedule. I was late getting back to Gdansk to clean up the debris from the down military plane. That was why the Poland National Security Group was able to gather some of the wreckage.

Fact six: Did you hear about the Secretary of Agriculture being gunned down across the river in McLean, Virginia? How about the Secretary of Veterans Affairs assassinated in Pittsburgh, PA? The Secretary of Education in Germantown, Maryland? The

Secretary of Housing and Urban Development in Detroit, Michigan? The Secretary of Health and Human Services in/over Glasgow, Scotland? The Secretary of Interior in Gettysburg, PA? The Attorney General in Washington, D.C.? That one inside the Justice Department courtyard. And the Secretary of Defense in Ocean City, Maryland. My brother-in-law! My own sister's husband."

Implicating himself in the conspiracy to assassinate his own brother-in-law, Mr. Noarc became extremely upset. He hung his head low. He fought desperately to hold back tears. To hold back emotion. He fidgeted with his plain gold wedding band. He was not able to compose himself and began to cry and sob.

He mumbled, "My sister's husband. My own sister's husband. God have mercy on my soul. What have I allowed to happen?"

Tommy comforted Mr. Noarc.

"That's okay Mr. Noarc. Take your time. Take a few minutes. This is hard for you to do. But you're doing the right thing. You need to get this off your chest. You need to tell someone about this. You made the right choice. You need to let someone help you. Please, when you're ready, continue. This'll be good for you. We're here to help you."

Mr. Noarc sat in silence. He continued to fight to hold back his emotion. He took a napkin from Tommy and wiped his eyes. His head still low.

After a few minutes, Mr. Noarc looked deep into Tommy's eyes and said, "Thank you, Tommy. Thank you."

He turned away from Tommy. He took a deep breath.

With the sound of relief in his voice, Mr. Noarc continued.

"Okay. I must continue. The most recent assassination, the Secretary of State in Brussels, Belgium. That one you may not know about yet. That one occurs on my way here. One, two, three, four. Oh, one more, the Secretary of Commerce, Gdansk, Poland. Yes, Jan, Gdansk, Poland. That is ten out of fifteen. Those are the ones I know of."

Sarge interrupted.

"That can't be so. Ten out of fifteen. Okay. I believe this can happen, but to the numbers you claim. I don't think so. That is an elaborate conspiracy. One to involve officials at the highest level of Government. To reach all the way to the Office of President. The President or at least the Vice President."

"I now know, you understand what I say," said Mr. Noarc.

"You, you all can choose to believe it or not believe it. I'm getting relief just telling you. I'm trying to right a wrong that I let myself perpetrate. How I'm going to right that wrong with my sister, I don't know. I hope she can find in her heart to forgive me. I just don't know. Yes, you can believe it if you want. These facts are going to be hard to believe. And if you all are having trouble believing these facts, how do you think the public is going to respond? They know far less about how the Federal government works than we who sit in this room. They are a very ill-informed bunch."

"No way. No way. The Office of President is involved? The Vice President. No way. That I have a hard time...I don't believe that," said Bertha.

"Well madam, you can believe it or not. You better believe it, though. I sit before you, the leader, the coordinator, of the clean-up team," Mr. Noarc said. "You see, as the assassination team moves in place to assassinate the Secretaries, the FBI sends out a clean-up team. I'm responsible for dispatching the clean-up team and to ensure nothing is left behind. I report directly to the Director of the FBI."

Tommy placed his hand on Mr. Noarc's right shoulder. In a low, comforting tone, Tommy asked, "Walter, how do we prove this? Who, besides you, in the FBI can help us get the facts we'll need? How do we show the citizens of the United States that what you say is true? Where do we get the facts, the evidence to show the ill-informed that what you say is the truth? Please, help us. Help yourself."

Mr. Noarc looked to Tommy.

"Well Tommy, if we can get help. If we can get the facts, the evidence, who do we take it to? We can't take it to the FBI. The Secret Service is suspect because of their closeness to the President and Vice President. I don't know if they are involved or not. So, do we take it to Congress? Who in Congress? The Chair Person for the Appropriations Committee so those blowhards can shut off the funding to the Office of President. Stop funding the FBI or Secret Service. We need to think about this. Once we have evidence, where do we take it? It appears there may be no stopping this out of control train. This out of control conspiracy. I don't have immediate answers to all your questions. This is the first step, I'm here."

Tommy replied, "We're listening. We're listening to you. We want to help you. Perhaps the Inspector General at Justice?"

"Well, maybe. Or an Inspector General. Search out one we can trust. But then to whom do they take this information?"

"We're going to have to trust someone at some point," said Sarge. "We can decide that as we gather and organize the facts. The evidence."

"Remember, if ten Secretaries have been assassinated, then ten IGs have jurisdiction. They can conduct independent criminal investigations. And, thinking with the end in mind. I know we have facts to gather and organize, but thinking with the end in mind. We could get all ten IGs together in one room and brief them all at once. Though only one or two may act, all the IGs

314

know the other IGs have the information. And it would be interesting to challenge the IGs, at some point in the briefing, to contact their respective Secretary to see what response they get. After all, they can pick up their telephones and call the Secretaries directly. Remember what Bryan Hallmark said, *They told me she was on a national security assignment and could not return my call.* So that would be interesting and a compelling finish to the briefing."

"Oh, my. That is good. I think that will work. I think that will actually work," Bertha said. "Sarge that's good. We could even have Mr. Hallmark speak before the IGs about the particulars with his mother."

"Yes. That's good. Really good," Jan said.

"Like I saw on the street in Manhattan. I saw you guys were good." Mr. Noarc added.

"It'll only work with the information you provide Mr. Noarc. You see, and I know you know, you're going to have to work with us. You're going to have to provide FBI internal files of commands and directives by high-ranking officials. That'll include the Director of the FBI. If you do that, you agree and accept the fact that you'll be living here at the Embassy of the Republic of Poland. Perhaps living here the rest of your life. How do you feel about that?" asked Sarge.

"I came here today on my own free will. I didn't know how today would go or what would happen when I told you what I knew."

"Alright. Mr. Noarc you have to go back to FBI headquarters and download all your files. You must gather every bit of information on this plot you can carry out. Will you do that? Will you do that today?"

"No."

Everyone in the room stopped and immediately looked at Mr. Noarc. Everyone was puzzled by what he just said. His nonverbal signs, for the first time since he came into the SCIF, displayed an ease about himself.

Mr. Noarc looked about the SCIF and made eye contact with each of the team members. He stopped at Sarge.

"No. I don't have to. I have everything I can get on this thumb drive."

With a slight smirk, Mr. Noarc reached into the outside left pocket of his suit coat and retrieved the thumb drive. He laid it on the conference table and slid it toward Sarge.

"There's everything I can get from my involvement with this operation. It's all under Operation Red X. We can continue now?"

Tommy said, "I guess I'll be the one to address the elephant in the room. Is it possible, what is unfolding to be, this massive conspiracy, isn't stoppable? Who can we trust? Are we going to saunter over to the U.S. Attorney's office in the District of Columbia and lay this case out to them with the hope they accept it for prosecution? That they open a case? Who's going to be the person, the first person ever to indict a sitting President and co-conspirators? What U.S. Attorney will take out key high-level government officials? I know we could find a Federal prosecutor quick to make a case against a Secretary of the President's Cabinet. Make a case against a sitting member of Congress. But a sitting President? The first sitting President who self-proclaims African roots. I say, who are we going to get to do that?"

Tommy just placed the harsh reality on the huge black conference table. His candor forced the group to think about the huge degree of difficulty. They all fell back into their chairs and silence came over the SCIF.

Jan finally broke the silence.

"Well. Let's break for lunch. I think we all need a short break from this. People, we can do this. We must do this for the people of Poland. For the people of the United States of America."

The team members mumbled agreement. They got up from the conference table chairs, slid them into the table and exited the SCIF on their way to the Embassy cafeteria. They took Mr. Noarc with them. Jan, the last person out, watched to ensure the SCIF door closed securely. He pulled on the door handle to make sure it was secured. Jan paused, with his hand still on the knob, deep in thought about what Tommy just said. He then walked behind the rest of the group.

USA, Florida, Orlando
325 South Orange Avenue
Grand Bohemian Hotel

1747 Hours   Outside the Secretary's Hotel Room

"Sir, what time do you want to go to dinner tonight?" asked the Detail Leader.

"How about 630? Can you find the Ace Café?" replied the Secretary of Transportation. "That's where I want to go. If the President sends me down here for this wasteful event tomorrow, I'll make the best of this. Right? A high-speed rail line from Tampa to downtown Orlando. Give me a break. It doesn't even have a stop at the theme parks. Why is the federal government putting billions of dollars into this project? There's already an interstate highway here."

"Okay, Sir. We'll leave at 630 and go to the Ace Café. I'll be outside your door for 630. Thank you."

As he started to close his hotel room door, the Secretary replied, "See you at 630. Thank you."

317

1830 Hours

"Detail Leader to Limo Driver, we're moving your way."

"10-4 all clear."

The Detail Leader and the Secretary of Transportation entered the hotel elevator. The doors closed and it descended to the lobby floor. When the doors opened, the Detail Leader was immediately met by the Shift Leader who stood post by the elevators in the lobby. The Detail Leader motioned for the Secretary to follow the Shift Leader who led them through the lobby, out the front entrance of the Grand Bohemian Hotel, and to the two-vehicle motorcade. At the limo, the Shift Leader opened the right rear door and maintained control until the Secretary entered the limo. Once the Secretary was inside, the Detail Leader took control of the door. The Shift Leader moved to the follow vehicle and took the driver's position. The Detail Leader closed the right rear limo door and slid into the front passenger position. The Limo Driver remotely locked the limo doors.

The Detail Leader broadcasted, "Move."

Secretary of Transportation Motorcade in transit

The two-vehicle motorcade drove away from the Grand Bohemian Hotel, northbound on North Orange Avenue.

The Shift Leader, now operating the follow vehicle, immediately broadcasted, "Traffic coming up on the right. Unable to block the motorcycles."

The Detail Leader broadcasted, "How many?"

"Five motorcycles, two riders each."

"Hey, are those bikes I hear," said the Secretary from the right rear seat.

He moved around to see. He was a vintage motorcycle enthusiast, a member of the Vintage Japanese Motorcycle Club, and the owner of ten Japanese and four British vintage motorcycles of various manufacturers.

The Advance Agent, now the Limo Driver, took evasive actions. He accelerated the speed and maneuvered the limo in a gliding manner from the right fog line to the left fog line. He knew he had to keep the motorcycles from coming up and riding alongside the limo.

The Shift Leader did the same evasive action, only opposite from the limo. When the limo glided right, the follow vehicle drifted left.

Then, without any prompts, in a horrified tone, the Shift Leader broadcasted, "They tagged the limo. Limo tagged."

There was no reply. The Detail Leader and the Limo Drive knew the meaning of the broadcast. Everyone in the protection profession knew "the limo is tagged" meant the end. There was no defense for such an attack. No one could respond quickly enough to this attack to save themselves or the protectee. It was also a call sign for the God-fearing law enforcement officer to say one last prayer in final contrition to their maker.

Then, as the Shift Leader watched with fear, the limo exploded. The explosives placed on the roof of the limo had a downward directional force and caused the limo to abruptly stop and explode into a ball of fire. The Shift Leader, in a state of shock as a witness to the attack and the explosion, was unable to steer away. He plowed into the massive ball of fire, and the follow vehicle exploded.

The five motorcycles were occupied with a driver and passenger on each. Each wore black military-style uniforms and light blue

319

helmets with a dark tinted full-face shield. The assassins gathered in a formation a block away. One of the five motorcycles broke formation and drove to the burning motorcade.

The passenger dismounted the motorcycle and moved as close to the burning motorcade as the intense heat allowed, knelt on one knee as his left hand moved toward his left side cargo pocket. He retrieved an aerosol paint can. First, he shook the contents. Then he painted a large red X on the pavement. Near the X, he painted the number 14. The light blue-helmeted rider stood and threw the aerosol spray paint can into the inferno, and it immediately exploded. The assassin returned to the motorcycle and remounted. The motorcycle roared away from the burning motorcade, joined the other four, and all five fell into formation. All the assassins looked toward the burning motorcade as if they were admiring their work. The motorcycles roared off and passed the approaching law enforcement vehicles.

23 October, Saturday

USA, Washington D.C.

0800 Hours   A telephone call

"Good morning," said Bashir.

"Good morning Bashir," replied the President. "Can you hold on for a couple minutes?"

"Yes."

About five minutes later, the President said, "Okay. I'm finally at level five on this damn bird game my daughter wants me to play. What's on your mind? You call on a Saturday morning? You're not out on the golf course practicing for our next outing, so you have a respectable showing. So, I don't kick your ass on the course as I always do."

"That's where I'd be if something didn't come up that we need to discuss," replied Bashir.

"And what's that? Another white racist police officer shoots an innocent black man? Do you want me to call the boys and get them out protesting? That way we can scare the public into supporting our gun control policies and continue to promote civil unrest. Those stupid ass citizens. They're so willing to give their constitutional rights away."

"No. This is much bigger than that. I think one of the FBI Special Agents with Operation Red X, which helps with the cover-up, has a change of heart about his support for the cause. He coordinates the clean-up team."

"Well, I don't see that as a problem. Kill him. Then he can't talk to anyone. I'm way too close to my third term to let one person get in my way."

321

"Sir, it's not that simple.

"Yes, it is."

"No. The Agent is the son of one of your top donors. I don't think he'll like it if his son is killed, murdered. Killing his son-in-law, his daughter, and his granddaughters are one thing. Sons are important in our culture."

"Yes, that is true, sons are important in our culture. In our culture, to kill a son is not right. He's not a Muslim. You are confusing cultures just like you did in Chicago. If you have to kill his son, kill his son. We're way too close to accomplishing our plan. Besides, how's he going to know it's you?"

"Me! I take my orders from you."

"So, you want me to take care of him? The assassination team takes orders from both of us, but you expect me to handle this. What's the difference if I call the assassination team or you call them and tell them to kill this guy? I really don't care that he's the son of a top money contributor. This donor isn't going to matter once the cabinet is gone. When I spin the assassination of the cabinet members to the ill-informed citizens of the United States, who do you think is going to want to be a Secretary of any of the departments? That group is such an elitist, lily-white group of babies. It's pathetic. They'll be running and hiding. And then the plan will start to unfold, a change to America. Who do you think will run for Congress with me telling the world that Congressional Representatives are the next targets? That I have intelligence that Senators and Representatives are the next targets. I'll be able to turn the hill back into a garbage dump. There won't be anyone running for those offices. That group will be running to hide too. Well, you know the plan. The hope for Muslims, for Allah. The change to America. Remember my campaign slogan."

"Okay. As soon as I find the Agent, I'll have the assassination team kill him."

"Find him! What do you mean? Sounds like things are out of control on your end."

"And now you know that. I'm glad you understand that."

"You better find him and find him fast. How do you lose one of your employees? Call the NSA. Ask them what towers his last cellular telephone calls hit. Ask for his last keystrokes on his computer. Come on. You know that's why I let the NSA continue to gather the mega data. This should not be that difficult with all the federal agencies tracking all the citizens."

"Well, apparently he's off the grid."

"Well, apparently he's off the grid. Well, apparently, he's off the grid. Well, apparently you have work to do. You can go and do it now."

"Okay. Talk to you later."

"I have to get back to the bird game. I can't let my daughters or wife beat me. I don't like to lose. Talk to you later."

Embassy of the Republic of Poland

0800 Hours   SCIF

"Good morning everyone. I trust everyone is well," said Jan as he addressed the group. "We have a lot to do today if we're going to take our information to the Inspectors General on Monday. Monday is the day. We have a lot of work to do today and tomorrow. First, we'll invite only the IGs from cabinet-level departments. Now, where will this meeting be? Should we invite them here?"

"Yes. I think it should be here," sounded Sarge. "Here on Poland soil. No matter what happens, no action can be taken against the witnesses or us or the evidence we have. We'll have diplomatic immunity as leverage."

"I think Sarge is right. We should have it here." Tommy said. "That will work in our favor. If it's too far to come, then the IG's don't come. This is our first attempt to find someone. Some U.S. entity to assist with this massive conspiracy. I agree with Sarge, have the briefing right here. Here's where we're going to be able to freely speak. Speak with clarity."

"How are we going to entice the IGs to come? They have to be busy people. How do we know they're all in town and available to come?" asked Bertha.

Jan said, "How about we create a one-page briefing sheet. We'll have the embassy messenger service deliver it to the IGs and ask the IGs to sign a delivery recipient. It's Saturday, we'll have two days to complete the one page and get all the names of the IGs and addresses. First thing Monday morning, the messenger service will deliver it to the IGs. If they show, they show. We need to move this thing along."

"You're right Jan," said Tommy. "We need to move this thing along. We don't know who is in town, who'll come, how busy they are or if they will take this seriously. We have to take action now."

"Okay. I like it," replied Jan.

Sarge injected, "All we need is one to show up. That one will spread the word for us. That one will reach out to the IG community and be way more convincing than us. Our goal is to have one IG attend. It would be nice to a half dozen. But all we need is one."

The group acknowledged approval with the collective nodding of their heads. Each uttered yes.

"The one-page briefing should provide about six bullet points to request their presence," said Bertha.

"Request their presence to discuss a matter of mutual interest. A mutual national security issue. I don't think we should mention anything about a conspiracy, an assassination operation or evidence."

"I agree," said Jan. "Remember, this is our first attempt to gain a U.S. ally who believes the evidence we lay out in the briefing. Bertha, will you write the one-page briefing sheet, please?"

"Yes, I will."

"Good. You coordinate all the necessary details."

"Yes, sir."

Tommy said, "Jan, if I may suggest. You know Wayne Norchenski is staying at the embassy to help us with Bryan Hallmark. I propose that we ask him to work with Bertha. He's retired from the IG community. He knows his way around the IG community. Though he's retired, he's still in daily, weekly contact with the IGs or their confidants. He probably has a list of the IGs names, addresses, and telephone numbers. Probably direct phone numbers if I know him. He could be a real asset with contacting the IGs and writing the briefing sheet. He may be able to convince many of them to come to the meeting."

"That sounds great," said Jan. "Bertha, will that help you? Do you want his assistance?"

"Yes. Of course, I want Wayne's help. His help will expedite this task. And I agree with Tommy, Wayne is our best hope to convince the IGs to attend our meeting. I think Wayne will be a huge help here."

"Great. Tommy, reach out to Wayne. Let's get him on board with us. Bertha, please help Tommy get Wayne clearance for Poland credentials."

USA, Washington D.C.
Georgetown

1130 Hours   Residence of the Secretary of Labor

"Mi Chica Bonita, what are we doing today?" said Raul, in a thick Hispanic accent.

In a soft, timid, sexy voice, Bianca Carlos replied, "Honey, I just want to relax. I don't want to think of anything. I don't want to be concerned with anything. This being Secretary of Labor is demanding."

"Okay," said Raul. "Hey. I know. Let's go for a ride in the country. We'll take the vintage Honda Gold Wing. You can just sit on the back and let the wind blow through your hair. You know, like on the island."

"Raul. And then I guess you'll want to go down a backroad and find a grassy meadow and run naked?"

"Well if that'll help you relax, I'm all for that. I'm just trying to help my beautiful wife. What do you say?"

"I say let's go. Let me change."

"Are you going to wear your leathers? You're so hot in them."

Showing her timid and shy side, Bianca replied, "Okay, Raul. Go get the bike ready. I'll be right down."

"I'm just saying."

"Thank you, my adoring husband. Now go get the bike ready. Hurry. Hurry."

Raul jumped out of the chair by the fireplace. He left the bedroom and headed to the unattached eight-bay garage where Bianca stored her vintage automobiles and motorcycles.

Raul and Bianca knew each other since they were children in Puerto Rico. The island as they called it. Raul, born to the poor working class and Bianca, born to the wealthy, politically affluent class. Neither Raul's nor Bianca's parents approved of their dating and marriage. Right after they were married, they moved to Miami, Florida. As they referred to it in Puerto Rico, the land of opportunity. Bianca and Raul moved to create distance between them and their overbearing parents. They did not need an opportunity; Bianca was independently wealthy. Wealth from a multimillion-dollar trust fund left to her by her grandparents on her mother's side. So, when they arrived in Miami, Bianca became interested in politics. Before they knew, they were living in the Georgetown area of Washington D.C. Bianca's wealth, charm, Hispanic heritage and background in Puerto Rico's politics landed her first as the Executive Director and then the Chairperson of the Democratic National Committee. That was her springboard to Secretary of Labor. Raul took care of the house and Bianca.

Without the distraction of Raul, Bianca quickly dressed into her leather riding outfit. She took one last glance in the large wall mirror and said out loud to herself, "Raul's right. I'm hot."

Bianca left the bedroom. She walked through the large Georgetown home without any distractions. Out the back door, across what seemed like a football field size covered patio, to the unattached eight-bay garage, to start what she knew would be a relaxing ride.

She thought to herself, "Raul really knows me. A motorcycle ride in the country is just what I need to relax. And if we find a grassy meadow, all the better."

Her thoughts created a huge smile on her face. There was a joyful bounce in her walk.

When she arrived at the opened overhead garage door, Bianca immediately said, "Where did you get the light blue helmet? That's new. And a full-face shield with deep tint. No, I'm not wearing a full-face shield."

Just then, four other individuals rose from behind the vintage automobiles. All wore light blue colored helmets with a dark tinted full-face shield and black military-style uniforms. The fifth individual Bianca mistook for her husband turned and faced her. Without warning, without a word said, in unison, all five assassins raised their military long guns to their shoulders and commenced to fire automatic bursts at the Secretary of Labor. Her body danced in different directions from the different trajectory of the many bullets striking her. When the automatic firing stopped, her lifeless body fell to the gray painted concrete garage floor. A pool of thick red blood quickly formed about her body. If she were alive, Bianca's eyes would be looking into the lifeless eyes of her dead husband.

The assassins maintained weapons ready. The Secretary showed no signs of life and one of the assassins, with his left hand, retrieved a white rag from a left rear pocket. The assassin soaked the white rag in the Secretary's blood and near her lifeless body, drew a large red X. Near the X, he wrote the number 11. The assassin tactically stood up, dropped the blood-soaked rag, turned and followed the other four assassins out the rear garage door. There, five motorcycles with drivers waited. The assassins mounted the rear seats, and in a loud roar, the motorcycles drove off in a formation.

USA, Washington D.C.

1300 Hours   Somewhere in the underground tunnels

"Abdul. Abdul! Are you there?" said a faint voice.

328

A surprised Abdul said, "What are you doing here? How did you get away?"

"Listen. I don't have a lot of time. My wife thinks I'm shooting hoops. Security thinks I'm upstairs in residence."

"Shoot some hoops, with all we have going on. You're crazy. You're one crazy guy. You're nothing like your weak brother in Kenya."

"Okay listen. How many more of the cabinet secretaries are there to kill?"

"There are one, two, three, four. No. Wait a minute. Akram. Hey, Akram. Come here now."

"Yes, Abdul. Wait, is this him? Is this him?" asked Akram.

"Akram, focus here. Don't worry who this is. Focus! Did you hear from the team today?"

"Yes, I did."

"Well?"

"Well, what?"

"Well did they accomplish their mission?"

"Well, yes. Why won't the assassination team accomplish the mission? This is like, as the infidels say, *shooting fish in a barrel*. There's no resistance. They don't have security. Today is Saturday. It's the weekend here in America. They don't have security on the weekend. They only have security Mondays through Fridays. Why would you ask such a question? We are twelve for twelve. Three more to kill. We only wait for the command to go. I add the only concern I have is the FBI getting

329

there quick enough to clean the scene. Those people have a weak stomach."

"Okay, Akram. You can go."

In a quiet voice, Akram said to Abdul, "Can I meet him?"

"No. Just go."

Akram disregarded his leader's command. He quickly turned to the person and bowed with respect.

The faint spoken person, without hesitation and from what appeared to have been years of conditioning to do the same, bowed back.

Akram walked away.

"There. 12 for 12. Are you giving the okay for the last three?"

"Yes. I'll call you with the locations."

"It'll be done as you command."

"And there may be more."

"More will cost more."

"That's not a problem."

The person with the faint voice walked away from Abdul and back through the tunnel from which he came.

Abdul turned around.

"Akram. Akram. Come here."

"Abdul, I'm right here. You don't have to shout."

"Finish this. I want this done by tomorrow. I want the remaining Secretaries killed no later than Sunday. I want to get out of these tunnels and back to the luxurious Embassy living."

"Me too. I'll get this done by tomorrow. I too can't wait to get out of here and back to the embassy. Let me gather the team and dispatch them. I'm still concern about the FBI cleaning it up."

"Call that guy. What's his name? Bashir. Walt. It's Walt. Call Walt. If you think you're going to have problems with the FBI cleaners, you better call Walt. Is that his name?"

"Yes. I will if I need. Three in less than twenty-four hours is something the FBI cleaners may not have the stomach to do. Walt will need to organize this. Those FBI guys are not like the CIA people back home."

USA, Washington D.C.
Georgetown

2245 Hours

"What a lovely party," said Anthony. "What do you think Consetta?"

"I guess," replied Consetta. "You know I don't like them that much. His wife is rude to her house staff. All he does is brag about himself."

"Thank you for going."

"I enjoy the food. Now that's one thing I must compliment. The food is always good."

"Yes. That's true. I wonder what all the other Secretaries are working on. Did you notice only the Secretary of Treasury, Energy and myself at the party? For about the last month, many of the Secretaries are away from the city working on some type

331

of National Security issue. In the cabinet meetings, the President doesn't say what they're working on. He only says they're away working a National Security issue. I wonder what it is."

"I hope you don't have to go. I don't like it when you're out of town."

"Here we are. I think I'll put the car in the garage. You want out here or in the garage?"

"I'll get out in the garage."

The Secretary of Homeland Security waited for the garage door to automatically rise. Once completely opened, the Secretary eased the white Land Rover Range Rover Sport into the garage. As he did, the roar of motorcycles filled the driveway and spooked the Secretary and his wife. As the Secretary looked into the rearview mirror, he was blinded by the five headlights of five motorcycles lined across the garage door opening.

The Secretary froze for a moment. He watched in the rearview mirrors as five shadowy figures dismounted the motorcycles. The shadowy figures advanced to the rear of the white Land Rover. They formed a crescent shape tactical formation. Without warning, they raised their fully automatic weapons and commenced a fierce volley of fire. The prolonged gunfire riddled the Secretary of Homeland Security's personal vehicle in a fashion that caused the vehicle to rock side to side. The lights began to flash on and off. The car alarm sounded. When the gunfire stopped, one of the five attackers tactically moved to the driver's side of the Range Rover with his weapon still raised in the ready position. He looked down over the weapon to the Secretary riddled with bullet wounds, bled profusely and appeared to be dead. The assassin lowered his gun and maintained control of it with his right hand. With his left hand, he reached through the shattered-out driver's door window and checked to ensure the Secretary was dead.

With an affirmative nod that the Secretary was dead, another assassin quickly moved to the passenger front door and checked the Secretary's wife. This attacker too gave an affirmative nod that the Secretary's wife was dead and moved back into the formation.

The driver side assassin retrieved a white rag from a rear pocket, reached into the vehicle and soaked it in the Secretary's blood. With the blood-soaked rag in hand, the assassin stooped down by the driver's side of the Land Rover and on the side of the white Land Rover, drew a large red X and next to the X, wrote the number 18. The assassin stood up and dropped the blood-soaked rag into the vehicle. With a tactical shuffle step, the assassin returned to the formation. The formation unfolded as the assassins moved back to the motorcycles, mounted them, and then drove off in a roar.

The FBI cleaners swooped into to clean the scene.

24 October, Sunday

0735 Hours

Five motorcycles, engines roaring, popped out onto the roadway from the rear of a white colored trailer attached to a light blue colored Kenworth tracker truck. Each had a driver and passenger. Both, the driver and passenger, wore a black military-style uniform and a light blue colored helmet with a dark-tinted full-face shield. Slung over the back of the drivers was a military weapon. The passengers held their military style weapon in a front low ready position.

The five motorcycles, in a formation, turned right onto Boyers Mill Road and broke the country silence in a tranquil urban setting that was once robust producing farmland. They passed a sign of urban sprawl, an elementary and middle school to their left. Also on their left, they passed what looked like a tiny church. Swaying with the curves, the formation of motorcycles continued to their destination as they tracked the narrow, two-lane, curvy, country road. They crossed over a bridge that spanned a lake. Fog rose from the lake water. The morning sun started to shine, and rays danced about the lake's shoreline. The leaves were shades of yellow, red and gold. Fall's aroma permeated the crisp morning air temperature.

As the formation of motorcycles reached the end of the bridge, they negotiated a slight bend to the left and a rise to a residential intersection. At that intersection, a black Mercedes-Benz SLK 350 with black leather interior turned left and merged onto Boyers Mill Road. The top was down, and there were two occupants, a male driver, and a female passenger. The driver aggressively operated the SLK 350 to get out in front of the motorcycles. The vehicle fishtailed onto Boyers Mill Road and almost went out of control. Once brought under control, the SLK was accelerated to stay ahead of the motorcycles and to negotiate the roadway incline and curves.

The leader of the assassins tactically motioned to follow the car. Though the plan was to turn left onto Eaglehead Drive, the leader knew their target had just pulled out in front of them. The motorcycle formation continued Boyers Mill Road, now in pursuit of the Secretary.

From inside the SLK, the passenger said, "Slow down Bill. You know I don't like it when you drive fast. You don't know how to drive fast."

"My dear Jill. Hold on. You're in for a thrill of your life. Bill is driving. Grab your undies and hold on tight. Here we go."

Bill continued to accelerate up the hill. They passed a small old fieldstone church on the left. The road eased to the right and then immediately back to the left. The black SLK drifted into the opposite lane of the narrow two-lane curvy country road.

"Watch this Jill. I'm going to lose those motorcycles. I don't know why they are on my ass."

"No. Slow down, Bill. This is why I don't like to go with you when you drive this car. I asked you not to get it. No. No. You just had to get it. Slow down!"

"Hold onto to whatever you can grab. Here we go, baby. See you later motorcycles."

Bill mashed the accelerator. The engine's torque pushed him and Jill into their seats. Jill pulled her seat belt tight. Bill looked into the rearview mirror, and to his surprise, the motorcycles were not only still there but were gaining on him.

The roar of the motorcycles became louder and louder as they closed the distance between them and the SLK. Two of the motorcycles broke formation and accelerated to opposite sides of the SLK. As the two motorcycles paced the SLK, the passengers, in unison, throw a brick-shaped object into the small cargo area directly behind the seats of the driver and passenger. Instantly, the two motorcycle operators stopped accelerating and braked hard to create distance between them and the SLK. As the distance was increased, the SLK exploded into a ball of fire. The force of the explosion caused the car to come to an abrupt stop in the middle of its travel lane. The SLK rested there, engulfed in flames.

One of the two motorcycles returned to the formation, a distance back from the carnage. The other maneuvered as close to the inferno as the intense heat allowed.

The passenger dismounted, knelt on the roadway and retrieved a can of spray paint from his left side cargo pocket. He shook the can and spray painted a large red X on the pavement. Next, to the large red X, he painted the number 5. The individual stood and threw the aerosol paint can into the inferno. It immediately exploded. The passenger returned and mounted the motorcycle, and it roared away from the inferno and fell into formation with the other four. In a formation, all ten assassins turned and looked in the direction of the carnage. They held their pose momentary as though they were admiring their work. Then the motorcycles roared off, retracing their direction on Boyers Mill Road, back to the small rural town of New Market.

On Old National Pike, Route 144, near the New Market Post Office, the motorcycles roared up the ramp to the waiting white trailer from which they emerged. As the light blue color Kenworth diesel tractor shifted through gears, a long ball of black smoke left the erected shiny dual chrome exhaust pipes. The huge truck bounced into motion, and the white colored trailer was pulled away from the curb. The ramp automatically retracted. The overhead door automatically closed and locked.

Back at the raging inferno, witnesses to the assassination leaped into action. Unnoticed by the assassins, seated in the garage to a small red brick home, were three brothers and their wives. They had gathered at the residence early this fall Sunday morning to continue to tend to the roasting of a whole pig for the annual family fall pig roast.

The brothers and wives sat and drank coffee and beer. They talked and enjoyed the aroma of the roasting pig. Unknown to them, they just witnessed an assassination. The carnage unfolded before their eyes. Though they had no idea who the motorcycle riders were, they immediately recognized the black Mercedes-Benz SLK 350. It was the SLK the Secretary of Treasury owned and drove. There was no mistake by the brothers and their wives. Many times, the Secretary of Treasury used more than his half of the roadway as he drove on, not only Boyers Mill Road but all the narrow country roads to and from his vast Lake Linganore lakefront home and the city of Frederick. Many times, the brothers and their wives had to involuntarily use the rough, grassy, shoulder, to avoid an accident with the Secretary. Though every time this happened, the Secretary gave them a big robust wave out the opened top of the two-seat convertible.

Rushing to the carnage to help the Secretary and his wife, the brothers and their wives were met by the intense heat of the inferno which kept them at bay. There was nothing they could do but summon emergency services.

As they waited for emergency services to arrive, they endured the horrific moans from the Secretary and his wife who were suffering an unimaginable death from burns and affixation. Their cries echoed through the sublime fall countryside. The smell of burning oil, gasoline, leather and human flesh quickly replaced the fall smells of the crisp morning country air.

As soon as one of the witnesses ended the cellular call to the Frederick County 911 emergency services, all the witnesses observed emergency vehicles speeding up Boyer Mills Road from the direction of Lake Linganore. When the emergency services arrived, perhaps surprised, somewhat befuddled, the witnesses did not know why their uniform badges identified them as the FBI. Also identifying the emergency personnel as the FBI was the on-scene supervisor; or as she condescendingly referred to herself, the Major Event Site Supervisory Special Agent.

When one of the witnesses asked why the FBI was here and another asked how they arrived so quickly, the female Major Event Site Supervisory Special Agent said, "This is a National Security event. I cannot speak to you about this major event. You would not have the necessary Federal government security clearance, even if you had a need to know. And you do not have a need to know. Your government thanks you for calling emergency services. Please leave. Thank you."

All the witnesses slowly walked backward then turned and continued to walk back to the garage. When the Major Event Site Supervisory Special Agent threatened them with arrest for obstructing a Federal Law Enforcement Officer, they knew they did not need to be there. They just needed to go back and tend to the roasting pig.

As they seated themselves and became comfortable again, they sat in silence as they watched the cleanup of the carnage.

One of the brothers broke the silence and said, "That's the first time I've ever seen a Federal agency involved in the cleanup of an automobile accident."

Another brother said, "I don't know. Do you think those motorcycle riders caused the accident and then left the scene of the crash?"

And the third brother contributed, "Where's that FBI agent who lived over by you on Horn Court? I bet he could tell us why the FBI was cleaning up this accident. What's his name?"

Jeannie, a wife to one of the brothers, said, "Tommy. His name is Tommy Slatski. I never did know what he did. And you know, he was not around much either. I wonder if he did anything like this, cleaned up accidents involving high-level government employees."

Brian spoke again, "I don't think that was an accident."

USA, Washington D.C. NW

1340 Hours

The Secretary of Energy and his wife emerged from their residence. George greeted them.

"Good afternoon, Mr. Secretary."

The Secretary replied, "Good afternoon, George. Sorry I had to call you guys out on Sunday, your day off. This was much unexpected. But when the President called and told me my expertise was needed at the Iran treaty negotiations. Well."

"We'll get you and your wife to the airport and over to Brussels."

The Secretary entered the limo and greeted Dodge.

"Good afternoon Dodge."

"Good afternoon Mr. Secretary."

Likewise, when the Secretary's wife entered the limo, she too greeted Dodge.

"Good afternoon Dodge.

"Good afternoon."

"Will you be going to Brussels with us?"

"No, I won't. Fred will be going with you all."

"Okay. Thank you."

George closed the Secretary's door and entered the limo himself. Dodge locked the doors.

George broadcasted, "Move."

The two-vehicle motorcade moved down the narrow, mature tree lined street to merge onto the main city artery and into the traffic flow. The Secretary was in the right rear seat and began to read the Sunday edition of the Washington Era. The Secretary's wife, in the left rear seat, rummaged through her purse.

George whispered into the cuff of his left hand, "George to Hope."

"Go George."

"Make the notifications."

After a brief lull. "Notifications made. Fred is positioned to meet us at Andrews."

The two-vehicle motorcade eased to the intersection at the same time a light blue tractor with a long white trailer, eased into the intersection and blocked it. George and Dodge immediately looked at each other. George slowly slid his right hand to his right thigh and continued to slide his right hand under his suit coat to his government-issued duty sidearm on his right hip. Under his suit jacket, George gripped his 9-millimeter Glock, with fifteen rounds in the magazine and one round chambered, ready to draw. Dodge continued to drift the limo toward the intersection. A defensive, protection tactic, so the limo was not a stationary target. At the same time, Dodge positioned his right hand on the column-mounted gear selector. He prepared to ram the gear selector into reverse for a tactical evasive maneuver.

Instantly, there came a roar of motorcycle engines that broke the silence of the quiet, residential street. Dodge scanned the limo's rearview mirror and saw five motorcycles in a formation. They accelerated down the street, each with a driver and passenger. The drivers and passengers wore a black military style uniform and a light blue colored helmet with a dark-tinted full-face shield. Each driver had a military weapon slung over their back. Two of the passenger's military weapons were at the shoulder ready position. The three other passengers held their guns in front in a low ready position.

As the motorcycles closed the distance between them, and the motorcade, the sound of automatic gunfire reverberated to the rear of the limo. The follow vehicle was under attack. It was quickly riddled with bullets. After a prolonged volley of fire, directed at the driver and passenger door windows, the rounds found their intended targets. The follow vehicle started to drift toward the limo.

George broadcasted, "What was that? What was that? What did they do?" He tightened his grip on his duty sidearm and drew the weapon from its holster. He kept it under his suit jacket.

Just then, there was a thud sound to the rear of the limo. The follow vehicle drifted into the limo. The impact caused the limo to lurch forward. Dodge gripped the steering wheel tighter at the nine and three o'clock positions. He pressed as hard as he could on the brake pedal. Dodge rose in his seat from the pressure he applied to the brake pedal. Dodge did not want the limo to get wedged between the white tractor-trailer and the follow vehicle.

Then there were soft thud noises about the limo; one each on the rear driver and passenger side doors and one in the middle of the roof.

Into his left French cuff sleeve, George broadcasted "What was that? What was that? What did they do?" He tightened his grip on his sidearm which was still under his suit jacket.

There was no response. The two Special Agents in the follow vehicle were unable to respond. They took no defensive actions. They were dead, killed in the ambush. Unlike the Secretary's limo, the follow vehicle had no armor or ballistic glass for protection to provide time to get off the X.

George shouted to the Secretary and his wife, "Get down. Get down on the floor. We're under attack."

The Secretary and his wife froze into their black leather seats from fear. They did not move.

The intersection started to clear, and the light blue and white tractor-trailer rig eased out of the intersection. Dodge lowered back down into his seat as he eased up on the pressure he applied to the brake.

George shouted, "Go. Go. Go. Get us off the X. Go!"

As Dodge started to transition his right foot from the brake pedal to the accelerator pedal, the Secretary of Energy's limo exploded into a raging inferno. The engine compartment hood flew high up into the air and landed on the roof of the follow vehicle. The trunk lid flew off and landed in front of the limo. The force from the positioning of the explosives cut the limo in half. The burning rubber tires caused a plume of thick, black, smoke which rose from the inferno. The intense heat instantly incinerated the interior of the limo. The extreme heat ignited the follow vehicle, and it too exploded.

The five motorcycles and the ten assassins positioned themselves in front of the Secretary's house, to the rear of the carnage. They were in a formation and gazed at the carnage. They seemed to admire their work. One of the motorcycle drivers motioned to another, and a motorcycle drove out of formation toward the carnage. When the motorcycle got as close to the limo as the intense heat permitted, it stopped. The assassin dismounted and bent down on one knee. The assassin took an aerosol spray paint can from a left side cargo pocket, shook it and spray painted a large red X on the road surface. Next to the large red X, he painted the number 15. The assassin threw the spray paint can into the raging inferno that was once a government motorcade. It immediately exploded. The assassin tactically moved back to the motorcycle and mounted it.

The motorcycle moved back to the formation. The five motorcycles roared down the quiet city residential street and passed the burning motorcade. The emergency vehicles stopped to allow the formation of motorcycles to turn right and merge onto the main city thoroughfare. A half a mile down, the five motorcycles turned left and then immediately turned right. They entered through the side gate of the Islamic Center of Washington and disappeared into the underground garage.

USA, Washington D.C.
The White House

1945 Hours   Oval Office

"What the hell are you doing in here?" said the President. "Did anyone see you come in here? How did you get in here?"

Abdul replied, "I used the tunnels."

"You used the tunnels? Who showed you the tunnels? You can get around in the tunnels?"

"I followed you the other day."

"You followed me? Why?"

"I wanted to."

"You wanted to?"

Abdul ignored the President's conversation.

"I'm here to tell you it's done. All the members of your cabinet are dead. We are ready to move on with the plan. We continue tomorrow."

"That's a little soon for me to coordinate a press briefing."

"You're Muslim. You'll get it done. This, Allah, asks of you."

The President turned in his chair and gazed out his oval office window.

"Very well. The sooner we do the press briefing, the sooner I can move onto my third term. After what I tell the ill-informed, government program dependent citizens, no one, none of the lily-white spoiled rich people will want to hold any Federal office. Who will want to serve in my cabinet? Who will want to serve in Congress? Yes. This is going to work out well for me. This is what Allah asks of me. This is Allah's plan. I'll get it done."

The President turned his chair back around to look at Abdul.

"Abdul. Abdul where are you."

He looked about the room for Abdul but only noticed the hidden door from his office to the tunnels close.

25 October, Monday

USA, Washington D.C.
Embassy of the Republic of Poland

0800 Hour   SCIF

"Good morning everyone. Shall we get started?" said Jan. "We have a lot to do. First order of business, Bertha and Wayne, did you get the briefing sheets delivered?"

Bertha said, "Yes. We sent them by embassy dispatch. Wayne had all their addresses. Wayne had a good idea of which IGs were in their offices on a Monday morning. Those that Wayne thought were in their office, he called to give them a heads up hoping they would instruct someone to sign for the delivery. For the IGs Wayne did not reach, we had them ask for a signature from the person with whom they left the envelope."

Wayne contributed, "We have compiled all the delivery records and information into one spreadsheet for a sign in or check off sheet today. The meeting was scheduled for 1500 hours."

Bertha continued, "We had the embassy staff ready the main floor SCIF for the briefing room. Everything was set up for us."

Jan said, "Excellent. Thank you, Bertha. Wayne, you are in the SCIF with us? Yes."

"Yes, sir. As you wish."

The telephone rang. Bertha quickly answered it. She said, "Okay put it through. Thank you." She hung up and said, "Jan, turn the television on. Intel is sending us a live feed."

Without hesitation or comment, Jan turned the television on, and everyone adjusted their seats to watch.

"Good morning viewers. I am Kate McGuire, sitting in for Bryan Hallmark, of Now What's Happening in Government, the Fact News Center.

Fact News Center reports the President of the United States of America will hold a press briefing this afternoon. We don't know the subject. We're waiting for the President's Press Secretary to send out the final details, to include the time. At this time, we don't know any details about the subject of the press briefing. Please stand by with us for further details. We have to go to commercial break now."

The group sat and waited for the commercial to end. The five were deep in thought.

"Welcome back. During our commercial break, we received notification that the President of the United States of America, accompanied by the Vice-President of the United States, planned a press briefing from the west wing press room in the White House today at 3:30 p.m. Fact News Center Monday afternoon regularly scheduled programming was suspended. We will bring you live coverage of the press briefing. The White House did not say what the topic was for the briefing. Now, What's Happening in Government staff tried to determine more details. We'll be back, live, at three o'clock today to begin our coverage. See you back here," Kate reported.

"Now what?" Sarge asked.

Jan said, "I don't know what to think of that."

Bertha said, "Let's think on that. Now we need to go to the first floor SCIF to practice our briefing. Time is moving fast on us today. I'll have Embassy Audio Support prepare a live feed to the first floor SCIF in case we want to show the Presidential press briefing during our presentation. And I'll have Intelligence watch the newscast and determine if we need to stop and show the telecast."

Wayne said, "That's a good idea. I suggest we plan to show the President's press briefing to the IGs. If you all agree, I'll tell that to the IGs who call me this morning. I am quite confident I'll be fielding calls. They'll be calling me for any information I have on this meeting."

Jan said, "Great. Thank you, Bertha. Thank you, Wayne. Shall we go?"

The hotshot investigative team rose from their chairs. Today, no one bothered to organize the workspace before leaving the SCIF. They had too much on their minds. Especially after the news report they just watched. Everyone knew their brief had to project the utmost professionalism to establish credibility. Their efforts to clear Poland from the conspiracy needed the weight of the United States Inspectors General.

Embassy of the Republic of Poland
1st Floor SCIF

1500 Hours

During their preparation for the briefing, it was decided Jan was the main speaker. Sarge and Tommy were seated at a table to the left of Jan and the podium. Bertha was positioned by the door to the SCIF. Wayne was free to move about the room and interact with the IGs. Everyone agreed, it was vital that the IGs had access to Wayne when they arrived, during the briefing and after the briefing. Jan, Bertha, Sarge and Tommy realized and understood the value Wayne brought to the team.

Jan said, "Welcome ladies and gentlemen. Thank you for coming. My name is Jan Sklodowski. I wish to speak to you to discuss a grave concern to the Republic of Poland."

Bertha approached Jan at the podium and in a quiet voice said, "Intel said we need to go to a live feed of the U.S. President's press briefing. We need to do this now so the IGs can watch."

347

"Please excuse the interruption. Your President is giving a press briefing. I don't want you to miss it. Before I continue, let's watch the live feed. Please direct your attention to the television screens around the room. Thank you."

The televisions were cued up, and the audio began.

"Good afternoon. Welcome. I am Kate McGuire. This is Now What's Happening in Government. Thank you for joining Fact News Center's live coverage of the Presidential Press Briefing. The subject of this press briefing is being held close to the vest. My long time reliable sources in the Federal government, as well as other sources, do not know the subject of this press briefing. It appears only the President knows the subject. Typically, the White House Press Secretary dribbles some insight about the subject to spin up the news outlets interest so the news outlets can inform you the viewer, so the President has a sizable audience. Not this time. Nothing. From my experiences and observations, I believe the President is the only one who knows what he's going to talk about. Puzzling here is why the President doesn't want anyone to know the subject of his press briefing until he speaks. This is quite unusual in my experience."

"We now go live to the West Wing of the White House, to the White House press room for the live Presidential Press Briefing."

The aid to the President announced, "Ladies and gentlemen, the President of the United States of America."

"Good afternoon. Today, I come before the American people with a heavy, heavy heart."

The President collected himself. He was visibly distraught. He fought to hold back his emotion.

"Today, I have to report."

Again, he paused. He lowered his head. The Vice President of the United States moved to the President and put his left hand on the President's right shoulder to comfort the President. The Vice President patted the President on his back, leaned in and spoke into the President's ear. The Vice President remained near the President's side with his hand still on the President's right shoulder.

The President cleared his throat and straightened his posture. He cleared his throat again and raised his head and looked directly into the news cameras. The clicking of the digital SLR cameras sounded. Flashes from the cameras brightened the press room as the news reporters took still pictures of the President struggling to speak.

"Today, I report, over the course of this month, during October, the United States of America was under attack. Under attack by the Republic of Poland. The reasons and the purposes of the outrageous acts of brutality carried out by Poland were not disclosed. Throughout October, Poland systematically attacked my cabinet Secretaries and assassinated them all. The Republic of Poland murdered all fifteen of my cabinet members. Photographs, very, very graphic photographs were sent to me as proof of the vicious capabilities of the Republic of Poland."

The President looked to his right, to the television monitor which played a sequence of photographs of the assassinated members of the Presidential Cabinet.

The President continued as the graphic pictures were shown on the monitor.

"The photographs showed the horrific deaths suffered by the Secretaries and in some incidents, their wives and family. All the photographs contained a large red X and a number written by the red X. The number represented the Secretary's position in the line of succession to the Office of President for the continuity of government. The large red X was a means for the assassination team to taunt the United States of America. That we were unable to get the Secretaries off the X. Evacuated to safety to protect the Secretaries. The photographs run in order of the Secretary's succession to the Office of President. Again, the photos depicted the horrific event of the assassinated Secretary's and their families. I showed them to you to keep my campaign promise for transparency in government.

Earlier in the month, unable to contact some of my cabinet members, I summoned Bashir Bashshar al Bazir, my Director of the Federal Bureau of Investigations to my Oval Office. Director al Bazir relentlessly investigated this matter and briefed me twice daily since then. I valued his professional abilities. Mr. al Bazir advised, and I agreed, nothing should be released to the public to give the Federal Bureau of Investigations time to investigate this matter. So not to taint the criminal investigation, I agreed not to make this issue public until today.

I want the citizens of the United States of America to know the Federal government is in control, is functioning and is operational. All departments and agencies are open for business. They are following their continuity of government and operational plans. Where necessary, career government officials are acting in the capacity for the leadership that is missing. These employees are exceptionally capable of handling the day-to-day operations of the Federal government. I ask the great citizens of the United States of America to go about business as usual, knowing your Federal government is here to protect you.

I will not take questions today. My heart is heavy for the loss of my hand-picked cabinet members and their families. Some close personal friends. All passionately served me and my land."

The President, with the Vice President, turned and walked out of the White House press room. The Vice President continued to comfort the President.

In a controlled chaotic manner, the Press Corps members started to muster to leave the White House press room. They were off to provide live coverage to report to their viewers. They all stopped when they heard from behind the curtains, in the direction that the President and Vice President just went, a loud cry from the Vice President, "God save me. God save me. No! No!"

Then they heard the President, in a muffled voice, say, "What're you doing? What're you doing Abdul? This isn't the plan."

The Press Corps members glanced back and forth from each other to the direction of the voices. A deafening silence came over the White House press room, and expressions of bewilderment held the faces of the Press Corps members.

Then, their bewildered expression turned to shock as the members of the Press Corps were presented the President on stage. Individuals who wore black hoods with openings cut for their eyes, nose, and mouth, controlled and maneuvered the President as they wished. The President did not resist. An expression of fear was frozen on the President's face. Each of the black hooded individuals controlled the President by his arms with one of their hands. Their other hand was armed with a sword. One of the swords had blood dripping off it. The other sword glistened in the White House press room lights.

Closely behind and filing through the same entrance of the White House press room was a flood of individuals also fitted with black hoods with openings cut for their eyes, nose, and mouth. They also wore black military-style uniforms and carried military-style automatic long guns. They moved with tactical precision and positioned themselves in a line in front of the stage, weapons in the low ready position. Dressed in black uniforms and black hoods, their mission was evident. They guarded those who were on the stage.

Then a black hooded individual appeared on the press room stage and in each hand, carried a decapitated head. Holding the two decapitated heads high, the individual sauntered to the Presidential podium and placed the two decapitated heads on it. He positioned himself to the rear of the podium, crossed his arms

351

over his chest and stood. He surveyed the Press Corps and the press briefing room.

The Press Corps immediately recognized the decapitate heads as the Speaker of the House of Representatives and the President Pro Tempore of the Senate. Many of the members of the Press Corps became ill at the gruesome sight of the decapitated heads. Some dry heaved, others vomited. When some of the Press Corps members started to walk toward the exits, the line of black hooded individuals standing in formation in front of the press room stage raised their military-style automatic rifles in the air. They fired quick automatic bursts. The Press Corps members knew what that meant. It was a warning to stay in the White House press room or be killed. The members of the Press Corps stopped and returned their focus to the stage.

Following this direct warning, another black hooded individual sauntered onto the press room stage. He carried a decapitated head. The individual walked directly to the Presidential podium and placed the Vice-President's decapitated head on the Presidential podium in the middle of the other two.

He announced.

"There is your weak and foolish Vice President of America. In the name of Allah and as the Quran commands, the Christian is dead. To the citizens of America, to you infidels, your government is no more. It is not the Republic of Poland who assassinated the successors to your Office of the President. The Islamic State is the assassin of your succession to your Office of President. Anyone who attempts to fill these positions will meet the same fate – beheading. We tell all government workers to leave and do not return, or you will meet the same fate – beheading. The once big and powerful United States of America has fallen into the hands of the followers of Allah. The United States of America is no more."

Again, many of the Press Corps members dry heaved. Others now violently vomited. Still, others held their heads in their hands as they sat in the White House press room shocked at what unfolded before their eyes. The superpower of the world, the United States of America, the Federal government was taken down, taken over by terrorists.

The black hooded speaker remained behind the Presidential podium. He continued to speak.

"We show our devotion to Allah with this."

He turned and with a nod, signaled to the black hooded assassin, with the sword glistening in the press room lights.

As the black hooded assassin, still holding the arm of the President, raised his glistening sword, the President, whose face was frozen in shock, supplicated for his life.

"Abdul! No! No! I'm one of you. Don't kill me. I'm one of you. Abdul, you know me. You know me from our years together in Jakarta. Osama bin Laden is not here because of me. Because of me, you are now the leader. I'm not a Christian. I'm not a citizen of the United States of America. I'm Muslim like you. I bow to our global support. As children, we pledged to follow Allah and the Quran. Remember? We planned to bring down the United States of America for its oppression in the world. I commanded the infidel soldiers to leave the Muslim lands so you could control those lands. The economy of the United States is weak because of my fiscal policies. To further our cause, Iran has the nuclear bomb to use on infidels. Iran has its money back to support and finance the Islamic State. Support and finance, you. The borders are open because of my policies. The free flow of illegal aliens to the United States of America to establish the legions of Muslims in preparation to carry out Allah's plan. Preparation for them to rise now. My command reduces the size and budget of the military, so the followers of Allah meet no resistance by the nonbelievers. Law enforcement is weak from my direction to our brothers to kill them. So, the followers of Allah meet no resistance from the police. This is my third term. I am the supreme ruler of this land. I am the Caliph of this land, the United States of America. That is Allah's plan."

The President wept uncontrollably.

Still, from behind the Presidential Podium, the black hooded speaker again spoke.

"Yes, you did all those things. You said you did them for Allah, but I knew you did them for yourself. You lived too long in the West. You became like the infidels. Your allegiance wasn't to Allah, it was to yourself. Everything you did, you did for yourself. Allah spoke to me and told me to kill you."

The President of the United States begged.

"No. No. The Caliph of this land, this western conquered land is me. That is what the Caliphate of our homeland says. Me. You know that Abdul, from our last visit together to our homeland."

Unmoved by the President's begging for his life, the black hooded speaker gave the final nod.

On live television. Before the United States of America and all the world to see. In a swift flowing motion, the black hooded assassin, with his sword glistening in the press room lights, swung his sword high in the air. Then, just as swift, he swung the sword down. The President of the United States was decapitated. The President of the United States was dead.

The black hooded assassin picked up the decapitated head of the President of the United States of America and held it high. He moved it from left to right like a trophy. Like the victor of the Super Bowl with the Lombardi trophy. He then placed the President's decapitated head on the podium, next to the other three decapitated heads of the successors to the Office of President. The successors to the most powerful office to lead the free world.

The black hooded speaker, who gave the command to assassinate the President of the United States, drew a white rag from his right cargo pocket. With purpose, he moved to the front of the Presidential podium. He knelt on one knee. He soaked the white rag in the blood from the decapitated successors to the Office of President that had pooled at the base. He took the blood-soaked rag and drew a large red X on the front of the podium, intersecting it over the seal of the Office of President. He re-soaked the bloody rag. By the large red X, he wrote the capital letters POTUS. These gory actions the news media broadcasted around the world uncensored by political correctness or special interest sway

The black hooded speaker stood in front of the Presidential podium. He dropped the bloody rag, paused and turned to the Press Corps, to the television cameras. He looked deep into the cameras.

"The Islamic State is here. The Islamic State declares Sharia Law. The Islamic State is coming through our newly conquered land to purge it of infidels. Those who do not pledge allegiance to Allah will be beheaded. I tell all members of the Islamic State here in waiting, rise now and please Allah. Rid our newly conquered land of the infidels. Install Sharia Law. Take down the American flags and excrete on them. Burn them. Raise the Islamic State flag across our newly conquered land. Raise it high."

He raised his arms into the air. In a loud voice, the black hooded speaker exclaimed.

"The United States of America did not respect Allah. The United States of America IS NO MORE! I am the Caliph here in our newly conquered land. **Al-ḥamdu lillāh**."

www.ingramcontent.com/pod-product-compliance
Lightning Source LLC
Chambersburg PA
CBHW071247250626
47163CB00002B/359